Angst

David J. Pedersen

Odysia Press

Cover art by
Alessandro Brunelli

Editing by:
Angie Pedersen http://www.angiewrites.com
Danielle Fine http://www.daniellefine.com

Angst font:
Comodore Paper by Reza Mfck
http://comodorepaper.blogspot.com/

© 2010 by David J. Pedersen
Odysia Press

ISBN 978-0-692-99104-6

Acknowledgements

I wanted to take a moment and thank everyone who has been so gracious to help and encourage me in completing this. The short version is simple. Thanks to my family - every single one of you.

To start out the longer version I have to begin by thanking Darren for offering the first true critique that kicked my butt and made me get serious. Holly, who is sometimes Rose and other times is not, for your sincere editing and encouragement and patience and. Matt, for helping me realize that all characters need descriptions, and always asking for more chapters. Mike for your great suggestions, and for helping teach my characters to curse. Allie, you are no doubt the princess and my ego. I am grateful for your constant enthusiasm and for always fixing things. Susan, for waiting so patiently. Becky and Matthew, for your encouragment and ideas. Michael for your insight and suggestions. BJ, for your thorough attention to details. My parents who I know thought I was born in the wrong era. James and Joanne for every time you said, "You're doing great Dad, good job."

Most important, thank you to my lovely wife Angie. Without her I'm certain this novel would appear to have been written by a fifth grader. Not only did she grasp what I wanted to say, but edited the entire book, twice, in a way that retained my voice. I could not have done this without her, as is true with everything I do.

Finally, thank you for reading this. I've wanted to write it since High School, and I hope you enjoy it as much as I have.

Addendum

It's hard to believe five years have passed since I originally released "Angst." What an incredible adventure! I've had the honor of entertaining people all over the world with this story, and the pleasure of meeting many who enjoy what I write.

Five years ago, my wife, who is a published author, edited "Angst." Friends critiqued it, I made changes, more friends critiqued it, Angie edited again, and I released my novel into the wild. The results were positive, and the reviews have been great. When I finished the sequel, Angie was busy writing another book and couldn't edit "Buried in Angst," so I found an editor, Danielle Fine. Her fine-tuning was an eye-opener!

Because my wife knows me so well, she made certain unconscious allowances, but Dani didn't. I may have cried tears, of blood, but the end result was a better book. She makes me a better writer. (Though, Dani may disagree since she sees my rough drafts.) After she completed editing my third Angst novel, "Drowning in Angst," I asked her to go back and line edit "Angst." My goal was consistency, but being the amazing editor she is, Dani dug deeper.

Nobody has complained about "Angst," the story or the grammar, but she made some solid recommendations. My writing has evolved over the last five years, I have learned a lot, and we leveraged that to clean up a few things in the first book.

There have been no changes to the story, I haven't made any significant 'retcons', but this should be a much cleaner read than the previous version. Personally, it's been hard to go back and update a story I thought was done five years ago. I spent easily a month reviewing, editing, and formatting. But, at the end of the day, I feel really good about this.

My sincere thanks to Danielle, and my wife, Angie, for their efforts to make this a quality novel. Also, I couldn't be more grateful for my readers and their support—you are truly the reason I keep writing! I hope you enjoy this revised edition, and I sincerely hope you enjoy my Angst!

Map of Ehrde

Books by David J. Pedersen

Angst Five Book Series:

Book 1: Angst
Book 2: Buried in Angst
Book 3: Drowning in Angst
Book 4: Burning with Angst
Book 5: Dying with Angst

Young Adult / Middle Grade Fiction:

Clod Makes A Friend

1

Angst was not happy. This was not an uncommon occurrence, or a fleeting concern caused by a recent event. Unfortunately, this had been his state of mind for years, and today's project reaffirmed everything he believed to be wrong with his life. His expectations lay heavily on his shoulders, making them droop like the nearby tables burdened with enormous stacks of paper and parchment. He sighed at the discouraging mess, which almost reached high enough to block the hint of sunlight creeping through the castle window. Paper dust filled the air, giving the light a solid quality that seemed to point to the door.

He walked around the desk and reached for the light as though grasping a handful of silk then opened his hand to find it still empty. Was it empty hope that he would never escape his personal trappings, procrastination and daydreams? Or merely a tease that couldn't illuminate the room? He lifted a nearby candle and used it to kindle others around the smallish office. Noon approached, and the sun would soon rise over the castle, stealing the small bit of natural light and warmth this room offered.

It was the last day of summer. His wife and friends were outside enjoying that light and warmth, while he spent his weekend filing papers. Angst sighed once again to cleanse his bout of procrastination and pouting. He reached for a nearby stack of bureaucracy when the office door flew open with a loud bang and slammed against one of the tables. The candle nearest the door went out, and several pieces of parchment were blown off a nearby table, rocking in the air until they landed on the dusty floor. Angst watched as hours of sorting slowly drifted to the floor.

Bad news entered the room on two well-fed legs. The younger man had a greasy disposition and wore a dark scowl. He walked up to Angst and stood within smelling distance— unfortunately, as he reeked of yesterday's work clothes and last night's mead. The visitor peered down his nose at Angst, straightening haughtily to tower over him.

Angst didn't care about being short, but he felt worn out. Years of sitting and pastries and gravity had abused his body. He'd developed a middle he'd sworn he'd never have, making him the unbecoming combination of short and pudgy. His thick dark hair had grayed and thinned until there was more growing out of his ears than the top of his head. Angst didn't enjoy getting older, but realized that time is precious and confrontations like these wasted it.

Lifting a beefy hand, the visitor pointed his sausage finger, poised to direct his words with it like a conductor. "I been looking for someone all morning, and heard a noise in here," the man said with a thick tongue.

"Right. Well, what can I do for you?" Hiding his irritation, Angst bent to retrieve the parchment that had fallen to the floor.

"Dis Mr. Milt, he calls himself, does some masonry by use of his infliction," said the walking slab of beef. "Dis needs ta be stopped. Now."

Angst took a step back. "I'm sorry, who are you and what are you talking about?"

The man stuck out his chest and jabbed at a symbol on his shirt that indicated he worked for the mason's guild. "I'm in charge, and dis Milt is breaking de law with his magics."

Angst shook his head quickly and attempted to translate. "You are with the mason's guild and there is a man using magic to do mason work. Is that what you're trying to say?"

"Dat's what I *said*. You need ta listen." He worked hard to take a deep breath and wiped his fat, sweaty brow before pointing again. "Dis man is breaking de law and messing with our business. As assistant co-leader, I demand you make him stop."

The true source of the complaint was greed—the fact that masonry work wasn't being done by a guild member, but rather by some independent, magic notwithstanding. A smart guild, and some were, would hire the person and pay them for their work, thus making the use of magic legal. This guild wanted justice, pronounced 'intolerance.'

"And his name was Mr. Milt, is that correct?" Angst questioned politely as he pretended to scribble a note.

"Yes, and we will be pressing full charges. Do ya hear?" said the assistant co-whatever as he banged on Angst's table with a meaty finger.

Angst looked up from the parchment in his hands and raised an eyebrow. "Full charges? Who do you think I am, the local constable? I'll pass this along, and maybe speak to the man, but there are no charges pressed at this station."

Now the mason was hot with anger, his face red, his finger still conducting. He obviously intended to use the full power of his size to intimidate Angst. "I been wandering around dis castle for hours, and now dat I found someone, I want something done. Dis Mr. Milt needs ta be locked up or put down or whatever's done with dese inbreds."

Angst did his best to speak calmly. "Your 'charges' have been noted. You can leave now."

"Mebbe ya don't understand me, but we're gonna march over ta Mr. Milt and fix dis right now." His finger was now stabbing Angst's chest instead of the table.

The finger didn't hurt as much as the stream of insults spewing from the man's mouth. Angst's jaw set as a wave of frustration crashed against his patience. He glanced over to confirm the door was mostly closed then took a half step forward and raised his right hand, which was surrounded by a bright blue aura.

The mason tried to step back. "Wha'?" he said, his eyebrows

coming together in a thick frown that seemed to weigh down his thick forehead. "I can't move muh leg?" He removed his finger from Angst's chest and began pulling at his left pant leg. His foot had sunk into the solid stone floor and was now buried to the ankle.

Angst's cheeks flushed with anger and the familiar surge of energy now filled his body. It wasn't enough—he wanted to scare this intruder—so he held his hand over one of several large tiles protruding from the floor. The word *Magic* had been cleanly chiseled into the tile, giving it the ominous appearance of a very wide grave marker.

He willed the tile to rise. It lifted into the air pulling along with it stone-wrought shelves like an enormous dresser drawer that pulled up instead of out. He'd formed this underground storage from the very bedrock beneath the castle years ago. This storage kept papers from becoming piles around the cramped office, and out of the hands of overly ambitious politicians. It would've taken four strong men a frustrating hour with crowbars and pulleys to wrench one of his hidden shelves free, but Angst could move them in seconds, with little effort.

The man had paled, but he hadn't passed out yet, so Angst pulled up the rest. Like saplings instantly sprouting into trees, a forest of shelves grew before them. The man's head jerked each time another one appeared. When the floor stopped moving and they were completely surrounded by shelves jam-packed with parchment, the man braved a look at Angst before staring at his own feet as if waiting for one to grow beneath them.

Angst glared at the frightened man. It would take nothing, absolutely nothing, to file this man in the shelves and hide him with the other nonsense. Or, he could simply push the mason's chest. With his foot stuck firmly in place, his ankle would break as he toppled to the ground. How much trouble could he get into for breaking a man's ankle? He sighed. All of it. All of the trouble that the kingdom could muster. Angst took a deep breath and, as always, let it all go.

The mason was now visibly shaking and sweating profusely.

His leg freed, he stumbled toward the entrance. He aimed his favorite pointing finger at Angst. "You...dis was wrong wut you did! You'll get reported too. All of you need to be gotten rid of."

As the man fell through the door, Angst was left shaking his head. His heart was still racing, and that familiar anxiety gripped his insides. His emotions had gotten the better of him, and yet he'd backed away from someone who truly deserved some educating. As always, Angst felt he'd accomplished nothing and was disgusted with what his life had come to. It wasn't supposed to be like this.

2

They laughed. They all laughed. The sort of infectious laughter that forced even the storyteller to lose some modicum of control. Angst clutched his belly with one hand while wiping away tears from his cheeks with the other.

The pretty young redhead sitting across from Angst was the first to recover. For Rose, the moment of levity was brief. She angrily grabbed an empty carafe and marched up to the bar.

"Watch out, Graloon, here she comes," yelled Tarness in his deep booming voice.

The others at the table watched Rose stomp off, pitcher in hand. The aging barkeep, Graloon, looked up from his flock of customers to see her approaching. Having experienced that storm on many occasions, he hustled through a doorway and into the kitchen. Rose sidestepped the bar and crossed that pretend line which protected bartenders from the more aggressive patrons. A bartender hopped out of the way as she proceeded into the back room as well.

Angst looked at the other two men across the table, and they all burst into laughter.

"She's half his size," said Tarness as he laughed, bracing himself with a tight grip that seemed to make the table wince. The large man picked up his oversized steel stein, and his muscular black arm flexed as he lifted the mug to his bald forehead, trading sweat for cooler condensation.

CHAPTER TWO

"I don't know, Tarness. Right now, I'd say she's the biggest person in here." Hector peered around the room with his sharp blue eyes while running his hand over the remaining grays of his military haircut. His taut, weatherworn face was decorated with several well-earned scars and a bit of stubble. "Did anyone find out if Dallow was going to make it?"

"I only saw him once this week," replied Tarness. "I'm sure he'll make it. He always does, even if he's usually the last to arrive."

Angst looked around and smiled. The Wizard's Revenge was more than just their favorite pub. It was the greatest spot he could imagine to sit and watch people. Being one of the few establishments that openly welcomed "their kind," so all hallowed these halls. There were several hundred known magic-wielders in Unsel, each making an appearance at some point throughout the week. Some came to enjoy company of friends, others to eat, and all to share rumors about the kingdom and their murky futures. The room was filled with inspiration and perspiration, with those who sought answers, and those who thought they had them.

It was a loosely guarded secret that magic was entertained, and entertaining, at the Wizard's Revenge. A swirling black hole appeared over a nearby table, depositing food and drink for the happy patrons. A new row of sticky wood bar tables had appeared in anticipation of more guests. The room always adjusted to the number of customers in it, while still offering a cozy atmosphere, no matter how many there were.

Angst loved the patrons of the Wizard's Revenge, and struggled to temper his people watching. A cursory glance of the crowd was always met with familiar smiles and polite nods, but that told no tales. Actual watching, or even worse staring, would often be met with clouded eyes or pent frustration. The untold story of wielders in Unsel hid behind long draws of mead in a smoke-filled bar. Youth just learning to want something more, and elders longing for what they couldn't have, all came here to find out nothing had changed. Yet.

Past the angry and tired crowd, a tall man entered the pub. As the door closed behind Dallow, he took in a deep breath of mead and lingering smoke, and sighed out a bit of marriage and age before searching the bar. Pushing long blond bangs aside, he squinted, instead of admitting his years and putting on glasses. Dallow was older than Angst and Tarness by several years, but somehow appeared younger than all of them. He was almost as tall as Tarness, yet lean as a teenager. Dallow found the group and made his way over. They all rose at his arrival to clasp arms and pat shoulders.

Rose came back with a full carafe and sat across from Angst, setting the port wine on the table with a thump. "You can go ahead and save your tips for me," she said before noticing Dallow had arrived. "Nice of you to show up."

"It is nice of me," Dallow replied, smiling slyly. "Not to mention, I don't tip minors. Isn't there a law against underage workers?"

Rose slugged Dallow's shoulder with one tiny fist. She was fifteen years younger than the rest of them and glad to remind everyone of it. Almost too thin, yet still curvy, when she walked, she threw her curvy hips around in a way that left a lot of men wide-eyed and slack-jawed. Her long, straight hair was dark red, and her eyes were dangerous—large dark pools that were easy to get lost in, which Angst found himself doing until he realized he'd just been caught.

"Stop it," she said sincerely, and reached across to punch him too.

Hector had brought Dallow up to date on Angst's filing misadventures and was now speaking in length and breadth on the bad and the worst of some guilds, especially the masons.

When Hector directed his attention to Rose and Tarness, Dallow leaned over to Angst and whispered, "You could get into trouble for that bit with the mason. Think you can ask for a pardon in your not-so-secret 'meeting' tomorrow morning?"

Angst grabbed his friend's arm and leaned in. "How... What meeting?"

CHAPTER TWO

Dallow rolled his eyes. "We've known each other almost our entire lives. You may be clever, sometimes, but you can't hide things from me. I'm just trying to tell you, be careful. If I know that you are meeting with her, so do others."

"It doesn't matter; I'll take the risk. She..." Angst paused and thought for a second. "I'm needed, and I can't turn away from that."

"You're needed, or you need? I don't think that's a completely honest answer you are giving yourself," his friend whispered.

Angst shrugged and reached for his goblet. While he probably should've been concerned that Dallow knew about tomorrow morning, or that others might know, the incident with the mason was more distressing. Angst had wielded magic when it could get him in trouble, but was he upset at the idea of getting caught, or that he hadn't finished what he'd started? The mason had deserved a good bending. It had been a long time since Angst had experienced such blatant, overt, in-your-face bigotry, and he'd started losing his temper. He could've taken the man down without using magic, and using magic defensively was illegal, so he worried a bit.

"What about you?" Angst whispered back. "Late for a real reason, or does she even know you're here?"

Dallow sighed, and his shoulders dropped. For a moment, his age showed. "I—"

The new pub waitress finally bustled up to the table. Young, blond, and very attractive, she was also completely lost. Her pretty eyes grew wide at the mostly-full carafes of mead. In a practiced effort to procure tips, she bosomtastically leaned over the table and breathily asked, "Is there anything at all I can get for anyone?" She smelled like cheap perfume sprinkled over the musky scent of hay and sweat.

"No," said Rose loudly, breaking the general stupor that had overcome the table. "I did your job for you, and if I have to do it again, they can pay me your wage for the night."

The waitress looked Rose up and down and huffed noisily before stomping off to another table.

"Whore," Rose said quietly, but not too quietly.

"You're going to put poor Graloon out of business one of these days," Dallow said with a laugh. "He's either going to have to go outside the city to find new barmaids, or stop giving you free meals every time you get upset."

"I can't help it. He shouldn't hire stupid prostitutes to serve us." She made no apologies, ever.

Hector coughed uncomfortably and tried to change the subject. "Why doesn't Graloon ever give me free meals when I'm upset?"

"Because you don't walk funny like Rose does," Angst replied.

They laughed, and Rose struck Angst again with her tiny stick arms. He feigned pain.

Hector looked after the waitress. "Wait, she's a prostitute?"

Rose rolled her eyes and shook her head.

Hector winked at Angst. "So what are we in trouble for doing this week?"

Angst's heart felt heavy and he sighed. "I read the new laws as they are delivered, but there's no keeping up with them. Every week, the queen dips a quill in hate and scribbles on scrolls of bitter...and she never seems to run out of either." He took a draw of port and poured another. "There wasn't anything that directly affects what we do at work, but they want to restrict magic to be used *only* for work. That translates to no magic at home."

"How do they enforce that?" asked Rose.

"The last time they tried that, they quickly followed up with strict restrictions at pubs and inns," said Graloon in a gruff voice. He'd approached the table with more port. He looked over at Rose. "This place wasn't always called Wizard's Revenge. Ten years ago, we called it Wizard's Retreat. There were new restrictions on magic almost every day, tensions were at an all-time high. Then, 'mysteriously,' a fire burned down the pub. Three times in one week."

"Three times in the same week?" Rose shook her head.

Graloon's droopy expression looked even wearier than normal. "Each night the Wizard's Retreat burned to the ground, it reappeared the following morning. The third and final time, a member of the queen's guard also lost his home to a fire."

"Wouldn't that have made things worse?" Rose asked, her eyes filling with surprise.

Graloon shook his head. "Nobody died. The guard and his family woke the next morning in a barn just outside the city. Wizard's Retreat was gone forever, but a fire resistant, stone building had appeared in its place. We named it Wizard's Revenge, and that was the last of the fires."

"Also the last time they tried to get so strict," said Tarness. "Well, until now."

"Stone?" Rose asked, looking at Angst.

He quickly took a drink to avoid her gaze. An uncomfortable silence enveloped the table.

"Are you sure she's not a prostitute?" Hector said, trying once again to change the subject.

Graloon walked over and slapped him firmly on the shoulder. "If you're talking about the new waitress, that'd be my niece."

Hector began stuttering an apology as he stood to face the barkeep. Graloon couldn't keep a smirk from creeping across his mouth.

Hector shook his head. "Ohhh. You, sir, are an ass."

Graloon laughed and gave Hector a much lighter pat. "I don't have any nieces, and if I did, I wouldn't let them anywhere near you lot. I just hired her because of the nice view."

Everyone at the table laughed. Well, everyone but Rose.

"Enjoy your drinks," Graloon said respectfully then left to barkeep.

"So you all built the Wizard's Revenge?" Rose asked skeptically.

"On that note, I leave this party in your capable hands." Dallow stood and nodded to Angst.

"You haven't even had your fifth glass yet," Angst quipped.

"I barely saw him finish his first," said Tarness.

"Next time," Dallow replied with a polite bow to the table.

"I'll join you, I need to head out as well." Hector nodded his goodbye to everyone. On their way out, he whispered something to Dallow, and they both laughed.

"I thought they didn't get along that well. When did that start?" Rose asked as the two men walked out the door.

Angst could do nothing but shrug, disappointment weighing him down. Could their weekly outing really be ending already? Their visits were becoming shorter every week. How long would it be before they stopped altogether?

The three remained quiet for a few more minutes when Rose finally stood.

"You old people get boring when it's past your bedtime. Have a good weekend." She waved an awkward goodbye at Angst and Tarness, glowered at the waitress for a moment, and made her exit.

Angst and Tarness stared at each other. Angst finally broke the silence. "You don't have to stay, just to be polite."

"Okay, thanks, Angst." Tarness stood, thumped Angst on the shoulder, and left.

Angst stared at the two full pitchers of port, and watched condensation drip to the table. There was a time when their gatherings closed the bar, and they stumbled out together, dumb and happy—a great distraction he sorely missed. What had happened to them? What had broken?

It wasn't long before his wife, Heather, entered the pub. She greeted several friends on the way to the table. Like Angst, Heather was getting older. Her long, curly brown hair was peppered with gray. She complained about being overweight, but he didn't see it. Angst only saw her smiles—the one on her full lips, and the one in her eyes. Neither of them were twenty, or even thirty, but forty wasn't so very old as it looked. He enjoyed taking in the view of Heather as she sauntered over and sat on Angst's lap.

"Instead of pouting alone and gawking at the new barmaid, you should come home and help me make a baby," she said, wrapping her arms around his neck.

CHAPTER TWO

Angst smirked, looked at the empty seats around the table then looked into his wife's brown eyes. "How could I possibly turn down seduction like that? Let's go."

3

The next morning Angst found himself alone in a small courtyard with Victoria, which made him shuffle his feet nervously and suck in his gut a bit. She stood before him, not noticing, or maybe ignoring, his awkwardness, and smiled. Angst very much wanted to breathe in deeply, and sigh for about a half hour. The trouble wasn't so much in the need for the sigh itself. He had sighed many times in front of her, and another would be easily dismissed as being very Angst. The trouble was proximity. She stood so very close, a step past that invisible line typically broken by make out sessions or the socially inept. Taking a deep breath would overwhelm him with strawberry-scented dark hair and delicately-perfumed pale skin, and he really didn't think of her that way. Often.

* * * *

Angst had met Victoria two years ago, when she was seventeen, and he was too old to be talking to a seventeen-year-old who wasn't a daughter or niece. He'd been sweating in uncomfortable formal attire, in an uncomfortable formal room, listening to the queen drone on and on about some sort of treatise between various dukedoms and so much *blah blah blah*. Why was he even invited—well, ordered actually—to attend these things? Nobody asked his opinion, which was readily available in vast quantities. There were no notes to take, barely even mental ones as there were no follow-up actions that needed doing. He could only conclude that the queen hated him, and the meetings were a sort of punishment. Not only for being who he was and doing what he could do, but as a result of some deeper personality clash.

Angst didn't hate the queen, but a terrible deep and grating dislike for her filled his heart. He disliked everything about her—from how she treated those like him, to how she spoke to him, to how she carried herself—but especially her voice. Her nails-on-a-chalkboard high-pitched raven-squawking voice that made everyone's shoulders visibly tense. The queen's unique version of a bizarre highborn accent required that she roll her *rrrrrr*s and pronounce some of her vowels different than those of improper lineage.

This mutual lack of admiration often inspired Angst to do things he shouldn't, rather like a petulant child. During her longer speeches, he feigned such close attention to what the queen would say that he often made eye contact. One didn't do this with any royalty, and especially not with the queen, but what could she do in the middle of a speech? On this particular day, however, during this particularly long and high-pitched opera of boredom, he snuck out. He was driven by his desire to breathe and not to be smothered by the wickedness of doldrums.

His sneaking brought him to an area of the castle he hadn't explored. While elated to be out of the meeting, he was still frustrated at having wasted his morning. This dichotomy brought about a great amount of mumbling, and he paid little attention to where his feet took him. When he pushed his way through a pair of elaborately carved doors into a small courtyard, he was taken aback at the beauty around him. Ivy and roses covered the stone walls, and an open ceiling offered a welcome glimpse of the blue sky. Ornate white marble planters and several stone pedestals had been thoughtfully placed around the polished white marble floor. In the center, a beautiful fountain featured a very naked statue of a young woman pouring water from a pitcher. It was a very relaxing place, and Angst took a moment to breathe in the solitude.

Other than the sound of bubbling water, it was quiet, and he couldn't help but feel he was disturbing something. His frustration had abated slightly, but after several seconds of looking around, he resumed his mumbling. This quickly grew from mere distracted behavior to near performance level volume as he began his somewhat poor yet recognizable impersonation of the queen. It was a great way to release pent up frustration. It was a bad, very bad, way to get caught doing something very stupid.

"Angst!" spittle spittle. "Take these documents immediately to yourrrrr hovel in the celarrrr and file them and yourrrrrrself away forrrreverrrr." He stood straight, stuck out his chest, and straightened his shirt by pulling forcefully on the sides. "Make cerrrrtain that you don't use magi—"

His speech was abruptly ended by a quickly stifled giggle. It took several minutes of peeking behind pillars and bushes to find the attractive young teen in hiding.

She was crouched over with her hand covering her mouth. At the sight of Angst, she stood quickly, arching her back in a somewhat pompous manner, and tried not to smile. She was skinny in an awkward sort of way, as though she hadn't properly grown into her body. Her lips were too full for her face, her fine black hair reached her waist, her attire was quite ornate, and she wore a bit too much makeup for her age. The combination almost made Angst a little uncomfortable as he really couldn't discern how old she was. She was attractive in the way young women often are, and fortunately didn't seem upset that he was there.

Rather than apologize for being where he probably shouldn't, Angst questioned the young woman. "So, did you like my impersonation?"

She seemed quite surprised, even taken aback by his directness, as if expecting something else. Her surprise passed quickly, and she stepped a bit closer to him. "Not quite haughty enough. I've heard her speak many times, and you are very close, but your 'Rs' aren't quite right..."

Smirking, Angst nodded once and tried the queen's voice again. "I am so honorrred to make yourrrr acquaintance." He cleared his throat to ensure his voice returned to normal. "My name is Angst."

She laughed, and very ladylike, held out her hand. "Please call me Tori."

Angst leaned forward in a very exaggerated bow, playing along with her formality, and slowly kissed Tori's hand. "It is my pleasure." He gave her a cheeky grin.

Tori blushed prettily then giggled. "So, Angst... Your name is really Angst?"

"Yes," he answered politely.

"Angst, what is a man of the court doing wandering around this particular courtyard?"

"To be perfectly honest," he whispered, "I'm in hiding."

Tori's fine eyebrows raised in mock skepticism. "What could a brave knight like yourself possibly be afraid of?"

"Me? A knight?" His heart skipped a beat at the compliment. "I could only dream. Actually, milady, I fear a slow death brought on by stuffy bureaucracy and, specifically, meetings." He went on. "Hours and hours of talking and re-talking about the same...something, until most of the day has been spent coordinating the placement of planters, or the removal of rocks, or the digging of moats, or countless other equally exciting ventures. All done in the name of progress. And in the same time that one of these meetings took place you could have removed all of the rocks from Unsel, dug, filled and re-dug new moats around every keep, and carved new marble planters for every man, woman, and child." He sighed. Noticing he was losing his audience, he quickly added, "All that, and the queen hates me, so I'm hiding from her."

Tori had seemed politely bored at Angst's complaints, until he mentioned the queen. "Really? The queen hates you?" she asked almost hopefully.

"I'm certain of it." She'd clearly warmed to this, and he

couldn't help but take the bait. "It's not just how she looks at me, or speaks to me, or speaks to others about me...she also hates me for what I can do. Or maybe she hates me for what I can do, and the rest comes with the package, I haven't yet decided."

There was an uncomfortable pause in their conversation. Tori cocked her head to one side, an expressive eyebrow raised with curiosity. "What can you do?" Her eyes widened, and she shifted closer to him then whispered, "Do you mean that you are inflicted with magics?"

"Inflicted?" Angst smiled and widened his eyes too. "Well, I may mean that. I may know something about magic. That wouldn't make you hate me, would it?"

"Oh no. I'm not like the queen," she said adamantly. Her eyes sparkled mischievously, luring him down a path they shouldn't walk. "Would you show me?"

"Really? Using magic, here in the open, is more than a little illegal." Then he whispered again with mock concern, "Like I said, it's one of the reasons the queen hates me."

She stepped too close, and Angst's cheeks warmed. "It will be our secret, I promise."

He shuffled back, returning to his comfort zone. What was this game she played, entering his personal safety bubble where Heather was allowed but beautiful teens weren't? Her presence was overwhelming, intoxicating, and Angst knew his judgment was askew. Was she being honest, or overly curious? He steeled himself and looked into her eyes. Deep down, beyond the flirt and wonder, was a wisdom and sincerity that took him by surprise. "I believe you," Angst decided aloud.

He kneeled and reached toward the marble stone at their feet, his brow furrowing in concentration. He touched the fingertips of his right hand to the marble then cupped his hand over it. Slowly, very slowly, a small stalk of marble grew out of the stone. Tori gasped, but he remained focused. It had been a while, and his hand began to vibrate with the stress of willing this thing to happen, an aura of blue light surrounding his palm. The marble stalk continued to rise until it was twice the length of his hand. A bulb appeared at the tip of the stalk and then opened to become a beautiful rose. The animation of the stone rose blooming was meant for effect, and Tori drew in a little breath. Several marble leaves furled out from the base of the stalk, and slowly, a vein of gold wove amongst the leaves and petals.

Angst took a deep breath and wiped a tiny bead of sweat from his brow. He plucked his creation from the ground, made a gentle bow, and handed the beautiful marble rose to the attractive young woman.

Her eyes were wide and her expression so stunned, for a brief moment, he feared she would yell for help. Instead, she reached forward and took the rose. She looked as though she would smell it then thought better of the notion.

"I know," Angst said, "pretty evil thing I'm 'inflicted' with." His father once said that timing is everything, especially bad timing. As if on cue, the ground began to shake, a gentle vibration that quickly intensified.

Tori let out a short scream and braced herself against a pillar, staring at Angst. Earthquakes never happened at the castle. He was alarmed, and embarrassed. This wasn't supposed to happen. Had she really flustered him that much? The shaking became more violent, and some pillars toppled. Grabbing Tori's arm Angst pulled her away from a falling pillar. Having lost her footing, she clung tightly to him. When she was close, the room continued to shake, but they did not.

"How did... Did you...?" she began to ask.

Angst closed his eyes. He stood very still, and reached out both hands. Concentration scrunched his forehead into his nose as he turned his palms down and willed the ground to stop shaking. Tori still clung to Angst, as they were both bathed in the blue light of magic he had summoned. He willed, and he willed, though it took all his strength and effort. Even while he forced the ground to stop shuddering, he berated himself for being a showoff.

The courtyard, now in shambles, was once again quiet. Water

sputtered out of a new crack in the fountain wall and puddled at their feet. Angst was sweating as much as he had during the boring meeting.

Tori let go slowly and took two steps back.

"I'm very sorry about that," said Angst, quite out of breath. "That hasn't happened in a long time. I must be out of practice."

He knew his excuse was lame, but Tori's shoulders lowered slightly. She almost smiled at Angst, but then suddenly screamed again. Angst found himself on the ground, the remainder of his breath knocked out. The courtyard was quickly filling with soldiers and knights and footmen and what appeared to be the rest of the kingdom. Angst attempted to take a few short breaths, but it was hard to do so lying on his back facing the tips of so many swords and halberds.

Quiet returned once again, and a path was cleared to the entrance of the courtyard, save for the few heroes who'd knocked Angst senseless and kept their pointy things aimed at his face. The queen, of all people, entered the courtyard and walked straight to Tori. She seemed petrified, and Tori looked somewhat petulant.

Angst wanted to say that it wasn't Tori's fault, but only got as far as coughing out, "Wait," before he noticed that, behind her back, Tori was making a stopping motion with her hand. The odd moment had become surreal, and Angst had to wonder if he'd landed on his head.

"Daughter... Victoria, are you all right?" the queen asked, facing Tori, her unique dialect almost completely lost in the face of her obvious concern.

Angst's eyes grew large and his jaw hung low. The shock immediately found his stomach, and squeezed hard. He hoped silently that he wouldn't throw up in front of the princess.

"Of course, Mother," Victoria replied. Those three words were bitten out with more defiance than the rest of the combined room had the bravery to muster. It was refreshing to see someone face the queen like that, and he couldn't help but close his mouth and smile slightly.

The queen ignored the tone and turned slowly to face Angst. "For endangering my daughter...death."

"Wait!" Victoria yelled. "He saved me! The ground started shaking, and Mr. Angst ran in and pushed me out of the way of this falling pillar." She stepped to her mother and grabbed the queen's sleeve. "He saved me, Mother."

The queen seemed surprised by her daughter's reaction, though not entirely convinced. Finally, she looked over at Angst. "By all means then, a hero," she said mockingly. At her nod, the guards withdrew their weapons and helped Angst to his feet. Several dusted him off, though a bit roughly.

"You have the queen's thanks," she said and reached out her hand to Angst.

He knelt and kissed her ring, though not the same way he had kissed her daughter's hand moments ago. He felt very fortunate that he still hadn't thrown up on anyone.

Tori's shoulders dropped and she nodded once at him, and he knew everything was all right. While Tori was considerably younger than Angst, her knowledge of all things royal were years beyond him.

The queen nodded. "Please stand, Angst," she spat his name. "Everyone leave but my Captain Guard."

They waited a minute in awkward silence until everyone was gone.

"And now, Angst, you can thank me for your life. Do you know where you stand right now?" the queen asked. At his quizzical dumbfounded look, she continued, "This would be the Maiden's Courtyard. You are one of the very few uninvited men to see this place and live."

"Mother, I told you, he ran in and saved me!" Victoria said.

"Don't lie to me girl, I'm no fool. *Mr. Angst*? I thought he was saving your life, not in here making formal introductions to the royal princess." The queen continued to spit as she spoke. She looked down at the broken marble rose on the courtyard floor then looked over at Angst. "Fine work, *Mr. Angst*. As I'm sure you remember, non-commissioned magic is as illegal as it is dangerous." She looked over at her daughter. "You, young lady, are in such trouble—"

"Your Majesty," Angst interrupted the queen.

The Captain Guard looked up, his eyes pleading for Angst to stop, and a hush fell over the courtyard. Nobody interrupted the queen. It was as though the water stopped flowing from the fountain, leaves stopped rustling in the gentle wind, and the entire kingdom became momentarily quiet to hear the words important enough to interrupt the queen.

"Please, Your Majesty, Tori did nothing wrong." His intention was noble, for he didn't want the princess to be in trouble simply because he was a flirt, but the words fell out of his mouth before he could stop them. How on Ehrde would he know to call her 'Tori' if he'd just run in to save her life?

Victoria shut her eyes slowly, defeated by the gaffe.

The queen's anger was calm, and dangerous. "*Tori?* Yes, of course. *Tori.* I see." She breathed deeply to regain control. "Victoria, you should know better than to even speak to those inflicted with the magics, much less to find a man here and not report him, especially one so dangerous! We will discuss this later in great detail." She turned to Angst and stabbed a finger in his face. "I will say this, *Mr. Angst.* If I ever catch you in this courtyard again, if I ever see you speaking with the royal princess again, you will be banished and hunted and killed. In that order. Do I make myself clear?"

Angst was stunned, but his anger seeped through. His cheeks burned red, and he really wanted to share a few of his sharper thoughts. Inflicted? Dangerous? Victoria gave him a hand signal that screamed "no," and so he stopped himself, bowed, and said simply, "Yes, Your Majesty."

"You may leave, Angst," the queen spat out his name again.

He bowed once again, walked to the broken flower, picked up the pieces, focused for a moment, and then handed Tori the repaired marble rose.

She smiled.

"It's been an honor to serve Your Majesty," he said to the

princess, bowing respectfully. He turned sharply on his heel, and left the comedy of errors.

* * * *

After the queen's command, the courtyard became their meeting place. Who would ever consider looking for them there? The princess had initiated the meetings by sending him polite invitations at first. He thought she was crazy, but when she returned the rose, he felt obliged to see her. The first visit led to several, and several became many. Often he found her in tears, or shrouded in a cloud of anger, and so he went to listen, and to support. She would ask him questions about magic, and ask him to make things. "To practice without destroying the castle," was her excuse. Sometimes he'd even get a chance to complain, though rarely about her mother. Oddly enough, they became friends.

Angst enjoyed their friendship, but visits also meant an equal measure of fear and excitement. And lately, something else. A growing awkwardness. Tori was becoming Victoria. Her full lips had remained full, her hair had remained long, but her body had grown into its own respectable shape. She never appeared to notice these changes, from what Angst could tell, and he tried to do the same. He teased, and flirted on occasion to cause trouble, and she would laugh or smile or pretend to be shocked. But lately she had taken to standing very, very close when they spoke. She pretended it was for secrecy's sake, but he had to wonder why their meetings suddenly required that.

The princess smiled and grabbed his hand with both of hers. "I just found out, I get to go to your party."

Angst smiled, too. "I will be honored by Her Majesty's presence." He stepped back, gracefully removing his hand from hers, and bowed dramatically.

She ignored his teasing and took a half-step toward him. "I've been asking for weeks. Mother kept saying no, but Tyrell told her he would assign personal guards, and she finally agreed." He was certain she hadn't taken a breath. "This is my first party, and I may even get to drink wine. I'm not sure what I'll wear—"

"You'll have to be careful with that dangerous combination. A fancy dress and some wine, and you'll need those personal guards to fight off the boys."

She giggled. He'd rarely seen her this excited. "I have no interest in boys."

"Um, have you told the queen about this? It could be a problem for future heirs."

She laughed and gently hit his arm. "I hear you're giving the first toast. I also heard mother say she hopes you do awful."

"Well," Angst said, a bit defensive, "I'll strive to disappoint."

4

If it's possible to sprint in a small three-room cottage, he did so. From room to room, Angst scrambled. Every bit of the house not attached to the floor and light enough to lift was moved for a third time. He, again, grabbed a stack of papers, sat at the old dining table, and rummaged through it.

"How could I possibly have misplaced it? I had it a second ago," he said a bit louder than necessary. He looked up to Heather for an answer, only to notice stern eyes under a severe frown. Angst's shoulders dropped. Her expression meant trouble. He had lost his toast, and had snapped at her while looking for it, several times, unintentionally pushing her to that quiet place between anger and pain. It was a toss-up whether or not she'd start yelling or break down in tears.

"Heather, I'm sorry. This is just so important, and we're running later than usual." His shoulders slumped a bit more, and he again looked through various bits of parchment that should've been thrown away long ago. Not there either. "This is the last random stack of papers I can find."

Angst leaned his head on his forearm, which rested flat on the table. He took a deep breath, and let out a long frustrated sigh. As his clothes shifted, he heard the quietest sound of paper crumpling. He patted his tunic, and trousers and cape to find his speech neatly tucked in a cape pocket.

"Oh, good, you found it," Heather said, in a polite and calm

'I'm going to beat you later' tone.

Angst stood, ran his fingers through his graying hair, and attempted to straighten out the now-bedraggled dress clothes. "I really am sorry. I must be getting old."

Heather raised an eyebrow, but said nothing.

This is going to be a fun evening, Angst thought sarcastically then stepped forward, opened the door, and forced a smile. "Shall we?"

Heather still glared a bit, but was obviously relieved that the great panic was over. She followed his lead through the door to the cobblestone walk.

* * * *

The party was an annual fall event held in honor of the bureaucracy that supported the crown. Almost everyone was invited—from the town crier to the local librarian. Often, several knights would appear in dress armor to pass along thanks to those who helped the cause. Dignitaries or visiting officials would attend to show support as well as pick up a few tidbits of gossip from those who worked at the castle. It could be fun, when he was able to sit with his closest friends, but more often, this event was a place to feel claustrophobic, eat bad food, and make small talk with people whose company he couldn't stand. Attendance was not optional.

Under normal circumstances, Angst could arrive fashionably late, and leave early with a "sick wife" or "busy day tomorrow." For some reason, he'd been asked—ordered, actually—to toast the "success and progress" they'd enjoyed this year. The toast was to be quick, to the point, and would mark the official start of festivities. Somehow, he was certain that being forced to give this short speech was yet another punishment. Either the queen had learned of his apathy for the event, or some unknown archnemesis had submitted his name with the devious plan of making him the fool.

They were late. At a normal pace, he could meander along the cobblestones for fifteen or twenty minutes before arriving at the castle, but they had ten. They rushed, further upsetting Heather, and making Angst sweat. After twelve minutes at an uncomfortable pace in awkward dress clothes, they could hear the low murmur of party conversation.

The entrance of the courtyard hosting the party was impressive. Four guards in full dress armor stood on each side of the stone walkway. Lamplight reflected off their breastplates, creating a gentle glow. Beyond the guards, thirty tables were filled with people talking to, or avoiding, those around them. Serving girls wandered, topping off glasses of wine or mead. A small quartet of singers entertained one corner of the party, while a jester juggled for the opposite corner.

Important people sat high on a platform before the courtyard, with the queen at the head of the table, Princess Victoria on her left, and the Captain Guard on her right. A general and several high-ranking cabinet officials filled out most of the remaining seats. After a brief overview of the scene, Angst was absolutely confident they were the last to arrive. He purposefully avoided making eye contact with anyone considered royalty, grabbed his wife's hand and weaved through tables to find friends.

Just as they arrived at a table of familiar smiles, a knight approached and placed a hand on Angst's shoulder, a bit more heavily than necessary. "Your seat is already reserved. Please follow me."

Though he obviously took no joy in ushering Angst and Heather, the knight led them to the head table. Heather looked at Angst, who shrugged, surprised to find himself looking at two seats at the end of the long table.

The knight held out a chair for Heather, but before Angst could sit, said, "The queen would like to speak with you."

Heather squeezed his hand in support then Angst followed the knight, feeling a bit ill in his stomach. They stopped before the queen and the princess, who both seemed somewhat perturbed but said nothing. The queen was covered in gaudy, with enough gem-encrusted red velvet to drape every room in the castle. The princess was stunning, her frustration replaced with a blush as

Angst stared a little longer than he should have. She wore a fitted purple satin dress probably cut a bit lower than her mother had wished. An almost conservative diamond tiara sat atop her long black hair, which had been curled for the occasion, falling in layers across her shoulders and back.

"You are late, Mr. Angst," said the queen in her high-pitched voice, spitting out his name as though she had corn in her teeth.

"Your Majesties." Angst looked from princess to queen. He bowed slowly, mustering up all his formality. "May I be so bold to say that you and your daughter look absolutely stunning?"

One corner of the queen's mouth made the barest of twitches. She held out her signet ring. "You may be so bold, Angst, but only tonight."

Angst briefly kissed the queen's ring then turned to the princess. Victoria held out hers as well, but Angst missed, kissing her hand instead. He looked up quickly and winked with the eye furthest from where the queen sat.

The queen coughed, and Angst stood to face her. "If you are ready, let's get this over with," she said warily.

Rose, working at the event as a server, conveniently arrived just then and handed him a goblet of mead. She leaned forward and whispered, "Don't screw up."

Rose topped off the princess's wine glass, bumping her hand in the process. They stared at each other for the briefest of moments. The princess looked Rose up and down in that scrutinizing way only women can manage. Rose nodded at her with painful respect then left to watch Angst from a distance.

Angst smirked, raised his goblet, and said very loudly, "Friends."

The courtyard slowly became quiet as he held his goblet high, desperately hoping not to spill anything on the queen. He winked at Heather, looked at the nearby table of friends, and braved a glance at the royal princess.

Without looking at the speech in his pocket, he began, "Friends and family, I would like to toast. Every day, we are faced with challenge, and work, and unfairness, and life." He paused, looking around at nodding heads. "Whatever it is you strive for, whether it be something better, or something more, on rare occasions, you'll get to enjoy brief moments that remind you what all your efforts are for. That moment may be as simple as a sunset, or as complicated as giving a speech in front of the queen herself." Everyone chuckled, and Angst nodded politely to Her Majesty. "We have to recognize those moments, and be grateful for them, because they are so very rare. Tonight is for you. It is one of those moments in which we are all thanked for our good efforts. To you, I raise my glass in toast." He turned to the queen, "and to you, Your Majesty, for your kindness and generosity in this recognition."

The queen nodded, and everyone drank. Some applauded politely. Tarness yelled, "Does this mean it's finally time to eat?"

"Let the festivities begin," Angst declared.

This was followed by more cheers. Angst bowed once again to the queen and princess, who appeared pleased with his toast. He walked over to sit with Heather.

She kissed his cheek and whispered, "I'm so proud of you, and you didn't even need your notes."

"Thank you. May I throw up now?" he asked, a thin smile across his face.

She laughed. He didn't.

The evening was filled with food and drinks, performers and contests. Dinner was served in eight courses, and between each course there was entertainment. The first round came from a bard who sang a humorous song about a princess who'd lost her prince to a spell. He was forever to be a duck until she kissed him, so she spent her life traveling the countryside kissing ducks. After the song, they were served duck and laughed at the "coincidence."

Shortly after that course, a small troupe of five acrobats flipped and jumped and rolled into an opening between the tables. Four came from each corner of the courtyard, and the fifth flipped over the princess at the head table, causing her to yelp. She looked down the table at Angst, blushing, which made him smile.

Between the fourth and fifth course, the crowd enjoyed a contest. The centerpiece of the courtyard featured a gigantic decorative broadsword resting on a marble stand. The metal blade of the sword was just shy of five feet in length, and two feet wide across the flat. This statue was a monument to another time, even the words etched into the marble were in a lost language. It weighed...well, it weighed as much as the world, for it had been commonly decided that the old statue was anchored to its marble base.

The challenge, of course, was to lift the sword and become a knight. Every new employee was pressured to try, as a sort of hazing ritual. Of course, there were also the stubborn few not willing to believe it was a joke who continued to try year after year as though it were some lottery. The contest was the cause of much laughter, and for those unknowing suspects, a bit of disappointment.

Before the dessert course, a children's choir stood at the back, singing several songs and finishing with Unsel's anthem. Heather and Angst had been unable to have children, and she held his hand tight as they stood for the anthem. Children singing so beautifully and, Angst suspected, a little wine, made Heather emotional. Fortunately, a chocolate soufflé cured her ails.

At the official end of the evening, the queen and most of her court would leave so the festivities could continue in a less supervised fashion. The princess, who'd apparently been allowed some wine, wanted to stay, but the queen was stern and made her walk in front so she couldn't sneak off.

As they passed Angst and Heather, Tori leaned forward. "Goodnight, Angst."

The queen actually grunted at this un-princess-like behavior, and Angst couldn't help but smirk.

Heather squinted at him with an admonishing wife look.

"What? Obviously the young princess can't handle a little mead. Youth, you know?" He feigned complete innocence.

CHAPTER FOUR

Shortly after the royal departure, Heather and Angst stepped away from the head table and joined their friends.

"You are such a kiss ass," said Hector rather loudly.

Dallow stood, bowed low, and kissed Heather's hand, much as Angst had done with the princess, ending with a loud smack of the lips.

Angst's cheeks went very red.

Heather fluttered her eyelashes quickly and looked at Dallow with overdramatic appreciation. "Why, whatever would my mother think?"

Everyone at the table laughed. Well, everyone but Angst.

He looked around the grounds, trying not to encourage his friends' performances. Several tables over, Rose poured more wine into a knight's goblet. The knight was being a bit grabby and pulled her down to whisper in her ear. She slammed the pitcher on their table and stomped off toward Angst.

"You okay?" he asked when she arrived. "Who is that? Sir Ivan?"

"Yes. He's just being a pig." She sat next to Heather, who leaned toward Rose and whispered in her ear. "Angst, I was wondering. Did the queen threaten to arrest you for making out with the princess's hand?"

This was cause for more laughter, and the only person who seemed even a little sympathetic was Wilfred the Short. His more official title was Wilfred the Wise, but most of Angst's friends didn't like him nearly as much as Angst did. Being 'Wise' also tended to mean you were a know-it-all, so he was redubbed 'the Short.' This wasn't so bad, since Angst was the same height, if not as round as Wilfred, and he really preferred that someone, anyone, else have that title.

Rose sighed and shook her head as someone waved her over. "Back to work. Save me some mead."

The harassment at Angst's expense continued for a short while before Hector began telling stories. Angst's gaze drifted from Hector, and he watched the crowd thin. Rose waved at friends who were leaving then wandered around cleaning tables.

She was near the center of the courtyard, clearing off a table, when Ivan approached her with several cronies in tow. Standing next to her, he was enormous, a menacing sight in his full plate. Angst looked over at his friends, who were lost in conversation. He tried interrupting but couldn't seem to get anyone's attention.

The knight's back was to Angst, but he could see Rose and she was obviously offended by what he was saying. She tried to walk around him but the cronies blocked the path and she was forced to back away toward the nearby sword statue. Ivan towered over her, his armor making him appear almost as large as Tarness. She finally lost her temper and yelled at him. He laughed and stepped close then reached around and squeezed her ass. She spat in his face before taking a pitcher of mead and pouring it over his head.

The few remaining partygoers near the scene did nothing but watch and laugh. Ivan, now quite aware of the extra attention, decided to be offended. He grabbed Rose's wrist and lifted it high so she was forced to balance on her toes. She looked so very small next to the knight. He lifted his right hand and balled it into a fist, barking angrily in slurred speech that couldn't be understood from a distance. He pulled the fist back in a dramatically wide arc. When his hand finally reached the apex of its swing, it hit a wall, accompanied by the familiar ringing of metal. Those watching gave a quick gasp. Ivan looked to see what he'd inadvertently struck.

Next to his hand was the broad side of an enormous sword. The harrowing width of the blade was easily four times the size of Ivan's hand and emitted a dark blue glow. His face went slightly pale, he swallowed hard, and lowered his right arm. His eyes slowly followed the edge of the blade to two extended arms, which were rigid and unshaking.

"Let. Her. Go. Now!" Each word was separated by the briefest pause, and rang loud enough to be heard far beyond the confines of the courtyard. Angst seethed with anger. Not the anger or frustration of embarrassment caused by a serving girl. No, this was genuine bitterness. The kind of anger that came from deep in his gut, and drove him to do unexpected things—such as lifting the sword that was supposed to be nothing more than a statue.

As with many fish tales, this one was told and retold and embellished and elaborated. In the years that followed, Angst heard many variations. One version claimed Angst had miraculously grown to be twelve feet tall after lifting the sword. Others would say that he swung that sword and tables went flying throughout the courtyard. Some would say the knight wet himself in fear of Angst the giant. However the tale was told, everyone shivered a little at the prospect of someone actually picking up that sword.

The knight paused, disbelief widening his bloodshot eyes. His left arm was still outstretched and holding Rose, but she was too busy gaping at Angst to take advantage of the distraction. Then, Ivan let go. He smiled drunkenly, put his right forearm against his waist and bowed slightly. "Of course, Sir Knight. I didn't realize she was with you."

5

The queen stared into nothing, concentrating and contemplating. Isabelle ignored the "good mornings" and the "Your Majestys" as advisors entered her war room, but still felt their gazes, and the weight of their fears that echoed her own. She couldn't remember miscalculating so badly throughout her reign. Rather than showing weakness, she had attempted to cover her mistake in elaborate formality. Her bold crimson dress was intricately detailed with gold embroidery. The queen's crown rested on coifed white hair, and her handsome features were covered in a heavily applied layer of makeup that attempted to hide the weariness of crown and daughter.

These distractions may have worked on her advisors and staff, but certainly not everyone. Victoria must have immediately perceived Queen Isabelle's worry, waking far earlier than normal for a teenage princess to see her before this meeting. The princess' insight that everything would work out was kind if not comforting. Captain Tyrell simply returned her worried looks with his own, which didn't help.

Unlike most of the kingdoms of Ehrde, the queen had welcomed those inflicted with magics into her borders. She had even graciously employed some into her court and her staff. Inclusion required constant attention to balance the needs of those who could wield and those who hated them. Ten years of laws and controls had put that delicate balance in place, and the thanks she received for these gifts were defiance, at best, and at worst, alienation from what she thought of as an entirely different race of people.

In recent years, the balance had irrevocably shifted. Tensions were already high, and they now had someone to rally around. Isabelle grimaced at the very name. Angst. She had despised the man ever since his courtyard visit with her daughter, and loathed how fond Victoria had become of him. The queen wanted Victoria to be strong, and that day in the courtyard she'd shown strength in her defiance. But did it have to be for him?

Isabelle had never seen Angst as anything but a stubby magic-inflicted rock carver with a melancholy demeanor. He was always distracted, offered very little at their meetings, and was ungrateful for the many opportunities she'd bestowed upon him, including his job. Angst was a good tool to keep in her pocket, and not only for his popularity with those like him. More importantly, he could be used as leverage with her daughter. She'd been waiting for the day the princess forgot about Angst, for any fondness to pass, so she could dismiss him from Unsel, but she had waited too long, and completely underestimated his potential.

The queen rarely underestimated people. After the courtyard incident, spies had kept watch on Angst and his friends. The only thing remarkable about him was how much he dreamed and how little he did. He appeared happy on the outside, but bitter on the inside, and seemed to twist and turn in his own trappings. She'd dreaded reading the incredibly tedious reports about him, but had never been concerned. Until now. Now, her entire kingdom may be in danger because she'd let them in.

Straightening her dress, she sat up and looked around. The room had filled with people and apprehension. Everyone whose opinion mattered had been mustered out of bed at first light. Meeting in the war room seemed somewhat overdramatic, but this was one of the few private rooms in the castle that could host this many. The over-decorated soldiers sat at the large oak table opposite the well-respected advisors, each of them pining to present their unique knee-jerk assessment of the event. Everyone began to settle and await her nod.

The queen closed her eyes and listened. When the room became perfectly quiet, she simply said, "Go."

Words came from around the table as those in attendance spoke freely, fighting for the queen's recognition with the advice they provided.

"What is it?"

"I guess we now know it isn't a statue."

"That's not necessarily true. Angst can use magic on stone. Maybe it was all for show."

"His name is really Angst?"

"Back to my question, what is it?" The room became quiet again. "Okay, if we don't know what it is, what isn't it?"

"I still say it isn't a statue."

"I think it's a weapon."

"Did someone actually invite you?"

"Don't be insulting. Obviously it's a weapon, because it's a sword. People have reported that the sword was glowing. That says magic to me, and probably dangerous."

"Just because something glows doesn't mean it's dangerous."

"A glowing blue sword that nobody has been able to lift in recorded history, and you don't believe it's dangerous? In my world, if it looks like fire, it probably is fire. I say magic, and I say dangerous."

Most mumbled in agreement at this.

"Is it possible that we were supposed to be guarding it?"

"I don't follow."

"A dangerous, magic, glowing weapon that is securely fastened to a pedestal within castle walls. It may be a leap, but I'm guessing we weren't supposed to be using it as a party favor, but instead keeping it out of hands."

"Whose hands?"

"Angst's would've been a good start."

"Where's the sword now?"

"He has it with him."

"You let him leave with it?"

"He looked angry."

"Does anyone else have a problem with this?"

"It's bigger than any of the guards, and he carries it like a stick."

"So, you're telling me that this could be a weapon with unknown magical powers and it's in some cabin in the middle of town."

"It's not like he's going to sneak out with it."

"What do we do now?"

"Killing him would be easy. I hear he drinks a lot."

"Maybe he could be an asset. A new weapon against what's going on out there. We aren't exactly winning."

"Does that mean we have to make him a knight?"

"One of them? A knight? Are you serious?"

"Speaking of them, it's not going to take them long to rally around Angst like he's accomplished something."

"We can't kill him. That could just make him a martyr. The magic wielders are already in an uproar about all the new laws."

"Stop." The queen held up a hand, and the room grew quiet once more. "What happened last night was significant, and requires thorough understanding, not just conjecture. We need information, and we need to keep Angst occupied without causing riots. You've all given me much to ponder. If anyone is able to obtain further information about the sword, bring it to my attention immediately. Wilfred, Tyrell, General Mirot, please remain. Everyone else is dismissed."

The meeting dispersed, with only a few noticeably sneering at those chosen to remain. Captain Guard Tyrell and General Mirot stood at attention, while Wilfred seemed to lounge, enjoying the recognition in front of his peers.

"We all heard the same theories, now we need to come up with a plan, but let me be clear on what we're discussing. Our primary goal is to protect the kingdom. The people living in Unsel would be completely defenseless against the magic-wielders. If it means making that sap a knight to avoid rebellion, so be it. Our forces are spread too thin along the borders to defend against our own people, especially those who can wield magic." Isabelle looked around the room to make sure everyone understood. "General Mirot?"

The general's shoulders drooped from the weight of decoration and recognition. He tugged on his limp gray moustache and peered at the queen through dark, calculating eyes. "Your Majesty, he's an unknown element. We're already losing men to bizarre attacks on our borders, which, may I remind you, also seem to be of a magical nature. With Angst dead, we're safe."

"Are we safe, General?" Captain Guard Tyrell asked, tugging at the hem of his conservative navy uniform, a single bar on his chest the only evidence of his advanced rank. "You've told us that defending the kingdom by traditional means has been unsuccessful. What if this is our untraditional answer?"

"Sounds dangerous," Mirot huffed. "We don't even know what he's capable of with that statue he's carrying."

"Your Majesty, I offer my blade to test him," Tyrell said. "We've fenced in the past. I know his capabilities and could tell if something has changed."

"And if he has?" Isabelle asked.

"Kill him before it's too late," Mirot said, his jaw tight.

The queen sighed heavily. "General, I doubt we'll kill him, I agree that the wielders don't need a martyr. But, what if he is more powerful? Do we actually knight him?" Queen Isabelle asked, shuddering at the prospect.

"Angst spent some time training with the soldiers and knights before it was discovered he could wield magic," Tyrell said. "He's familiar with what would be expected of him."

"The military would be fiercely opposed to knighting a wielder!" Mirot's words exploded as if personally offended.

"He's well respected," Tyrell argued calmly, brushing the general's spittle off his arm. "Even liked."

"But not trusted," Mirot said between deep, calming breaths. "He already holds too much power for one man, and if the sword augments that power...even those who like him would be fiercely opposed to his knighting. There has to be an alternative."

"If he has become more powerful, and we even decide he could be an asset, how do we avoid knighting him?" Isabelle asked.

Mirot stared off as if upset that Angst wasn't dead yet. Tyrell frowned at Wilfred quizzically, who was the only one in the room smiling.

Isabelle narrowed her eyes at Wilfred, "You're never this quiet. I will hear your advice, but I weigh it with the knowledge that Angst is your friend."

"Thank you, Your Majesty. I would hope my service to your court balances any bias you might perceive." He paused until she reluctantly acknowledged this with a nod. "Your Majesty, what you have now is a new representative for the underdog, so to speak. If he is, indeed, more powerful, Unsel could use him. But, his loyalties lie with his friends, his family, and, forgive me for saying so, your daughter, not with you. He won't come to your side just because you ask it."

"I don't see where this is going," she said, fidgeting with the brocade on her sleeve.

"Angst has always wanted to be a knight, and by lifting the sword, he has won that chance," Wilfred said, his words rushed. "Make him earn it. Send him away on a mission, some long menial task through the heart of danger, with the promise of becoming a knight should he succeed. Something important enough that he can't refuse."

"And dangerous enough that he may not come back," Mirot said in agreement.

"Temporarily rid yourself of Angst and his friends," Wilfred continued. "In the process, you garner the support of all those who believe in him."

She looked at Wilfred, letting this idea sink in. "What is it you have in mind, exactly?"

"Wheat, my queen. Wheat."

She shook her head, not understanding.

"We've lost three scouting parties to whatever's going on out there, and haven't seen a trade shipment from anyone in over a month. With winter coming, our stores of wheat are certain to run short if something isn't done. Send Angst and his friends on a mission to Fulk'han, to free the blocked trade routes."

"It could take months," she said hopefully, the stiffness in her shoulders loosening slightly.

"Get rid of Angst while sending him on a 'noble' mission for the kingdom," he continued.

"Chances are he'll just get eaten," Mirot said.

"There's little to lose, Your Majesty," Wilfred said, sticking out his chest proudly. "What's the worst that could happen?"

The queen shot Wilfred a cool, direct look. "He could succeed."

6

It was unquestionably the longest morning Angst had ever endured. He was awoken by courier shortly after dawn with a polite note from Captain Guard Tyrell advising him not to come to work and to expect to hear from someone later in the day. This required an exceptional amount of pacing and worry on Angst's part. The constant barrage of 'what ifs' and 'what nexts' drove Heather out of the house to visit the market, leaving Angst alone with his hopes, his concerns, and the sword.

He'd tried setting the sword on their old wooden table, but the table had buckled and creaked before he could even let go, as had the wall of their cottage when he attempted to lean it in a corner. So the sword rested unceremoniously on the floor, in the middle of everything, waiting impatiently. Angst tried to ignore it as he paced from room to room, but the sword taunted him. Every time he passed, it glowed just enough to see from the corner of his eye, but the glow was always gone when he looked directly at it. The first time, he ignored it as a figment of his imagination. But after several passes, Angst was convinced the glow was real. He unsuccessfully tried to catch the blade in the act by whipping around, walking backward, or peeking from around a corner.

Angst finally dragged a battered chair across the floor and slammed it down a mere foot away from the beast. He stared at it awhile. It wasn't an elaborately designed weapon made by some legendary craftsman. The sword was crude, like a giant metal stick with a handle. The edges were straight and sharp until they finally bent to form a tip. There was no decoration or writing engraved anywhere. Most broadswords had a fuller, a groove through the center of the blade to make it lighter, but this one actually featured a riser, with more steel down the center instead of less. The grip was thin, looking almost silly in comparison to the rest of the blade. It was so wide and so long it seemed to fill half the room, making Angst feel small as he sat and pondered.

He continued staring, waiting for something to happen, before finally asking, "What? What do you want?"

As though relieved, the sword began to glow blue once more, though subdued this time. Angst could barely hear something, but it was so very quiet that he leaned toward the floor. After realizing that didn't help, he gripped the hilt, holding it for the first time since last night's mess.

The sword was singing. It was a chorus of musical instruments unlike any he had ever heard, and he worried it would disturb the neighbors. A quick glance out the door at some uncaring pedestrians passing by gave him the impression the song was for him. The music quieted, sounding as though he'd begun humming to himself. The song wasn't beautiful, but it was nice to listen to. At first he didn't recognize the tune, but it became more familiar the longer he listened. If he could just concentrate enough, maybe he could…

"*Chryslaenor*," rang through his head like a bell, and he dropped the sword. It fell with a loud bang, cracking parts of the wooden floor where it landed.

"What was that?" asked Heather, walking in with a bag of food. "What happened to my floor? Are you okay?"

"It talks," was all Angst could say. Goosebumps covered his arms, and he couldn't take his eyes off the sword.

"Very funny," Heather replied.

"No. Really. It talks. Sort of." Angst kneeled by the sword, and it started glowing again. "The sword has a name."

"Angst, I know you're excited that they might make you a knight, or something, and I'm sure you're exhausted after last night, but a talking sword? Maybe you should sit down." She walked past him and set her groceries on the table.

"It's not really talking. It kind of sings. I can't explain it, but I think it's trying to communicate with me." He reached for the hilt again.

"Maybe that's not a good idea," Heather suggested, but it was too late.

Angst had picked up the sword once more and concentrated as he had before.

"*Chryslaenor*," it sang once again.

"I was right. It does have a name." Angst cocked his head to the side. He felt detached, as though he was trying to explain a conversation he was having in another room at the same time. He pointed the tip at the ground so that the sword was upright, the hilt now over his head. Heather jumped out of the way when Angst let go, but the sword remained vertical, resting on its tip.

"How did you do that?" Heather asked, more curious than concerned.

"It taught me," he replied, then looked at her. "You couldn't hear any of that?"

She shook her head.

There was a knock at the door.

Heather startled, her head whipping back and forth between the door and the sword. "Can't you lie it back down? We don't want to scare the neighbors."

The knock was louder this time.

"Angst, are you in there?" It was Hector, and they both sighed with relief.

Angst opened the door. Hector was standing before him in formal black leather armor with several soldiers behind him. His bushy eyebrows were furrowed and his piercing blue-gray eyes looked oddly guilty. Sweat trickled down his friend's cheek to rest in the deep scar running along his square jaw.

"May I come in?" Hector asked.

"I think everyone should come on in. Thimes, Rook, Simmons, please. You are all welcome." Angst bowed formally and waved them in.

The soldiers looked at each other, clearly unsettled by this breach of protocol. Armed soldiers on official business weren't typically presented with casual invitations. Angst smirked at their reactions, and winked at Heather to let her know all was well.

"I'll make tea," she offered.

"No need, Heather. Thank you, but we won't be staying long." Hector stepped inside and immediately leapt away from the giant sword resting on its tip. "What in blazes is it doing?"

"Actually, *it* has a name. Chryslaenor. Chryslaenor doesn't like to lie on the floor."

"Right," Hector said, sounding dumbfounded, staring at Chryslaenor warily as if it would fall over at any second. "That answers that question. So last night wasn't just you wielding stone or metal, was it? That wasn't all for show?"

"I'll take some of the credit, I picked it up, but no, it wasn't just me," Angst replied.

"I have an invitation for you." Hector tore his eyes away from the sword. "It's from the Captain Guard. He would like to fence with you."

Angst smiled, but Heather didn't. "Isn't he the best? Angst, didn't he break your wrist once by accident?"

They both answered at the same time. "He's one of the best." "It was an accident."

Angst put his hands on Heather's shoulders and looked into her worried eyes. "Tyrell is a good man. I trust him, and I trust Hector. It'll be fun." He turned to Hector and asked, "When?"

"Now," Hector replied politely.

Angst nodded and took Chryslaenor from its resting position. As he approached the door with it, the guards moved away nervously.

"I really don't think this is a good idea," Heather said.

"Honey, it wasn't really a request."

7

Angst, Hector, Tyrell, and the three guards arrived at the training grounds. They were instantly enveloped by heat, dust, and air thick with humidity. Several acres stretched out before them. Areas had been marked off with short stone fences, each designated by wooden signposts. Classes were in session, and groups of sweaty young men busily trained with swords, halberds, in hand-to-hand combat and horseback riding, or simply did pushups.

Captain Guard Tyrell walked in front, his long gait making everyone scramble to catch up. Tyrell was forty-ish, like Angst, and while his body was in much better shape, his face seemed older from the heavy weight of responsibility. He was thin, all sinewy muscle, which stood out along his neck and jaw. His light brown hair was cut short, and his long nose and jutted chin seemed to point from his pale face. Many thought the man preened a bit much—the way he arched his back and lifted his chin made it seem as though he was looking down at everyone— but Angst had always felt that Tyrell was simply on duty at all times, and that his confidence and pride were often mistaken for haughtiness. Tyrell had reason to be confident. He was the only person Queen Isabelle trusted, and he was considered one of the best swordsmen in all the kingdoms.

Tyrell checked the nearest sign and waved for everyone to follow. Chryslaenor rose high over the party. There was no easy way to carry it. Angst had to rest the sword on his shoulder as though carrying a long beam of timber. Students, teachers, and sometimes entire classes came to an abrupt stop when they passed. Some stared, a few pointed, and one was struck upside the head by his sparring partner.

In spite of the heat and humidity and dust and attention, Angst was smiling. Tyrell had stated on the hike here that this would be nothing more than a friendly fencing match, to see if Angst could do anything more than threaten drunk knights, but Angst wasn't fooled. This was a test. He could only guess what the queen and Captain Guard were looking for, or what the results of the test could mean for him, but he too wanted to know what Chryslaenor could do in his hands.

"I haven't been here for a long time," Angst reflected as he nodded at several onlookers.

Hector smiled slyly. "You weren't really that bad...twenty years ago."

"Wait, I haven't been away that long, have I?" Angst asked, jerking to a stop.

"No, you only stopped coming about ten years ago. Just saying that twenty years ago, you were pretty good." Hector grinned mischievously.

"Here we are." Tyrell stopped next to a *Dueling and Fencing* sign. He glanced around the dirt-strewn space then casually looked up at the distant castle, which loomed over them like a mountain. While the castle wasn't close, someone with a good spyglass could see everything.

"So," said Rook, admiring the weapon still leaning on Angst's shoulder. "Any chance I can give that thing a swing?"

Angst shrugged. Until now, nobody else had asked. "Sure, why not?" He pulled it off his shoulder, and, holding the blade, offered it to Rook.

Rook was a burly man with a tan complexion and light, curly hair. One look at his broad shoulders and strong arms and you would do just about anything to avoid arm wrestling with him. He reached for the hilt then yelped as Angst let go. Chryslaenor fell and landed with a solid thud, dust billowing up around it.

"What was that for?" Rook said, rubbing his hand with a perturbed look on his face.

"What was what for?" Angst replied defensively, picking up Chryslaenor. "It really isn't that heavy, just awkward." He held the sword out to Rook again, who refused it this time.

Hector stepped forward and grabbed the hilt. He gripped tightly, but the sword immediately fell to the ground when Angst let go.

"That almost broke my wrist, Angst. What were you thinking?" Hector rubbed his forearm. "Not a great time for one of your jokes."

Angst shook his head in confusion. "I don't understand."

The Captain Guard rolled his eyes, familiar with Angst's abilities and often irreverent sense of humor. "Let's get this started. Angst, we brought training armor. You should pick out some pieces."

The soldiers ungraciously dropped several large bags in front of Angst and Hector with a crash.

Angst backed away, his eyes narrowing. He hadn't anticipated the need for armor. Wasn't this supposed to be a friendly sparring match? "Captain, I should be fine. I don't really need—"

"Not really a request, Angst." Tyrell's face was stone. "There's at least one at the castle who would try to see me in irons were you injured."

Angst pondered this for a second, and quickly decided it was best not to think about it.

Hector had been picking through the armor to find a few pieces. "Does this bring back memories? We never could find a full set of practice armor for you, even when you were a bit, well, a bit more in shape." Hector held up a leather chest piece that was a foot longer than Angst's torso. "The only things that are going to fit are the top half of some leg guards and maybe a helm."

"Hmm. That could be a problem," observed Tyrell.

Angst rested his sword on its tip then roughly grabbed a T-face helm in frustration. It rarely crossed his mind that he was shorter than most, nor did he dwell on the fact he needed to lose a bit of weight, but this was both the wound and some salt to rub in it. The smallest helmet was still large for his head. It featured a T-shaped opening for his eyes and mouth, but hung so low he could barely see. He then attempted to squeeze into plate leggings that were made for someone thinner and taller, making him feel more like a court jester in tights than a knight in armor. Hector helped unstrap and remove everything below the knee joint. They still hung over his knee awkwardly, but his thighs were protected. Everyone was smirking at him.

"Oh, this is silly," Angst said, shaking out his arms and legs, half-hoping that some of it would fall off.

"Her Majesty's orders, Angst," Tyrell proclaimed.

"I bet I know which *Her Majesty*," Angst muttered to himself.

Angst went to pick up Chryslaenor, but Rook grabbed his shoulder. "How about a little warm-up?" He handed Angst a wooden broadsword. "Let's see what you've got." Rook was still upset about dropping Chryslaenor, and Angst could tell he wasn't going to hold back during the "warm-up".

Angst took the sword and held it wrong, pointing it down awkwardly at a bad, almost defenseless angle. Hector, always the teacher, began to correct him, but Tyrell held up his hand. This was test time. Rook smirked, shaking his head at Angst's handling of the sword. He swung out at Angst's chest.

But Angst had a plan. Quickly correcting his stance, he held the wooden sword horizontal with one hand at both ends. He expertly blocked Rook's swing then moved in close. Pressing the flat of the sword against Rook's chest, he stepped around, sliding his foot behind Rook's left ankle. With a shove Rook tripped over Angst's foot. It wasn't a graceful fall or landing. Hector laughed, but Tyrell's expression was stony, staring on as if the entirety of Unsel was collectively disappointed with his shenanigans. Angst held a hand out to Rook, who slapped it away and stood on his own. Before Angst could say anything, Rook swung his wooden sword at Angst's head. Angst blocked, then blocked again, and again. Rook was relentless, swinging and thrusting all his frustration at Angst. Angst couldn't gain any ground; he could only defend against Rook's onslaught. He continued to block and parry until Rook finally swung at his leg and made contact. The wooden sword shattered against the leg armor, and would have probably broken Angst's thigh if not for the plate shielding him. He was glad, now, the princess had demanded the armor.

"Hey, Angst, I didn't mean..." Rook trailed off.

Angst smiled at the other man. "Can we say we're even now?"

Rook nodded.

"All right, not bad. You've obviously spent a little time with Hector," said Tyrell. "Let's see how you do with that...thing." He jerked his head in the direction of Chryslaenor. Then he looked at it more closely, finally squinting and rubbing his eyes.

Angst saw it too, the sword seemed to reflect a bit too much sunlight. Instead of glowing as it had on occasion, it now seemed blurry, as though shivering in anticipation. He frowned as he walked over to it, not quite understanding what was different. When he reached up to grab the hilt, Chryslaenor stopped vibrating.

Every time Angst held it, it fit. It wasn't merely an extension of his arm, or a tool to pick up and use. Chryslaenor seemed more like another limb that had always been there. Angst breathed in deeply and lifted it properly with both hands. A gentle blue aura surrounded the blade. He looked over toward Rook, who was in a basic attack stance, and now holding a large steel broadsword. They both nodded, and the duel began.

This time, the contest was different. Angst flawlessly blocked every swing Rook made. More than that, the blocks seemed effortless, his movements flowing smoothly. Angst stepped nimble and swung quick, like an over-excited twenty-year-old instead of a creaky, out-of-shape forty-year-old.

They paused long enough for him to notice Hector and the

captain sharing looks of surprise, and concern. Nearby soldiers in training were now making their way toward the duel.

* * * *

Hector watched the battle with a trained eye. He'd taught Angst how to fight, and seen him duel many times. This was like watching a different man. Someone who could do things he'd never seen. His swings were too effortless; neither Angst nor Chryslaenor were being tested by this match. Hector looked about quickly then grabbed a small shield from the armor pile. This hadn't been a part of the plan, nor did Hector really think it through. He drew a short sword and joined the fray.

Rook was used to fighting alongside others, so he automatically adjusted his stance to place Hector at his side. Angst's head jerked back and forth between the two men, all the while defending himself. After a brief moment of unsure footing, he seemed to relax and smoothly changed course. He continued to step back while defending himself against the two men. Within seconds, he appeared to hit his stride and smoothly changed course. Angst advanced, his steps sure and his swings accurate. He gently tapped Hector once on the arm and then spun to slap Rook on his leg. Angst's movements were so controlled that he never hurt the other men, yet still blocked every swing they made.

All the teachers and students had stopped their training and were now surrounding the combatants. The impromptu audience quickly divided itself, several cheering for Hector and Rook, while others rooted for the giant sword. The two guards who'd accompanied the group kept everyone a safe distance from the fighters, while holding their own weapons at the ready.

Even Angst seemed surprised to lift the giant sword over his head and block a sudden blow from Tyrell. The four men paused, assessing the situation for a moment, each breathing heavily. Angst lowered the sword and adjusted his helm. He made brief eye contact with each of them and smirked confidently.

"Fine, let's go," he challenged. Angst swung Chryslaenor in a wild arc, making Hector, Rook, and Tyrell all jump back. The crowd cheered loudly.

The three returned to the battle in force, stepping forward and working in conjunction against Angst and Chryslaenor. Two would swing, the third would defend. This strategy would've brought down any skilled blade master, if only by tiring him out. They were unrelenting, and soon quickened their pace. But even as they swung, attacked, and defended faster, so did Angst. The sword in his hand was glowing brighter, and Angst was now moving unnaturally fast. His arms, at times his entire body, were nothing more than a blur.

Angst blocked a double attack from Tyrell and Hector then spun and struck Rook in the chest with the flat of the blade. Rook flew several feet and fell to the ground with a heavy thud. He lay unmoving for a few tense moments, the cheers quieting to murmurs, then Rook suddenly sat up with a gasp, blinking rapidly. He waved to the others, signaling his part of the battle was over. The crowd returned their attention to the remaining fighters and were soon cheering again.

* * * *

Angst ignored the crowd, focused only on the battle and the sword. Chryslaenor was glowing, and whipped around like a blue streak of lightning. Angst felt like he was swinging a mountain, but knew how. He was conducting a symphony without knowing the music. He was aware of everything around him—his attackers, the crowd, even the queen at the castle watching him through the spyglass. Chryslaenor guided his movements, the song becoming louder and trying to seep into him as the fight continued.

Hector backed away, sheathing his weapon and holding up both hands. Angst immediately stopped attacking him, turning his focus solely on Tyrell. The crowd was now making bets, cheering for Tyrell, or just gawking at the spectacle before them, pleased with the unexpected entertainment.

The Captain Guard didn't lose, ever. A true master of the blade, he rarely got an opportunity that tested his skill. Now, the man was drenched in sweat and caked in dust, and, like Angst, grinning from ear to ear. They circled each other, swinging and blocking in a constant flow of metal and sparks. Both were hungry for more, but after five minutes, Hector stepped between them, unarmed.

Angst reared back mid-swing to avoid injuring him. The Captain Guard almost fell to keep from running Hector through.

Tyrell caught himself and slowly leaned over, hands on his knees. Gulping for air, he looked up at Angst suspiciously. "You used your magic," he accused.

Hector and Angst both shook their heads. Hector spoke first, "The explanation's not that simple. I never taught Angst any of that, and you know swordplay isn't his type of magic. If it *is* magic, it had to come from the sword."

Angst pulled off his helmet. His hair was drenched and sweat trickled down his dusty face. "That was fun," he said, unable to steady his voice. His hand shook and his heart pounded like angry bees circling their nest. He looked around at everyone, looked at his sword, smiled weakly, and everything went dark.

8

Angst crawled out of his deep slumber. His first breath was sweet, but there seemed to be a weight on his chest, and his mouth was too dry to open. Angst could only see blotches of light when he forced his eyelids open. His stomach was a yawning pit. It felt as though he hadn't eaten. Ever. Every tiny movement he attempted was thwarted by sore muscles or angry joints. The weight lifted from his chest as the room gradually came into focus.

"Angst?" said a voice that sounded young and fresh as the first day of spring. He could smell the gentle fragrance of strawberries.

"Tori?" He tried to sit, but didn't even have enough strength to rub the bleariness from his eyes.

The first thing he could see clearly was Victoria hovering over him, looking worried and surprised. Her eyes were red and puffy, as though she'd been crying, and her breaths included an occasional hitch.

"Ahem." The Captain Guard was somewhere behind her, and even now correcting Angst for using the nickname.

Angst was too tired to apologize and rocked his head to try to see more of the room. Behind Victoria's hair, he could make out Dallow and Hector, smiling and patting each other on the back. He smiled weakly at them, not quite understanding their enthusiasm, but someone had probably won a bet about when he would wake. It was obvious he was in the infirmary. The walls were painted white, the cot was uncomfortable, and the scent of 'scrubbed clean' was barely held back by Victoria's perfume.

"Your Majesty, let the nurse do her job," Tyrell advised politely.

The princess flashed the Captain Guard a challenging gaze and tried staring him down. Tyrell was not swayed as easily as her mother, and she slowly moved from a hovering position to one seated on Angst's cot, which almost gave the frustrated nurse and physician enough room to work. Angst came to realize she was holding his hand, which he still couldn't move.

Physician Nynette worked her way past Victoria, shaking her head in disbelief. She was older than Angst, though her brown hair was pulled back in a bun tight enough to smooth some of the wrinkles around her eyes. She'd spent too much daytime in rooms like this. Her skin was pale, and her dark blue physician robes too large for her frail body. Nynette was a bit wild-eyed, and she shook slightly while checking the pulse at his neck.

"What happened?" Angst whispered in a voice scratchy from exhaustion.

The physician replied in a strained, high-pitched voice, "When the guards carried you in, you weren't breathing. I declared you dead thirty minutes ago."

"Um, what? How could I be dead?" Shock infused Angst with a short burst of energy, and he tried to sit.

Tori put her hand on his chest so he would lie back down, and her hand was trembling, ever so slightly. "Angst, you were dead." Her pouty lip quivered and her worried eyes were bloodshot.

The nurse squeezed in behind Victoria, tipped his head back, and poured something gray and awful down his throat. It helped, a little. He looked over at Hector and Dallow, who had yet to say anything, eyeing him warily as if he shouldn't be there. The entire room seemed filled with a sense of awkward relief. But, what do you say to someone who suddenly stops being dead?

"I'm not dead now. I remember dueling, I remember beating

everyone up a little." Angst nodded toward Tyrell and Hector, both of whom seemed a bit chagrined. "Then, there was something... No, then I saw you." Angst looked at the princess. He wanted her to calm a bit, and flashed her an obnoxious ear-to-ear grin. "Wow, what a great way to come back to life."

Behind Victoria, Dallow rolled his eyes while Hector pretended to throw up. Even the nurse shook her head as she walked out of the room.

The princess closed her eyes and tried not to smile. "You know, you really aren't a very good flirt at all."

"Well, if you're flirting you can go back to being dead." Heather entered the room, followed by Tarness. Then she saw the princess and stopped abruptly. "Oh, Your Majesty, I didn't know." She bowed politely and waited at the door.

"Thank you, Heather, but there are more important things than formality right now." Victoria waved Heather into the room.

Tyrell bristled at this, sighing significantly, but otherwise kept his peace.

"Thank you, Your Highness." She nodded appreciatively then looked at Angst. "I heard you were dead. Sadly, it seems it was only a rumor. I had your replacement lined up already."

Angst feigned shock. "Not the *boy* who works the stables at Wizard's Revenge? He's a bit young, isn't he?"

Heather blushed a bit and her eyes grew large. "I do not know of what you speak."

"You didn't bring something to eat, did you?" Angst said, his voice still sounding like gravel crunching under a wagon wheel. His stomach growled, loud enough for everyone to hear.

The princess stared at Heather, shaking her head in disbelief. "She's as bad as you are." Victoria dropped his hand and stood to face Heather. "Weren't you worried?"

"I don't think I could get rid of him so easily." She chuckled politely, but her eyes said something different. Heather sat on the cot where Victoria had been. She took Angst's hand and held it. His hand was cold and damp, his grip weak from fatigue, but he squeezed hers gently.

Victoria hadn't observed the true concern in Heather's gaze. She smiled politely. "I'm glad you are all right, Mr. Angst. I wish you a speedy recovery."

"Thank you for being here," Angst whispered, but the princess had left before he could finish. Tyrell followed Victoria, and the physician smiled, rubbing her hands together.

Hector turned to Dallow. "He does play with fire, doesn't he?"

"He's braver than I am," Dallow replied then looked to Angst. "You're going to have to do something about that one day."

"Bah." Angst found he was able to sit up, and was starting to feel somewhat human again, though he was still famished. He looked down at his noisy stomach. "The princess and I are good friends, nothing else. Really, is there anything to eat?"

The room was quiet. Heather watched him with great concern, still holding his hand. "What happened?"

"We dueled. Tyrell, Rook, and I all fought Angst for about fifteen minutes or so," answered Hector. "When it was done, he collapsed."

Heather stood up suddenly and looked back and forth between Angst and Hector. "Wait. Why were three people fighting my husband? Was it everyone at once? Who knocked him out? Was it Tyrell?"

Hector looked at his foot to avoid her angry glare and drew his thumb along the scar on his chin. "Uh, well, not exactly. Angst started fighting Rook then I joined in. We dueled for several minutes before Tyrell stepped in too." He looked up briefly, but at seeing Heather's glare went back to studying his foot. "Angst knocked Rook senseless then I bowed out of the fight, leaving Tyrell and Angst. They dueled for another five minutes when I broke it up. That's when he passed out."

"What? What?" Heather asked, holding a palm up. "How is that possible? Fighting three men at once?"

Angst shook his head. "It's the sword. There was something

going on. It kept pushing me, or guiding me, or both." He shut his eyes, trying to remember. "It's hard to explain. Before I passed out, did you guys hear music?"

Blank, awestruck stares answered his question.

"No?" He shook his head. "I think I just need some more practice with it."

"After it killed you?" Heather cried, her curly hair disheveled and her cheeks blotchy red. "Is your ego so important that you'll die for it, Angst?"

He rolled his eyes and looked at Nynette, who'd been listening intently to the whole story. "Really, could I trouble you for a sandwich or something?"

Nynette ignored him, scribbling notes on a parchment that probably wasn't an order for food. Every time she looked up, her eyes were unsure. He didn't enjoy that look, from any of them, but the disbelief in their eyes didn't compare to the fury in Heather's.

"I'm sure *Tori* will be impressed when you kill yourself with that stupid sword," she shouted. "Forty years old and still pretending to be twenty! Do you want to die that badly, Angst? Is your life so horrible?" Heather threw his hand back to the bed and stomped out of the room.

"Could I please have just one more person kick the crap out of me today? That would be just great," Angst said to nobody.

"You're the one who likes to keep so many of them around," Tarness said with a broad smile.

"I think you're a sadist, personally," said Hector.

"So what are you guys doing here anyway?" Angst asked, trying to change the subject yet again.

"Hector sent word to Tarness and me that you were dead. Tarness fetched your wife while I went to tell Rose." Dallow said.

"Where is Rose?" Angst asked, looking around as though she were hiding.

"She, well, she got really angry at me when I told her the news then she stomped off. It was weird," Dallow said with look of bewilderment.

Angst wasn't surprised. Rose had lost her father when she was young, and had no tolerance for death. "Don't worry about it. I'll talk to her after I get out," he said, faking a smile. "So was I really dead? Is this going to happen every time I use that thing?"

Everyone shrugged.

Angst had no memory of passing out, but something tickled the back of his mind. He could still hear the music, though it was very quiet. There was a brief glimpse of memory, like a poor reflection in a choppy lake. Something about the sword, something about what it was made for and what it wanted. It had tried to tell him, or include him in something.

"Where is the sword anyway?" Angst asked.

"Right where you dropped it, Angst. You weren't kidding. No one else can lift it. Rook felt awful," Hector said apologetically.

It was Angst's turn to shrug. "Not to worry. This whole situation is beyond odd." He leaned back into the pillow.

"I'm curious. What kind of music did you hear, Angst?" asked Dallow.

"It's hard to describe. Not really music, but something similar. I want to hear more, though," Angst said in a quiet voice that trailed off.

"I've heard enough," Nynette said sharply, "Nurse, please bring in my alchemy kit."

Angst could hear a cart being wheeled down the hall. The sense of dread creeping up his spine was quickly forgotten by the smell of roast duck and spice bread. A man dressed in white pushed a cart of food into his room. It was the most magnificent, glorious cart of food Angst had ever seen, and delivered by the queen's chef himself!

"By Princess Victoria's command, I bring you some royal dinner." The chef dipped his white hat in a flourishing bow and winked at Angst. "Enjoy."

The physician growled loudly and stomped out of the room.

* * * *

"Just how bad was it?" asked Queen Isabelle.

They stood together in the viewing tower that overlooked the distant training field. Tyrell leaned forward and peered through a spyglass to see several guards standing by Chryslaenor.

"Worse than we'd expected. Did you see how he defended against all three of us?"

"All I could see was a blur, Tyrell. It looked as though he was out of control."

Tyrell pulled away from his viewing. "That's the frightening part. He was never out of control. If he had been, I'd be dead. He was actually having fun. You couldn't see his grin from up here. Angst was almost giddy the entire duel." He stepped away from the window and clasped his hands behind his back.

"We can't kill him?" she asked sincerely.

"I just watched him come back from the dead." The Captain Guard looked at the queen, meeting her gaze. "Mirot will be disappointed, but that option is definitely off the table."

They both stared at each other for an eternity, silently reviewing the few choices available.

"Your Majesty, I miscalculated. The *duel* should never have taken place in front of so many," Tyrell said in a disappointed tone. "By now the entire kingdom knows what happened."

"Thank you, Tyrell, but I believe there's no foreseeing what that weapon is capable of doing." Much of the queen's formality had been stripped away by worry and disbelief. She plopped down on a nearby cushioned seat and attempted to straighten her burgundy dress.

"I don't see how we can forcibly exile him. We're all concerned about what he can do with the sword now, but there is something else I found to be frightening." Tyrell paced around the small room. "As the duel progressed, he seemed to improve. It was almost as though Angst was trying to figure the sword out."

"What happens when he does *figure it out*? What happens

when he realizes its full potential? I don't think he should be anywhere near Unsel when that happens." Isabelle took in a deep breath and sighed. "That smug little bastard may be right."

"You're thinking of Wilfred's plan?" Tyrell asked, a bit surprised.

She nodded slowly. "I want Angst out of Unsel by the end of the week."

9

When opportunity knocks, it's typically hard and in the back of the head. Any time Angst heard the word 'opportunity' as part of an offer, tension immediately crept up his spine and into his shoulders. He'd always felt it was a bureaucratic code word, a way of saying, "We have a lot more work for you to do with little reward, except maybe our thanks if you don't mess up too badly." Angst muttered to himself while slipping his boot on. He wanted out of the infirmary and away from the evil genius doctor and the alchemy kit she kept threatening to use. His friends had departed and his stomach was full again. He now felt a great need to fetch Chryslaenor, make up with his wife, and sleep in his own bed.

"Angst? What do you think about the opportunity?" asked Tyrell. He had been waiting patiently for a response while Angst brooded.

Angst stood, pushing his foot the rest of the way into his boot. He liked Tyrell better when they were crossing swords. "Captain Guard, I'm sorry, I'm still a bit weary from the duel. What was that last part?"

"Of course, Angst," Tyrell stated in a formal tone. "The queen would like to discuss an opportunity over breakfast tomorrow morning. If you are up to the task."

Angst sighed, wondering what hoops he would need to jump through for knighthood. Had Tyrell even said they would be discussing knighthood? It was something Angst had always wanted, convinced it was the one thing that would fix everything he hated about his life. He vaguely recalled hearing the man say Angst could earn a 'title,' which could mean anything. 'Jester' was, officially, a title.

"Please tell Her Majesty I would be honored by the opportunity to breakfast with her," Angst replied with feigned gratitude. His response dripped with politic and irony, but it was enough of a response that Tyrell smiled, albeit curtly.

"Glad to see you're doing better. Tomorrow morning then." Tyrell bowed stiffly and turned to depart.

Angst followed, so closely that his proximity very obviously made the Captain Guard uncomfortable, until they reached the nurse. She stood abruptly and held out a threatening finger as if preparing to chastise Angst back into bed. But in the end did nothing more than open and close her mouth like a fish out of water. Following Tyrell that close had given the appearance Angst was under orders, and she wouldn't consider questioning the Captain Guard's authority.

As they exited the infirmary, Tyrell stopped and looked at Angst with a raised eyebrow. "Smooth. Is there anything else I can help you with tonight?"

Angst grinned, and clapped him unceremoniously on the shoulder. "That should do, thanks. See you tomorrow."

Angst walked away quickly to avoid any chance of contact with the physician or her nurse. He felt like he was suffering from a mild hangover and was desperate to clear his head with fresh air. He wanted to leave the castle, but had a nagging feeling that it would be best to visit Rose.

Within a few minutes, he arrived at the servants' quarters and knocked on her door.

"Go away!" Rose's command was embellished with several choice curses.

He knocked louder, and continued knocking until she stopped yelling and opened the door.

Her fine red hair was a disheveled mess, and her eyes widened more than usual at the sight of Angst. She was out of breath, and the bit of room he could see looked destroyed.

"Run out of people to beat on?" Angst asked politely.

Rose jumped forward, gave him the briefest of hugs, then quickly let go and took a step back. "Don't you ever die again."

"I can't even seem to do that right," Angst replied jokingly, but her stern gaze wasn't affected. He sobered. "I'll do my best."

Rose nodded and sighed.

"I was going for a walk to fetch my sword. I seemed to have dropped it when I died earlier. Want to come with?"

She smirked and rolled her eyes. "Well, if I stay here, I'll have to clean this mess up." Kicking a broken plate aside, she stepped behind the door and returned with a red cowl clasped around her neck. The cowl was heavy and made for winter, but Rose tended to chill easily. "Sure, why not?"

They left the castle and wandered toward the training grounds at a slowish pace. He was surprised at how much better he felt, only stopping to stretch out knots, which seemed to choose a different muscle every few minutes. Rose talked castle gossip, ranted about her job, and complained about the new idiot girl who'd been hired for her abilities in the sack. She never once asked him about the duel, or the sword, or the dying. Some would've considered this rude, but Angst found their conversation refreshing. During that short stroll, for those brief minutes, nothing had changed. He was still just Angst, and Rose would never let him get away with thinking anything more.

The air was crisp, and Rose hugged her cloak tight. Night was replacing dusk, and a bright moon illuminated their path. Angst was rarely cold, and had he been walking with Tori, he wouldn't have hesitated to throw an arm around her. To share body heat, of course. The princess was a hugger, who seemed to like popping his bubble. Rose was the opposite, vehemently defending her personal space. She would visibly shudder, or even lash out, when touched. Oddly, in spite of her aversion to physical contact, she was always willing to hit him for his occasional crude remark.

Gaps in conversation were filled by their lonely footsteps on the gravel path, and for Angst, the distant song of Chryslaenor. It became louder as they approached the training grounds, and he could make out the sword's blue glow in the distance.

Angst held his hand in front of Rose to stop her.

"Quit it," she said, struggling to shove past.

"Shhh. Something isn't right," Angst whispered quickly and pointed at Chryslaenor. "You see the sword? It's glowing."

"Doesn't it always do that? I thought its real job was to replace lamplights." She chuckled at her own joke.

Angst shook his head. "The last time it did that I was fighting someone."

There was nowhere to hide, so they moved forward quietly until the scene became clear. Two guards were lying on each side of the sword, unmoving, as though tossed aside. Five or six silhouettes of animal-like creatures surrounded Chryslaenor. The creatures made clicking and guttural horting sounds. They took turns trying to pull or push the sword. It didn't budge, and obviously didn't want the attention, flashing bright blue every time they attempted to move it.

In the light cast by Chryslaenor's glow, their faces were strangely human. Each of them two or three feet tall, with rocky quill-like protrusions covering their heads and back. Their long claws clicked loudly when they moved. It would have been comical, if they hadn't been trying to steal his sword! Several of the creatures started digging around it, throwing bits of dirt and stone into the air. Soon others were helping, and Chryslaenor started to sink as they pulled away the ground beneath it.

There was no time to lose. With a deep breath Angst concentrated, reaching out toward the sword. His hand glowed brightly, and some of the beasts stopped digging and turned to look. When he focused on Chryslaenor, he could hear it, but it felt tethered to its resting place. He couldn't move the sword with magic, but, like the creatures, he could move the ground under it.

"Angst? That might not be a good idea," Rose stated, not quite whispering. She was rocking back and forth nervously, as though ready to sprint away at a moment's notice.

The ground around Chryslaenor shook as Angst willed the earth underneath to rise. Now, all the creatures had stopped digging. He had hoped they would scurry away like frightened rabbits, but instead they congregated and made more of their unusual sounds. The shaking became violent enough that one of them fell. A dozen bright red eyes suddenly looked up and they advanced toward Angst and Rose.

"Bad idea, Angst. Bad idea!" Rose looked back and forth between the path and their attackers, finally drawing a dagger from somewhere near her hip. "We can come back for it. Let's go."

"Chryslaenor is mine!" Angst declared in a hollow voice.

"Angst?" Rose asked, her voice filled with concern.

Sweat trickled down his cheek and the aura surrounding his hand became even brighter as he willed the ground to push Chryslaenor. Like a stormy ocean beating a rocky shore, waves of earth crashed toward them, lifting the sword and carrying it on a crest of flowing dirt and stone.

The sword came slowly at first, as Angst had never done anything like this. But as he became more familiar with the process, it gained speed. The upswell of ground threw the beasts aside. They screamed in frustration, but rather than landing, dove into the ground as though it were water. The waves of earth abruptly stopped. Chryslaenor launched into the air and landed in Angst's hands.

Three of the monsters leaped out of the ground, grasping the sword with long bear-clawed fingers. Two more dove at Angst and one ran straight at Rose. She screamed and drove her dagger into the chest of her attacker. The beast grabbed at her arm with its sharp claws, tearing away at her sleeve. She spun in a full circle, trying to shake it off. When she stopped, it slid off the blade and flew into the air. It landed on its feet and raced toward Rose once again.

Angst quickly stepped in front of her. Chryslaenor's song was loud, filling his head, and his strength had returned. His aches and pains were completely gone, and everything felt right.

CHAPTER NINE

Angst swung at the creature jumping toward Rose. The animals still hanging on the sword were thrown into the air, and bits of the claw-like fingers were instantly severed by Chryslaenor. The song grew louder and power flowed through him. Rose gasped as Angst became a blur. He sliced her assailant in half, gloppy innards splattering them both. He quickly dispatched two more and stopped suddenly. Holding the sword high into the night Angst ran at the three injured creatures, roaring maniacally. The monsters dove into the ground, and everything became quiet.

"What were those things?" Rose yelled, stomping in place and shaking bits of monster off her tattered cloak. "Aaaah!"

Angst kneeled down to check on the soldiers. "It's Rook! He's alive, they both are, but these cuts look bad." He turned on his knee to look at Rose. "Are you all right? It looked like one of them got your arm."

"No, I'm fine," Rose assured him. She stood away from the soldiers, holding the arm that had been attacked out of sight.

Angst lightly slapped the men in an attempt to wake them, their only response was weak moaning, neither woke fully.

"I can't wake them, and I don't want to stay. Those things could come back with friends. Maybe I can find some rope and we can drag them back." He stood and everything began to spin, his vision fading in and out. "Not now," Angst whispered to himself, dropping Chryslaenor. He fell to one knee and fought the sudden and pressing need to pass out.

Rose yelped from behind him, but he couldn't turn. "Are you all right?" he croaked, still fighting to clear his head.

"Yes. Yes, I'm okay." Her voice had become husky. "One of them is waking up."

"Angst, is that you? What's wrong?" Rook asked.

Angst couldn't respond. He had to force himself to breathe. Rook grabbed under both arms, pulling him to his feet.

Chryslaenor had been quiet after the fight, but the music began once again, a song he didn't want to hear right now. He needed time to think, to try to understand what it wanted of him.

But it appeared there was no time, so he listened and let the power of the song fill him with energy once again. After several moments, he took a deep breath.

"I'm fine." Angst stood and lifted Chryslaenor. He hefted it over his shoulder and onto his back then let go. The sword stayed in place as though resting in a sheath that wasn't there. The hilt rose high over his right shoulder, and the tip mere inches above his left ankle. Both Rose and Rook stared in awe.

"I just sort of figured that out," Angst said with a shrug.

"Um, never mind. No offense, but I really don't want to know," Rook said, shuddering at the sight. He walked over to the other soldier, placed his hands under the man's arms, and lifted him.

Rose shot Angst a quirky smile. "Freak," she chided. She circled the area and collected the monster claws he'd removed with Chryslaenor. "Look, souvenirs!"

Her cloak was stained with blood, and the sleeve shredded with claw marks. "Are you sure you're okay?" He pulled at her arm to check it for wounds and was surprised to find it untouched. She jerked it back and scowled at him.

"That thing tore my cloak, but I'm fine," she said, hiding her arm behind her back.

Angst didn't believe Rose but arguing would be useless. "Let's get him to the infirmary." Angst said to Rook.

They both took an arm and slowly made their way back to the castle. It was an awkward walk for Angst. If he bent his knees even slightly, the sword tip dragged on the ground. If he stood up too straight, the man's head flopped back and hit Chryslaenor's hilt. Rose chuckled on occasion, but didn't offer to help.

Several guards ran to them as they came into view of the castle. "I'll go with him to the infirmary. I should get checked out too," Rook informed Angst and Rose. He paused for a moment. "Thank you, both, for saving my life."

"Thank you for guarding my sword, Rook. It obviously needed watching." Angst clasped arms with the man.

Rook smiled then followed the guards.

"You did pretty good out there. For a girl," Angst teased Rose.

She struck his arm. "I don't even understand how you did all that, but you can explain it some other time. I need sleep."

"Me too. I get exhausted every time I use Chryslaenor."

"It looked to me like you just needed to relax a bit," Rose offered.

"Huh." Angst considered Rose's comment, and knew he would have to give her suggestion more thought later. "Well, sorry for getting you involved in all that."

"Eh. Thanks for not dying this time." She handed him several claws, keeping the rest for herself, before returning to the castle.

Angst stared at the claws. He decided he was done with surreal, with which the day seemed far too full. He walked straight home, startling several couples on the way with the view of Chryslaenor towering over his shoulder. A light was on inside his cottage, and he opened the door slowly.

"Angst?" called Heather. She got up from the table and greeted him with a hug. "Are you okay? I'm so sorry. I've been so worried."

"I'm sorry too. I'm sorry about this whole mess," he said, holding her tight.

She pulled away, looking him over with worried eyes. "You look terrible! What happened?"

"Everything," Angst said.

He set Chryslaenor in the corner, sat in a chair, and told her about his day from the beginning.

10

This was not breakfast. Breakfast is toast and milk, or porridge. Maybe an apple. This grandiose combination of breakfast, lunch, and dinner was enough to feed his friends, wife, and distant cousins for a week. After all that had happened to Angst over the last several days, it was the height of irony. He hadn't been shocked by picking up the sword or what it allowed him to do; he was shocked by breakfast, that there was so much. Fancy toasts dripping in syrups, gravy and steak (for breakfast), five different kinds of eggs…and it all smelled so good that his mouth watered. Someone had actually gone to the trouble of peeling every bit of fruit that decorated the table. Angst couldn't help but wonder how the princess had remained so thin, and now knew why the queen had not.

"*Angst!* Your sword, *sir!*" The Captain Guard barred his way, hand on the hilt of his short sword, and face curdled with anger. Angst had been ignoring him again.

The spread of food was so ostentatious that Angst had completely forgotten Chryslaenor looming over his right shoulder. It must've stood out like a sign that read in big bold letters, "I'm here to kick your ass." Carrying any weapon in front of the queen was more than a *faux pas*, but hefting this beast in her presence must've seemed like an overt act of war.

Angst shook his head to clear his thoughts then stepped back from Tyrell. "My apologies. These last few days have been a bit...overwhelming."

"*Remove your sword now!*" Tyrell was still yelling, even after Angst apologized.

Now Angst was getting upset. It seemed Tyrell wouldn't even give him a moment to speak. "Fine," he said curtly. Chryslaenor fell from his back, the tip chipping a fist-sized piece of marble out of the floor just before the hilt landed with a loud boom. "Anything else?"

The Captain Guard, having been extraordinarily lenient in matters concerning Angst and the princess, had no tolerance for any disrespect of the queen. He raised a threatening finger and leaned down so the two men were nose to nose. Tyrell's pale cheeks were blotchy red with anger, and he took a breath deep enough to blow out a campfire.

Like a refreshing spring breeze, the princess floated in, grabbed Angst's hand and pulled him to the queen, who was already seated at the table. The move was so quick, so smooth, that neither Angst nor Tyrell had time to react.

"Thank you so much for joining us, Mr. Angst. Our chef prepared a little extra, not knowing what you would like." She made eye contact and nodded slowly as though trying to extract the merest bit of etiquette from him. She jerked her head once toward the queen then let go of his hand.

Angst tore himself from thinking of Tyrell's verbal assault, and bowed as best he could. "Your Majesty, my sincere gratitude for your invitation to breakfast this fine morning. I am honored."

The queen, who'd completely ignored everything that had happened to this point, held out her hand so Angst could kiss the royal ring. He kissed it with the tiniest of pecks, quickly, as though to avoid contaminating his lips. Isabelle offered a strained smile. Today, the queen wore a mauve dress that seemed slightly less flowing and embroidered than her usual pageantry. Her white hair rested on her well-fed cheeks, and her crown was nowhere to be seen. Had she tried to dress down for the occasion so he would be more comfortable?

"I would like to see it," she commanded politely.

"Your Majesty?" Angst asked, perplexed by the queen's request.

"The sword, Angst. I would like to see it." Her gaze was steady, her eyes absorbing and assessing everything he did.

"Um, of course, Your Majesty." It made no sense to Angst, especially after the altercation with Tyrell.

"Your Majesty, it is by your own command that weapons should never be carried in your presence, save for your own personal guards." Tyrell's feathers were evidently still a bit ruffled.

"Tyrell, from what I understand, if Angst intended to attack us with that thing, he could've taken out half the castle by now." The queen's tone wasn't rude but rather matter-of-fact.

Angst walked by Tyrell to fetch Chryslaenor. It took every ounce of strength not to stick out his tongue, stick up his nose, or stick out his finger at the man. He could sense the princess holding her breath, and feel Tyrell's eyes boring into his skull.

He lifted the sword then looked down at the dislodged piece of marble. "With your permission, Majesty, may I repair the floor? My sword seems to have damaged it."

The queen nodded once, examining him closely. Angst knelt down. A gentle blue aura surrounded his hand, and the marble melted back into the floor. He stood and walked to the queen, holding out Chryslaenor for her to see. She reached out and touched the blade curiously. Tyrell loomed, appearing ready to pounce at the slightest provocation.

"Please, be careful. It could harm you if you were to try to lift it," Angst warned with genuine concern.

"So I've heard, Mr. Angst, but thank you for the warning all the same." The queen took her hand away. "It seems surprisingly unremarkable. Is it...intelligent?"

"Well, I don't believe it's stupid," Angst replied without thinking then realized he should've spoken more formally. "Sorry. I mean to say, I'm not certain, but Chryslaenor seems to react to things, which would indicate...something. I honestly don't know what that means, just yet."

Isabelle nodded then casually waved to the nearest corner. "Set it aside and let's breakfast."

Breakfast was actually, sort of, nice. For the briefest of moments, the queen appeared almost human. She liked eggs, and ate her fill of three different kinds. A young servant had prepared a plate of fruit for the princess, who pulled her feet up to the chair, wrapped her arms around her knees, and nibbled on grapes. Tyrell ate more steak and eggs than Angst had seen even Tarness down. Angst wasn't hungry; anxiety seemed to be marching through his stomach. He was, however, curious, and snacked on the dishes he wasn't familiar with.

Conversation was filled with safe generalities. In fifteen minutes, they covered summer, fall, family members, visiting dignitaries, and breakfast, not once mentioning anything relevant or controversial. While he felt he was intruding on a family meal, it was nice to sit near Victoria, in the open, without getting yelled at or stared down. The queen was diplomatic, seeming both casual and careful with her choice of topic. She even held back rolling some of her Rs.

Dishes were efficiently removed at the end of their stuffing, and all became quiet.

"Your Majesty, what can I do for you?" Angst finally asked.

"Angst, that was the right question," she said with a politic grin.

The queen's brows knit together as though they were trying to form the word 'opportunity.' He sensed that it may have been the wrong question.

"You wielding that sword has been both complicated and timely," she began.

"Would these have something to do with being timely, Your Majesty?" Angst dropped one clawed finger from the prior night's battle onto the white tablecloth.

The queen waved at one of the servers, who hurried over to scoop it up then whisk it away to Tyrell.

The Captain Guard took the claw and studied it. He seemed surprised at first then a little worried. "Angst, where did this come from?" It was the first time Tyrell had spoken directly to him since their altercation.

"When I went to fetch the sword last night with my friend Rose, some creatures were trying to take Chryslaenor. We killed several, and scared the rest away."

"You killed some?" Tyrell asked in disbelief, looking up briefly. "We've been defenseless against the gamlin since they appeared a year ago."

"I don't understand. What do you mean defenseless?"

"Our weapons can't penetrate their hide. The best we can do is capture them, but even then we haven't been able to hold them." Tyrell looked at the queen and nodded, as though confirming something.

Angst braved a glance at the princess, who flashed him a quick wink but offered nothing more. He then faced the queen.

Isabelle sat straight in her high-backed chair, her face pained as she fought to form the words. "Angst, Unsel is in need of your...abilities, and I'm prepared to offer you title in exchange for your services."

Angst wanted to ask if the 'title' being offered was knight. He wanted to know what that would take to achieve. But this wasn't an award ceremony for winning a lottery—this was politics. "I assume you aren't asking about my filing services, though with Chryslaenor, I could put away documents faster than ever."

The princess chuckled, familiar with Angst's humor, but the queen shifted uncomfortably in her chair. "In light of current events, I believe a promotion is in order."

Angst couldn't help but smile. The anticipation was almost too much.

As though reading his mind, the queen answered his unspoken question. "Angst, as you know, not just anyone can be a knight of Unsel. It requires more than family, more than strength or prowess on the battlefield. Knights are something...well, something more. Making you a knight because you picked up an old sword would be like making you a king for finding one in a stone. The protection of Unsel is more important, more sacred, than tradition."

What the queen said made sense; it was very logical and struck hard enough to crack Angst's stained glass window. He couldn't bring himself to say anything at that moment for fear his voice might also crack. He couldn't bear to look over at Victoria, so Angst merely nodded in acknowledgement of what she was saying and sank a bit in his seat.

"Knighthood, Angst, cannot be won. It must be earned." As though this were an unrehearsed performance, the queen nodded at the Captain Guard, indicating his entrance cue.

"Angst," Tyrell began. "We would like you to undertake a mission, on behalf of Unsel."

Angst remained low in his seat. He wanted to be a knight, and the prospect of doing the queen and Tyrell some favor without that reward made this entire meeting feel like a waste of time. "What did you have in mind?" he asked warily.

"The gamlin have been wreaking havoc along our borders, and we believe they're blocking major trade routes."

"You're kidding?" asked Angst, no longer in the mood for formality. "Those little things?"

"Nobody else can seem to kill 'those little things.' Neither the Kingdom of Melkier nor Unsel have received a shipment or communication from Rohjek or Fulk'han in months." Tyrell handed the claw back to one of the servers, who returned it to Angst.

Angst held it up, and looked at the Captain Guard in disbelief. It sounded like a bad joke. "No offense, Tyrell, but I have a hard time believing those creatures are the cause."

"Which is why we need you to investigate. You can obviously handle yourself around them. In two weeks, you can make it to Rohjek. Another week to Fulk'han, if necessary, then come straight home."

"By myself?" Angst asked, not quite believing the simplicity of the mission.

"No." Tyrell was smiling as though getting away with selling a bag of horse manure. "You need to put together a team, a group you can trust. We'll provide mounts, provisions, and traveling expenses, and you will all be rewarded handsomely for your efforts."

Angst looked around the table. Tyrell and the queen were smiling and nodding in unison, as though they hoped Angst would feel obliged to join in. He looked at the princess, this time not bothering to sneak a quick glance or steal a smile. Instead he spent a moment just looking at her. Victoria was staring at her knees, her face shrouded with concern. She looked up at Angst, concern still on her face, and slowly, reluctantly, nodded yes.

He turned to face Tyrell once more. "I can bring anyone?"

"We will have final say, but I can't foresee any restrictions." Tyrell's smile had grown even more. "I would recommend bringing more people who can do...some of the things...you can do."

"You do realize," Angst asked, sitting up a bit, "that would mean the use of magic, openly?"

The queen covered a harrumph with a cough then strained her way through a commitment. "We have an official document you can travel with, decreeing that your party may openly use magic."

"Thank you." Angst sat up in his seat, and for the first time felt breakfast may have been worth it, after all.

"Was that all?" the queen asked with raised eyebrow.

"How will anyone know that I represent Unsel? As I'm riding through the countryside fighting monsters, I won't always have the opportunity to present decrees to citizens of Unsel, or friends in Rohjek or Fulk'han."

Isabelle actually smirked, as though Angst's desire to negotiate pleased her. "The armor worn by our knights bears the seal of Unsel. We will commission armor for you that will also carry the seal. Everyone will recognize you as a knight, Angst, though any title you earn will be solely based on the success of your quest."

Angst couldn't help but chuckle at her unwillingness to commit; it stunk of bureaucracy. "Your Majesty, Captain Guard,

I would be honored to undertake this mission," Angst replied. "How soon should I plan to depart with my team?"

"It is of the upmost importance that this issue be resolved quickly. We expect you to be on your way in three days, by any means necessary." The queen seemed pleased at this notion. "Princess Victoria is planning a gathering for you and your team, in recognition of you wielding the sword and to send you off properly on your...quest."

Angst was surprised by this, and wondered about the queen's underlying motivation. "That's very kind, Your Majesty."

Queen Isabelle stood. "Thank you, Angst. I'm certain you have much to attend to. Now, unless there is something else?" she asked with firm finality, her tone making it obvious she considered the meeting over.

Angst smiled broadly and stood. "Actually, if I'm to leave in just three days, there is one more thing."

11

Angst pushed through the double doors of the breakfast room to find Hector waiting outside. He was holding a piece of parchment, a look of surprise and a broad grin on his rugged face, as though he'd just won something and couldn't wait to tell a friend.

"What did you do?" Hector asked almost accusingly as he walked in step with Angst down the hallway.

"Everything I could think of," Angst replied, a bit mischievously.

Hector shook his head in disbelief. "I just got a promotion, a raise, and if I read this correct, we're going on an adventure? To Rohjek?"

"The queen has requested that we run a little errand. A quick trip to Rohjek, maybe Fulk'han, nothing we can't handle. I'm going to spend the day putting the team together." Angst spoke quicky, unable to retain his excitement. Hector didn't seem reluctant to go at all, and he was hopeful everyone would feel this way.

Hector ran his fingers through the short gray hair that stuck up from his head, and his dark eyebrows furrowed over his intense blue-gray eyes. "That's why I rushed down here. We stick to the highways, we should be safe, in spite of the rumors. We shouldn't need more than four of us."

"Exactly what I was thinking," Angst replied. "A group large enough to defend ourselves, if needed, but small enough to get around quickly."

"Then we agree. I'll let Rook and Hanson know," Hector offered, making a huge leap in logic. "They're good men, both respect you, and they have a lot of experience in small group missions."

Angst stopped walking. "Wait. Why them?"

Hector stopped before turning to face Angst. "I assumed you'd want to travel with people who knew what they were doing."

"Look, I'm sure they'd be fine under normal circumstances, but they aren't who I had in mind," Angst replied.

"If you don't like them, I guess I can come up with a couple other names," Hector said, sounding surprised.

"I don't think you understand, Hector. I'm bringing Tarness and Dallow."

"Angst, no, we can't do that." Hector shook his head in disagreement, completely dismissing the notion. "I'm sure they'd appreciate being invited, but it's dangerous out there." He smiled politely. "We'll take Rook and Hanson. They know what they're doing."

"They know what they're doing against what? The gamlin?" Angst said in a louder tone. He didn't want to sound defensive, but not only did he have to get through to his stubborn friend, he was now arguing with a ranked officer who assumed he was the chain of command. "What are they going to be, human shields?"

Now Hector raised his voice. "They are veterans. They've been in battles. I trained them myself, I've been out there with them, and I can't think of anyone I'd rather have cover our backs."

"Under normal circumstances, yes, but they can't do anything against these creatures."

"Angst, if you think the gamlin are the only problem out there, you're a fool." Hector was yelling now, obviously frustrated by Angst's stubborn refusal to listen to reason.

"I'm not that stupid, thank you." Angst's pale cheeks flushed with anger. "It's exactly why we need Dallow and Tarness. It took magic to kill those creatures. And since Dallow and Tarness can wield magic, at least with them, we would have a fighting chance."

"Look, they're my friends too, but this isn't one of our camping trips. This is going to be dangerous, and we need people who know how to fight." Hector was now glowering so hard it looked like he was going to start growling.

"Last time Rook fought these things, he ended up face down in the dirt. No, we aren't bringing either of them."

"So are you planning on bringing Rose too? How about Heather and the princess? Why don't you just take the ladies out?" Hector's tone dripped with sarcasm. "Don't you see what a mistake you're making? Make this easy. Rook and Hanson are the right choice."

"Rose isn't going. She has some sort of magic so she can fight them, I've seen it, but it's not safe," Angst said, considering this notion. "You, me, Tarness, and Dallow. My decision is final."

"Your decision? Who do you think's going to be in charge?" Hector asked, and Angst began to understand what was really bothering his friend.

"I'll be taking lead on this trip, Hector," Angst stated, a bit more quietly than before.

Hector's gray eyes became cold and he sliced at the air with his hand. "What? You've never been in charge of anything. That big hunk of steel on your back doesn't make you a leader."

"Actually, it does. If you don't believe me, take it up with Tyrell, or the queen, or whoever you want, but work it out. You are coming with, I'm leading, just as the queen has commanded," Angst said, pointing at a parchment in his hand. "But I'm not going to spend the next month arguing with you about every decision I make." Angst sighed deeply and fought to regain composure. "I need to go find Dallow and Tarness. To tell them what's going on."

Hector looked as though he'd been slapped in the face.

Twice. By his mother. His gruff voice seemed somewhat hollow. "Dallow won't be at the library until later, but Tarness is at Wizard's Revenge."

"Why is Tarness at the bar so early?" Angst asked.

"He was fired this morning. Something about a dead horse and a stable wall?" Hector answered, still sounding dejected. "It's a bad situation."

"The princess is planning a reception of sorts, two nights from now. Please be there. The following morning we'll meet at sunrise out by the training grounds before heading out." Angst looked his old friend in the eye for several moments, and it began to sink in just how the rest of this day would unfold.

* * * *

Graloon greeted Angst at the door, smelling of soap and greasy cooking. His eyes flicked up to Chryslaenor's hilt looming over Angst's shoulder while he spoke. "You're never here this early. Did you get fired too?"

Angst shook Graloon's hand to find it wet and oily. "No, I came to speak with Tarness." He looked around the room, which was smaller than he was used to seeing. Its dimensions had adjusted automatically to accommodate the few people scattered amongst the tables.

A frown grew on Graloon's face. "He's been here an hour, not in good shape either. I've been slow to deliver him drinks, but I can't tell him no. He's too big to argue with. Over there." He thumbed in the direction of a dark corner table.

Tarness was slouched over a tankard of mead, his large back facing away from the front door. Angst thanked Graloon, and made his way over. The big man sighed deeply and stared into his empty mug. Even seated, he was as tall as Angst.

"Hi, Angst," he said, not even bothering to look up. His deep voice was full of defeat and disappointment.

"Bad day?" Angst asked, seating himself on the stool next to his friend.

"The worst." Tarness rested his face in his hand. He had yet to make eye contact.

He didn't sound drunk—it took a lot of alcohol for him to get even near that state—but he did sound somewhere between more than a few drinks and really upset. Tarness was a walking contradiction of scary large muscle and passive kindness. If you were to find him in a dark alley, you'd piss yourself and slip in the puddle trying to run away. But Tarness would be the first to pick you up and then offer you his shirt to dry off. He had dark black skin and bristly hair that was receding from his large forehead. Tarness's eyes were close to his nose, and his caterpillar eyebrows made him look like he was in a constant state of rage, when he was actually nothing more than concerned and worried.

"I hated that horse, Angst, but I never meant to hurt it." Tarness seemed on the verge of tears. "The boss came over and started yelling at me about something. He hates me because of what we can do. There was this stallion, a big gray beast, and I was cleaning out his stable." Angst had to wonder how huge the horse was if Tarness called it big. "The boss kept yelling, threatening my job, calling me names, and I was getting upset. I think the horse knew because he was shuffling around the stall, all nervous like."

Angst listened attentively, nodding for his friend to continue.

"Finally, it kicked me right in my chest. There was this awful cracking sound, and the horse fell. His rear legs broke when they hit me. I was really angry at being kicked, Angst." He stopped and looked up at Angst, shifting uncomfortably.

"Go ahead, Tarness, it's all right." Angst prompted his friend.

Tarness reluctantly continued. "I lost my temper, so...I picked up the horse, and threw it."

Angst's eyes widened, and he shuddered at the thought of a man picking up a horse and throwing it. And through a wall, no less. Tarness was incredibly strong on any given day, but get him riled up and he was virtually unstoppable. "Wow. So, um, did you throw it at the stable boss?"

Tarness shook his head and snuffled a bit. "I wanted to, but at the last minute I turned and threw it through the brick stable wall." Tarness was on the verge of tears. "I didn't really mean to kill the horse, Angst, it was an accident. And now they fired me. I think they even wanted to arrest me but were afraid."

Angst reached out and gently patted the part of Tarness's shoulder he could reach.

After several moments, Tarness looked up. "Angst, I've got no wife, no kids, no job. I have nothing."

"I'm sorry, old friend. What if I have an opportunity for you?" He cringed at using the word, but it fit.

"I thought you hated opportunities," Tarness said, before loudly blowing his nose in a napkin.

Angst smiled and offered his big friend another one. "Well, what if I had a new job for you? Something fun, with friends, a bit of adventure?"

"The last time we had fun like that I ended up in jail and lost my girlfriend." Tarness looked at Angst suspiciously.

Apparently, he wasn't selling this very well He decided to change his approach and handed Tarness a copy of the queen's decree stating that his team was free to use magic. "I promise; this time is different."

Tarness looked over the parchment and sat up a bit. His voice lost some of its upset and became serious. "Angst, what is this? What's going on?"

"It's a job. We're going to Rohjek. You, me, Hector, and Dallow. We head out in two days. Ride there, ride back, get paid. That's it," Angst said enthusiastically, hoping Tarness would get caught up in the moment.

Concern showed on Tarness's dark face. "Are you crazy? It's dangerous out there. I don't have one of those things." He gestured toward Chryslaenor. "It's not like I can throw a horse at everything that attacks us."

"Tarness, you just said you don't have a job, you don't have anything here. What could possibly keep you from going on a trip with old friends?"

"I'm not crazy, is what. Just because I'm upset doesn't mean

I'm looking to die." Tarness sighed deeply. "Angst, thank you, but no thank you."

It was Angst's turn to sigh. Eyes closed, he reached into the breast pocket of his jacket. "Tarness, by the queen's command, you are joining me on this mission. In two nights, we have a reception at the castle, and the following day, we leave." He handed Tarness a parchment.

"What's this?" Tarness asked, looking over the document. "I don't understand. You mean I *have* to go?"

"Look, Tarness, it's better than going to jail for killing a horse," Angst said then immediately regretted it when Tarness took a deep sobbing breath.

"You may not see it now, but it really is the best thing for you," Angst suggested. "A few days away with friends, that's all this is. And we get paid for it."

"I'm not stupid, Angst. This is dangerous, but I won't refuse the queen's command. If she wants me to go, for whatever reason, I will." Tarness looked even more defeated than when Angst had first arrived.

He felt like he'd stolen a toy from a child. "That's great, Tarness. You won't be disappointed. Do you still have your guard armor?"

"I doubt it fits, but I've got it." Tarness nodded.

"Bring it to Teedle's shop tomorrow morning, first thing."

"Okay, Angst." Tarness looked up at him. "I don't know what you've got us into, I think it's a mistake, but thanks for the job."

"Sure, Tarness, anything for a friend." The fact that Tarness showed gratitude made Angst feel worse. He patted his friend on the shoulder once more then found Graloon and gave him enough coin to cover Tarness's tab.

* * * *

Dallow sat in front of a pile of books with his eyes shut and moving rapidly beneath the lids as though he were in a deep sleep. A gentle white aura surrounded his hands where they rested on two separate books. Angst hated visiting him at the library. He always felt like he was interrupting. Dallow opened his eyes slowly as Angst arrived, his irises opaque and glowing like his hands. Angst waited for them to go back to green.

"That has to be the strangest thing I've ever seen," Angst stated. "I don't know that I'll ever get used to it."

"Just getting caught up on some reading." Dallow smiled knowingly.

"Right," Angst replied.

They sat at a large marble-top table in the middle of the enormous library. The room was three floors tall and featured a square, forty-foot atrium covered with a glass ceiling. Sunlight flooded the room, showing off tall marble pillars and staircases. Shelves containing thousands of books circled each floor. The library was stunning, though Dallow frequently complained about it. The sunlight made it easy to read the books, but aged them prematurely. The glass ceiling broke almost every winter, allowing the weather to cause irreparable damage. And not to mention the beautiful atrium was an ineffectual use of space that could've been used to shelve more books.

Dallow studied Angst as he looked around the room. "So, to what do I owe the honor? You aren't here to harass me about my short visits to Wizard's Revenge, are you? You know how my wife hates it when I'm away."

"I should harass you, but no. I need your help. I'm being sent on a mission, of sorts." Angst was trying a different approach this time. Maybe asking for help would work better.

"Really? That sounds fun. Are you in need of maps? I know of an excellent atlas. How about a compendium of some rare creatures you may come across?"

Angst cut him off. "Actually, I need you to come with."

Dallow laughed. "I love your jokes, Angst, but this isn't the best day for jokes. I've got a lot of reading to get caught up on."

"I'm not joking. I'm headed to Rohjek in a couple of days and need you along."

"Look, I really can't," Dallow said gently. Never wanting to offend anyone, he smiled in spite of a frown shadowing his fore-head. "Traveling to Rohjek isn't the safest thing to do right now, from what I understand."

"That's why you have to join me. You know, well, you know everything in this library. I need that knowledge. I need you by my side." It was coming out a bit more desperate than Angst had intended.

"Look, Angst, I appreciate you asking, but it's not a good time. My wife and I, it's complicated, believe me that it's just not a good time. I'd love to go on one of your adventures, but I can't. Thank you but no." Dallow had all but dismissed Angst, and he put his hands back on the books.

"Dallow, I really need this. Can't you help me?"

Dallow gave a fake, polite laugh. "I really can't, old friend."

How was it that not one of his friends would willingly join him? His voice took on a hard edge. "Look, I've supported eve-rything you've ever done. I have been there whenever you've asked, and even the times you haven't asked. I was there when your wife was going to leave you. I was there when you were arrested. I've never asked *anything* of you, except this."

Ignoring him, Dallow set his long fingers back on the books, his eyes becoming opaque again.

Angst pulled a folded parchment out of his pocket then slid it under Dallow's left hand.

His trance broke immediately. "Um. This says... This says that...did I read this correctly? I *have* to go on this trip?" His eyes clearing, he scanned the handwritten decree to confirm what he'd sensed. Dallow's eyebrows jerked up, and he stared at Angst in disbelief.

Angst nodded.

"What have you done? I can't leave. My wife, she won't tol-erate this... My work...I can't waste my time on some silly trip!"

"You hate your job, you hate your marriage. I can't think of anyone who needs a break from their life more than you," Angst pointed out. "In two nights, there's a reception. You need to be there. In three days, we leave, and you are riding out with us, whether you like it or not." Angst stood and stomped out of the library.

* * * *

Angst was fed up with his friends, and so lost in frustration he didn't notice Rose standing directly in front of him until he bumped into her. He jumped back. "Whoa, I'm sorry."

"Now you're so old your eyes are going bad too?" she said with a laugh. Rose wore her simple gray server uniform, her long red hair pulled back tight.

"Sorry, Rose. My day isn't going very well," he started with a sigh, grateful to finally speak with someone who would understand. "The queen is sending me on a mission to Rohjek, and I just talked to the boys about going, but nobody wants to join me."

"Well, at least one of us wants to go," Rose said, a hint of hope in her voice.

"Really? Who did you talk to? Did Hector shake off his attitude?" It was the first good news Angst had heard about his friends.

Rose seemed quite pleased. "No, Angst. Me. I'm the one who's excited to go."

Angst stared at her, slack jawed. "You?"

"I'm going with," she declared.

"Rose, no. I'm sorry, you can't." Angst shook his head. Things had gotten worse. "I would love you to be there, but it's dangerous. If you were... No, I can't. I'm sorry."

"But you guys need me. You know I can handle myself." Her face plainly showed her disappointment. "You can't just leave me here for a month."

Angst attempted to reason with her. "Rose, it's not only very dangerous, it's traveling. You told me you hate to travel. You've never even come with us on our camping trips."

"I hate it that you remember everything I say," she grumbled under her breath. "This is different. I think you guys can really use my help."

Angst sighed. This hurt more than any reaction he'd faced so far. Here was a friend who actually wanted to go, a friend whose company would keep him sane. But he refused to put her in danger. "No, you aren't coming. I'm sorry, but you can't."

She looked like she was going to punch him in the mouth. Then her chin started to quiver and her large dark eyes became wet. She turned on her heel and walked away.

"Rose, I'm sorry," Angst offered weakly, but she didn't reply. He had never seen Rose cry, and it was crushing to think he could be the cause.

"I guess all that's left is to go home and tell Heather about the trip then everyone can be angry with me," Angst said to nobody. He looked around the hallway for just one smiling face, or even a glimpse of someone being amazed by Chryslaenor, but he found himself very alone.

12

"They say armor makes the man, but I'm not seeing that." Teedle cleared his throat, barely holding back a chuckle. "It seems the standard set of battle armor just isn't going to work for you, Angst."

Even after lifting the visor, Angst had trouble seeing over the helm's chin. When he spoke, it sounded like he was at the bottom of a well, and possibly drowning. "I thought armor was supposed to protect you."

The blacksmith barked out a laugh and a muscular hand came down on Angst's back hard, making him glad, for a brief moment, that the armor was there. Teedle was a short, square old man as wide with muscle as he was tall. The hair that should've been on his head had grown from his thick curly sideburns all the way to his chin. Teedle's pale head was so bald it shone, and his wild eyes were hidden behind coal-blackened smudge marks like a mask.

"You wouldn't think that if you saw the armor that comes back to my shop these days," he cautioned, his raucous laughter quickly replaced by worry. "Let me put it this way. If I'm sent a piece of used leg armor, there's usually a leg still in it. I don't know what's carving people up out there, but if I didn't laugh, I'd go crazy."

Angst had an itch between his shoulders that he wouldn't have been able to reach under normal circumstances, no doubt caused by a trickle of sweat. The armor was bulky. Not to mention being made for six-foot-tall beasts who spent their lives training to lift it, use it, and fight in it. Angst wasn't weak, but his body was the result of misguided attempts to balance exercise and cake. Battle armor was a full suit of heavy plate, and there was no way he could maneuver in it the way the sword seemed to want. He shifted his frame uncomfortably in the hope that something, anything, would bump the itch.

The blacksmith laughed again at the sight. Angst slowly moved the hinges near his knees, and wobbled his way around to face him, looking like a child playing in his father's clothes. This was the second time in two days someone dressed him in armor and laughed — it had to be a conspiracy. "I thought Tarness would be here by now. Have you seen him?"

"He was in last night. We did some minor alterations but everything seemed to fit," Teedle replied. "Are you guys really going out there? I've heard some mighty awful stories."

"That's exactly why the queen is sending us," Angst said proudly.

"That's good, I guess," Teedle said hesitantly, shaking his head. "But how am I supposed to have you armored up by tomorrow?

Angst shrugged, which wasn't at all visible. As he lowered his shoulders the additional weight seemed to create a pinch in his back muscles, right next to the itch. He grunted in frustration. "Would you help get this stuff off me?"

They struggled for the next fifteen minutes, each piece coming off slower than the one before. Angst only fell over twice. "What do I do if I want to lift my arms over my head?"

"You don't," Teedle replied.

"What if I have to pee?"

"You don't," Teedle said again, "or you do, but I don't suggest it."

"How will I swing that beast of a sword?"

"You can't, so quit asking," Teedle said, cutting him off.

"This won't work," said Angst in exasperation. The queen

demanded he have armor, and gave him no time to have it made. It was like she wanted him to look silly. Angst was beginning to get the idea that might just be her real mission.

Teedle shared his agitation. "I don't see how we can do this without you looking the fool. There just isn't time to make you something from scratch that would actually fit. Even if I could make armor your size, it wouldn't allow you to do what you need to do with your, you know, stuff you do." His head bobbed nervously, and he waved in the general direction of Chryslaenor.

"So, the queen demands traditional armor? By any means necessary?" Angst asked hopefully.

Teedle peered at him warily. "What exactly do you have in mind, Angst?"

Completely out of the armor, Angst mopped sweat from his forehead then itched his back against a nearby post. He raised an eyebrow mischievously and grinned. "Have no fears, my friend. I'll be back in an hour or so."

* * * *

Angst returned with three people in tow. A dark-skinned overweight woman walked beside him carrying an overstuffed cloth bag. Another blacksmith followed them, appearing every bit as muscular as Teedle, though quite a bit younger. Behind the blacksmith was a long-faced Dallow, who carried a large book and a sour expression.

Dallow reached forward to shake Teedle's hand. "Hi, I'm Dallow."

Teedle met his grip and nodded.

"This is Raena." Angst nodded respectfully in the direction of the woman.

Teedle smiled and bowed his head politely. "Ma'am." He then turned to the third, "Aren't you Shint? Didn't you win last year's shoeing contest?"

"Yes, sir," replied Shint, pleased by the recognition. He, too, shook hands with Teedle.

Teedle looked each of them up and down before turning to face Angst. "What's all this about?"

Angst nodded at Dallow, who gently set an enormous old book on a nearby stump that acted as both a chair and table. Dallow opened it to a page conveniently saved by his finger. Angst should've gone to Dallow first, but knew his friend was still upset about their pending trip. Eventually, though, he'd decided there was no choice—the man knew every book in that library, literally. It had only taken him a handful of minutes to find a history book with an armor design that could work for Angst.

The page was titled *Armour of the Zyn'ight*, and featured detailed diagrams of armor that looked quite different than modern battle plate. The book was old, and some would say the design appeared dated. But oddly enough, the first picture showed the seal of Unsel impressed onto the chest piece. Teedle's eyes widened, and he shook his head in disbelief. When he glanced at Angst, his shoulders dropped.

"Angst, armor like this hasn't been made in a thousand years or more. I've never even seen anything like it." He flipped pages of the book to see guidelines and specifications that went well beyond the sword and board get-up of a normal soldier. Several of the pictures showed the wearer wielding staves, or bending in ways that normal armor didn't allow. "I just don't see how I'm going to make this in time."

Shint touched Teedle's arm and said, "If it won't upset you too much, there is time."

The muscular young blacksmith picked up a steel bracer from a nearby table and studied it for several minutes before setting it down. Donning his heavy blacksmith gloves, he used tongs to hold a flat piece of iron against an anvil. With his other hand, he pulled a steel mallet from his belt. Then, without heating up the iron, he preceded to pound on the steel. Teedle looked about ready to stop Shint and correct him for doing things out of order but stopped when Shint's arms began to glow. The metal at the end of the tong turned bright red. It was quickly shaping into the gauntlet Shint had studied. In a matter of minutes, the young blacksmith had hammered out a gauntlet identical to the one lying on the table nearby.

"The magics," Teedle whispered, visibly shaken.

Angst cleared his throat. "Teedle, Her Majesty did say 'by any means necessary,' right?"

Teedle nodded, staring in awe but slowly collecting himself. "So, if you can do all that, *whatdoyaneedmefor?*" His words ran together, and he sounded a little upset.

"Sir, I've never made armor before. I may be able to make simple things quickly, but I have none of your knowledge or expertise," Shint said in an incredibly respectful tone. "I can't do this alone."

"All right then," Teedle said begrudgingly. "But how on Ehrde are we to make sense of all...that?" He began reviewing the book again.

"I understand almost all of it, but I have no means of applying what I know," stated Dallow. His voice was somber, and he still refused to make eye contact with Angst.

"Fine, okay, all right. So we may know how, and we may be able to do this fast enough, but these measurements would require an engineer." Teedle was obviously looking for an escape.

Angst nodded at Raena.

"I am the personal seamstress of her Royal Majesty, the Princess Victoria," said Raena in a sharp, high-pitched tone. She waited for the awe to subside, though everyone merely nodded courteously.

"The Princess Victoria, for some reason," she paused and glanced at Angst, "has asked, as a personal favor, that I assist in the fitting of this...armor."

Shint and Teedle exchanged shrugs and a questioning glance before the older man spoke.

"We're not sewing the armor, ma'am," Teedle said.

Shint covered his mouth, failing to hold back a chuckle.

Angst coughed politely. "Raena is the absolute best seamstress in all of the court, and without a doubt, the reason the royal princess always appears so radiant."

Raena accepted this as her due and couldn't help but smile.

"This armor is different than anything you've ever made. Dallow explained that it should allow for the movement I need, that this armor was actually created for people who could do magic." Angst pointed at places near joints and behind the legs. "It's missing steel in certain spots to make it lighter, and seems to measure tight across the chest, but offer a lot of space around the shoulders."

"But Angst, there's so much unprotected," Teedle observed.

"From what you tell me, my friend, there's little to protect me from what's out there anyway." Angst let Teedle consider the heavy comment. "Can we do this?"

"Why not? Let's see if we can't figure it out," Teedle said, looking around at the odd group Angst had gathered.

The day, and night, were long, and frustrating, and tiresome, and inspiring. Angst arranged for food to be delivered throughout the project, so there was rarely a break. Arguments erupted between Shint and Teedle, or Teedle and Dallow, or Angst and all of them, but often Angst calmed everyone down with some story or a bit of nonsense that distracted from the argument, allowing the makeshift team to refocus.

Raena was commanding, and guided the other three in the specifics of what they were building. The inside of the suit had a unique padding of soft leather and cotton that supposedly allowed for absorption of some shock. She was every bit as efficient in measuring and sewing as Shint was at hammering.

Shint made many mistakes as he was more familiar with hammering out simple objects quickly, and nothing near the complexity this required. In the end, they found if Shint held the steel, concentrated on the picture, and let Teedle hammer out the armor, the pieces came together faster.

When the morning sun began to climb over the buildings, the armor appeared finished. But the last page of instructions left everyone bewildered.

"I just don't get this. There's a way of hardening the armor, making it many times more durable than it should be, but it requires a spell." Dallow was tired enough that he didn't stop himself from talking to Angst.

"Then, why don't you just, um, do your thing?" a tired Teedle asked.

"Spells are more complex than the magic we cast," Dallow explained, looking around the room. "What we do is simply what we know, maybe by accident or necessity. Spells are something that require training, and years of practice. It's a deeper sort of mag—"

Angst touched Dallow's arm lightly. "Let's not worry about it right now. If you don't mind, make a note of the spell for me and we'll save it for later."

Dallow shrugged, and yawned. "So aren't you going to try it on?"

"I'll get plenty of opportunity to wear it, and I don't see that there's much more we could do. The individual pieces fit fine." Angst walked around the room, shook hands with each of them, and gave Raena a hug. "Thank you all so very much. I don't think I could ever repay you for this kindness."

They all nodded and thanked one another, and then everyone wandered off to get a short rest before the day's activities. Teedle was staring at the armor and shaking his head incredulously, though smiling a little. "We really did it. That young Shint, well, he did just fine by me. I'll have to work with him a bit more, but I'm going to request that he be reassigned as my apprentice. He has potential."

"Thank you, Teedle, for that too." Angst smiled, and felt almost giddy. It was one of the few times he could remember everything coming together, just right.

"You know, Angst, they're going to hate you for wearing that."

"I know," Angst replied with his trademark ear-to-ear grin. "But it was the queen's idea. She did say 'traditional.'"

Teedle winced as he helped Angst pack up the armor.

13

There were two types of knight in the Kingdom of Unsel. The queen knighted some who found her favor for tasks performed in service to the kingdom. This act conferred the title of 'Sir.' It was a title only, no lands or gold or staff were awarded, but significant in terms of public respect and prestige, and the title was forever.

The traditional knight, the man who strode around in shiny plate armor righting wrongs and saving fair maidens, was something altogether different. These were the heroes, the elite, and they included an exceptional few. Those chosen to be knights were typically the best soldiers, those individuals who would sacrifice anything for Unsel and often did. They were supposed to be heroes who lived by an unwritten code of honor. This sort of knighting represented an exceptional achievement for most, and an unprecedented feat for someone like Angst.

A person who could perform magic hadn't received a title, any title, in all the eight kingdoms for over a thousand years. Rumor had spread quickly that Angst could possibly be the first magic-wielding knight, and people wanted to be a part of it. The castle was packed with every duke and dignitary who could get there within three days, including the king from neighboring Melkier. Outside, there was a growing crowd of people and turmoil. Some were upset and showed their bigotry and hate openly. Others were enthusiastic and proud of this change in direction.

The considerably larger mass of protesters stomped around the city yelling catchy phrases like, "No More Magic" or "Keep Knights Human." At times, the magic protestors carried signs, or human-shaped dolls attached to poles. These would often spontaneously combust, turn into wild animals, or disappear. A much smaller group, comprised of those who could wield magic and a few of their supporters, would laugh at this but stayed near the guards for safety. The guards were exhausted.

The 'small party' Princess Victoria had thrown together to recognize Angst and his friends had commandeered the castle's largest dining hall for two hours. Hector, Dallow, Tarness, and Heather waited with Angst in an antechamber hidden near the dining hall entrance. His friends took turns making sour faces at him while they watched attendees arrive. Their room was large enough for ten people to sit next to each other uncomfortably, and small enough to give Angst claustrophobia.

His armor had fit, perfectly. The entire suit was a dusky black rather than a polished shine, as though left unfinished. His tiberius helm had a rounded top that covered everything from the back of his neck to his forehead. His face was left unprotected, save for a steel noseguard. The chest piece was a half cuirass that fit like a sleeveless shirt cut off below his pectoral muscles. Chain mail hung around his midriff like a curtain. The front of Angst's arms and legs were guarded by the dark plate, but an inch-wide strip was left exposed in the back of his legs and inside of his arms to keep the armor light. The inside of his elbows and back of his knees were also missing steel for the sake of mobility, covered only by dark leather padding. On close inspection, it appeared a lot of Angst was exposed.

After seeing how dark the armor was, the princess had Raena make a red cape "for formal occasions" that attached to both shoulders and his left wrist. He felt it was ostentatious, but wasn't going to argue, as he knew he had no taste.

Angst stood in the center of the antechamber, almost afraid to move. The armor was as comfortable as armor could be. It was made for mobility, he could bend his joints freely, and it actually fit. The room, however, was stuffy, and he was nervous, and he was afraid moving might take off someone's ankle with the tip of his sword. The only thing he could do was sweat and sigh.

Anxiety pervaded the room. Heather didn't want any of this, and her eyes were red and blotchy from crying. Hector, Dallow, and Tarness didn't want to be there and barely spoke a word to Angst.

The door opened, and a young man's head peered into the room. "We will begin in five minutes. Please take your seat."

Heather looked at Angst with sad eyes, squeezed his hand, and then slipped out the door.

Dallow, Tarness, and Hector stood before him and eyed the armor.

"It turned out all right," Dallow approved stiffly.

"I wouldn't want to meet up with you in a dark alley," stated Tarness with an admiring grin.

"I don't think you'd see him," Hector took a stab at teasing. "Try not to make the rest of us look bad by throwing up."

That didn't help, and it was the end of the conversation. Angst spent the remaining eternity of the next four minutes alone in thought. He took the sword in hand and held it aloft. It felt comfortable, it felt right. It was the worst time to be questioning himself, yet he couldn't help but wonder. This was what he wanted, right? With this sword, this armor, there was still time even at his age to do some good, wasn't there? It had all happened so fast. Angst had spent his life wanting to become a knight, and now he had the opportunity, but opportunity always came at a cost. Heather and his friends were already upset. What else would he have to sacrifice?

The usher returned, and yelped a bit at the sword being out. Angst hastily returned it to his back. "Uh, sorry about that."

The usher shuddered. "This way, everyone."

The group followed him into the hall.

* * * *

CHAPTER THIRTEEN

Rows of tables outlined the enormous room in a 'U' shape, providing space in the middle for Angst and his friends to stand on display. Hundreds of attendees sat at the tables, lost in a low buzz of conversation until the four of them approached. At the sight of Angst, his sword, and his new armor, the crowd's murmur immediately became louder. Several at the front tables looked visibly offended, and a few in the back stood to point. The queen reached up to her temple with a finger and pressed hard as if to quell a sudden headache, squinting with pain.

Queen Isabelle stood and stared for a moment at his Zyn'ight armor. It was obviously making more of a statement than he had intended, and Angst felt the urge to run, or maybe tell a joke that would relieve the palpable tension in the room. He pulled the sword from his back, which was met by a gasp from the crowd. He rested it on its tip, and knelt. Dallow, Tarness and Hector looked at each other then decided to follow Angst's lead.

This seemed to work for the queen, and she spoke. Isabelle's tone was formal enough to roll all of her Rs, yet tense enough to squawk a bit higher than usual. Whether it was due to the echo of her voice in the hall or the mood of her subjects, she paused between each sentence as though choosing her words carefully.

"We live in a time of change and challenge. The great sword Chryslaenor has been wielded for the first time in recorded history, and will be championed on behalf of Unsel by these four men. While there is no tradition on which we can rely to acknowledge the sword or its bearer, the crown does recognize Angst, Tarness, Hector, and Dallow. We are grateful for your willingness to meet the challenge we have set before you."

The queen raised a glass silently, as did the attendees, though several seemed reluctant to do so. A few tables in the back hosted members of the community who could wield magic, and they began to clap. Others in the crowd felt obliged to join in. When the princess started clapping enthusiastically, all the attendees followed suit, yet many still looked upset. Angst couldn't help but flash his friends a satisfied grin.

Soon the applause died away, and they were ushered to a table near the front. It took only seconds for Tori to pull Angst from his chair. The princess and Tyrell spent the rest of the evening taking turns dragging Angst across the room for another introduction to an unknown leader of some province or dukedom he'd never heard of. Every chance Angst thought he might get to hide amongst his friends, or snack on the attractive meal, was smoothly thwarted.

King Gaarder of Melkier was gracious to a fault before diving into questions about Angst, the sword, his armor, and how all things magical were handled in Unsel. He was a curious old man, with long white hair and longer moustache. His robes were a rich crimson, and his friendly smile reached his eyes with a twinkle.

"I suppose it would be too forward, Mr. Angst, if I asked to hold it?" The king held out his hand.

"Your Majesty, I would be honored, but I've found out recently that I'm the only one able to lift it. Anyone else who attempts it suffers injury." Angst tried to be good-natured about saying no, and to his surprise, Gaarder understood.

"It only makes sense, or others would've picked it up before you. It's obviously your destiny. But too bad you didn't have the opportunity to wield it when you were a bit, um, younger."

"Yes." Angst tried to keep his wince internal. "I guess it just wasn't the right time for me."

"I understand you took out a full garrison that night. Very impressive," the king joked and winked. "Don't you just love tall tales? I've found a 'full garrison' tends to be one frightened man pissing himself."

Angst laughed out some tension, grateful for the king's charming nature.

"Are there many swords like that one?" he asked.

"To my knowledge, Chryslaenor is unique," Angst said, tilting his head in curiosity.

"Hmm," Gaarder thought aloud while tugging at his long beard. "I'm not so sure, it looks—."

Just as the conversation had become interesting, Princess Victoria interrupted. "Your Majesty." The princess curtsied and held out her hand.

After bowing, Gaarder kissed her hand gently. "How you've grown, my dear. I can only imagine that your poor mother has to fight off the line of suitors."

Victoria blushed prettily. "You are too kind, Your Majesty. If I may," she said, as she took Angst's hand. "My mother has requested Angst's presence."

"Of course. Angst, it was a pleasure to meet you." As the two men shook hands, the king held on for a bit. "You should come and visit some time. I believe we have much to discuss about swords and things."

"I would like that, Your Majesty." Angst bowed before hurrying to keep up with the princess.

Victoria led Angst through the crowd, still holding onto his hand. "Your hand is sweaty. You need to relax."

"Right, I'll do that now," he replied. She giggled. "So, why does the queen want to see me? She loves the armor, right? I knew she would."

"She doesn't love the armor, nor does she want to see you. I thought I'd save you from politics you weren't familiar with, and I figured you'd enjoy my company much more than King Gaarder's."

Angst smiled gratefully. "You aren't going to make me dance, are you, Your Majesty?"

"I'm not that mean," she replied. "According to Rose, you dance like a hobbled elephant."

He blushed. "She said that, did she?"

"That and some other things, but she told me to save those. Though I can't imagine what for."

Angst rolled his eyes and made a mental note to return the favor. They'd arrived in a corner, almost separated from the masses. Fortunately, her being the princess kept most visitors at bay.

She looked at Angst with concern. "I won't be there tomorrow to see you off. Please be careful."

"Because my mother is sending you off to die," Angst said mockingly as he finished her sentence.

"Don't say that! And don't put words in my mouth!" She looked at someone nearby and smiled graciously, nodding in a royal manner. "You don't know everything that's been set into motion. You're going to be in great danger, and I—"

"Have some faith in me. Everything happens for a reason, including this." Angst reached up to rap on the hilt of Chryslaenor with his knuckle. "It's not like all of Ehrde is going to war."

Tori looked like he'd slapped her. Apparently she didn't find the comment as funny as he had intended.

"Or, maybe I've been given the sword for a reason. Maybe, it's possible that I have a chance to do something good."

"You were doing good, Angst. You've never given yourself credit, but just being who you are helps people. You've certainly helped me. It's in your nature to do good."

"Thank you. Know that you've also done worlds of good for me. Your friendship has really filled a hole in my life, Tori. Please don't ever forget that." He smiled at her. "But the king is right. You, young lady, will soon find yourself surrounded by suitors wooing you and vying for your attentions. You may not believe me, but you're going to move on to better things, and your need for time with an old man will dwindle. I will probably have to team up with the queen to keep them at bay. Imagine your mother and I banding together." Angst made a comical, cringing expression.

She laughed. "You won't get rid of me so easily, 'old man,' nor will I let you get old so quickly." She'd begun sounding queen-like. "This trip is far more dangerous than it sounds. I have faith in you, Angst, but please remember to have faith in yourself. You will need it."

14

The morning they were set to depart, the air held a touch of fall. A wet bitterness that worked its way through pores, sank into the muscles and settled into the bones, leaving you with a creak that was more annoying than painful. In his youth, Angst had loved these days. It was the early freeze that killed the pollen and cleaned the air. To the chagrin of people in their forties, he would remove his shirt on these cool mornings just to revel in the steam rising from his strong muscles, laughing at those older than him, bundling themselves in cumbersome traveling cloaks and extra sweaters.

Angst wasn't laughing now. Now, he shivered, in part from that very cold—yet another sign of age—but also in anticipation. He had asked and finally demanded that his nearest and dearest join him for a grand adventure. Angst had justified to himself that they would wrong some rights, solve some puzzles, kill a few monsters, and return as heroes. His justifications were so strong and so rehearsed that he'd almost completely muffled the voice screaming from deep inside that this was all one big ego trip. This quest was the desire of an aging man trying to feel like a young man, no matter that the cost could be the lives of his friends. Since being 'assigned' this mission, he'd successfully ignored that voice, set it aside, busying himself to the point that he almost couldn't hear it at all. Almost. Today, though, he shivered, and the voice rang in his head like a crystal bell.

Heather squeezed his hand tight, her face more worried and upset than he'd ever seen it. She faked a smile every time she caught him looking, but he knew her heart wasn't in it. The smile on her lips wasn't in her eyes, and he felt bad that she would be alone for so long.

"I'm sorry, Angst, for arguing last night," she said quietly, her voice scratchy from crying. "You didn't deserve that the night before your big trip."

If an argument was a gentle spring rain, last night was a hurricane. Armageddon had swept through their kitchen. He'd gotten lost in that storm, somewhere between her screaming and her crying. His hope for a bit of lovemaking and an early night was replaced with stress, three hours of sleep, and a belly full of stomach pains.

He shook his head and touched her face. "You are the love of my life, and we've never been apart for more than a few days. I'm sorry to have upset you. I'll do everything I can to come back quickly, and to be safe. I promise."

Heather nodded, and attempted to smile again. She was being so very brave, and it broke his heart. She looked over his shoulder, to the throng of people behind him. "Well, Angst, this is what you wanted. They're waiting for you."

"But..." Angst hesitated. Maybe there was something more he should do or say.

"Go. The sooner you leave, the sooner you return." She kissed him on his cheek. "I love you. Now go be a hero so you can hurry home to me."

That made him smirk, and she flashed him one genuine smile, eyes and all. He nodded, said, "I love you too," and turned to face everyone.

What had begun as a quiet departure with friends and family had expanded to a hundred curious, unwanted well-wishers who had no business being there. Nor did they all wish him well. He didn't want them there, hadn't invited any of them, yet couldn't help but smile. Angst and Heather stepped forward, holding hands. Angst wore his dark armor, the huge sword hovering against his back like a large metal tree trunk. Chryslaenor impressed and intimidated the crowd enough that many stepped back when he came toward them.

"Hector, everyone's here. Can we go?" Angst asked his friend, who seemed to be in a rather surly mood.

"No, we're waiting for Captain Guard Tyrell," Hector snapped. He tugged down on his sleeveless leather chest piece, his hairy arms flexing impressively. Having spent his entire life in the military, Hector didn't do late, and he was almost as anxious as Angst.

"Pfft, this is crap," said Angst. "What about supplies? Do we have everything we need?"

"Yes. Still. We still have everything we need," Dallow said, resting a calming hand on Angst's shoulder.

Angst looked Dallow in the eyes and smiled, grateful for his patience. "Thanks."

Dallow simply nodded like an old friend who knew exactly what to expect. In spite of the man's reluctance to join Angst on this adventure, he now appeared more open to going, almost calm. His wife was nowhere to be seen.

Angst looked from where they stood on the training field toward the castle. It was still a reassuring sight, and he wondered again if he was being watched from the tower. He peered over the throng of people to find two riders approaching.

"That should be him," Angst announced, pointing toward the riders.

A knight in full plate armor and closed helm accompanied the frustrated Captain Guard. Tyrell dismounted and walked forward to shake hands with Angst.

"Thank you," Angst said, hoping to expedite their departure. He looked back at the horses, the gear, and his friends. "For everything."

"Of course, Angst. I want to see you succeed." Tyrell paused before continuing. "Please walk with me for a moment." The Captain Guard led him beyond the crowd and curious ears. "Before you go, I have a few things for you. One you will appreciate. The other you will not."

The Captain Guard looked at Angst with a wary expression, handing Angst a package and a note. "First, these are from Her Highness, the royal princess."

Angst took the unexpected package. "Well, uh, thanks."

"I was told you should open it upon receipt." Tyrell said.

"Oh, of course." The envelope had been marked with Victoria's seal, a decorative letter V set in a rose, which had been undisturbed. He cracked it open and read the note inside. It smelled of berries. *'Please bring this back safely. Love, Tori.'*

Angst opened the package, a bit embarrassed. In spite of being away from the crowd, they were all watching, including Heather. Inside was a deep red travel cloak—light yet warm to the touch. The material was nothing he recognized, and probably worth more than his home. When he lifted it, something fell to the ground. Angst leaned forward and picked up the stone rose he'd made for her when they first met. He smiled, heartened by Tori's show of faith that he would make it back.

Tyrell's eyes widened at the cloak, and he shook his head. Angst looked at him curiously. "Well, Angst, I could be mistaken, but I believe that cloak to be made from the queen's favorite comforter. She claims not to have slept well since it went missing."

"Ha!" Angst blurted out in surprise. "Please tell the princess that I will gladly do as she commands." He nodded at the note in his hand. "And thank her for the very thoughtful gift." He dramatically threw the cloak over his shoulders, clasped it at his neck, and set the rose inside a pocket.

The Captain Guard nodded once.

"I can't imagine the bad news outweighs the good news."

"Uh, yes. About that..." Tyrell cleared his throat and handed Angst another envelope, this time with the queen's signet imprint on the wax, the letter I set over the royal crown. "I was opposed to this, Angst, for the record. The queen is sending one more to accompany you on your trip."

Angst looked quizzically at Tyrell then down at the parchment. His jaw dropped as he read the queen's command. "What?" he exclaimed. "This is ridiculous!" His gaze jerked up to meet Tyrell's then he looked over at the knight, who'd remained on his mount.

The knight lifted his visor to reveal Sir Ivan, the man who had assaulted Rose at the banquet. Ivan rode over, his arrogance pouring from the open helmet. Flared nostrils and an obnoxious sneer hid Ivan's otherwise handsome features. Dark bangs hung over his dark eyes, which were untrusting and watchful. "I suppose the queen wanted someone with an actual title to keep an eye on you, freak."

Angst quickly lifted a glowing hand and aimed it at Ivan. The knight yelped as he flew off his horse. The crowd laughed, and Angst casually turned his back on Ivan, who was struggling to get up. He faced Tyrell. "This has to be a mistake. This man shouldn't even be a knight. Not to mention, he can't even defend himself against the gamlin. He's going to make this trip even harder."

"I'm sorry, Angst. I understand your concern, but these are the queen's orders," Tyrell replied apologetically.

Ivan lunged at Angst's back with a broadsword. Several onlookers screamed, while others yelled warnings. In one blurred motion, Angst grabbed his sword, turned to face Ivan, and knocked him back with the flat of Chryslaenor. Ivan flew ten feet into the air and landed directly behind his horse, who stomped the ground in alarm, kicking up dirt. Before Ivan could even consider sitting up, Angst was standing over the fallen knight. A hush came over the crowd.

Angst returned Chryslaenor to his back, leaned forward, and held out a hand. "You have one chance, Ivan. One. Either you're with me, or you won't make it back alive."

Ivan slapped Angst's hand away and rolled to one side, pushing himself back to his feet. "I represent the queen, and don't need your placations. Now get out of my way before I split your face open." Ivan's twitching sneer strained to hide the fear and humiliation behind his eyes.

Angst looked him up and down, let out a deep sigh, then turned once again to face Tyrell. "Any other good news?"

The captain spread empty hands and smiled as though nothing had happened. "Good luck, Angst."

Angst walked to his friends, shaking his head. Not only was he surprised by the fact that Ivan was now joining them, but why hadn't Tyrell defended the knight when Angst attacked? Heather took his hand and looked lovingly into his eyes, instantly dissolving his frustration. She gestured over her shoulder toward the crowd. He hadn't had any plans to say something, but maybe he owed it to the people who'd come to see them off.

"Opportunity is a sword. On one end is a blade and on the other a handle." Angst mounted his horse. "There's no guarantee that if you pick up and swing that sword, you won't cut yourself, but if you never lift that sword, if you never swing it," he lifted his own sword high overhead, "you'll never know if that sword, that opportunity, was the one you needed to succeed."

The crowd remained silent, merely nodding in agreement, and Angst wondered what they'd been looking for. He sought Heather's eyes one last time, gave her a cocky wink, then looked over his companions. "Let's go."

They didn't gallop off heroically, the crowd didn't cheer or sing, their horses simply strode down the path somberly. Angst shivered and pulled his new traveling cloak tight.

15

Angst reveled in the glory of their first day on the road. A combination of friends and nostalgia, spiced with a little excitement, all wrapped up in a cool fall day. After the very quiet and slightly awkward first hour of riding, Hector had begun telling stories. Several of the stories Angst had never heard, and a few of those he'd even been a part of. The resentment everyone felt toward Angst quickly melted away with laughter, and the distance from their lives left behind.

The day passed quickly and less painfully than anyone had expected. Angst missed Heather, but was enjoying himself. More than that, he'd known this time with his friends would be like this. Three hours away from home, Angst wanted to yell at everyone, "I told you so! Is this so bad?" They weren't being eaten by giant hairy one-eyed monsters, they hadn't been attacked by crazy brigands or roaming thieves, and there was no sign of gamlin. And Ivan was riding far enough behind that Angst could only barely feel the hate from Ivan's glare boring into the back of his skull.

The group had agreed to stop early after finding an ideal camping spot. They filled their bellies with food before settling around the campfire. Angst wrapped himself in the cloak Tori had given him, which made his friends roll their eyes. Hector had brought a bottle of port that everyone took several swigs from. As the evening progressed and starry dark filled the sky,

Angst's friends relaxed. It was male camaraderie at its finest, and in spite of his best efforts, Ivan almost cracked a smile before crawling into his tent.

For the first time in weeks, Angst was able to fall asleep immediately. The combination of fresh air, full stomach, progress, and exhaustion had opened the door to quick slumber. At home, before Chryslaenor, he always fell asleep late and woke early. It was an ugly cycle that left him tired, forcing him to work harder than he should have at being happy. When he finally did sleep, it was a deep and dark thing filled with odd dreams. Throughout his life, the few dreams he could fleetingly recall were all too real. Days or weeks later something would happen that Angst vaguely remembered dreaming about—bits of nothing like lifting a pen or hugging Heather. The whole thing was confusing, and he tended to avoid dwelling on it.

He'd heard of true seers, of course. There were stories of individuals gifted with the ability to envision the future. Angst couldn't see the future, only muddied waters, brief recollections of things to come. Now he longed for those dreams, his dreams, which were gone and replaced by visions. It was as if the sword was now serving his mind someone else's memories without any explanation as to why.

Every day, Angst heard Chryslaenor's music. It seemed nothing more than a push, a nudge, a gentle invitation to something he didn't understand. Since collapsing on the practice field, every night the song became a promise in his mind's eye. His dreams were filled with what he assumed to be the past. He would see Chryslaenor being held by others. He experienced their triumphs, their losses, and their incredible power. A power he could wield, if only...something. Each night brought more images, and they pushed, insisted, until finally he would wake with a start.

By morning, his memory was but a fleeting shadow. His waking haze quickly clouded the night's visions. Angst could only remember glimpses of those who'd wielded Chryslaenor before him, and what they could do with it. He found it increasingly frustrating. Angst wanted to know what the visions were about, and he wanted to understand the song's invitation. He simply couldn't accept the invitation without knowing more, and Chryslaenor tried to teach him.

* * * *

In spite of his desperation to sleep, his first night on the road, Angst found himself in one of Chryslaenor's dreams. Dissociated from his body, he hovered, and watched three men standing beside a wall of ominous misty darkness. Two were dressed in traditional plate, not yet dirty from war and battle. The third wore only chausses and aketon. He was a tall man with a strong jaw and wore his bright blond hair pulled back from his forehead.

"General Drake, what lies beyond this wall of dark?" questioned the man without armor.

"Death, my Lord," replied the general, a short stocky man with a bald head and several scars behind his right ear.

"We have ordered everyone into the black, but not one has yet returned," stated the third man. He had the same strong jaw as the unarmored man, but his hair was a dark brown.

"The odd thing is, Lord Farkus, it's...quiet," said the general in a worried tone.

Lord Farkus pondered the dark wall, brushing his fingers through his blond hair. He dropped his head and knelt for a moment in silence, concentrating on something while the others waited patiently. Minutes later, he stood up straight and pronounced, "It's time."

As Farkus began untying one of many large satchels from his mount, General Drake walked over and put his hand on the tie string. "Lord, I don't know if this *is* the time yet. If you're wrong, it's like falling on your sword and making everyone join you." Drake looked at the darker haired man. "Semiya..." he trailed off pleadingly.

"You will know when it's right, brother," Semiya said to

Farkus, his voice lacking both fear and encouragement. "Isn't that what that strange old man told us?"

"Told *me*, Semiya, and then provided me with this." Farkus opened the satchel and pulled out a gleaming, pearl-white chest piece. He set it on the ground, and began removing other pieces of armor. The legs, helm, gauntlets, and boots all shared the same unnatural pearly sheen. It was obvious that the armor hadn't been crafted by human hands. "As I said, it is time. Now help me get this on, so I can use this great power to end the darkness that threatens."

"Are you so sure, brother, that you know the source of this darkness? Are we fighting for balance, or should we be fighting against magic?" Semiya asked.

"There is no longer time for that discussion, or one of our petty fights. Men are dying in that darkness, and soon we will all face a similar fate. There is no time."

Farkus reached down for the leggings then abruptly dropped to the ground as the flat of Semiya's blade struck the back of his head. Farkus lay face down in the grass, a small trickle of red dripping from the wound.

Semiya's sword was pointed at the shocked face of General Drake. "Now, Drake, you will help me prepare for battle."

"You killed him?"

"He won't die. I saved him, as I will save us all. He was going to do it wrong. You and I both know what has to happen today. Help me suit up."

The general looked from Semiya to Farkus then quietly nodded. "How do you know the armor won't kill you?"

"We are of the same mother. We have the same blood."

Drake cut him off. "It was meant for Lord Farkus. That's what he was told!"

"Or so he said. I agree with one thing, there is no more time. Look," Semiya said, pointing at the dark wall which slowly crept toward them. "It's getting larger."

Drake shook his head in frustration and Angst could tell the general felt this was wrong. He picked up each piece with a sigh, or a worried glance, but still handed them all over to Semiya. Angst had struggled plenty with armor, but never like this. Every new piece seemed more challenging than the last to put on. Semiya became more and more uncomfortable, shifting and adjusting as he was encased in the milky armor.

When the helm was all that remained, the armor sealed itself around Semiya. Joints and hinges and holes melded together to form a solid white suit. He visibly relaxed as though an ordeal had passed and breathed a sigh of relief. The unnatural suit rose and fell with his powerful chest like a cotton shirt.

"I wish I had more time," Semiya said as he admired the stolen armor. "You have never...experienced..." His voice drifted off for a moment then he abruptly commanded, "The helm."

Drake knelt to pick up the final piece of armor, warily watching the younger man. He paused for a moment, looking at it and then at Semiya.

"I'm not going to kill you, General," Semiya said, answering the general's wary look. "We are on the same side, you and I. Wait and see. This is not a mistake."

The general walked behind Semiya and held the helm high over the man's head. The headpiece seemed reluctant to set down. The general pulled, and tugged, and slowly, so slowly, the helm lowered to cover Semiya's head.

Angst, watching the scene in horror, tried to yell to warn Drake, but the dream wouldn't listen. The general couldn't see Semiya's face. Semiya's eyes were wide with panic, his mouth open, and what should've been a scream ended up being a trickle of foaming drool that fell from his lips as though the armor prevented him from making any sound. To Angst, the despairing look on Semiya's face made it seem as though he realized his brother had been right all along. The helm sealed with a click.

"There you are, my Lord," Drake said, wiping a bit of sweat from his bald brow. "I agree with you. Now rid us of magics, once and for all." He took a step back.

This was good, because Semiya began to shudder. Slowly, at first, then violently until it seemed even the air and ground around him also shook with fury. Drake started to move forward, reaching for Semiya, but reluctantly took a step back, and another. Semiya rose into the air, and the shaking white armor made him appear more apparition than man. The vibrating stopped, and there was a horrendous pop, as though a seal had broken. Semiya dropped to the ground and lay there for a moment, face down and unmoving.

"My Lord?" asked the general, in a very quiet voice.

Semiya stood as though nothing had happened then turned to face the general. Drake stuttered as color left his cheeks, and he reeled, stepping back to balance his footing. This obviously fierce and battle-worn general was clearly afraid.

The helm had sealed itself to the breastplate. Near his left shoulder, where the heart should've been, a new, ugly crack crossed Semiya's sternum and crawled downward around the right side of the chest piece. Dangerous black and orange smoke spewed lazily from the crack. The armor had broken, completely rejecting its host.

Small slits in the helm had widened to show Semiya's face from eyebrow to cheekbone. A black haze hovered around the edges of the openings, and an orange glow surrounded his eyes, which were now pale and unblinking. It wasn't Semiya, or if it was, he had gone insane.

The white suit of armor walked to Semiya's sword, black wispy smoke trailing in his wake. Without a word, it made an unnaturally agile leap onto Semiya's horse and rode directly into the black void.

The general shivered before attempting to follow Semiya, but the darkness blocked him. When Farkus mumbled, Drake spun about and walked over to the fallen body of his lord so he could tend to his injuries. Farkus lay there, oblivious to what had transpired. Minutes passed as the general doctored the wound at the base of Lord Farkus's head, wrapping it in bandage while he explained what Semiya had done.

Angst saw the frightening realization slap Farkus across the face. But before Farkus had any opportunity to speak his thoughts, existence blinked. Everything that was, simply left, and then returned. Lord and general both heaved out the contents of their stomachs. Together, they slowly looked up and saw that it was gone. The dark misty wall, the black sky…all that remained was an empty battlefield and ominous silence.

Farkus attempted to stand. Without a word, General Drake helped him. Angst followed their progress to the edge of the battlefield, which was now a large, round, blackened nothing. Lord Farkus stepped onto the black ground, crossing over the line that separated life from this space of death. He looked at General Drake, who nodded, urging him forward.

Drake pointed at the distant center of the field where something rose from the ground. When they neared the center, Farkus let go of Drake and moved, as quickly as he could, to his brother. Semiya lay still, eyes open, and somehow alive. The armor was gone, but a large sword rose from Semiya's chest and pinned him to the ground. The blade seemed to be the same width and placement as the armor's crack, and Angst immediately recognized it as Chryslaenor.

Neither Lord nor General were able to budge the monstrous sword. Semiya lifted his arm, and Farkus knelt by his brother, gripping his neck and pulling him close. "I was right, brother," Semiya said in a whisper. "The magics are gone now. I saved us all." And with those words, Semiya died.

16

The silence of the early morning was shattered by a scream. Angst had woken with a start to find he couldn't roll over, he couldn't lift either leg, he couldn't move. Every muscle, every joint, every fiber of his body ached and throbbed.

He heard another scream, and then pain-induced moans from Tarness and Dallow.

"I can't move," Dallow whined.

"Are you guys all right?" Angst gasped.

"I don't know, Angst. Everything feels horribly wrong," Tarness called out dramatically. "This is all your fault!" He swore vehemently.

Hector shook his head and clicked his tongue in mock sympathy as he bustled about a small cooking fire. "We're going to get nowhere fast if you three can't handle a bit of horseback riding. My old granmama with a gimp leg and an eye patch doesn't complain this much."

Their continued laments made the campsite sound like wounded on a battlefield as the three heroes dealt loudly with their old, unused muscles. Not nearly as enthusiastic about the hours of travel ahead as they'd been the night before.

Angst remembered hangovers that felt better than this. The remnants of last night's dream made his head throb. Body aches like these typically came with black eyes. Not to mention, the sweats. It had to be some sort of illness, there was no way he was this out of shape!

Sitting up in this condition was a job for younger men. After long moments of indecision, Angst gracefully rocked from side to side until finally rolling over to his stomach. He pushed himself awkwardly onto his knees, shaking like a newborn deer. Several muttered curses later, he had successfully crawled over rocks and roots to leave the tent. He paused to seek out those remaining muscles that weren't strained and hadn't magically turned into knotty tendons overnight. It was a nearly impossible task. The few spots that weren't sore had been chafed by the horse and armor—it felt as though to the bone. "Who's making breakfast?" Angst growled.

"Already done, but you have to come over here to eat it," Hector taunted, sounding too happy for his own good.

"This is *not* going to work. How are we supposed to defend the kingdom if we need an infirmary every morning?" Angst said, rising to his knees. He looked up from the ground to find Tarness and Dallow in similar conditions.

Ivan, already in his armor, walked over to stand behind Angst. "You three just need a swift kick like any new recruit," he barked, pulling back his leg. "Hey, I can't move my foot!"

It was an easy bit of magic for Angst, and this trick had always been one of his favorites at the castle. With only the slightest bit of concentration, he could will the ground to hold someone's armor in place.

Angst looked up at Hector and winked. He stood, slowly, letting out a long grunt, and then turned to face Ivan. "No rules out here, Sir Ivan. I'm happy to humble you all the way there and back again."

Ivan gave up on fighting his immobility. A thin smile crawled across his lips, obviously forced. "Just joking, Angst," he muttered through gritted teeth.

Angst looked him up and down, and with a wave of his hand, released Ivan's foot. He walked over to Dallow and Tarness and helped them to their feet. "Let's eat."

They ate in relative silence, well, save for the popping bones, creaky tendons, and moans when muscles were unexpectedly stretched for the first time in a decade.

"Are you certain we didn't bring any meds that could soften the blow a bit?" Dallow asked Hector desperately. "I don't know if I can get back on that horse."

"Meds? We have a few bandages. Maybe I can wrap everyone's mouth so they stop complaining." Hector sounded frustrated. "You're the smart one. You go find something out there." He waved off into the woods.

Hector's words acted like a trigger, and Dallow replied with a considering, "Huh." His green irises and dark pupils gradually clouded over and began glowing. His eyes moved back and forth quickly, as though reading some invisible text unimaginably fast. Dallow cocked his head to one side and a satisfied smile spread across his face as his eyes returned to normal. He slapped Hector on the shoulder.

"Good idea," Dallow acknowledged before wandering off into the nearby wood.

Angst looked at Tarness, shrugged, and the two of them followed. Ivan stood back with a disgusted look on his face, but said nothing.

Dallow started pulling moss off various trees then grabbed some wild mushrooms from around their base. "I need these ground up, quickly."

Angst held out his hands for the materials. "I do this at home for Heather all the time," he explained. He placed the ingredients in his breakfast bowl then picked up a small rock, wiped it off on Dallow's leather jerkin, and dropped it on top of the moss and mushrooms. The rock began to spin, bouncing off the bowl's edge and crashing against the vegetation. After several moments, the rock had ground everything into a fine paste that smelled of musty carrots and vinegar.

Angst peered into the bowl and quickly jerked his nose away. "I get it. You're poisoning us so we die instead of hurting. Good plan."

"Yeah, don't eat that. You'll be sick for a week." Dallow

scooped up a skosh of the concoction with two fingers and rubbed it along the inside of his legs. "Ahhh. Try it."

Without hesitation, Tarness grabbed a huge handful and slathered it all over his legs and shoulders. He sighed with relief. "It feels like a warm bath. Dallow, you're a genius."

Angst mixed the remainder of the plants then scooped a generous handful and worked the paste into his sore muscles. It burned, tolerably, where his legs were chafed, but his muscles relaxed as though he were bathing in a hot spring.

"Dallow, this is great. Where did you get the idea?" Tarness asked.

"An old medical herb book," Dallow said, pleased with himself. "We're very lucky. The mushrooms die quickly when fall arrives."

"We should keep this stuff on hand, you know, just in case." Tarness seemed eager.

"I'll collect more of the moss and mushrooms while you both pack camp," Dallow agreed.

Angst and Tarness returned to find Ivan and Hector arguing. Hector appeared ready to leap at Ivan, his wolf-like eyes narrowed to dangerous slits. His short gray hairs reminded Angst of a dog's hackles, raised before a fight.

Ivan immediately stopped when they arrived, looking slightly nauseated. He pinched his nose and reared his head away. "What is that smell?" He almost gagged. "Did you roll around in a dead animal or something?"

"Dallow made a salve to help with our sore muscles. I feel like new!" Tarness sounded ecstatic.

Hector took a step back. "You don't smell like new. I hope your armor covers that stench."

Dallow returned with more mushrooms and moss, which they decided to pack separately, as the smell was easier to contain when the ingredients were unmixed. The armor covered a small portion of the scent, but it was strong enough that Hector rode well in front of the group, and Ivan followed far behind.

They made slow progress over the next several days, since it was necessary to locate campsites with an ample cache of moss and mushrooms. Angst had wanted to ask Hector what he'd been arguing with Ivan about, but his friend seemed most offended by the smell and avoided the three of them.

Each day's ride required a bit more of the paste until Dallow announced, "I believe that's all we get."

"Finally!" Ivan exclaimed.

"What do you mean? We've only been using it for a few days," Angst asked, not wanting to face riding sore for the next week.

"It seems to be losing potency," Dallow informed them. "Either because summer is over, or because we are using too much."

Hector seemed happy for the first time in days. "Then we have a new requirement for tonight's campsite — a creek. You three need a bath!"

17

A cool morning breeze crept through the window and into the queen's chamber. Isabelle pulled at her blankets then shivered and opened her eyes when she realized her comforter was still missing. She sighed deeply, already aware it would be impossible to go back to sleep. But mornings were always like this, her mind started to-do lists even while her body longed for precious rest. It was pointless to just lie in bed, but she continued to do so anyway. She pondered and justified. Didn't she deserve one late morning? With the tiniest amount of sacrifice, the queen had removed the trash, and all her burdens, from Unsel. It had been days since she'd rid herself of Angst, and of Ivan, and she still felt smugly triumphant. The thought of this win was comforting. Her eyes were just beginning to make a feeble attempt at shutting when Isabelle heard it. *Click, click, click.*

Was she dreaming, or maybe stuck in that half-waking, early morning state? The queen sat up, but her sleep-laden eyes required a certain amount of knuckling before they would focus. She peered at a bird-shaped silhouette blocking the early morning sunlight. From across her bedroom, it looked like a huge raven. The kind someone might mistake for an eagle or a hawk when it flew high overhead.

The queen rose from her bed, pulled a heavy violet cloak over her shoulders, and slipped her feet into violet morning shoes. She shuffled across the thick Meldusian carpet, with the intent of shooing the thing off, but stopped fifteen feet away. The bird remained still as if it owned the windowsill. It was disconcerting, but at least now she could now see her visitor clearly.

Early morning light reflected off velvety purple wings. Its chest was a dark crimson, and seemed covered in soft gosling fur where one would've expected bird feathers. The legs were almost thick as her arm, and its talons were the size of her fingers. As the bird shifted slightly, the legs and beak shone in the morning sun like polished metal. Its silvery beak was a long thin thing that was almost handsome, making it appear majestic. When she met its eyes, a fan of feathers popped up, like a peacock but from the bird's neck rather than its back end. They surrounded its head in a feathery purple half circle, each feather displaying several crimson eyes that matched the ones on its face.

Isabelle was mesmerized, and slowly moved closer. She couldn't tear her gaze away from its watchful eyes. It cocked its head, studying her as she studied it. Such a magnificent creature, so regal in nature, it belonged at the castle with her. Isabelle stopped a reach away. Holding her breath, she spread her arms wide and prepared to capture it in a giant hug. Then the eyes blinked, both on the bird's face, and on the feathery fan. They all blinked simultaneously, then narrowed with intent.

"Wait, that isn't right," Isabelle said.

She wanted to take a step back, but was already leaning forward to catch it. The creature dove at her face, its long, handsome beak aimed directly at her eyes.

* * * *

Tyrell was doing morning calisthenics in his bed chamber when the queen screamed across the hall—the type of bloodcurdling scream that crawled through your bones and into your nightmares. Without pause, he grabbed his short sword and tore through the double doors of his room.

The guards posted outside the queen's room fumbled to unlock the doors then scrambled out of the way as Tyrell rammed through them.

Isabelle lay on the carpet of her room with her arms extended, holding off a giant purple bird that stood on her chest. The queen's arms were barely long enough to protect her face from its talons. Unfortunately, they weren't long enough to keep its beak away. The bird paid no heed to Tyrell or the soldiers, and instead continued digging in the queen's right eye.

One of the guards gasped, the other cursed.

"Tyrell!" Isabelle screamed, panic gripping her voice.

He struck the creature with all his might. It rolled to the floor, shook slightly then ran back to the queen. Tyrell moved forward quickly to intercept.

Victoria ran into the room, but one of the queen's guards held her back. "Mother!" she screamed, her body bent over the guard's restraining arm, straining to push through. "Let me go!"

The bird paused, looking from queen to princess, then expanded its massive wings and flew to Victoria.

"Get her out now!" Tyrell barked. He leaped forward and tackled the beast.

Tyrell and the bird rolled, its metal talons tearing at his bare chest. He gripped the creature's neck with one hand while grappling to better position his sword.

One guard attempted to wrestle the princess out of the room, while the other grabbed the queen's arm to drag her away. Blood poured from Isabelle's face as she held her hand against her eye. She screamed for Tyrell, and flailed as though the bird still attacked.

"What have you done!" Tyrell roared at the bird creature.

The bird's strength was astounding, and he struggled to position himself on top of it. He jammed his short sword into the creature's chest. The impact made it cough, but Tyrell's blade couldn't penetrate the bird's crimson coat.

"Fine," the Captain Guard explained to the bird in frustration. "We'll do it this way." With all the rage Tyrell could muster, he rammed the creature's head with the hilt of his sword. He moved his hand off its neck and shoved the sharp beak aside while continuously smashing at its head.

The bird became agitated, tossing and writhing until it was finally out of Tyrell's grip.

"Get the window!" Tyrell commanded, but the guards were busy helping Isabelle and Victoria. Others had arrived, but they were too far away.

The large purple bird hopped to the windowsill then turned and looked at Tyrell. It opened its mouth wide, let out a loud shrilling sound, spread its wings, and flew off.

* * * *

Later, Tyrell and the princess sat outside the physician's room and waited. Tyrell had stopped pacing to sit by Victoria, who seemed to choose different spots on the wall to stare at. He would have expected a storm of tears — she deserved every one of them — but instead the princess surprised him, again. She hadn't panicked when she'd walked into the chaos of her mother's chamber. She'd actually wanted to help fight, and had taken charge of the guards when the battle was over. Even now, her poise was impressive. She was obviously upset, but she also seemed thoughtful. Tyrell couldn't help but wonder, had Princess Victoria just become queen?

Physician Nynette entered the waiting room. Her hair, once gathered in a tight bun, was a disheveled mess, exhaustion plain on her haggard face. Her blue robes were splattered with royal blood.

She knelt in front of Victoria and looked up at her intently. "Your mother is alive, Your Majesty," the physician said.

Tyrell and Victoria let out a sigh of relief.

"I would like to see her now," Victoria said in stoic voice.

"She's sleeping, but you may see her," Nynette agreed. "Before you go in, I need to share my concerns."

The princess took a deep breath, bracing herself for the news, and nodded.

"The queen's right eye is gone. It will have to be replaced

with a glass eye to minimize the chance of infection. She has some deep wounds around her eye, some of which will heal, but there will be scarring." Nynette took a deep breath. "Her Majesty will need a lot of care and attention. An attack this damaging often leaves most people frightened and bewildered."

Victoria held up her hand, stopping the physician. Her voice was very serious. "The queen will be fine. She is not *most people*, and if anyone asks, that is exactly what you will tell them."

The physician seemed surprised by Victoria's response. She stood and stepped back, but said nothing.

Princess Victoria rose and went to the infirmary room where her mother was resting.

Tyrell caught himself almost smiling, once again impressed by the young woman. "What are the rest of your concerns?" he asked the physician.

"I've seen other patients with dagger wounds to the eye. The results are horrific. People can go crazy, or die a slow death as a result of damage done behind the eye. I did everything I could, but it's impossible to tell how deep the queen's injuries are." Her voice was filled with worry.

"Thank you for telling me, but the princess is correct. Nobody outside of this room will ever learn the extent of her injuries." Tyrell placed a firm hand on her shoulder, looking directly into her eyes. "You understand this?"

Nynette nodded.

"Is there anything else?" he asked.

"We will need to continue administering medication so she remains asleep until her glass eye is in place. I wouldn't recommend waking or moving her for several days."

"That isn't a problem," Tyrell acknowledged. "I will station a dozen guards outside the doors. Nobody will be allowed in save your staff, the princess, and myself."

Nynette crossed her arms and tsked in annoyance. "I thought this was an animal attack? What kind of animal requires that many guards?"

He peered around the door to see Victoria sitting beside her mother in the examination room as she'd done only days before with Angst. The princess held the queen's hand, and gazed intently at her face. She didn't appear aware of Tyrell and Nynette's conversation.

Tyrell didn't want misinformation to spread, but the queen's presence might mean danger for the physician and her staff. "That wasn't just any animal. It was magical, and it was trained."

18

Another day passed. The road they traveled was devoid of traffic, not what one would expect of Unsel's busiest highway. Old wagon ruts hadn't been filled in and were starting to grow over with weeds. It had obviously been some time since the road had seen regular attention, and Angst spent much of the day trying to understand what could possibly halt all forms of commerce. It left him uneasy.

Angst, Tarness, and Dallow rode sore, but smelled better, after finding a shallow creek for a quick rinse off. Ivan still trailed twenty or so yards behind, but at least Hector would ride with them now.

"I've been wondering, what were you and Ivan arguing about the first morning?" Angst asked Hector.

Hector didn't appear to enjoy the memory, and he sneered while casting a dark look over his shoulder at Ivan. "I really don't understand how that man became a knight. First he reminded me of his higher rank and then ordered me to help him attack you. Supposedly so he could be in charge. Ivan believed the two of us could take you."

"Well, thanks for telling him no. I appreciate you sticking up for me." Angst grinned smugly.

"No? I told him yes." Hector chuckled. "I wanted to see you give him a beating. I figured it would shut him up for the rest of the trip."

"That sounds like a good idea," Dallow said. "But what caused the argument?"

"I couldn't help but laugh at his suggestion. He became offended. Then he proceeded to offend me," Hector said, fuming at the memory, his blue gray eyes narrowing dangerously. "Had you three shown up a few minutes later, the beating would've happened before you got there."

"Angst," Tarness interrupted. "Is something wrong with Chryslaenor?" He pointed at the giant sword.

A bright blue aura surrounded the great blade. They stopped their horses immediately and dismounted. Angst pulled Chryslaenor from his back and stared at it for a moment, concentrating. "I don't understand. We aren't being attacked." He listened closely, but Chryslaenor's song still chimed quietly in the back of his head, unchanged. "Hector, do you sense anything unusual?"

Hector cocked his head to one side and focused on their surroundings. "I don't hear anything sneaking up on us, nor do I smell anything unusual." He shrugged. "I'd say we're safe."

Ivan caught up to the group. "Stopping for another respite, are we?" he quipped. Ivan looked agitated and was rubbing the back of his neck then stopped when he noticed the sword. "Why is that thing glowing?"

"Now you know why we stopped. Let's spread out and look around," Angst commanded the others.

"This is yet another waste of time," Ivan growled, his dark eyes peering at each of them with disgust. "Why don't we try something unique and hurry. We could still reach Oakhaven before sunset." He was still mounted while the others had already spread out and started walking into the woods.

"Ivan, get off your horse and look around or I'll drag you off the horse. Your choice." Angst was holding Chryslaenor in one hand, and was prepared to grab hold of Ivan with the other.

Ivan rolled his eyes, but dismounted nonchalantly. He began walking north, slowly.

"Angst, come over here," Dallow called from the northeast.

Tarness had gone south and turned around to catch up at Dallow's behest. Angst and Tarness lumbered through shrubs and tall weeds until they found their friend standing next to a road marker. The marker was an obelisk made of rich black marble. It had a foot-thick base and stood as tall as Dallow. Four decorative grooves were carved into each side. Ornately chiseled into the front of the pillar were the words, *Gressmore Towers*. The style of lettering was so dated it was almost illegible. Despite its obvious age, the marker appeared clean and new.

"What is Gressmore Towers?" asked Tarness.

Confusion and frustration wrinkled Dallow's face. "I don't know. I've been standing here trying to remember if I have ever read anything about it, but I have no mental reference of its existence."

Ivan had made his way over. He looked at the sign and seemed confused to the point of annoyance. "Gressmore? I've never heard of it. And what are you all looking at, this isn't even a sign! It's a blank marker pointing up."

"Actually, it's pointing that way." Angst walked around the sign. Like some optical illusion, the words always faced him, even while the marker leaned in a northeast direction.

Hector dropped out of a nearby tree, making Ivan startle. "I don't know what that marker is about, Angst. I've traveled this highway a hundred times, and I've never seen any sign like it. I've never even heard of Gressmore Towers. Even stranger, fifty yards ahead is a path that looks freshly cut. You can guess which direction it goes."

"That seems a little convenient," Tarness observed warily.

"Maybe because that's where we need to go," Angst suggested.

Ivan grabbed Hector's shoulder and pointed at Angst. "I told you your boy there is crazy." Ivan's eyes went wild and he grasped at the air as his feet started sinking into the ground.

Angst's hands were glowing, and he peered angrily at Ivan.

"Stop!" He held out both hands. "Look, I'm just saying with all the attacks we've heard about, it's obvious that this could be a trap." Ivan stopped sinking. "Let's not make it easy for whoever, or whatever, is out there to kill us, okay?"

Angst continued staring at Ivan. His gut told him to take the path, that they should go to Gressmore, but Ivan's logic was sound. "You're right. We'll keep moving." He reluctantly made his way back to the road, waving for his friends to follow.

* * * *

It was late in the afternoon when Angst suddenly stopped his horse in the middle of the road.

"What is that?" Hector asked, also stopping. He cocked his head to listen.

"You hear it too?" Angst asked, squinting in concentration.

The high-pitched squeal was faint, as though the wind had carried it a long distance.

They waited in silence, listening until Hector finally spoke. "I hear it, but I don't know what it is. I know I don't like it."

The woods around them became quiet once again, and they decided to continue.

The squeal became a scream, and it sounded closer. Dallow looked at everyone, his eyes huge and his face pale. "It couldn't be," he exclaimed, his voice thick with worry. Without saying another word, he turned his horse south and rode straight into the woods.

Angst immediately wheeled his horse to follow Dallow. "Let's go," he called.

Hector and Tarness hesitated for only a moment then followed Angst and Dallow. Angst glanced back to see that Ivan remained on the road. He wore his helm as though ready to fight, but didn't move.

Branches and twigs grabbed at their faces as they tore through the woods. Within moments, they found the source of the screams.

It had hands. Undeniably, whatever it was, it had hands. Only three fingers, wide and grotesque with short, cracked nails that looked to be an inch thick, but there was no doubt that they were hands. The rest of the body wasn't as easy to categorize. The creature was four times the height of a man, with the haunches of a bear, maybe, though without hair. It looked uncomfortable in its standing position, as it had no front legs to balance the rear. Its chest and arms appeared human, though its skin was covered with red and white blotches. The nose and mouth protruded from its face like a snub-nosed dog's. Above those sat one large black eye. This monster was not of Ehrde.

Dallow and Angst had stopped just fifty feet away at the edge of the small clearing. Dallow seemed uncertain what to do next, as though he wanted to attack immediately but was trying to figure out what the creature was.

Tarness caught up with them. "What is that thing?" he asked in a horrified voice, sounding as though he were swallowing bile. He drew his sword and shield.

Hector pulled his horse to a stop next to Tarness. "Looks like practice to me." He hopped up to stand on his horse, whipped out a long dagger that had been hidden in his armor, and held it in his mouth. He then leaped to a nearby tree, easily scaling the trunk.

Tarness looked over at Angst, who shrugged. "Let's wait for Hector to get into position. Dismount, and we'll move in slowly." He paused to analyze the situation, leaning his head forward for a better view. "Uh, what is it holding?"

They dismounted and inched closer. The creature stood in the middle of a glade, staring at its hands. It was holding what appeared to be a thin, wobbly stick in one, and part of a horse in the other. The horse had evidently been lunch. When they were twenty feet away, they could see that the stick was moving. The stick screamed, startling the creature. It began to growl, apparently unhappy that its toy was making noise. The monster looked ready to throw it, or bite its head off, or something else nightmarish that none of them really wanted to see.

"Help me, you idiots," yelled a familiar voice.

"That's what I heard before," Dallow pointed frantically, his eyes wide. "It's Rose!"

There was no more time to wait for Hector to get in position. They ran toward the monster as fast as they could. Adrenaline helped Angst ignore his pains as they jumped over fallen logs and crashed through more branches. Knowing his friend was in danger helped him ignore his fear.

Angst swung Chryslaenor in a wide arc that ended deep in the beast's right calf. It howled in pain as Angst attempted to re-move the sword. The monster bent over and slapped him aside. Angst flew into a large bush. He hadn't been knocked out, but everything hurt again. He caught his breath in time to roll out of the way as the half-eaten horse hurtled toward him.

Tarness positioned himself in front of the creature's swinging arm. He caught it, steadied the giant hand in his strong grip and stabbed the back of it with his sword. The giant jerked his arm away, but Tarness held onto his sword as it lifted him into the air. After a failed attempt to shake the man loose, the monster peered at him with confusion and pain in its one dark eye. Tar-ness yanked out his sword and hauled himself up the arm.

As Tarness made his way to the neck, Hector dropped down from a tree, now with a dagger in both hands. He landed on the shoulder opposite Tarness and worked his way to the beast's head.

Dallow stood back and watched the right hand that held Rose captive. It rocked back and forth, closer to the ground with each swing. The giant seemed to have forgotten its prisoner, focusing instead on the attackers. Dallow waited, timing the swings, then ran in and struck the monster hard on the wrist with his staff. The well-timed smack forced the creature to drop Rose into his arms. He set her down, and they sprinted back to the horses.

The monster bellowed in anger, and lurched forward to grab Rose.

"Down!" Hector yelled.

Rose dove away in time, but Dallow was struck by the giant hand. He flew ten yards into a tree, landing in a crumpled heap, where he lay, unmoving.

CHAPTER EIGHTEEN

Angst picked himself back up and yelled *"Dallow!"* but there was no response. Anger filled his veins, his jaw jutting forward as the magic overcame him. The giant let out a horrible roar as the ground beneath it shook violently. Tendrils of dirt and stone reached up, grabbed the monster's legs, and drug it into the earth. Angst willed the earth to pull the monster deep enough to trap it without burying Chryslaenor.

Just then Hector launched his own attack. The giant's howl of frustration and pain sounded like a tree being snapped in half as Hector stabbed its eye. From his seat on the creature's shoulder, Tarness hacked at the enormous neck. Angst took advantage of the distraction of their attacks, and ran forward to yank Chryslaenor free. He spun about to face the creature before it could react. Angst held Chryslaenor in front of him with both hands and focused. Tendrils of earth pulled at the monster once again until it was buried to its knees. Angst moved forward, slashing across the monster's stomach with his sword, and a steaming pile of guts and undigested horse poured over him. The giant grabbed at its entrails with a loud roar before falling back dead.

Angst gagged as he carved his way through the guts he'd let loose. Tarness tried to help, but lost his footing in the thick pool of blood. They awkwardly helped each other slide away from the mess, taking careful steps as if walking on ice. With the adrenaline gone, Angst grabbed his chest where he had been struck. "Ow," he said pitifully. He approached Rose and Dallow. "Rose, is he all right? Are you?" His voice was shaky from a sudden wave of exhaustion.

Rose was facing away from everyone, shivering violently. She must've been reeling with shock after being held by the creature they'd just killed. He moved forward, but she lifted her hand to stop him. Her shivering eventually subsided to an occasional tremor, and she took a deep breath before turning to face them. Tears streamed down her cheeks, making Angst fear she was hurt or Dallow dead.

But Dallow stood, patting along random spots on his body as though shocked everything was still intact.

"Are you okay?" asked Hector. "That throw looked pretty rough."

Dallow's eyes were wide with surprise as he stared at Rose.

"Thank you," she said to Dallow before he could speak. When he didn't respond, she elaborated. "For catching me."

Dallow nodded slowly, seemingly in shock himself, and wiped his sweaty blond bangs from his forehead. "How do you feel?" he asked Rose.

"Just scared, but really, I'll be fine." She smiled.

Rose and Dallow stared at each other for a long time, while everyone else looked on awkwardly.

"Ahem," Angst interrupted, wiping monster bits from his armor.

Rose tore her gaze away from Dallow and looked at everyone. "Eww. Um, thanks."

Ivan conveniently arrived, smirking at the mess of them. He took one look at Rose and scoffed. "Where did the bitch come from?"

Angst reached out, and Ivan flew from his mount. Angst turned away and walked over to the heap of dead monster. He shook his head in disbelief. "What was it?"

"It's not one of ours," replied Tarness.

Everyone looked at him in disbelief.

"My dad and I used to hunt," he explained, "and I know all about cleaning game." Tarness pointed at the monster's crotch. "There's nothing to reproduce with. This thing didn't come from Ehrde."

Hector and Angst both looked at him with some surprise. "Good catch," agreed Hector.

"What is that smell?" asked Tarness.

A drifting spiral of black smoke rose from the dead body. It hovered unnaturally as the giant slowly deflated.

"I wouldn't recommend taking any deep breaths right now," cautioned Hector.

They all stepped back. Ivan had returned to his feet, eyeing Angst warily. The pile of creature continued to disintegrate, until there was nothing but a disgusting, smelly ooze staining the forest floor.

"Let's head back to the road," Angst suggested, nodding his head in that direction.

"So is that what we're facing out here?" asked Tarness as they walked alongside their horses.

"I hope not," replied Hector. "Had there been two of those things, they'd be enjoying us for supper." He looked over his shoulder to Angst. "You need to get your crap together."

"Me? Didn't I bury it in two feet of earth before gutting it?" Angst asked defensively.

"After it beat you senseless. You fought as gracefully as you dance. What happened to those fancy sword moves of yours?"

Angst merely shrugged. Hector was right, though Angst wouldn't admit it. Sure, they had won, but it had been an ugly win. It didn't go at all like he would have hoped. There was nothing musical or glorious or artistic in the nature of this battle. Everyone was bruised, covered in guts, or both. He was relieved they were all safe, but wasn't overwhelmed with feelings of success or heroics.

They made their way back to the road. Ivan looked at Rose with a sneer. "How exactly are you getting back home?"

She stepped toward him, making a tiny, threatening fist.

"Are you talking again, Ivan?" Angst asked, backing up her threat.

Hector stood behind Angst and Rose, placing a hand on both their shoulders. "Unfortunately, he's right, in a way. What are you doing here, Rose?"

She handed an envelope to Angst, its seal adorned with the princess's signet.

Everyone saw the signet and moaned. "She made Rose deliver a love letter all the way out here?" asked Dallow, shaking his head.

Ivan raised an eyebrow but said nothing.

Angst wiped his hand off on Dallow before taking it. He opened the note and looked it over. Then he read aloud, *"You will need her. Keep her safe.*" He didn't bother to read the '*I miss you, Love Tori.*' part out loud, knowing it would be misunderstood.

"Pfft," was Ivan's eloquent response as he mounted his horse.

Hector removed his hand from Angst slowly and wiped it off on his leg. He nodded at the messy armor. "Was that your horse, Rose?"

Rose stopped glaring at Ivan to look around frantically as realization struck. "It was my horse," she said to Hector with a sigh. "That monster picked me up hours ago, I don't know where any of my things are. This travel outfit the princess gave me is all I have left. The rest of my gear is gone."

She wore a corset-like top with long sleeves, tight brown leather riding breeches, and high dark leather boots. The outfit was strikingly different from anything she normally wore and accentuated the curves on her tiny frame. Rose coughed purposefully when she noticed everyone staring. She shook her head and rolled her eyes.

"You're welcome to ride with me," Angst offered hastily, having forgotten he was covered in monster.

"Um, I'll ride with Dallow," she replied, and followed the tall, thin man to his mount.

Angst shrugged, feeling a bit put out.

19

Like guests at a dinner party, they separated to their own conversations for the remainder of the afternoon. Anxious to make Oakhaven before nightfall, Ivan rode ahead of the others, attempting to set pace. Tarness and Hector followed closely behind. Rose and Dallow trailed far enough to be seen without being heard, and it was obvious to all they preferred it that way. Hector had suggested Angst stay downwind until they could find a creek, as he was still covered in monster and the smell was not improving.

Hector patted Tarness' arm and nodded at Ivan. The knight was rubbing the back of his neck. It caused an annoying racket in his full plate as he attempted to massage a spot just under the armor.

"Injure yourself in the battle, Ivan?" Hector asked.

"I'm just not used to sleeping on the ground," Ivan replied sullenly. He stopped reaching and stretched out his arms before finally cricking his neck to one side, making an audible pop. "I typically make Oakhaven in a day." Ivan's tone was almost polite, and his typical sneer had been replaced by, perhaps, a more professional demeanor.

Hector glared at him until Ivan let loose a sigh.

"You're right. I should've fought alongside everyone as commanded by Her Majesty. I'm not completely sure I would've done much good though."

In spite of Ivan's surprising candor, Hector was skeptical of anything the man said. "I'm not sure I follow you, Ivan."

"There are only a few knights and soldiers who've lived through attacks from unnatural creatures. I've heard stories, not of that monster, but of others just as horrific. Clements, a friend of mine at one of the border outposts, lost an arm to such an attack. He was...is a fierce fighter with little fear. Clements told me he couldn't even scratch the monster he fought. The beast ate his arm then threw him aside to eat his horse." Ivan shuddered then looked back toward Angst. "It must be the magics."

Hector nodded thoughtfully. "That's an interesting theory. In all honesty, I felt that the thing died pretty easily, considering how large it was." He smiled at Tarness's surprised look. "Well, it was a bit messy, and we all have a lot to learn about fighting together. But I've heard about other battles like ours and these things don't die."

"So Clements's monster was different than our monster?" Tarness asked.

"You all were able to kill this one, which is a difference," replied Ivan. "He didn't like discussing the details, but it sounds like it was about the same size, and just as grotesque. I seem to recall something about his monster having human ears and horns."

"Huh," Tarness replied, while making eye contact with Hector.

In this brief moment of apparent frankness, Hector really wanted to ask the knight why he was such an ass. It was as though they were all meeting a different Ivan for the first time.

Ivan gave up on his scratch and stopped fidgeting. "This whole situation is damned frustrating. Monsters I can't fight, surrounded by people who can do, well, you know..." He waved his hand around in a motion that apparently included every reference to magic in all existence. "Nothing I can do but tag along and hope the queen forgets what happened at the banquet." He looked back at Rose.

Hector leaned toward him. "You should hope we all forget

about what happened at the banquet."

Ivan snorted and rolled his eyes at Hector before speeding ahead to lead again, distancing himself from the others.

"You really don't give him much of a chance," Tarness said, shaking his head at Hector.

"Angst gave him a chance, now I'll just help keep him in line." Hector peered at Ivan as the man rode ahead. "Maybe as a scout, he could be useful. You know, yell a warning as the next monster takes a bite."

Tarness chuckled. "I'm sure we'll know we've caught up to poor Ivan when we start seeing parts on the trail. 'Oh, look, a hand. Everyone get out their weapons.'"

"See? Even if he can't do 'the magics,' he's plenty useful." Hector smiled mischievously. "I'm going to go check on the hero."

Hector slowed his horse to a trot, letting Dallow and Rose pass him. They looked up and nodded, but said nothing more. When Angst caught up, Hector flashed his friend a broad grin that wasn't returned. He positioned himself close enough to talk quietly, but a breath ahead of smelling distance.

"You okay back here, stinky?" Hector asked.

"Fine," Angst replied, practically biting out the word. He was pulling at bits of creature that had gotten lodged in the chainmail around his midsection.

"You aren't upset about being ditched back here by yourself, are you?" Hector asked.

Angst sighed. "I have to admit, I feel like I'm being punished for doing a lot of the work."

"Nobody wanted you to smell like carcass, but it doesn't hurt for you to think about what happened."

"Oh, really?" Angst said darkly. His words then exploded as if the top came off a kettle boiling with frustration. "So, if you could take a moment to be constructive instead of offensive, how exactly could I have done better in that battle? What did you do the last time you fought a giant one-eyed monster?"

Hector looked around for help. Maybe he should have

brought Tarness, these sorts of confrontations weren't his favorite. His goal was to cheer Angst with banter, not get into a fight. He stroked the long scar along his right jaw with his thumb as he thought of a way to broach the subject gently. "You attacked the giant like you were fighting a normal person. It looked to me like you were trying to fight instead of letting the sword do its thing."

"That's it? All of the insults and insinuations, and that's the great advice you have for me?" Angst's jaw jutted forward in anger. "What about your participation in the fight? You couldn't share some of your great wisdom and tactical knowledge before going monkey-feline and jumping into a tree?"

"I thought you were taking lead, Angst?" Hector retorted, unable to stop himself.

"I thought you were here to help? Do I actually need to order you to provide tactical advice for us?"

Hector shifted in his saddle uncomfortably. They rode in silence for several minutes when he finally said, "Well, we should be at Oakhaven in about twenty minutes."

"That doesn't exactly answer my question," Angst said to him with a raised an eyebrow.

"Eh," he said with a small shrug, looking around hopefully for another monster.

* * * *

While Angst had never been to Oakhaven, he imagined it to be like other small towns he'd visited. A busy center of commerce and community during the day, and peacefully quiet at night. Oakhaven's very name sounded like 'nice little place you'd like to visit.' Because of this, and the prospect of a bath, he was very much looking forward to their first major stop.

Anticipation was slowly replaced with concern as they approached the first farm on the outskirts of town. Dusk had fallen, and it was going to be one of those nights that seemed darker than usual. Even from a distance, candles and torches shone weakly through the early evening haze.

CHAPTER NINETEEN

"From here, it looks completely abandoned," Hector observed, sounding worried. "I could take a quick look, but I'd recommend we scoot to town. It's getting late."

Angst was surprised that Hector was giving advice instead of orders. Maybe his friend had gotten his point. It shouldn't have been hard; Angst had said it loud enough. "Hopefully nothing's wrong, and the outskirts are just abandoned. I agree that we should keep moving."

They rode past another farm, and then a third, each as dark and quiet as the first. After twenty minutes of riding warily in the thickening dark, they approached Oakhaven. The houses surrounding the town were lifeless, but before they reached the center, they found it protected by a makeshift barricade. Wagons, carts, doors, chairs, and small trees were bound together between houses and shops. The sight wasn't intimidating; it was desperate. Flickers of torchlight peeked out through gaps in the blockade, and a baby began crying when they stopped their horses.

Angst looked at his friends for suggestions and found they were waiting for his cue. "Hello?" he called out.

There was no response, so he tried again, "Is anyone here? My name is Angst. I'm from Unsel."

Without warning, a torch flew over the barricade to fall in the middle of the group. The horses shuffled nervously.

"They don't look like monsters," a voice whispered loudly through one of the gaps.

Hector removed a foot from his stirrup, no doubt preparing to run off into the shadows for a bit of reconnaissance.

"Not yet," Angst whispered.

Hector's expression twisted into a scowl but he said nothing.

"We mean you no harm," Angst shouted. "We're on a mission for Her Majesty and seek food and lodging."

There was a brief murmur of discussion then more torches were lit.

"Are you a knight? I've never heard of Sir Angst," a young man answered, his voice quavering.

"Not exactly..." Angst replied, unsure how to respond.

"This is Sir Ivan," Ivan interjected. "What's going on here?"

A head popped through a hole between a wagon wheel and a wood desk. Even in the dim light, he appeared gaunt, and scared, and boyish. He was a dark-haired twenty-something with a wide nose. Young stubble covered his dirty face.

"Sir Ivan?" the young man asked. "This is Manst, I was the stable boy during your last visit?" Almost everything he said came in the form of a question. "Who's with you?"

Ivan looked at Angst, who nodded, encouraging him to continue. "These are friends. We've been sent by the queen to investigate concerning stories. We've been ordered to help, if we can. What happened here?"

"For weeks, we were attacked by small creatures until a one-eyed monster appeared and killed them," Manst replied. "Every night since, the one-eyed monster has attacked? We keep feeding it livestock, but we're running out?"

"We killed a one-eyed monster on the way here," Angst replied.

The people shuffled noisily behind the makeshift wall until Manst shushed them. "How do we know this is true?"

"If you let us in, you'll be able to see that Angst is still covered in monster," Hector said, jerking his thumb at Angst.

More heads rose from behind the barricade.

"I can't promise we killed your monster, but we killed one, and we're here to help if there's another," Angst promised.

Manst argued with someone behind him before turning to face them again. "This is the first good news we've heard in a month. Please come on in?"

The townsfolk removed enough makeshift protection to clear a small path, though it surely wouldn't have taken much effort to push through the entire wall. They dismounted to squeeze single file through the barricade opening. There appeared to be thirty townspeople, ranging from young children to old men. These survivors were tired, and ragged, with a cloud of desperation hovering about their weary bodies.

"Does this stuff actually protect you?" Ivan pointed at the wall of junk that supposedly kept the town safe.

A middle-aged woman turned away to hide her tears. Ivan's trademark flavors of rude and tactless had once again failed to impress his audience.

"We did what we could, Sir Knight, but we lost so many?" Manst replied, patting the woman on the shoulder.

"What you could? How about a ditch around the barricade? How about—" Before Ivan could continue, Angst laid a heavy hand on the knight's shoulder. Ivan faced him, surprised at being interrupted. "I'm just saying, Angst."

"You need to stop making words again. Now," Angst whispered very firmly to Ivan.

Ivan's dark eyes widened and then narrowed to glower at Angst, but he remained quiet. With a grunt, he pulled his horse toward the nearby inn.

"Pardon me, Manst. Sir Ivan hasn't been feeling well since we left," Angst offered in an attempt at an excuse, though he knew it was a poor one.

Manst looked concerned. "Sir Ivan has been through here many times. That was ruder than he usually is."

Hector leaned over to Dallow and whispered, "Maybe he's fallen off his horse too many times?"

Angst shot Hector a sly look. "These are hard times, Manst, and we're trying to find out why. Is there somewhere we can rest?" He glanced down at his armor. "And maybe get cleaned up a bit?"

The old woman who'd been crying blurted out, "Rest? What if that thing, that monster, comes back? Every day it comes and takes something, or someone. What are you going to do about that?"

"If there is another, we'll have to kill it. If we don't kill it, maybe it'll eat one of us instead of one of you." His reply was deadpan, and honest, and seemed to appease her.

A young woman stepped forward. "We have room for you at my inn, and some food, but not much," she said. "We can scrounge up some water for your, uh, mess." She regarded Angst's armor with distaste. "Manst can take your horses to the stables, as they're empty now."

Angst could only barely see, but she appeared very pretty in the light of the torches, and he couldn't help but smile. "That would be wonderful, thank you."

"Sir, did you actually say your name was Angst?" Manst asked.

Manst asking a real question caught Angst off guard. As he turned away, the young woman walked off. "Yes, well, it's a long story."

"You seem...no offense, but...aren't you kind of old for a knight?"

The comment struck Angst right in the ego, but he knew that courtesy and fear didn't typically coexist, so he winced it off. "Like I said, I'm not really a knight. It's the new thing in the kingdom, give old guys big swords and strange armor then throw them headfirst into a pot of boiling danger. Crazy times we're in," Angst replied rather nonchalantly.

Manst chuckled warily, as though unsure it was actually a joke. For the first time, he noticed Chryslaenor looming over Angst's shoulder and stopped chuckling abruptly. He took the reins of their horses and pointed everyone in the direction of the inn, never taking his wide eyes from the blade.

The interior of the inn was a welcome change from the depressing and dreary surroundings of a town that had seemed to be slowly imploding. The first floor appeared to be a tavern with polished wooden floors and walls. Most of the light came from a fire in a beautiful stone fireplace in the center of the room. The smell of sweet spices and freshly cooked meat wafted past the entrance and into his nose then pooled as a bit of drool under his tongue. This wasn't an inn; it was an oasis. Angst swallowed hard, and Tarness's stomach growled loudly.

Angst had stepped inside the doorway then immediately stepped out for fear of dirtying the room with the crusty monster bits stuck to his armor.

CHAPTER NINETEEN

The young woman who'd spoken earlier came through a pair of doors that obviously led to the kitchen. In spite of what the town had dealt with, she seemed to embody a confident and almost cheerful bearing that was contagious. Long, curly blond hair draped loosely across the shoulders of her low-cut peasant blouse. Underneath the blouse and her long skirt, she was quite curvy. He looked at her pretty green eyes as she approached, and smiled in spite of himself.

Her full lips quickly widened into a broad smile at everyone's reactions to the food. "Now you know why most travelers heading to Rohjek make this their first stop."

"Do you have enough to feed us? If not, we have some food we travel with," Dallow offered.

"We can still hunt during the day," she replied. "We typically see the monster at night." She was obviously upset and kept talking to cover the faint quiver in her voice. "We're short on dry goods, like wheat and flour, but we've got plenty of meat."

"We should be able to spare something," said Angst, anxious to win another smile. He wasn't disappointed.

"What time does your visitor show up?" asked Tarness from the doorway.

"We have a couple hours, assuming it's coming." She looked Angst up and down. "The stables out back have some buckets of rainwater for washing that armor. We have baths too."

Manst returned to the room. "Anything you need help with, Marissa?"

"Could you see everyone to the rooms at the end of the hall upstairs?" she requested. "I'll show Angst to the rainwater and bath." She flashed a grin at Angst as she walked past the group.

Rose gave Angst a gentle push from behind, combined with a knowing look.

"What?" he asked innocently then followed Marissa out the door.

"So, did you really destroy one of those things?" Marissa asked Angst as she led him to the stables.

"It was a bit messy, as you can see, but it was dead and gone when we were done," Angst said proudly.

Marissa spun around so abruptly that Angst almost ran into her before stopping. "How? How did you do it? In spite of your strange armor, you don't look like a knight. Was it that thing?" she pointed at Chryslaenor.

He needed to be careful. Everyone's reaction to magic was different. Marissa could get upset, or scared, or hateful, and he really didn't want her to stop smiling.

"So, are you going to tell me or just stand there staring at me?"

Taken by surprise at her abrupt nature, he laughed out loud. "All right. Well, the truth is, we used magic. I can wield magic, almost everyone I'm with wields magic...and the sword helps quite a bit."

She blinked several times then glanced up at the sword and back at his face.

"Now you're the one staring," he teased. She laughed loudly, and Angst continued. "The 'magic thing' we do is the reason I was hesitant to share. Most people don't take that news very well."

Marissa shrugged. "Probably because it's illegal, right? As long as it works, I don't think anyone here will care. That's not true for all towns, but there are a few here who can do a bit of magic and nobody seems to mind." She turned away and beckoned him to follow. "So why did you tell me the truth?"

"I felt I could trust you," he replied to the back of her head. Her blond hair smelled like lavender.

She pointed at a rain barrel outside the stables. "You can wash your armor here." Marissa walked toward the back of the inn.

"So, do you run this place?" Angst asked, attempting to keep the conversation flowing.

"I do now." Marissa was still facing away. "My husband and I...Well, he... It's just me and my daughter." Her words trailed off, and she kept walking. She lifted a finger to her face, probably to wipe a tear.

"I'm sorry. I didn't know," Angst said quietly.

"Of course not." She turned to flash him a forced smile before lighting a torch on the inn's back wall. She lifted one side of a double door that seemed to lead underneath the inn.

Angst opened the other and was met with a waft of steam. "What is this?"

"The inn was built over a hot spring," Marissa replied. "This is the 'haven' part of 'Oakhaven.'"

"This is incredible. I think we should stay here for several months...just to protect the town, of course."

Marissa laughed politely. "Thanks for telling me the truth, about how you killed the monster. My husband was a strong man, and I never understood why he couldn't... Well, thank you."

"You're welcome, Marissa. Thank you for this, and every-thing."

She winced and pinched her nose. "You still stink, sir. Hurry up so you can join your friends for dinner."

* * * *

Angst returned incredibly relaxed. The hot springs had washed away all the knots he'd collected on the road. He found Marissa standing near his friends, chatting. She was strikingly pretty and her cheer affected everyone. She seated him nearby, since the table where his friends sat was full. After refreshing everyone's drinks, she served him a plate of roast and potatoes then sat down to join him. He was happy, in that twelve-year-old gift-receiving way, as they discussed everything that wasn't monsters. This was his element, and he was very grateful for his first true distraction since picking up the sword. He told her about the first leg of their journey and the trials of traveling when you're old and out of shape. She laughed at his humorous spin on the trip, which made Rose roll her eyes several times. After an hour of losing himself in talking about nothing, Angst felt a hand on his shoulder and looked up to see Hector.

"It's time to see if we have another monster to kill." Hector then spoke to Marissa. "That meal was amazing. Hopefully we can have a second helping in several hours?"

"I'll be waiting." Marissa put her hand on Angst's arm. "Be careful."

Rose grabbed his other arm and pulled him out of the seat and toward the door. "We'll all be careful."

Angst flashed Marissa a boyish grin then stepped out with the others.

"You just can't help yourself, can you?" asked Rose in a harsh whisper. "Wouldn't Heather be upset?"

Angst screwed up his eyes a bit. "At what? Talking to pretty girls? If that were the case, you and I wouldn't be friends."

Rose shook her head in disbelief before giving him a shove. "Go kill something."

Everyone, including Ivan, made their way back outside the barricade. Manst covered their exit then waited behind the wall. They circled the wall several times before searching the surrounding town. The first hour passed quickly, but the second hour felt like they were watching someone empty a large jar of molasses. Halfway into hour three, Angst had to wake Hector.

"Um, Manst, how are we doing?" Hector called over the barricade.

Manst sounded cautiously optimistic. "The monster has always come by now. I don't know what we should do?"

"How about some more dinner?" Tarness rubbed his hands together in anticipation.

20

During the queen's three days in the infirmary, her bedroom had been scrubbed, washed, painted, and returned to its original immaculate state. Where the staff was unable to clean blood from the carpet, they used dye. Damage to the windowsill and floor done by her attacker's steel claws had been stained and buffed. The quality of work was a testament to her court's dedication.

Isabelle's room wasn't the only thing restored. A team of artists and glassblowers from the city had spent days perfecting several replacement eyes for the queen. The eye wouldn't function, of course, which was part of the reason such effort was made to mend her room as completely as possible. Victoria and Tyrell desperately hoped that familiarity would promote healing and help her adjust to the loss of half her vision.

Isabelle had been moved from the confines of the physician's office to her bed chamber. Tyrell and Victoria stood on opposite sides of her bed, watching and waiting for the medications to wear off. She lay still, her heavy cheeks drooping unkindly. Her white hair was bed-matted, spread about the pillow, unbrushed from days of rest.

"How soon until she wakes?" asked Tyrell, his voice thick with guilt and apprehension.

"Within the hour," Victoria replied nervously.

The princess seemed uneasy, pulling at a long strand of dark hair that rested on her shoulder, winding and wrapping it within her fingers. After the physician's warning, he had the same worries. Would the queen be the same strong ruler Unsel respected? Or would she be too scarred to see to her duties?

Tyrell's expression gentled upon seeing her concerned face, and answered in a comforting tone. "You will be a great queen, Your Majesty. I've seen that side of you these past few days. You can lead. I believe you will do great things as queen of Unsel, when it is time."

Victoria blushed and looked to the floor shyly. "That's kind, Captain Guard, but I hardly feel ready to lead a nation."

"Your mother was only two years older than you are now when she joined your father on the throne," he said, smiling warmly, trying his best to comfort the young woman. "Have faith in yourself, and one day soon you could—"

"I'm not done yet." Isabelle's high-pitched voice was scratchy and seemed to reach for them from the depths of slumber.

"My queen?" Tyrell jumped slightly at her sudden response.

"Mother?" Victoria asked, her voice gentle.

Queen Isabelle opened her eyes. She blinked as the left eye adjusted to the light and focused on the canopy over her four-poster bed. Isabelle covered her left eye and pulled her hand away, blinking several more times as realization sank in. With a look of defeat on her, she gently touched her right cheek.

"It's glass," Victoria stated hesitantly, a brief catch in her voice that hinted at tears. She took a deep, fortifying breath before speaking again. "It looks amazing. Nobody will notice."

Isabelle's face was sad as she drew her hand away, and the one eye shifted to look at Victoria. "I will notice," the queen replied groggily. She reached for Tyrell's hand.

Tyrell offered her support, helping her rise from the bed. She sat up and turned awkwardly, setting her feet on the Meldusian carpet. Instinctively, her toes curled and flexed, massaging the thick rug while she centered herself. She gripped Tyrell's hand and pulled herself to a standing position.

"Your Majesty," he almost whispered, his eyes grew moist as guilt flooded his chest and drowned his heart. "I wasn't fast enough, I couldn't..." His voice trailed off for a moment before he said, "I'm sorry."

The queen looked at Tyrell for a long moment before patting his cheek gently. "Don't be sorry. You saved me. I remember everything."

Tyrell felt the merest bit of relief and his shoulders if dropped only a quarter-inch, but it was the most he had relaxed in days. He leaned over and held out his arm for Isabelle, which she refused.

Like a toddler taking careful steps, Isabelle slowly made her way to the windowsill. She stared outside the closed window and pondered for a moment. "What was it?"

"We've been looking for it. There've been no signs, but we have men still combing the city and the nearby woods." The Captain Guard slipped into business mode, but words left him as he trailed behind his queen. He watched her every move and hovered as though ready to catch her.

"That's fine, but what was it?"

"We don't know," Tyrell replied, unable to hold back his disappointment. "All indications are that it was magic in nature."

The queen nodded and considered this for a moment. Tyrell and Victoria waited, giving her the time she needed. "Is this one of the creatures that have been appearing at our borders, killing our soldiers?"

"I don't believe so, Your Majesty. This thing had, well, it seemed to have intent." When the queen turned away from the window to face Tyrell, he continued. "The princess entered the room to help, and it went straight for her. Your Majesty, I believe this could have been an assassination attempt."

"By the magic wielders? By Angst?" Isabelle asked accusingly.

"Mother, no," Victoria pleaded, instantly defensive. "How could you assume that? Of Angst?"

"Your Majesty, I have to agree with Her Highness," Tyrell

said, surprised by the accusation. "With that sword, it's obvious Angst wouldn't have needed any help killing you or anyone at the castle. You said so yourself, at breakfast last week."

Queen Isabelle walked over to the spot where the bird had pinned her down. Tyrell and Victoria exchanged a look. Should he stop her, or maybe distract her with more conversation? Isabelle stared at the floor and ran her foot over the freshly-polished wood.

"I need to get cleaned up, change, and eat. After that, I'd like a meeting in the war room, two hours from now." The queen's tone was returning to its commanding, formal nature. Even a few of her distinct rolling Rs had returned. "I expect to be brought up to date on everything that's happened since I've been out of commission."

"Of course, Your Majesty." Tyrell clicked his heels together and bowed formally. "I'm not completely sure how to ask this, but—"

"Don't be sensitive with me, Tyrell. Speak your mind as always," Isabelle interjected harshly.

"Thank you, my queen." Tyrell still sought the words. "I believe you need to be under protection at all hours, even when you bathe and change. I realize it will be awkward, but you will be safe."

Isabelle looked at Tyrell like he was the one who could be going crazy. Before she could say no, the princess spoke, "I could stay with you, at those times, to provide warning to the guards."

"But, you too could be in danger." Tyrell didn't seem to approve of this idea at all.

"Thank you, Victoria. I think that's an excellent idea, but there will be times I need to be left alone, and this is one of them." Isabelle stopped their protests with a hand. "I promise to keep the window closed. Tyrell, advise everyone about the meeting. Victoria, please have the kitchen prepare a meal. I would like to dine with both of you in an hour. Now go."

"This is a terrible idea," Victoria warned as she turned on her heel and stomped out.

CHAPTER TWENTY

"Respectfully, I agree with the princess." Tyrell waited for the queen to give in, but she merely stared at him with that 'I gave you a command, now go' look. He sighed deeply. "As you wish, Your Majesty." Tyrell left the room.

* * * *

After the room emptied, after the doors closed, Queen Isabelle took a deep breath and gradually let down her guard. She walked to a nearby mirror to inspect her face and eye. Several fresh scars near the right eye were too puffy to be successfully covered with heavy powder, but some would heal. The false eye did look strikingly like her real eye, except that it didn't move and the pupil remained the same size.

Isabelle had never felt beautiful like her daughter, but the loss of her eye, the attack in her own room, made her feel helpless and in a constant state of danger. She held herself tight and choked back a sob. Tears streamed down her left cheek. It may have been the thing that bothered her most; the false eye hadn't produced any tears. It was another thing taken from her, her eye, her tears, and ultimately her sense of safety. Isabelle allowed herself this sense of loss and mourning for only a few moments before pulling herself together. She was still queen, her heart beat strong and tears could be wiped away. But, despite the sense of duty that set most of this aside, Isabelle could feel the gentlest tickle, not quite an itch, behind her new glass eye.

* * * *

Two hours later, the usual combatants had arrived in her war room, and sat themselves in their usual places as though the seats were assigned. The typically robust drama-filled debate was replaced with surreptitious whispers and awkward silence. Some looked at Queen Isabelle with genuine concern, for which she was silently grateful. But when others around the table caught her eye, opportunity flashed in their vulture-like gaze.

Isabelle peered coldly at those advisors until they were forced to turn away.

The queen wore a fitted, overly formal burgundy dress with a built-in corset that held her tight. Something about it made her feel safe, and maybe even confident, like armor would a knight. She had applied extra makeup, and wore her crown, which was typically saved for special occasions. Several members at the table had seemed surprised, but it was clear as morning after the first frost, Isabelle was here and in charge.

Discussion had required prompting, and the queen gladly worked over each member of her counsel to provide the most recent updates of events taking place in her kingdom. Not much had changed while she was bedridden, but leadership of this group fit as comfortably as her favorite slippers. As always, the round table discussion ended with Tyrell.

"My primary task has been to reinforce our defenses at the castle, and locate Her Majesty's attacker," Tyrell updated the advisors solemnly. The queen respected him for being the first to make mention of what had happened. "We have yet to find a single lead beyond my observations that it was possibly an assassination attempt, and the creature was magic in nature."

Wilfred coughed at the end of Tyrell's brief report. When everyone turned to look, he swallowed hard. "What indications do you have that it was magic?"

"I wasn't able to harm it, and I didn't miss," Tyrell said dryly. "The only person able to damage any of these new beasts is Angst, with his magic sword."

"Well, that doesn't mean the creature attacking Her Majesty was magic. Even if other monsters are magic, there's no indication they all, somehow, come from the same source." Despite his contrary words, Wilfred didn't seem to be challenging Tyrell, but offering another opinion.

This was the point where the queen would typically close her eyes and let her advisors loose, but "typical" no longer applied to her life. Instead, she questioned Wilfred. "What information do you have?"

Wilfred stuttered a bit. "Your, uh, Your Majesty. I have no information, per se, simply trying to offer a logical analysis..."

"Fine. If you have no solid information, tell me Wilfred, what have you done to investigate my attack?" Isabelle peered around the table. "I recommend everyone prepare their answers carefully because I'm going to ask this of you all. I was attacked, I represent Unsel, therefore Unsel was attacked. Wilfred?"

"I'm sorry, Your Majesty." Wilfred spread his hands apart helplessly. "I have nothing."

"You are dismissed," Isabelle stated in a firm, resonating tone.

Wilfred looked at Tyrell with wild eyes then back at the queen.

"You are welcome back at this table when you have something of value for me. Now leave." She waved him off and turned to the next advisor. "Do you have anything, Komlen?"

A heavy-set, middle-aged man with a bushy brown mustache shook his head stiffly, as if he wasn't completely committed to the answer. The queen didn't say a word, she waved him away from the table too.

Isabelle stood, placed her hands firmly on the table and leaned in. She pierced each of them with her uncanny one-eyed stare. "Does *anyone* have *anything*?" she bellowed.

Young advisors, generals who were brave veterans of war, and everyone in between squirmed. None of them had expected this of their damaged queen with the false eye, and all sat in awe and surprise as she continued to assail them.

"Let me state this in a way everyone in the room can understand. We've been attacked at our borders, our trade routes are being blocked, and now we've been attacked at our castle. We are at war!" She pounded on the table with her fist. "I don't care if this war is with the crazy magic wielders, or some nation we would never expect. I want to know who. I want to know why. And I want to know *now*. Or you will all be replaced with competent advisors who can provide me the information I need to keep Unsel safe. Do you understand what I am telling you?"

Everyone nodded as though their mother had yelled at them for breaking a prize vase.

"You have two days to return with something useful or don't come back! Dismissed!" Isabelle glared at every advisor as they quickly gathered themselves and rushed out of the room. Only Tyrell remained. "What?" she spat at him.

"You're right, and it's good to have you back," Tyrell replied with relief.

21

The sun seemed to rise early the next morning for Angst, as he and Marissa had talked late into the night. They were the only two showing signs of being tired. His friends had eaten their fill, bathed in the hot spring, and slept in beds. The rest of Oakhaven's residents enjoyed their first full night's sleep since the attacks began.

In spite of Ivan's protests, Angst decided to leave half their dry goods with Marissa and the town, only sorry he couldn't give more. "These won't last you long," he apologized.

Marissa smiled gratefully as she brushed a lock of blond hair from her face. She still looked quite amazing after their late night, whereas Angst couldn't rub all of the sleep out of his eyes or make his graying brown hair mat down.

"Marissa, I really don't think that's the end of the monsters," Hector said. "Your best strategy would be to pack up what you can and head to the capital until we get this thing fixed."

"Angst suggested that last night. It's a good idea, but I don't think they'll leave. These people are frightened, and the idea of traveling is probably too much."

"Well, consider my other suggestion, if you can convince everyone it will work," Angst said as he stepped through the door into the brisk morning air.

"If that's our only other option, I don't think they'll complain much." Marissa followed them out of the inn and handed Angst a small bundle. "A bit of jerky for the trip. The marinade is a family recipe." She gave Angst a hug. "When this is done, and everything is 'fixed,' you and Heather will have to come visit us."

"You can count on it. Be careful, Marissa," Angst said, smiling at his new friend.

Angst took the reins of his dark gray stallion from Manst and led it through the barricade opening.

Hector stood next to Angst as he mounted, looking back at Marissa. "What is it with you?" he asked, shaking his head.

"What?" Angst replied with all the innocence he could summon.

As they returned to the highway, Rose leaned over from Dallow's horse to ask, "How many clothes did she have on when you were giving that advice?"

"As many as you have on when you and I spend time together," Angst replied, playful yet sincere.

Hector and Tarness laughed as Rose reached over to slap his armor.

"There are a few in the town who can wield magic. I suggested they should be the ones to fight if any monsters return," Angst answered Rose's unasked question.

"Wait, you what?" asked Ivan in disbelief.

"What's your problem now, Ivan?" Hector asked.

"First he gives them half our food then he tells them about your magics. Are you trying to get everyone killed?" Ivan looked like someone slapped him in the mouth, and his lips curled in disgust as he mouthed the word 'magic.'

"I told them how to survive," Angst snapped.

"Don't you realize there are towns of people out here that hate you, all of you? They would rather see you hung than be saved by you." Ivan shook his head in disbelief. "I, for one, don't care to be killed for wielding magics."

"Looks like we're going to have to change some opinions, whether people like it or not," Angst said with finality.

Ivan took off and separated himself, "leading" from so far

ahead he was almost out of view.

Several hours later, Ivan stopped abruptly, practically jumping from his horse. He came out from behind bushes as everyone approached, his face pale and blotchy.

"Are you all right, Ivan?" Hector asked.

Ivan's eyes grew large with desperation. He turned and bent over, emptying his stomach on the side of the road.

"I believe that was deserved," Dallow said to Hector with a broad grin.

Ivan stood straight again, wiping his mouth. "Give me a minute before we continue."

"Ivan, we can head back to Oakhaven or set up camp here. There's no need..." Angst began.

Ivan merely shook his head and sat on a nearby stump. "I'm not sick. I don't understand. My stomach isn't in that much pain." He eyed Angst warily. "This isn't you, is it?"

"I wouldn't know how," Angst replied.

Ivan nodded, took a deep breath, and remounted. Without further explanation, he took off down the empty highway, riding ahead of the rest, once again almost out of view. Angst merely shrugged at everyone and followed, as there was nothing further they could do to help.

* * * *

An hour later, Hector was the first to spot Ivan, lying beside his mount as though he'd fallen off. The group followed Hector as he rushed forward to see what had happened.

"Is he dead?" Rose asked, sounding hopeful. She corrected her tone and said more somberly, "is he dead?"

Hector and Dallow dismounted to check on the knight. Dallow removed Ivan's helm to find his dark hair matted with sweat. Ivan's eyes were open, and he was breathing, but his body was otherwise rigid as a statue.

"Nope," Hector said, sounding not quite disappointed. He looked around the nearby woods, and then along the path. "No sign he was attacked. He's got to be sick."

Angst

Dallow's eyes began to glow as he searched through the catalog of ailments in his head. "The symptoms don't match anything I've read about. He's not feverish, or cold, but he's still sweating. I don't understand why his muscles are locked up."

"This doesn't feel right at all," Tarness said, gripping his reigns tightly.

Angst tilted his head, listening to Chryslaenor's song. There was a subtle sense of urgency to it but nothing more. "Tarness, why don't you and I ride ahead to check things out?"

"Do we have to?" Tarness asked, his tone was joking and almost completely covered a slight quaver.

They took off at a gallop. As they continued, the song grew louder, but there was no other indication of danger. Angst relaxed and was about to turn around when Tarness' horse reared in the wrong direction, smashing into his. Angst's horse neighed in panic as it tripped, collapsing before the edge of a twenty-foot cliff that had eaten the road.

In the end, the reins saved Angst. The sudden stop tossed him from the saddle as the horse toppled. Gripping onto the reins with strength that only comes from panic, he flipped over the cliff edge and crashed into the wall. The horse lay on its side, unable to get up with Angst hanging from the reins, and trying not to look at his pending fall.

Tarness was breathing heavily from the sudden burst of adrenaline. "Angst, I'm sorry, I just pulled the wrong way..." He stopped talking.

"Tarness? Tarness, are you all right?" Angst called while attempting to pull himself up. He hung there for a minute, wondering exactly what to do next. He looked up to see Tarness's big black head, followed by his large arm reaching down, nearly blocking out his view of the sky. Tarness grabbed a handful of armor and effortlessly pulled Angst to safety.

"What just happened? I mean, thanks for pulling me up, but—" Angst began.

Tarness abruptly grabbed his shoulders and spun him around to face the cliff edge once more.

The thirty-foot wide chasm that cut through the road was amazing enough to warrant attention. It was as though a child had roughly dug into the ground with a stick, though, of course, this stick would've been the size of a house. Dirt along the chasm walls was dark and clumpy, as though never touched by rain or erosion. The most startling aspect of this freshly dug chasm was the orange ooze it contained. The gelatinous mass rippled and flowed like lava and smelled of sickeningly sweet honey mixed with maple syrup.

"I don't understand. What is that?" asked Angst, absolutely dumbfounded.

Their attention was drawn to the other side of the chasm, where a fox chased a rabbit, or a rabbit attacked a fox. Angst couldn't tell which was the predator or prey. Both creatures appeared disoriented as they came closer to their side of the gorge. They parried and tumbled in a strange and crazy dance until both ended up falling over the edge and into the orange syrup. Angst actually gripped Tarness's arm as the ooze swallowed the rabbit and fox.

The animals soon resurfaced. A chill of horror washed over him as the fox and rabbit transformed. Both animals howled as their bodies seemed to be pulled and stretched like so much taffy. Within minutes, the fox appeared to give up, and sank back into the orange mass, lost forever. The rabbit also disappeared, but only for a moment before pulling itself out. It had grown to the size of a large mountain lion, with a longer torso and claws large enough to be seen from twenty feet away. It clawed and fought its way up the cliff before realizing it could still jump. The once-rabbit-creature leaped up and landed spryly on the solid ground. The fur had become scales, and bony protrusions stuck out from its elbows and knees. It turned to face them with bright red eyes before darting into the forest at an unfathomable speed.

"I think it's my turn to throw up." Tarness said, always a master of understatement.

Angst let go of Tarness's arm, his fingers sore from gripping the armor. "Please go back and send the others here then stay with Ivan. I think it's wise to keep him away from that...whatever that stuff is."

* * * *

Hector, Dallow, and Rose arrived fifteen minutes later. Angst had been kneeling at the cliff's edge, and stood to face them.

"I think I figured out why we haven't been getting any wheat," Angst said in a mocking tone, thumbing the river of orange goop.

"You're quite the genius," Rose replied as they approached the edge of the chasm.

"Does this mean we can go home?" Dallow asked.

Hector merely gawked for a bit before turning to Dallow. "Any idea what it could be?"

Dallow reflected for a moment, consulting the vast compendium of information in his mind before shaking his head. "No." The color in his eyes returned. "I'm saying no too often. I think I need to find more books."

"I've been watching it for a while, and I've seen some things." Angst stepped away from the cliff's edge. "Animals don't fall in, they charge in. It's almost like they're attracted to it. More than half have died, but those that survived...changed."

"Into what?" asked Dallow, disbelief plain in his voice.

"Something else," he said, turning around to stare at the ravine. "Monsters, creatures, I don't even know what to call them. What I do know is, anything that crawls out of that soup comes out larger and meaner than when they entered."

Rose and Dallow obviously didn't believe him. They both rolled their eyes then glared at him impatiently.

"What? It's true," Angst said defensively. "This must be the stuff making all those monsters. The giant that had Rose, the others we've heard about. Probably the gamlin too." It should have made sense after his explanation, but they appeared unimpressed. "Didn't Tarness tell you?"

"Tarness is always the first one to support your pranks," Rose pointed out.

"I'm not going to argue with either of you about this. I think that," Angst pointed down into the chasm, "is what's making Ivan sick. We need to move him away from this flowing muck before it does some permanent damage, or sucks him in."

"You're serious, aren't you?" Hector analyzed his face then looked back at the chasm. "It would explain a lot. Why aren't we sick though?"

Angst closed his eyes, took a deep breath, and sighed. "The animals I've watched take the orange bath are just animals, there is nothing magical about them."

Dallow nodded slowly. "You think it's because we are already magic." Dallow considered this. "That would be plausible," he said finally.

"You believe him now?" Rose asked, incredulous.

"I think I do." Dallow's voice became hopeful for a brief moment. "So we really are going home now?"

"Home?" Angst stared at Dallow for a long moment. "This is just the beginning. We need to find out where this stuff is coming from before more people get hurt."

Hector put his hand on Angst's shoulder. "Dallow is right, Angst. We need to report back to the queen, and let her decide the next step."

Angst ripped his shoulder away. "No! No. It's not enough. What are you going to report? 'Angst found a river of orange syrup that changes animals into monsters.'" He stomped to his horse and mounted. "In case you three weren't in Oakhaven, people are dying out here. I'm going to go strap Ivan to his horse, backtrack a couple of miles to get away from that stuff, then head north to find the source. I hope I don't have to go alone." Angst took off at a gallop, leaving Hector, Dallow, and Rose looking at each other awkwardly.

* * * *

They'd been riding through the woods for several hours when dusk approached on the third night of their journey. The uncomfortable silence was only broken by Ivan's delirious mumbling. Angst had taken lead in the beginning, and did his best to find smooth ground or the occasional deer trail, but guiding a group of travelers through unmarked woods was new to him.

Soon, Hector pulled ahead, muttering loud enough for Angst to hear, "We'll never get there at this pace."

Hector found a clearing before nightfall, and they scrambled to set up their tents and make a small fire. They ate a quiet meal of bread and cheese, a tense frustration hanging over the campsite like an oppressive fog.

"I'm not tired," Angst declared. "I'll take the first watch."

When nobody replied, he stood slowly with a grunt and wandered to the edge of the circle cast by the firelight. Within minutes, he could hear Hector and Dallow arguing. What they said wasn't clear, other than his name, multiple times. Guilt swelled up in his chest, and he longed to go back home, but deep down, he felt this was the right thing to do. He watched the woods about him while absentmindedly running fingers along his arms where there was a gap in his armor.

"Hey," Rose said as she walked up behind him.

"Hey," he replied, desperately grateful she'd joined him.

"Everyone hates you right now," she said bluntly.

"I'm used to that." Angst shrugged before realizing it was too dark to see the gesture.

"Dallow says he's going home. I think he might head off tomorrow."

"Dallow didn't even want to come." Angst sighed. "Don't you see? Doesn't anyone see? We have to fix this...this thing that's happening. I don't think anyone else can. We have a duty—"

"A duty to whom? A bunch of people who hate us? I think Dallow is right, that we should head back before someone ends up dead." In spite of the desperation in Rose's voice, Angst could tell she was torn.

"Some may hate us, but it's still the right thing to do." Angst looked out at the woods again and filled his lungs with the cool night air.

"Are you sure this isn't for Marissa?"

"What?" Angst was taken aback by her question.

"Not Marissa specifically. Angst, you've always wanted to be a hero...a knight. You've always wanted the Marissas of the world to swoon at you and sigh longingly. Are you so sure that isn't what you're here for?" Rose hugged herself, shivering a bit.

Angst sighed again. "Maybe, Rose. Maybe you know me that well. And maybe I want to be a hero in everyone's eyes. But I also know what's right, and if we end up heroes, that just means we won." Angst tried to make eye contact in spite of the dark. "Even if this is selfish, even if I'm doing it for my own selfish reasons, it's still the right thing to do."

"But at what cost? Are you willing to risk everyone's life to become that hero?" She walked off with the last word, leaving Angst with that familiar nausea clawing at his belly.

22

As they made their way through the wooded terrain, color slowly bled from their surroundings like fresh paint washing away in the rain. The change was subtle at first, but gradually became disturbing when they finally entered Grayhollow Forest. Shades of gray seemed to coat everything, living or dead. Ten-foot wide tree trunks were wrapped in horizontal strips of papery pewter-colored bark. The forest floor was sparsely covered with decaying gray leaves and twigs; the dominant trees left little room for vegetation.

"What happened to my hair?" Rose asked, trying to pull bangs down in front of her eye. "It's gray."

"I ask myself that all the time," Angst said with a grin.

"The leaves from these graymowl trees filter color from the sunlight. Some have theorized that the trees actually live off color," replied Dallow, his thin lips smiling thoughtfully.

Rose shivered and leaned in closer to Dallow. "I don't like it. Something about the lack of color just doesn't feel healthy."

"Most people don't spend much time here," Ivan said morosely. "I'd advise keeping quiet and riding fast so we don't have to either."

"It's not too bad," Tarness stated, ignoring Ivan. "The trees are large enough to block most of the wind, and the path ahead is free of brush and hills."

"The path to where?" Dallow asked, but nobody answered.

The gray seemed to reflect Angst's mood. He felt alone amongst friends. After the argument, everyone had begrudgingly supported Angst and his decision to find the source of the orange ooze. Dallow had argued that there was no road to follow, Hector was concerned about rations, and Tarness wanted to know what they would do with unconscious Ivan. They sounded like weak excuses to Angst. They would follow the orange-filled chasm north and didn't need a road. Hector and Tarness could hunt for food if necessary, and Ivan could be tied to his horse until he woke. In the end, Angst won, but the cost was tense silence and angry glares.

Ivan remained unconscious the entire first day's ride. Angst had taken the lead once again, and guided Ivan's horse with the knight strapped to it. That day, riding far enough ahead that he could barely be seen by his friends, Angst had found another obelisk in the woods that pointed to Gressmore Towers. He didn't share the obelisk sighting with anyone, and circled back to change direction so they wouldn't see it. There was something about the obelisks that felt like a personal message left for him. Chryslaenor's song was relaxed and comforting as the blade glowed in the obelisk's presence. Angst wanted to go to Gressmore Towers even though he knew that would only incite more arguing.

Ivan regained consciousness the second day, and was able to ride without being bound to his saddle. Angst attempted to use Ivan's aches and pains as a gauge to stay away from the orange muck. But Ivan was a poor compass and worse company. Removed from the others, he took advantage of his captive audience and complained about everything. Every word that came out of his sniveling mouth made Angst's teeth grind. He considered heading east once more, just to make Ivan faint.

"I think we're getting too close," Ivan warned, gripping his stomach.

"You said that thirty minutes ago, before deciding you needed something to eat," Angst replied without pity.

"No, I think...this time..." Ivan unceremoniously leaned over and threw up.

Angst sighed, reaching over to grab Ivan's armored wrist to keep him from falling out of his saddle. Both horses had stopped and Angst looked back at the others as everyone caught up. They didn't want to be here, and it showed in their eyes. "We'll pull west a bit and see if that helps."

Ivan merely nodded and wiped his mouth before agreeing to move forward.

* * * *

Night came early in Grayhollow, the setting sun quickly hidden behind the towering tree line. The forest was dark and quiet, and their small campfire didn't seem to reach far beyond the circle of tents.

"I suppose I'll take first watch again," Angst announced, looking forward to time without uncomfortable stares and annoying Ivans.

"I'll join you," Hector said abruptly, stretching his legs as he stood.

"Me too," Dallow stated. He used his staff to push himself off the ground.

Angst sighed before faking a smile; their sudden interest in accompanying him sounded too planned for his comfort. "That would be great, thank you." He walked beyond the boundary of the firelight. Dallow grabbed an arm-length branch from the fire to use as a makeshift torch.

After a minute of walking through the woods, Angst stopped to face Hector and Dallow. "Are you both tagging along to argue more or simply to criticize what I'm trying to do?" He wanted to get their concerns out of the way or scare them back to camp as quickly as possible.

Hector shook his head. "You wallow too much, old friend. Everyone just feels a bit lost. We don't know where we're going."

"I still think we're doing the right thing, finding the source of the problem and not just discovering that muck," Angst replied defensively.

"I'm not arguing that, Angst. That's why we're all still with you. It's just that a guide would be nice, or maybe a path..." Hector paused and gripped Angst's arm. "Shhh," he whispered before Angst could question him.

Dallow placed the burning end of the stick on the ground, and stepped on it quietly to put out the fire. Darkness engulfed them and seemed to amplify every sound. After several incredibly long seconds, a hazy blue light rose from the ground. It seemed to be everywhere, stretching deep into the forest well beyond their view. The light was a stark contrast to their colorless day as it hovered low, waiting like a silent audience anticipating a singer's first note.

"A Mendahir Rise," Dallow whispered reverently. "This is truly a rare sight. I don't think anyone has reported seeing a Mendahir Rise in several hundred years."

A procession of shadowy figures floated up an invisible path. Hundreds of Mendahir appeared and disappeared like twinkling stars. Their shapes were illuminated by thin beams of blue light that shot up from the ground as the Mendahir passed. They moved through trees and branches like a river that never strayed off path.

Chryslaenor glowed softly, and Angst was surprised to hear the song in his head become a low, respectful dirge. "What are they?" asked Angst.

"Memories," replied Dallow quietly. "They were a magical race that lived in Ehrde thousands of years ago. It's been written that they haunt these woods, but they do as much haunting as a rainbow hovering over a waterfall. They aren't real. Well, they're a phenomenon, like a ring around the moon or an aurora in the northern night sky."

Angst nodded, though he didn't quite understand. "Then why are we being quiet?"

"The Mendahir, as a race, were killed millennia ago. They are no longer, and all that remains are these shadowy echoes," Dallow whispered solemnly. "It's tradition to be quiet out of respect."

"A bit of a coincidence they show up tonight, isn't it?" Angst asked as he stepped forward for a closer look.

"Angst, no," Hector whispered harshly.

Angst waved him off and walked to the edge of the Mendahir Rise. Standing closer, he could almost make out faces that seemed long and sad, as though wanting for something that couldn't be found. It took several minutes for Angst to realize that the faces were suddenly looking at him. The procession had stopped, and a tall floating Mendahir made its way over to Angst.

Angst's heart was racing. He considered reaching for his sword, but the steady dirge Chryslaenor sang gave no indication of danger. One of the apparitions stopped within arm's reach of Angst. It was mostly a tall, non-descript haze of dark fog, but for brief moments, the fog solidified enough to form a face. It had black eyes with glowing blue pupils, which looked up at Chryslaenor. The Mendahir's mouth grew into a smile too wide for its thin face.

"Hello," Angst stuttered, at a complete loss. "I'm Angst."

Its gaze caressed the sword for a long while before making eye contact with Angst. Trying to understand the Mendahir's expressions was as useful as imagining which animal a cloud looked like. He thought he saw a smile and a nod, but more oddly felt a sense of relief. The smile, or whatever it was, transformed to a frown. It lifted an arm and pointed over Angst's shoulder. In his mind, he heard an unearthly whisper, "Your guide is here."

Rose's scream echoed through the tall trees. Once again he was at a loss for words. Angst nodded respectfully at the ghostly Mendahir before turning to run. Hector had already left, but Dallow waited for Angst so he could follow the glow of Chryslaenor through the dark woods.

"I've never seen a rainbow do that, Dallow!" Angst yelled, tripping over a root and catching himself before falling.

"That wasn't supposed to happen. I don't understand," Dallow replied, shock and denial in his voice.

They reached the campfire to find Hector standing by Rose. Her hand shaking, she pointed at something over the fire. Ivan and Tarness were looking up with their weapons at the ready. Ivan was visibly unsettled, shaking in his armor, but stood his ground.

Floating five feet above their campsite was an enormous, glassy orb. It appeared mostly empty except for a pool of red sloshing liquid resting at its bottom. The bubble looked like any blown by a child during a spring day—if the bubbles were made from red soap, large as a cottage, and filled with a pool of blood.

"What now?" yelled Tarness. "Is that blood?"

"I don't know what that is. We aren't even supposed to be seeing colors," Dallow replied. He tried to step in front of Rose, protectively attempting to block her view, but she shoved him out of the way.

"What do you suggest?" Angst asked Hector.

"Are you kidding? We need to leave. Now," Hector said.

"Dallow and Rose, grab some torches," Angst yelled. "Ivan, Tarness, get the horses."

"Angst, the horses are gone," Tarness replied.

Smaller bubbles floated by their heads. One of the bubbles had apparently sucked in a family of rabbits, and was slowly making its way to the larger one. It melded with the giant bubble, that shortly after, reverberated with loud sounds of eating, the crunching of bone and the appreciative smacking of lips. The monstrous orb, or whatever was inside, had an appetite.

Angst looked away from the sphere to his friends and found everyone staring at it as though mesmerized by the hideous sight. "*Hey!*" he yelled, loud enough to get everyone's attention. They blinked quickly, tearing their gaze away to face him, slightly dazed. "*Run!*" he yelled. They ran.

More trapped animals floated by as if part of a gruesome parade. A frightened deer, followed by a fox, then a small angry creature nobody recognized trailed behind, each encased in an orb, which floated to the large one over the campsite. Everyone ran as fast as they could in the dark forest, for about fifteen seconds. Something seemed to keep them from rushing away. The ground became like wet sand, and then mud, and then small bubbles appeared at their feet.

Hector and Tarness immediately stabbed at the bubbles with their weapons. It was like trying to puncture a marble with a fork—the orbs deflected every weapon strike.

Angst didn't want to accidently hit anyone with Chryslaenor in the dark, so he focused his effort on the ground. He hoped that creating a small quake would free the earth of its orb-creating curse. Angst immediately realized his mistake. The bubbles came with more frequency, and the group was soon surrounded by them. The small bubbles merged and solidified, becoming a single ball that lifted them all off the ground together.

"Uh, oops," Angst said apologetically.

They all glared at him then stabbed and poked at their bubble prison.

Before they were a full foot off the ground, Angst carefully turned to face away from the bubble wall so his sword wouldn't stab anyone by accident. The tip of Chryslaenor tapped the orb, which instantly shattered. They fell, and quickly picked themselves up to start running again.

Their second attempt at running away was thwarted when another bubble quickly imprisoned them, but this time Angst was prepared. With sword in hand, he purposely popped the orb. They'd been carried faster this time, and were captured by another large bubble before reaching the ground. Three and four and five bubbles later, they continued floating toward the giant bubble that made loud chewing and smacking sounds. Angst stopped swinging.

"Wait, why aren't you popping bubbles?" asked Rose in a panicked voice.

"This isn't working." Angst held Chryslaenor in front of him, ready to defend against the oncoming threat.

"What are you talking about? We'll be there any second," Ivan yelled in alarm.

"You better get ready then," growled Hector, grinning wickedly. His wolf-like eyes flashed in anticipation of the coming battle.

They braced themselves as their bubble met its target. The two orbs didn't merge instantly, but instead slowly rubbed together as though positioning for a perfect union. The delay only made it worse as they waited for the bubbles to merge.

The interior was more disgusting than he could have imagined. The horrific gamey smell of freshly dead carcass was overwhelming. The bubble was lined with animal bits, feathers, and bones, all marinating in a shallow pool of fresh blood. At the center was a dog. If you could call it a dog. It was ten feet tall and black as night. The monster had six legs, one of which it was licking clean. Thin bony protrusions covered it like a dangerous black fur. It looked up at them with four glowing red eyes, and its three tails wagged, thudding loudly against the side of their prison.

Angst shook his head in disbelief. "Bad dog," he said coldly as he lowered Chryslaenor and popped the bubble.

They landed with a hard crash. Bones and blood showered the campsite. Exposed to the night air, the dog-thing yelped and howled in pain. The beast had fallen onto a tent and toppled to its side. Smoke rose from its body as it flailed and attempted to get up. Bubbles quickly began forming around the creature.

"Don't let it get inside another bubble," warned Dallow.

Angst picked himself off the ground and leaped forward, plunging Chryslaenor deep into the monster's side. Thick orange smoke billowed from the wound with a loud hiss.

The ground continued to produce bubbles.

"Everyone back!" Angst commanded. With a deep breath, he let Chryslaenor take over. In a whirlwind, he darted around like a hummingbird, destroying every orb as it appeared, until they finally stopped.

After the bubbles were gone, he watched in horror as their enormous, very hungry assailant completed its transformation, deflating into an actual dog. The extra legs withdrew back into its body and black fur replaced the boney protrusions. It was still alive, and they all stood back. Warily, a small black lab pup looked at them all with tired, sick eyes. It tried to get up, wagged its tail feebly, then fell over with a pitiful yelp. The pup whimpered in pain as the large gash along its side sputtered blood and smoke.

"Kill it," Ivan pleaded to Angst.

"No," argued Rose. She stepped forward, but Dallow held her back.

"That's not a good idea," Dallow warned, holding her arm.

Angst brought his sword to the fire and set the tip inside. When he felt that Chryslaenor was hot enough, he returned to the pup. "Sorry, boy." He held the tip to its side, cauterizing the wound. The dog howled pathetically before passing out, the soul-wrenching sound echoing through the dark woods.

"What was that all about?" yelled Tarness. He stomped around, brushing at his arms and legs as though trying to rid himself of what he'd just experienced.

"I was told that this is our new guide," Angst replied.

23

Public discord was good for business. Though Graloon would've preferred happier times, people didn't tend to cure depression, or oppression, with milk. How many revolutions had been started by angry men sipping lemonade? A few alcoholic beverages, sometimes a few more, some angry talk, and unfortunate circumstances could be the ingredients for brave souls, or foolish ones. For the last several evenings, his bar had become the headquarters for just such malcontents.

It wasn't unusual to find all the tables full at the Wizard's Revenge since the room would grow or shrink as needed to accommodate its guests. It was, however, unusual to have so many tables filling the room, and most with customers Graloon didn't recognize. With mugs of ale in hand, he made his way through the maze of patrons, both familiar and unfamiliar, listening to snatches of random conversations.

"...it was like they didn't even believe me. They kept asking me the same questions again and again!"

"I finally had to show them how I wield magic, like cleaning dishes could kill the queen. Then they started asking me what my friends could do, and they took notes the entire time."

"I heard they arrested Jeynson, that guy who could juggle balls of fire and water, when he said the queen deserved whatever happened to her. Guy never knew how to keep his mouth shut."

Graloon delivered the drinks to a few impatient customers before making his way back to Heather at the bar. She was dressed a bit more conservatively than his other barmaids this evening, but customers liked that her smile and laugh were genuine. Graloon chuckled. The other barmaids had been more than a little upset the night Heather started, when she made more tips by being herself instead of falling out of her clothes.

"Thanks again for the help, Heather. The crowd is getting bigger every night, and we'd be at a loss without you," said Graloon in his gravelly voice. "Are you all right? You seem a bit pale."

Heather straightened out her apron and smiled, pulling her curly brown hair back to keep it from her face. "Just tired. I haven't been sleeping well with Angst gone. I appreciate the distraction of working, though. It's so much better than being at home by myself."

"You know, I've been thinking about that. We have extra rooms here. You would be welcome to stay until Angst returns," Graloon offered. "With all that's going on, I'd feel a bit better knowing you're safe."

Heather cocked her head. "That's very kind. I'll consider it."

Graloon looked away from her to admire the full tables while rubbing his ample gut. Something about a group of men at the bar caught his attention, so he casually inched closer and listened.

"In my day, we would've taken the castle by force," slurred a drunken old man. He'd been perched on a nearby bar seat since lunch and was now deep in his cups.

"In your day, you would've been hung for saying that. Then hung again for wielding magic," retorted a younger man sitting next to him. "The laws have helped us more than hurt us. It's not like everyone is getting locked up or hunted down."

"You mean they haven't locked us up... yet," said a very tall, muscular man with a rich, booming voice. Most patrons near him went quiet, taking immediate notice of his impressive presence. He walked along the front of the bar, preening for attention. The man was thirtyish-years-old, with greasy blond hair pulled tight into a long ponytail, which rested on one shoulder. Unfortunate pockmarks dotted his long face and tall forehead. "Mind my words. They'll keep asking, and pushing, and taking away rights until there's nothing left."

A few at nearby tables nodded in agreement. Another young man thrust his tankard of ale upward, its contents sloshing dangerously, and yelled, "Yeah!"

Graloon didn't recognize the speaker as a regular, but did recognize him as the type of wannabe that lurked for opportunities. Graloon looked at Heather and rolled his eyes, jerking his head in the direction of the 'entertainment.' "Here's another one who thinks he can become a 'leader,'" he whispered grouchily. "One more know-it-all who knows nothing. Just taking advantage of all the frustration, if you ask me."

Heather chuckled, wiping her hands on her apron. "Isn't he the second 'ponytail' this week?" she whispered.

"Third, by my count," Graloon replied gruffly.

The pockmarked man wallowed in an overly dramatic pause before speaking louder so even more could hear. "Can any of you honestly say you want things to continue in this direction? The queen chisels away at our rights, while we do nothing. She gets attacked, and who does she investigate? We still do nothing. Soon they will be arresting us, for doing nothing. Look how many of us are here. We must number a hundred. How many does it take to start a revolution?"

It appeared to Graloon that several of the speaker's well-placed friends were spread around his bar, each about the same age and nobody he recognized. They did their best to muster support from all ends of the room.

The unfortunate-looking man was now loud enough for everyone to hear. "It must start now! It will start now! We can pull together, march to the queen, and demand change!"

"Can you all pay your tab first?" Graloon yelled. Everyone within earshot laughed.

The man's head whipped around, his ponytail slapping

against his cheek. He stared at Graloon with fire in his eyes. "Don't you understand?" He pointed at Graloon and then at his audience. "These people have had enough! This isn't the time for jokes. This is the time to fight!"

Graloon pulled an old towel from his shoulder and laid it on the bar. He stepped forward to face the young man. "Fight who, son? Queen Isabelle? It sounds to me like she's trying to protect herself. Now you want us to pose an even bigger threat to the queen? Why don't you and your cronies find what attacked her and bring about some real justice?"

"Bah," the man said, waving Graloon off, but when he turned back to look at the crowd, he found everyone had lost interest. His shoulders slumped as he looked to his friends. They were already getting up to leave, and he marched out of the bar after them.

"Well done," complimented Heather.

"I just hope it lasts. Angry customers are good for business, but dead ones aren't." Graloon returned to the bar and picked up his towel before tending another table. The front door opened again, and three clads of armor walk in. Graloon worked his way through the tables to greet them. "Tyrell?"

The Captain Guard was in a full set of armor, and in spite of his menacing appearance, he held out his hand. "Hello, Graloon. It's been a long time."

Graloon nodded and shook the man's hand. "I assume you aren't in here for a drink, Captain Guard?"

"I wish." Tyrell smiled politely. "I need to speak with one of your employees. Is Heather here?"

Graloon hesitated, but before he could deny Tyrell's request, Heather was standing beside him. "Tyrell?" she questioned politely.

"Hello, Heather." Tyrell bowed smartly with his head. "I'm here to extend an invitation to you."

Heather's eyebrows raised high. "I don't think I've ever had the pleasure of such a formal invitation from such an important person."

Tyrell chuckled politely. "Princess Victoria would appreciate your presence."

Graloon put his hand on her shoulder and whispered in her ear, "I don't think that's such a good idea."

Courtesy immediately left Tyrell's face. "We shall accompany you to the castle."

Heather patted Graloon's hand. "It's okay, Graloon. I appreciate your concern, but I trust the princess, and Tyrell knows there aren't enough soldiers in their army to protect them from Angst if something were to happen to me."

The accompanying soldiers paled a bit at this reminder. "The request is urgent, Heather," said Tyrell, "but I promise that it's friendly in nature."

"Please lead the way, Tyrell," Heather replied with a broad smile.

Graloon watched the four of them leave and sighed deeply. "Why do I have the feeling I need to replace another barmaid?"

* * * *

A short time later, Heather entered the maiden's courtyard and instantly felt out of place. Angst had described it on several occasions, but it was a surreal experience having only seen it through his eyes. Tyrell didn't accompany her; instead, he merely escorted her to the entrance and instructed her to wait inside. Heather wandered around for several minutes, feeling like she didn't belong, and even wondered if she was in the right place. At the moment she decided to leave, the royal princess arrived, and Heather fell into an immediate curtsy.

Victoria casually pulled her up. "Thank you, Heather, but as I've said before, that isn't necessary when it's just us."

Heather had a hard time with this. She knew the princess and Angst were friends, but she'd been far removed from this part of his life. Angst may know her, but she didn't, and felt the great need to be cautious. The princess was young, quite young, but not at all foolish. Heather looked the princess over, and felt her own years weighing heavily. Straightening her dress as she rose, Heather smiled her best smile, the one she usually saved for Angst when he got home late and smelled like the Wizard's Revenge.

The princess scrutinized her face, which surprised Heather. It wasn't the competitive female-to-female judgment of an opponent, but a more gentle and thorough observation.

"Thank you for coming, Heather. I regret I couldn't invite you myself rather than sending Tyrell, but I'm not allowed the luxury of leaving the castle."

"What can I do for Your Majesty?" Heather asked.

"Please call me Victoria when we're alone," the princess replied, sitting on a bench near the fountain.

Heather noticed that she hadn't asked to be called Tori, and the ends of her mouth began tiring from the smile. Victoria waited, so Heather sat beside her.

"I wanted to meet with you for several reasons," Victoria began. "You're the wife of one of my best friends, and I'm grateful that you've been supportive of that friendship. You know, Angst talks about you all the time."

"I'm sure he does," Heather couldn't help the sardonic tone in her voice.

Victoria laughed pleasantly. "It's true. He doesn't complain as often as you think. He loves you very much."

Heather nodded with fake appreciation while choking down the comment 'as much as you think.'

"I wanted to see you because I miss my friend, your husband, and feel a bit responsible for the danger he's in," Victoria said, looking down and wringing her hands.

"Responsible?" Heather asked.

Victoria shook her head, her long dark hair flipping back a bit too gloriously for Heather's mood. "It's complicated. Just, well, please know I've done my absolute best to protect him and help him. I don't want to frighten you, but he's in great danger."

"Have you heard something? Has he sent word about their mission?" Heather asked quickly, unable to contain her hope and worry.

"No, Heather, I haven't. I'm sorry."

"You'll pardon me, Victoria, if I say this conversation isn't helping much." Heather said, holding onto her knees to keep her hands from balling up into fists.

The princess responded with a tiny sigh, looking as though she wanted to say more but for some reason couldn't. Heather knew the feeling; she was biting her tongue so much it should have started bleeding. Heather felt like she was meeting the 'other woman,' who wasn't actually the other woman. She didn't believe for a second that Angst and Victoria were romantically involved—that wasn't Angst's way. He may push the envelope of her comfort zone, every day, but he wouldn't outright cheat on her. Still, Victoria was his friend, and the princess. Heather didn't know what was acceptable to discuss or how she was supposed to act. That uncertainty made her uncomfortable, so she faced it head-on.

"I appreciate your concern for Angst, Victoria. I have a lot of faith in my husband. I truly believe he can do almost anything, when he believes in himself." Saying this out loud was actually a reminder, she *did* believe in her husband, and it made her feel a little better.

Victoria nodded and smiled. "Thanks for saying that. I needed to hear it."

"So, is that why I'm here? I have to admit to feeling a bit odd consoling you because my husband's in danger."

Victoria giggled. "I was hoping we could support each other," she said then quickly sobered and went on. "But there is something else. I need you to move into the castle."

Heather gasped as if punched in the gut. "This is the second offer I've had to move out of my house today. Is something going on? Something more than a bit of aggressive questioning?"

"I believe you could be in danger," the princess replied, offering only another empty answer.

"From who, Victoria?"

"I'm not sure." Victoria's voice became very quiet and she

turned away from Heather. "Maybe from my mother."

"Your mother?" said Heather, her voice rising. "What is she going to do? Is she going to start having people killed? Do I need to warn everyone?" Heather stood suddenly.

"No. No, nothing like that." Victoria was careful with every word she spoke. "But I fear your life could be in danger if you don't stay."

Heather pondered this, and narrowed her eyes. "You aren't telling me everything. Actually, I don't feel like you're telling me anything."

"I can't tell you everything, Heather," said Victoria in an almost pleading tone that sounded desperate for Heather to believe.

"I should go. This doesn't feel right." Heather looked back toward the entrance. "Thank you for the invitation, but—"

The princess took a deep breath and stood. "You can't go. I'd prefer you to be my guest, but if necessary, I will order you to stay at the castle."

Heather turned to face her. "I don't understand, Victoria. You claim to be Angst's friend, but you threaten me with arrest?" She felt dizzy and her shoulders knotted up with tension.

"It doesn't need to be an arrest, and I'm doing this for Angst. It's the only way I can ensure you're safe. I can't tell you any more than that."

"And why is my safety so important to you, Your Majesty?" queried Heather defensively.

Victoria smiled, an affectionate expression washing over her face. "It's not just your safety, Heather. I want to keep your baby safe too."

Heather's eyes went wide, her swiftly conflicting emotions making her even more lightheaded. "I...I. What? I don't have a baby!"

Victoria grabbed her hand and squeezed comfortingly. "You didn't know?" she said in an excited, high-pitched voice. "You're pregnant."

24

Angst woke with a start to find Hector's concerned face leaning over him. Hector had been lightly patting his cheek while Rose and Dallow called his name to wake him up. He blinked rapidly as Chryslaenor's dreams slowly faded into the colorless forest of Grayhollow.

"What happened?" Angst asked, sitting up to lean on his elbows. He looked over to see the dog curled beside him. Its tail wagged sleepily at his attention.

"We kind of lost you again, after the whole thing with the dog," Dallow answered, his brow furrowed with concern.

"How long?" Angst asked. He looked around for water, his thin lips dry and smacking loudly.

"About twelve hours," Hector replied.

"Ugh." Rose stomped a tiny threatening foot. "I hate it when you do this!" she yelled, storming off.

"You're good at making her angry, aren't you?" Dallow asked with a mischievous grin.

"It's a gift," said Angst, shrugging one shoulder negligently. He stood, walked over to Chryslaenor, and returned the sword to his back. "Hector had suggested I let go so Chryslaenor could 'do its thing.' I did. I think it's getting better, and I don't feel nearly as tired as I have in the past."

"You still died," Hector said, rubbing the scar along his jaw line with his thumb. "Though it didn't take you as long to come

183

back. I wonder if there isn't some happy medium you could find."

Angst shrugged again and looked around the campsite. "Hey, where are Tarness and Ivan?"

"Hunting. Hopefully not each other," Dallow replied. "We're short on food since last night's attack."

Ivan and Tarness returned thirty minutes later, looking more roughed up than the small rabbits they'd killed. Ivan sported a fresh black eye, while Tarness had a fat lip, and an ugly cut on his hand. The wounds weren't life threatening, but the silent tension between the men was caustic.

Hector eyed them both up and down. "It looks like the rabbits should be carrying you."

"Ivan's lucky he made it back alive," was all Tarness would say. He threw the rabbits down near the fire in frustration.

"Don't speak to me like that, with your lazy, fat, black, magical—" Before Ivan could finish, the visor of his helm slammed shut.

"That's enough, both of you," Angst stated firmly. Ivan struggled to lift the visor, but Angst's power continued holding it shut. "We have enough to deal with, and don't need to be fighting each other."

"Angst, if he insulted you, or Rose, or any of us like he's been insulting me for the last two hours, you would've killed him," Tarness growled.

Angst turned to Ivan and glared at him in frustration. "Let's talk."

Ivan's entire suit of armor straightened and locked, forcing him to remain rigid as a statue. Angst willed the armor to lean back slightly, spin around, and follow him into the woods, like a doll being dragged by a child.

Locked in the armor, unable to bend or move in any way, Ivan bellowed, creating new curse words that made even Rose's eyebrows raise. When Angst felt they were far enough from the others, he forced Ivan's armor into a sitting position. Ivan's legs were spread awkwardly as he was leaned back against a tree.

"I don't know where to start, but you're getting worse." Angst paced in front of the knight, who continued to struggle in his metallic prison. "I realize that the orange river of muck seems to be causing you pain, but from what I've seen, it turns animals into monsters. I don't think it's the reason you're changing into more of an ass."

"I won't be spoken to this way!" Ivan yelled from inside his helm.

With a gentle flick of Angst's wrist, the visor flipped open. He leaned over to peer inside at Ivan. "Are you going crazy in there? Is this why the queen wanted to get rid of you?"

Ivan's face was red and his bloodshot eyes large and wild. He looked ready to explode as he spewed more curses at Angst.

"This is your last chance," Angst warned. "I'm not going to put up with your insults, your attitude, or your bigotry any longer."

"What are you going to do, kill me?" Ivan asked, spitting anger with every word.

"No, I'll leave you here to fend for yourself. Hopefully nothing hungry comes to visit while you ponder your life choices." Angst turned and began walking back to the others.

"Angst, no!" Ivan yelled. "Angst! Get back here!"

"Think about it," Angst yelled over his shoulder as he left Ivan alone.

Angst found his friends sitting around the campfire. Rose had returned and was cooking the rabbits. She gave him a bitter look but said nothing.

"Is he dead?" asked Tarness hopefully.

"We had words," said Angst simply. "He's...thinking about the things he said. I'll go back for him in an hour or so. Save him some food."

* * * *

It took three more days to make their way through Grayhollow on foot. They'd been able to gather their tents, some packs, and a bit of food, but had no luck finding the horses and could

185

only assume the worst. Everything else was gone, leaving them with an awkward mishmash of heavy gear to carry themselves.

The Mendahir Rise seemed to be a one-time event that Dallow couldn't stop theorizing about. His eyes flashed from green to white and back to green as he referred to stored books about the Mendahir. Angst appreciated Dallow's fascination. He appreciated even more the fact that Rose was so tired of hearing about it, she decided to walk with Angst for a while.

"I would've killed the horses a long time ago if that's all it took for you to talk with me a bit," Angst teased Rose as they made their way through the forest. "You've been...busy."

"You don't understand," she answered, avoiding the bait.

"I know the difference between flirting and something more than flirting," Angst jerked his head in Dallow's direction. "I understand he's still married."

"I understand that you are too, yet here we are, walking and talking," she snapped.

He could tell she had little patience for this conversation, so he let it drop. Angst looked back to find the dog sniffing a nearby tree. "Here, Scar. Come, boy."

"That's an awful name, by the way," she said in a surly voice.

"It's appropriate. What would you have named it?" Angst asked.

"What about Mighty?" she suggested hopefully.

"And that's why I named him," he replied, grinning obnoxiously.

* * * *

They head north to the Ruautu River, doing everything they could to avoid the orange muck while remaining close enough to continue tracking its source. The chasm had begun to split and fork chaotically, sometimes creating a single thin line across their path, and other times overtaking an entire open field with an elaborate spider web of glowing orange. They were often forced to backtrack and zigzag around the obstacles, frequently getting turned around. Any time they got too close, Scar would

186

whimper. Closer yet and Ivan became sick.

Ivan had little to say after his 'conversation' with Angst, only angry mutters that everyone simply ignored. Most of them felt Ivan was still upset at Angst and Tarness, but Angst knew otherwise, having seen the wild-eyed look of crazy steal over Ivan's features. He pondered the knight's continuing descent. Angst originally felt there was nothing more than a personality conflict between them, tainted by a large amount of bigotry. But the man was becoming increasingly irrational as they remained close to the orange muck. If that was the cause of Ivan's behavior, he should be kept away before it drove him mad or Angst killed him.

Angst also worried about his friends. They were covered from head to toe in exhaustion, not having seen a real bed or eaten a full meal for almost a week. Their food supply was low, the terrain was challenging, and everyone seemed testy and irritable. They were also alone, not having passed a road or a town since Oakhaven. Other than the occasional odd creature nobody recognized and a few rabbits, there was barely any sign of life. It was eerie and unsettling.

"We need to find a place to camp," said Angst, stopping to look around the nearby woods. Scar immediately yelped, and Ivan clutched his stomach and moaned. He was already turning pale.

"I feel like we're going in circles trying to avoid this stuff." Tarness huffed in frustration, flopping to the ground. Everyone followed his lead, taking the opportunity to rest their feet. "Are we even heading to the source anymore?"

Ivan remained standing, still holding his stomach. "Could we keep moving a bit? I think this is a bad place to rest."

Angst nodded in agreement and helped Tarness to his feet. "Let's go just a little further, until it gets better for Ivan and Scar."

Ivan nodded curtly and with resentful gratitude.

"We should continue east and then maybe north again until we can make our way around this thing." Angst tried his best to sound hopeful. "Maybe we'll come across a town and can pick up some horses."

"If I remember the maps correctly, we should be approaching the northern trade route," Dallow said thoughtfully. "There's a good-sized town on that highway."

"Ravenhill...I've been there," Hector said with a fond smile.

"Do they have beds?" asked Tarness.

"Large down beds for you, my friend." Hector smacked the man's shoulder. "And attractive barmaids for Angst. Something for everyone."

"Well, let's hurry then," Angst said with a grin.

They all reluctantly agreed, moaning and grunting with exhaustion as they continued. Scar's whimpers and Ivan's stomach quickly directed them north. Another half hour passed before they found a clearing in an otherwise thickly-wooded area. Several fallen trees were well placed, providing a spot to sit while eating. They'd just begun to unload their gear when Hector put his hand on Angst's shoulder and Scar started barking.

"What is it?" Angst asked, immediately on alert and drawing his sword.

"We have visitors," Hector replied, a longsword in his hand.

The group quickly positioned themselves in a circle to face the trees in all directions. Everyone had their weapon drawn, as prepared as they could be for the unknown. Guttural coughing sounds came from all directions.

"What is that?" asked Rose.

"Laughter," Hector said, sounding surprised.

A loud roar erupted as an enormous black bear burst from the woods. Angst rushed forward to face it, holding Chryslaenor up high so he could split the creature's skull.

"*Hold!*" growled a deep baritone voice from behind the bear.

It looked up over its shoulder as a twelve-foot man stepped out from behind the tree. He gripped the bear by the scruff of its neck, easily holding it in place. Scar ran up to the bear and continued barking, which brought on another round of the odd laughter. The large trees about them seemed to be casually pushed aside, making room for more of the giant men and women. Angst and his friends were surrounded.

25

"Are they giants?" asked Rose.

"No, I'd say they're Nordruaut," Dallow replied in amazement. "I've only read stories, but, well, wow."

"What are they doing?" asked Tarness.

"They're waiting to see if we're going to challenge them or welcome them," replied Hector. "I've met up with some in the past. They're good companions but be careful. They see things differently than we do and take offense when you wouldn't expect it."

Angst lowered his sword, setting Chryslaenor to hover on its tip. The five 'giants' murmured in curiosity. He spread his hands open in a welcoming gesture.

There were three men and two women, the shortest of whom was easily twice Angst's height. The Nordruaut were a striking sight. Feathers and beads had been woven into their long, platinum blond hair. Ceremonial paint covered the tan complexion of each face, and not one of them appeared overweight or disproportioned, simply much larger than other humans. The smallest woman looked as though she could pick up a calf with little effort. They were all draped in various animal furs and skins. Both women held longbows, and the men carried even longer spears.

"*Hail!*" yelled Hector, holding his hand up. "What brings a Tribe of the North to our warm lands?"

Rose leaned over to Angst. "What is he talking about, warm?

It's freezing out here." She was shivering.

"I think where they come from, this is balmy," Angst replied, trying not to shiver himself.

"We're here for the hunt, little neighbor," the largest Nordruaut replied. "There are creatures along the Vex'kvette that none before have seen. Some have even been a challenge." He touched a new scar across his cheek, and smiled proudly. "What brings you through these lonely woods?"

"We come to make camp here. Would you join us and trade tales?" Hector offered.

The apparent leader looked to his companions before nodding. "Thank you for your kind offer, little neighbor. We would enjoy your company and your stories."

A young Nordruaut man eyed Chryslaenor hungrily. He whispered something to the leader, who pushed him away roughly before speaking once again. "I am Jarle, and these are my companions, Niihlu and Paukka," he said, gesturing to the two men. Then he directed them to the women. "Our tracker is Feemi, and our scout is Maarja."

Hector introduced their party in much the same fashion. Jarle recommended that they set camp, and even offered to provide the night's meal. Niihlu, Paukka, and Feemi, the taller of the two women, all grinned with pleasure and ran off into the woods with surprising speed and grace, despite their size.

Jarle shrugged at Hector with a slight head tilt, as though this was what all young giants did at the prospect of a new hunt. Not only was he taller than the rest, but he seemed older than his companions as well. His handsome features showed more wear than those of the other Nordruaut. Harsh weather conditions and a life spent outdoors had stretched his skin to a leathery toughness. Jarle also sported the most war paint, with lines of red and white streaked across his forehead and vertically under his eyes. The dark furs and skins he wore bore evidence of much travel.

Maarja, who'd remained, seemed younger and more pristine than the others. She was covered in white fur and skins, and had a single line of white paint under each eye. Maarja was strikingly pretty, and when she proclaimed she would find wood for the fire, Tarness hastily offered to go with. The giant woman briefly eyed Tarness, looking him up and down slowly, then nodded once and lumbered off into the woods with Tarness scrambling to catch up.

"Your friend will find no warmth with that one. From what we can tell, she hates men," Jarle said with surprising candor.

Rose gave a sharp bark of laughter, while everyone else coughed and shuffled their feet. Jarle seemed to appreciate Rose's reaction and looked her over as if considering a purchase.

"How is it you only travel with one?" Jarle pointed at Rose. "How do you keep warm at night?"

"We take turns," said Angst.

Rose elbowed him in the stomach, where the armor gave the most. Jarle's eyes went wide, his mouth open to speak but nothing came out.

"I'm joking, Jarle," Angst coughed, rubbing his belly. "We actually spend our nights quite cold."

Jarle laughed out loud, which made everyone jump. He obviously found Angst's comment quite funny. Rose cocked her arm to elbow him again, but appeared to think better of it. Angst was relieved, not only because of the cultural hurdles that seemingly required translation, but because Rose's bony elbow hurt!

"This I understand all too well. We lost one to the hunt." Jarle's stoic features became somber.

"I'm sorry to hear that," offered Dallow.

"Why are you sorry? The hunt was good, the death brave and magnificent." He nodded once as though this explained all. "Where are your horses? We stopped hunting your pets long ago so you would no longer run out."

Hector held his hand out behind him, to keep his friends from asking what the Nordruaut meant. "We are grateful for your sacrifice. Ours were lost in the hunt."

This made Jarle smile. "You will have to tell your stories tonight."

"Of course," said Hector, nodding with respect.

The hunting party returned first, before Tarness and Maarja, with what could've been parts of a deer that had already been skinned and prepared for cooking. A leg was tossed to the bear, and a rib thrown to Scar. Both animals dug into their dinners, though Scar hesitated for a moment, eying the bear's larger meal. After a warning growl from the bear, Scar picked up his rib and scurried behind Rose to eat in safety.

"How brave," Ivan remarked dryly.

"I've heard tales, but I can't believe how quickly they came back with food," Hector whispered.

"It's scrawny, but will do," Jarle said to the three hunters. "I doubt the humans eat much."

Tarness and Maarja returned shortly after the others. Tarness looked flustered and out of breath as he rushed to keep up, his arms filled with enough wood for three fires. Maarja appeared to be carrying half a dead tree.

Jarle and the others nodded. "Kindling and firewood. It will be a good night for stories," Jarle said.

Thinking nothing of the large quantity of meat presented her, Rose stepped in and began cooking, with Dallow assisting per her directions. The Nordruaut didn't seem to mind, and appeared interested in the steps she took to prepare the meal. Rose pulled out the few remaining spices from their packs, trying to make a good impression.

The food was the best they'd eaten all week. Angst was certain he actually drooled several times during the meal, but didn't care. The Nordruaut politely enjoyed the venison, but drank a lot of water, indicating that maybe the spice was a bit strong, though none would admit it.

Throughout the meal, Niihlu eyed Chryslaenor, which remained hovering on its tip near the fire. Several times he walked over to inspect it, 'accidentally' bumping the sword on several occasions only to find it wouldn't budge. Jarle stared at Niihlu with disapproval, but said nothing.

After they were done eating, the Nordruaut began breaking off bits of Maarja's tree to feed the fire. The flames quickly grew in height, their heat driving Angst's group to the edge of the campsite. Now warmed, the Nordruaut chose this time to remove most of their furs and leathers, leaving on just enough to be almost considered clothed.

Tarness openly gawked at Maarja, who didn't seem to care she was falling out of her remaining animal hides. She beckoned him to sit by her, which he did gladly. Dallow and Hector exchanged a mischievous glance and some polite chuckling. In Unsel, Tarness had always been monstrously taller than any woman he was interested in.

Angst leaned over to Rose. "You're being very disrespectful to their customs," he whispered in mock disapproval.

"What? How?" she asked with concern.

"Shouldn't you be getting undressed too?" Angst said, nodding his head toward Maarja and Feemi, not bothering to contain a huge grin. Both women were clad in the scantiest of form-fitting leather undergarments.

Rose sighed loudly in annoyance, attempting to ignore his comment. "Where's Ivan?"

"He said he wasn't feeling well." Angst shrugged. "Maybe with him away, we can enjoy the evening."

Rose chuckled. "Now what's going on? Story time?" she asked, her tone thick with sarcasm.

Jarle crouched then made his way around the enormous fire slowly, as though stalking prey. He wore nothing but a loincloth, and his muscles moved sinuously with every step he took.

"Maybe story time is a good thing," Rose whispered in awe, and it was Angst's turn to roll his eyes and sigh loudly.

Jarle stopped and stared at the flames, bowing his head reverently before speaking. "The Great Hunter," Jarle began in his low voice, "captured dangerous Fire first, which he mounted in the sky to become the sun and the stars." He lifted his arms to the sky in a dramatic gesture. "The next day, he hunted Water, which spilled over the land like blood to become lakes and oceans and rain." Jarle brought his hands down, wiggling his fingers to simulate rain as he sat on his haunches.

"Powerful, lumbering Earth and quick, elusive Air were later trapped by the Great Hunter. Earth was crumbled into the very ground itself, and Air was shared with all to breathe and live," Jarle whispered as he spread his arms and hands expansively. He suddenly leaped to Rose, who yelped as he knelt before her on one knee. "Yet the hunt was not over, for Magic was the hardest prey to tame. It was everywhere and nowhere, hiding under Water and behind Earth. Magic could become one with air and then lash out with Fire." Jarle stood once again.

Rose took a deep breath, her eyes dreamy, either mesmerized by the story, or perhaps by Jarle.

"But the Great Hunter was patient and cunning and captured Magic, only to find it would quickly escape. He tried different prisons—objects and animals and people—but Magic was too clever to be trapped for long. Only the Vivek of Power could balance Earth and Fire and Air and Water, and only the Vivek could contain Magic. The Great Hunter guards the Vivek, and we will continue The Hunt!"

In unison, the five Nordruaut and Hector proclaimed, "and so it is said, and so it shall be told."

Angst wanted to stand and applaud, and ask questions. He flashed a look at Dallow, who appeared ready to do the same, but Hector covertly shook his head and both held their tongues. The Nordruaut waited, and after several moments, Paukka walked around the fire and shared the tale of a mighty horned beast they'd met near the Vex'kvette. The story wasn't as dramatic or practiced as Jarle's tale, which made the telling of their own stories less intimidating.

"The Vex'kvette must be what they call the orange stuff," Dallow whispered to Angst, who nodded in agreement.

When it was their turn, Dallow told the tale of the one-eyed monster that had captured Rose. Hector described how they'd battled Scar with his usual storytelling flair, only embellishing his participation a modest amount. It was entertaining, and relaxing, and the first time Angst had seen his friends genuinely smile in a week. He grinned and was trying his best to listen, but re-

mained haunted by Jarle's story. Angst wanted to leave everyone
and consider the story's meaning, or talk it through with Dallow,
or even question Jarle. Something about it seemed to click in his
mind, and once again, Angst felt a certain convenience in the
timing of this encounter with the Nordruaut.

26

The next morning, Angst found Niihlu practically salivating all over Chryslaenor, which he'd left hovering on point by the fire.

"I would very much like to have this," Niihlu stated, unable to tear his eyes from the blade.

"There are times I wouldn't mind being rid of it," Angst replied agreeably, watching Niihlu's confused reaction. "It's the greatest gift I ever received, and the heaviest burden I've ever carried."

"I don't think you understand. I would like to have this now," Niihlu growled threateningly.

"You're right, I don't understand. I also don't think you understand. It's not mine to give, nor yours to take," Angst responded.

Niihlu attempted to lift it for the hundredth time, but the sword still didn't budge. "Then I challenge you for it."

Jarle had been observing their conversation, and quickly joined them on hearing this. "Niihlu, what are you saying?"

"I challenged Angst for his sword," Niihlu answered firmly, as if Angst weren't standing right next to him.

"Niihlu, this was discussed. That blade is not for hunting, and we are not to covet," Jarle said disapprovingly.

"The challenge is made," Niihlu reiterated then stalked away from both men.

Jarle just shook his head and called after his younger companion. "This will not work in your favor." He then faced Angst. "Either you or someone of your choosing must fight in hand to hand combat for your right to keep the blade. No weapons can be used."

"This doesn't make any sense," Angst said irritably. "Even if he were to win, which he wouldn't, he couldn't even pick the sword up."

"Gather your people, Angst. I don't think this will take long." Jarle sounded discouraged as he walked to his companions, his shoulders slumped like a giant willow tree.

Angst sighed, and went to find Hector. Five minutes later, his friends all met around the campfire. Even Ivan left his sick bed to join them.

"Can you fight without the sword?" asked Rose.

"Oh, that's the encouragement I need," retorted Angst.

"She's right, Angst. Niihlu hits you once, and you're done for," Hector agreed.

Tarness had been staring at Maarja, and said distractedly, "I'll do it."

"Pardon?" replied Angst.

"I'll be your champion," Tarness said, still looking at the attractive Nordruaut.

"I don't need anyone to fight my fights," Angst said defensively.

Tarness tore his gaze away. "Angst, this has nothing to do with you. I think you could take him, but I have something to prove here."

Angst didn't quite understand until he looked over to see Maarja eyeing Tarness while winding feathers into her long blond braids. Obvious struck Angst in the head, and he reluctantly agreed. "Only if you're sure, Tarness."

Niihlu stepped in front of his group, and although he was one of the shorter Nordruaut men, he was still four feet taller than Tarness. He shed most of his furs and skins, allowing everyone to see that his wiry muscles were ripe with youth and power.

Tarness mimicked his actions, standing before Angst and removing his armor. He had muscles on top of muscles on top of several well-fed years on top of more muscles. Tarness was strong, though not nearly as fit or large as the Nordruaut. Glancing at Maarja, he quickly sucked in his gut.

Jarle stepped between them. "This is simple. The first man knocked unconscious or killed loses. There will be a break every two minutes if anyone remains standing." Jarle stepped back, raised his hand then lowered it. "Go!" he yelled.

With a roar, Niihlu took a running start at Tarness. Surprised by the offensive attack, Tarness was thrown off his feet, forcing Angst and Dallow to dive out of the way. The remaining one minute and fifty-nine seconds went much the same, a ruthless beat down of Tarness, at the end of which he still stood. Unfortunately.

Tarness limped over to his friends, his lip and right eye painfully swollen and bleeding. He coughed up a bit of blood, which he spat onto the forest floor. He was breathing heavily and caked in sweaty dirt. Several of the fingers on his left hand were bent in the wrong direction, and Tarness fought back a scream when Hector straightened them out.

"Tarness, I don't understand, why are you letting this man beat you?" asked Angst.

"I'm not letting... I just can't seem to focus. I don't understand, I can't seem to lose my temper." Tarness wiped a bit of blood from his dark cheek. "I'm simply not angry."

Ivan stood shakily and walked to Tarness. "This is going to take forever," he muttered in frustration. The knight leaned forward and began whispering in Tarness's ear.

His face transformed from distracted to furious. Tarness looked as though he would rip Ivan in half. Ivan grabbed his shoulders and spun Tarness around to face Niihlu.

"That was risky," Angst whispered to Ivan.

Ivan shrugged negligently. "I could care less if he wins or loses, but I need to get out of here."

Niihlu roared again, ready to repeat his previously successful strategy, and charged. To every Nordruaut's surprise, Niihlu collided with the immovable wall that was an angry Tarness. The shock of impact lifted everyone's hair, and Niihlu collapsed to his knees with a harsh grunt. Tarness smashed his elbow into Niihlu's face before his opponent could recover. He then lifted the giant man over his head and slammed him down hard. Niihlu bounced off the ground, and blood spurted from his mouth. Tarness kicked the giant in the side, flipping Niihlu awkwardly into the air. The Nordruaut landed on his stomach with a loud thud and remained motionless.

Tarness set his foot on the man's back and yelled, "Anyone else feel the need to challenge?"

Jarle was actually smiling, almost as much as Maarja. "Well done, friend!" He walked to Tarness and thumped him on the shoulder then looked down at Niihlu. "Hopefully Niihlu will learn from this."

Angst lifted the sword and returned it to his back. "The challenge has been met and won. For winning this challenge, we want her." He pointed at Maarja.

Jarle looked startled then outraged. "What?"

Angst was upset, and on the verge of getting angry. "I don't know what this nonsense was about, but we met your rules, now you can meet ours. Maarja will be our guide, so we can get Ivan safely away from what you call the Vex'kvette then she can return to you if she chooses."

Jarle stormed over to Angst and pushed roughly at his chest, but found Angst wouldn't budge. Jarle stepped back, his eyes widening at Angst's unexpected strength.

Angst looked at Jarle, and dusted the spot on his armor the Nordruaut had touched. "If necessary, we can have another challenge, but I'd rather just have your help."

The anger melted from Jarle's face as he eyed Angst with curiosity. Jarle placed both hands on Angst's chest then leaned and pushed against him as though testing to see if the first time was a trick. Again, Angst didn't budge. He merely concentrated on anchoring his armor to the ground with his power. Jarle stood, towering over Angst, and for the first time, thoroughly analyzed the armor, the sword, and the man.

"You didn't need Tarness to fight for you," Jarle stated matter-of-factly. "If she goes with you, will she be safe?"

"As safe as any of us," Angst replied.

"I didn't mean from the Vex'kvette." Jarle's stoic features showed genuine concern.

"We won't harm her," Angst stated, then in a friendlier tone, "We're so powerful we can't even find a path away from the Vex'kvette."

Hector and Dallow feigned a bit of laughter to keep up the appearance of being friendly. Jarle wasn't completely convinced, and went to Maarja. He spoke with her in harsh whispers. She nodded at Jarle and whispered something in response that appeared to upset him.

Jarle looked as though he'd lost all his money in a bet. "Maarja will guide you from the Vex'kvette," he confirmed. "You will be back on a road in three days at your pace. If I find that she has died by your hands, we will hunt *you*."

"That seems like a fair deal," Hector whispered loudly to Dallow.

Jarle reached out his hand as though no threat had ever left his lips. "Good hunting, Angst."

"Good hunting, Jarle," Angst repeated, and clasped forearms with the Nordruaut.

* * * *

"You walk slow," Maarja proclaimed as she waited at the top of a hill for them to catch up.

During the first several hours, it had been hard to tell if Maarja was upset about having to guide them. This concern quickly passed as it became obvious she actually enjoyed pushing them. Either Maarja had a cruel streak, or she was testing their limits. Tarness, who was sweating like an overworked ox, was the only one not complaining, despite his new limp.

"It's the armor," Angst wheezed as he tried to reason with the tall Nordruaut. "The armor and the years. You're like twenty-something, aren't you?"

"I'm no child, Angst. I'm sixty-seven, by your years," Maarja said seriously.

Angst sought to milk this conversation, hoping it would slow her down so everyone could catch their breath. "I would've said you don't look a day over sixty-six."

She smiled. "A Nordruaut can live for three hundred years. I am still young in many of my people's eyes."

"Is it normal for one who's a mere sixty-seven years old to be on the hunt?" Immediately, he regretted this question.

Maarja suddenly stopped, grabbing Angst's shoulder, and jerking him to a halt. She eyed Angst as though she'd stepped on something foul and needed to remove it from her shoe. "The others aren't so sure, but I know I could break you," she growled with a sneer. Everyone had stopped to watch this exchange. "We waste time. Let's go," she commanded and pressed forward faster than before.

Angst stood there for a moment, wondering exactly what that meant. Rose walked by at the new faster pace and smacked him in the back of the helm. Hector and Dallow were slower to follow, tears streaming down their face as they did their best to hold back laughter.

"I'd pay to watch her break him," said Hector, trying to catch his breath.

"I'm selling tickets," Dallow replied through chuckles.

The first day ended at sundown, and each one of them appeared exhausted in their own unique way. Only Ivan seemed to fare better since Maarja had guided them away from the worst of the Vex'kvette. Tarness, not wishing to show any sign of weakness, kept moving and made a small fire. Rose crashed onto a pile of blankets and appeared unwilling to move, so they choked down Marissa's jerky for dinner. Maarja didn't complain about the meal, but Angst could hear her stomach growling throughout the night.

They rose early the next morning to a gentle steady rain, each of them suffering silently. Tarness seemed much improved. The swelling in his face and his limp were both gone. Tiny Rose was the last to rise. Maarja offered to carry her, but Rose threw her a dark look and refused. She seemed to gather more energy after eating breakfast. Maarja tried to push the group to keep the prior day's pace, but Angst grew more insistent of maintaining a slower speed.

He attempted to persuade her at first with courtesy and humor. "Can we go a little slower for the short people?" By noon, he was trying reason. "We can keep up with you, and I appreciate your urgency, but there's too much going on out here for us to be exhausted." Later in the day, Angst stopped caring about diplomacy and simply yelled, "Hey! Legs! Slow down!" His requests all had the same effect, a scowl, a smile, and a slower pace, for a little while.

Shortly after noon on the third day, as promised, they approached a highway that apparently led from Unsel to Nordruaut. The rain had finally subsided, giving everyone another reason to rejoice.

"I need to return to Jarle and the others, or they will be quickly lost," she announced, chuckling at her own joke. Before Tarness could react, she kissed him square on the mouth. For five minutes, everyone stared off into the woods while she appeared to feast on Tarness's face. When she was done, Tarness had a glassy, far-off look in his eyes.

"I should stay and have my way with you," she said to him. Tarness's hopeful expression deflated with her next words. "But I need to return. Remember what I told you, where I am from. I would like to see you again if you live."

"You don't have to go back," Tarness pleaded.

"He's right. You're welcome to join us, Maarja," Angst offered. "We would certainly get there faster."

"Oh great, another ten mouths to feed," Ivan complained loudly.

"Tell me again why you wanted to save him?" asked Maarja.

"Good question," replied Hector.

"I thank you, but I haven't finished my first hunt. Maybe someday we will meet and trade stories again." She spat on Ivan's armored chest before nodding at Angst and the others. "Good hunting."

Maarja caught Tarness's eyes and held them with a hot stare before running back into the woods at an incredible pace.

"She'll be back to them by nightfall," Dallow said in wonder.

"We should be close to Ravenhill. We can spend the night there before heading back," Ivan proclaimed, wiping the spit off with a leaf.

"Heading back to where?" asked Angst.

Ivan looked surprised. "Back to Unsel, of course. This trip is over, and I'll be happy to report to the queen that this mission was the worst failure I've seen in my life."

27

"That's the entire reason he's here. The queen sent him to sabotage our trip, and ruin any chance of success." Angst was practically frothing at the mouth as he vented his frustrations to his friends.

Everyone remained quiet, waiting patiently for Angst to cool down. Ivan, feeling better now that they were away from the Vex'kvette, was once again in the lead, far ahead of the others on their approach to Ravenhill.

Angst continued to rant. "I've always known Isabelle hated me, but to undermine what we're trying to accomplish, when there are lives at risk? We've barely started!" Angst stopped suddenly and turned to face his friends. As a group, they awkwardly stumbled to a halt. "You aren't looking to give up, are you?"

"Will you hit me with the sword if I say yes?" Dallow asked.

"Maybe we should go back, Angst," Rose suggested. "You haven't failed at anything. You were supposed to find out what's stopping trade. We've done that." Her words had a slightly pleading tone.

"That's Dallow talking. Remember? You were the one who wanted to come?" Angst snapped accusingly at Rose then addressed everyone. "We've been over this. Ivan is right in the sense that we haven't accomplished anything. All we know is there's a giant ditch filled with orange crap that cuts Unsel off from every other country. How does knowing that help anyone?" Spreading his arms dramatically, he then let them drop to his sides in frustration. "There's something bigger going on, something much bigger than what I was looking for when I picked up this sword, and we're the only ones trying to figure it out. Everything that's happened, the monsters we've faced, the Mendahir Rise, the obelisk, doesn't it all seem too convenient? It has to mean something!"

"You're so desperate to become the hero that you're seeing conspiracy where there's none. Angst, you're going to get us killed," Dallow said in an equally frustrated tone.

"Me? I didn't create that stuff. It's the Vex'kvette that seems to be killing everything, not me." Angst suddenly turned and began walking again.

"I agree with Ivan. We should head back," Hector said to Angst's back. "I've known you for a long time, Angst, and, no offense, but this is a bit outside our abilities, even with that sword. This kind of stuff requires plans, and resources, and armies. We should get reinforcements."

"Hector is right. We should call this done," Dallow said.

Angst sighed deeply. "I'm going to get some rest in town before deciding what to do next."

* * * *

Total devastation cloaked the town in a heavy, thick sort of murk. The air was tainted with the scents of dry ash from old fires, wet earth, and the gamey smell of blood and death. Their arrival at the town of Ravenhill wasn't met with a weak barricade hiding hopeful eyes, or a safe harborage of soft beds, warm food, and fresh mounts. There was only a horrible silence and small ruins of buildings. The stillness was profound, as telling as a sign with bold letters posted on the city gates declaring, "Nobody came to save us!"

At Oakhaven, Angst and his friends had been prepared to fight, and then almost died of boredom. Having fought the monster before arriving—if that was truly what they'd done—had seemed like cheating. As they approached what would've been the middle of Ravenhill, Angst thought about the remaining inhabitants of Oakhaven, and of Marissa, and hoped they'd decided to go to Unsel for safety.

Tarness whistled softly. There was little left but char. A few blackened wood posts rose from the ground, marking the remnants of shops and homes. The white husk of a large, dead tree marked the former center of town, its branches missing and the bark blasted off by the heat of fire.

"I...I don't understand," Ivan said frantically. "I don't get this at all. Was it an army of those one-eyed creatures? What could do...this?"

"We should look around," Hector suggested. "Just in case."

"And look for survivors," Angst agreed.

Ivan didn't. "Look around? So we can be next? We aren't good to anyone if we get killed."

"We stay in groups, and within earshot. After fifteen minutes, we'll leave. We shouldn't stay here," Hector commanded, ignoring Ivan. He sounded nervous, and his voice was as raw as the air surrounding them.

Angst was annoyed with himself for not having said something similar, but shock numbed his mind and froze his tongue. Everyone looked quiet, or sickly. "Ivan, you're with me. I'll keep you safe."

Ivan peered at Angst hatefully but followed him as they split into three teams. Hector and Tarness went straight through the heart of the town while Dallow and Rose searched nearby rubble. They all wandered for a bit but never far enough to be out of view.

"Is anyone here?" Angst finally yelled in frustration, making everyone jump and turn toward him. "Let's get out of this place!" he commanded, and beckoned everyone to follow.

* * * *

There was enough daylight to hike back to the spot where Maarja had left them. Everyone had remained quiet. Everyone but Ivan.

Despite Ivan's lead, they could all hear quiet snippets of whatever the knight was muttering. He rubbed the back of his neck then suddenly stopped and stomped his foot. He knocked off his helmet several times, only to turn and flash everyone a wild, angry stare before picking it up and scrambling ahead to remain in the lead.

"I think Ivan is finally broken," Tarness observed.

"We should catch up and see what's going on," Angst said agreeably, quickening his pace.

As the distance closed, some of Ivan's mutterings became clearer. "Their magics are ruining everything! I need to get out. I need away from the bitch and those freaks."

"Hey, Ivan. What's going on?" Angst asked loudly, attempting to interrupt the crazy spilling out of the man's mouth.

Ivan shot him a mad look with wide, bloodshot eyes. His glare was so frightening it almost knocked Angst to the ground. Ivan was shivering, as though from sickness or anticipation. He took a deep breath to belt out a scream, but instead spat on the ground in front of everyone. Ivan turned to walk down the path even faster than before.

Angst sighed heavily. "I'm done with that man."

They set up camp far enough from the road that the fire wouldn't be seen by travelers. Ivan was missing, and they stopped looking for him when it became dark. Shortly after dinner, the knight returned. His helm and sword were gone, his face haggard, and some of his hair had apparently decided it needed to be torn out.

"Hey, Ivan, you're all right," Hector said, feigning interest in Ivan's return before getting a good look at him.

Without replying, Ivan walked directly to Rose and started cursing. The random combination of words didn't make sense, but every word was a sharp, cutting insult that left his mouth loudly and drenched in spittle. Dallow rushed to her defense, placing himself between Rose and the knight. Ivan paused long enough to punch Dallow in the stomach. Dallow, not expecting the blow, immediately doubled over.

Angst had had enough. He removed the giant sword from his back and rested it on its tip. Chryslaenor hovered over the ground, so unbelievably large it seemed to mock all other swords. Angst dropped his helm at the base of Chryslaenor, where it sat in the foci's reflective glow.

"Angst, wait," Hector called, trying to grab Angst's arm as he stomped over to Ivan. But Angst was in no mood to be stopped.

Rose had moved to kneel by the fallen Dallow as he clutched his stomach. Ivan looked up from Rose and screamed at Angst, "Are you going to push me around with your freakish magic, in the name of your bitch?" He balled up his fist and clumsily reached to punch Angst's face, but missed.

Angst slapped Ivan across the mouth. There was no great amount of strength behind the slap. No magic, no giant sword. Just the loud crack of hand striking cheek. Angst stepped closer to him, almost nose to nose, and delivered another harsh slap.

Ivan tried to move away, the wild look on his face met with a third and fourth slapping strike. For every step back he took, Angst moved forward, continuously striking Ivan's face with his open palm. Fear of Angst, of his magic, and the surprise of this unusual attack showed clearly on Ivan's face, now beginning to redden and welt. Angst was unrelenting, slapping and striking the knight's face over and over again.

There's a time in everyone's life that they remember being humbled, a moment when they're stripped of their shields and reminded of their humanity. Pride and arrogance are removed, sometimes forcibly, and replaced with a bit more of everyman, a bit more of that thing that makes us equals. For some poor souls, that one experience in humility goes far beyond the reach of its intended lesson.

Weeks and years of anger and frustration poured out of Angst's open palm. Angst wasn't just slapping him, he was beating Ivan's face with pure humiliation. It was a torrential onslaught meant to embarrass and disgrace. Ivan finally collapsed to the ground. Angst scoffed and shook his head. Ivan had been reduced to tears. Tears. A grown man, a knight of Unsel, slapped to the point of tears.

Angst looked at Ivan, cold fury still coursing through his veins. Saying nothing, Angst pointed to the highway.

Ivan looked away from Angst, pathetically attempting to hide his red puffy cheek from the others. He scrambled to stand then, without a word, ran into the woods.

Angst turned to look at his friends. Rose and Dallow had shied away, either embarrassed for him, or by him. Tarness looked at Angst as though through new eyes, obviously disappointed by the attack.

"Angst..." Hector said consolingly, but his voice trailed off.

Angst eyed each of them, feeling betrayed by their lack of response. "That's all the support I get? He deserved that, and you can all piss off." He walked to his sword, hoisted it, and stomped off into the woods.

He found a stone outcrop at the firelight's edge and sat down, facing the camp. Their voices were faint from this distant. They were arguing about something... about him. Actually, it wasn't much of an argument since the only one yelling was Rose, but he heard his name several times between loud curses. Who could blame them? He was surprised they weren't packing up to leave. Maybe they were.

He must have seemed as crazy as Ivan, attacking the knight like that. The very thought of the man made him grimace. Who says those kinds of things? Angst was no stranger to insults, and could handle the occasional bully, but don't poke his friends without expecting to lose a finger. What he did may have been wrong, no, it was wrong, but he would have done it again.

The distant argument faded, replaced by the sound of footsteps.

"Feel better?" Rose asked, crossing her arms in front of her chest.

"I didn't enjoy that." Angst's voice was low and husky. "He's not welcome back. I won't have you, or anyone, treated like that."

She dropped her arms, and her body eased. "Well, for that part, thank you." Rose stepped closer, and Angst made room for her to sit on the rock.

She hesitated, not uncomfortable but still cautious. Rose seemed to hover over the spot awkwardly.

"I promise not to make a pass at you, Rose," Angst offered, and she rolled her eyes. He wanted to avoid talking about what had just happened, and only one distraction came to mind. "I also don't need to be healed. I'm fine," he blurted.

She stilled, her large, pretty eyes widened with surprise.

"What?" Angst asked defensively. "I'm not a fool. We are friends, aren't we? You think I don't pay attention? I've always kind of known, but when we found you with the monster and you healed Dallow, I finally put it together. It took me a while, but I figured that's why you chose to ride with him, so it would remain your secret."

"Yes, that's part of it." She hesitated. He could tell she wanted to be upset but had no reason, so she just sat next to him, bumping shoulders in the process.

"I was going to wait for you to tell me, but I'm a little stressed right now," Angst explained.

Rose waited beside him quietly, and Angst worried that he'd hurt her by stealing her secret. "I think it was noble of you to heal Tarness the night after his fight with the Nordruaut," Angst said in an approving tone.

"I couldn't let him continue trying to keep up the pace in that condition," Rose said as though her actions needed justification. "Especially when he was trying so hard to impress that huge woman."

"I've been a little disappointed that you hold back. All the knocks and bruises we've been taking…but I assumed there was a reason."

"I'm sorry, Angst, but it hurts so much. I don't actually heal people, I take on their injuries myself," Rose explained.

"I'm not sure I completely understand," Angst said, confused.

Rose sighed. "Hold out your hand," she commanded.

Angst held his hand out in front of her. It still tingled a bit from striking Ivan. Rose quickly pulled out a dagger and cut deep into his palm.

"Hey! What the—" Angst yanked his hand back.

Rose threw down the dagger and grabbed his wrist. "Quit being such a baby." She touched his hand with her fingers, skin to skin, for the briefest of moments. The cut, and even the tingling, were instantly gone. Rose grimaced as she opened her own palm. The injury had appeared on her hand and was bleeding. Before his eyes, the skin reformed and the cut faded away.

"Wow," Angst whispered. "That has to hurt."

"The longer I make contact, the more I transfer. It's hard to touch someone injured, knowing I'm going to be instantly bathed in their pain. I remove both physical and emotional wounds. I experience the full brunt of it, but it passes quickly, because I heal incredibly fast. But you're right, it hurts. A lot." Everything Rose had been holding back burst out like water breaking free of a dam. She pulled on her long red hair nervously as she watched Angst's reactions. "You must think I'm a terrible person for not healing everyone more often."

Angst shook his head. "I'm not here to judge you, Rose. Not you or anyone. I've always had faith that if needed, you would be there. But this explains a lot. Thank you for telling me the rest of the story."

She smiled. "Thanks. You, uh, won't tell anyone else, will you?"

"It's your secret to share, I can't imagine why I would." Angst sighed. "If you don't mind, though, I came out here to mope and wallow. You're a bit too distracting for self-pity."

"And I've known you too long for you to be able to cover your emotions with weak flirting. Very weak flirting," she chided.

Angst laughed politely.

"Angst, that thing," Rose pointed at the sword, "seems to

weigh heavily on you."

"Nah, light as a feather," Angst said with mock cheer.

"Cute. I don't mean the physical weight. You seem to get disappointed and frustrated a lot more often and that outburst with Ivan was, well, a bit frightening," Rose said, a hand on his shoulder. "You seem so upset sometimes. We're all worried."

Angst looked at the ground. "I'm fine. There's just been so much change in so little time. I don't even know what I'm supposed to be doing. You'd think something this powerful would come with some sort of manual. It's embarrassing, especially after wanting this life for all these years. Some hero," he scoffed.

"I don't think you understand what I'm trying to say, Angst. I can listen, or I can take away some of the pain." Rose reached for his hand again. "I can heal some of what's making this hard for you."

Angst stood quickly to avoid being touched. "*No!*" he practically shouted.

Rose looked as though he'd struck her.

"You don't understand, but this weight, this burden won't just go away. It can't go away. Doesn't anyone see? Don't you? It drives me. I need it to drive me. It keeps me going. That means it has to stay." Angst sounded angry when he hadn't meant to. He was just desperate for Rose to understand.

Rose visibly reeled, obviously offended that he'd turned her down. "I couldn't have healed you enough to make you stop being an ass, anyway." She stormed back to the campsite.

"Rose, you don't understand," Angst called after her, but it made no difference. Her temper was as sudden and fierce as a lightning strike, and the mark left by that strike would take days to wash away.

What could he say? How could he explain that his dreams were haunted by people who used to wield his sword? That he now heard music almost all the time? Everyone would say he was as crazy as Ivan. Maybe he was. Rose couldn't possibly heal those visions. Who knew what it would do to her? Angst sat again, this time turning away from the campsite.

Scar brushed up against his knee, and he reached over to pet the small black lab. Scar wagged his tail, and Angst couldn't help but smile. "At least I don't have to justify everything I do to you." Angst rolled his eyes. "I'm now talking to a dog. Great. Pretty soon someone's going to start slapping me, and it will probably be Rose."

Scar's tail stopped wagging as he shivered for a moment. The dog whimpered then moved forward several feet and sniffed at the ground. Flickering light from the distant campfire reflected off a tall object in front of the dog. Angst stood with a grunt of effort and walked over, reaching out to touch the smooth surface of the object. He stepped out of the firelight's path for a better look, and realized it was another obelisk. It was too dark to read, but it had to be another signpost pointing to Gressmore Towers.

28

Fall winds blustered through the roads and pathways of Unsel, bringing with them a fresh crisp scent that hinted of snow. A whirlwind of leaves and dust danced along the wide cobblestone walkway in front of the castle. Samsen paid little heed to the elements since he was well-protected by several well-fed layers, covered with the tough leather hide of his guard's armor. He turned his head to watch an attractive young woman hasten by, unsuccessfully attempting to get her attention with a smile. Samsen assured himself it was the cold wind that had kept her from noticing him, or stopping to talk, or inviting him to a pub. But he admired the view anyway, coming and going, and was so distracted, he couldn't help but jump in surprise when something brushed his shoulder.

"Gave me a start, you did!" Samsen barked as he adjusted his considerable girth to face...something. What appeared to be a tall person had begun to form in front of him. The guard's thick brows furrowed, and he rubbed his eyes with meaty knuckles. Only the merest blurry impression of a body was visible, and Samsen strained to focus on anything, just to ensure his vision wasn't going bad. Blinking rapidly, he looked around to see nearby bushes that had already lost leaves to fall, blowing dust along the cobblestone walk, and a cracked stone bench. Everything else was clear and remained in focus.

This person would just have to stand still, and Samsen would be the one to tell him. He assumed the air of his formidable authority. With commanding intent, he took a deep breath, paused, and suddenly smiled. He could smell roast. And not just any roast, but the roast his mum used to make on holiday.

"Am I in Unsel?" questioned the blur in a whispery voice that sounded far away.

"Unsel, the capital city," the guard answered distractedly, still floating through memories of food and family.

"Good," said the voice. The blur slowly formed into a man. "And where might I find Queen Isabelle?"

Samsen took in another deep breath, and swiped self-consciously at the drool dribbling onto his chest piece. "Her Majesty is in the castle there," he said in a sleepy voice, pointing toward the castle entrance. "Maybe in the throne room?"

The man was now more clearly visible, with dark hair and a pale complexion. He nodded in approval of the guard's information. "You do fine work, don't you?"

The guard dropped his halberd, nodding in agreement. Samsen would agree to anything this man said, his mind abuzz with such wonderful scents. He recognized all of them from holiday meals. Tables of happy memories that made his stomach rumble.

"It's such a shame that you're so very hungry," the stranger crooned sympathetically. "Couldn't they feed you? Just the tiniest bit? For all your hard work?" The tall pale man leaned forward and gently blew in the guard's face.

The smell of roast had become so incredible and so overwhelming that the guard immediately lumbered off toward the castle entrance to find some. "Yes, just a little to eat. So very hungry," Samsen muttered to himself, too distracted to notice that the man was gone, leaving behind only a dry laugh and a dusty whirlwind of leaves that danced toward the castle.

* * * *

It was unusual for them to meet in the throne room, but Tyrell unquestioningly adhered to the queen's ever-changing whims.

He'd just finished describing to the queen, in great and boring detail, each dead end the advisors had brought to him. They'd either presented him with nonsense or nothing at all. Every report he received was tainted with insinuation and misdirection that blamed the attack on everything from the magic wielders to the weather. Advisors desperate to keep their jobs and their standing dramatically exaggerated any hint of a lead, but Tyrell knew better and wasted as much time disproving their research as they'd spent fabricating it.

When he finished, Tyrell stood in silence, waiting for the tirade he knew would ensue. They were the only two in the throne room since the queen had dismissed the guards, something she'd been doing with increasing frequency. Normally, he would've expected a stomping bout of anger followed by a stream of threats and possibly even the exile of an advisor or two. Instead, Isabelle fidgeted uncomfortably in her high throne. She stood to pace, pretending to analyze what he'd told her before sitting once again, but not still. When she finally reached up to her glass eye, Tyrell coughed.

"Her Majesty's physician has stated that isn't a good idea," he reminded her in an almost chiding voice.

"My physician should be kicked out with half my advisors," Isabelle grumbled. Her hand shook as she fought with her instinct, desperate to wiggle the glass eye. "You have no idea what this is like. Had you lost your eye—"

"I would rest easier knowing that you were safe, my queen," Tyrell finished for her.

"Fine," the queen harrumphed, dropping her hand. She stood to pace once again. "So, what you are telling me is that after three days, we still have nothing. There's no indication, whatsoever, that this attack was brought about by magic?"

"Your Majesty, we've been most thorough in our investigations, almost to the point of inciting protests. Not only have we been unable to find someone with the ability to cause that attack on you, there are very few who appear to hate you enough to do so."

"So we just wait?" the queen asked. She stopped to stand directly in front of him. "We simply wait for another attack?"

"I'm at a loss," Tyrell admitted in frustration. He watched her one good eye as it moved, while the other remained unsettlingly still. "What I do know is that this investigation hasn't made you popular with the magic-wielding crowd."

"That's easy to fix," she said, waving her hand in a regally dismissive gesture. "We loosen the reins a bit until they calm down." Queen Isabelle returned to the throne and tossed herself into the ornate gold chair.

The oversized doors at the entrance of the room crashed open, startling them both. Rook ran through the doorway. He stopped before the queen and bowed so quickly it could be considered rude.

"My sincere apologies, Your Majesty," he offered to the queen before turning to Tyrell. "Captain, it's one of the guards, he appears to be…well, it's hard to explain... Please come quickly."

Tyrell sighed and looked at Isabelle. She rolled her eye and shooed him off.

"I'll send your guards back in, and request that your daughter join you, Your Majesty," Tyrell announced, his bow interrupted by Rook pulling on his arm. He rushed out of the room with Rook before Isabelle could countermand his suggestion.

* * * *

Tyrell entered the kitchen to find Samsen lying dead on the floor. Samsen's armor was scattered about the room as if it had been on fire and removing it was an emergency. A large handful of uncooked meat scraps remained in one greasy fist, while the other hand gripped a basted ham hock. The guard's stomach distended grotesquely, well beyond the confines of his shirt and pants, as though he had consumed an entire lake. His cheeks and eyes bulged from his head. Tyrell leaned closer and saw what appeared to be several chicken bones protruding from the man's stomach and neck. The body was quickly beginning to smell of putrid bile.

"He beat off several members of the kitchen staff with his bare hands, and almost killed one of the chefs," Rook explained, shaking his head in disbelief. "Everyone else ran out to find guards. They told us Samsen immediately started gorging himself on every piece of food he could stuff in his mouth. Cooked or uncooked, it didn't seem to matter."

Tyrell circled Samsen, analyzing the situation before barking commands. "Get some bags, collect every bit of food in the kitchen, bring it to the training grounds, and burn it." He paused, considering, before letting out a long sigh. "Burn the guard too. Try not to touch him, though. Cover him with something and drag him to the fire as well."

"Captain? I don't understand," Rook said, looking utterly confused.

"We don't know if some disease floating through this man's head caused this, but I'm not taking any risks. Now go," Tyrell ordered, pointing to the entrance.

Rook rushed out of the kitchen to gather reinforcements. Tyrell continued circling the body, the whole time covering his mouth with his hand. He grabbed a fire poker and awkwardly flipped the guard over. The rolling was accompanied by ungracious burping sounds and more horrid stench. Tyrell refused to touch the body, but lifting arms and legs with the poker revealed nothing. There was no sign the man had been attacked or forced. It was obviously suicide, but by engorgement, which made absolutely no sense at all. The death was grotesque and sad and served no purpose other than interrupting his time with the queen.

With this realization, Tyrell's head whipped up and he tore out of the room as fast as he could.

* * * *

When he arrived at the closed throne room doors, Tyrell was

immediately relieved to hear the queen's laughter and just as quickly disturbed by it. Isabelle didn't laugh, hadn't genuinely laughed since the king passed away, unless it was to be polite, or mocking. Tyrell pushed the doors open to find Queen Isabelle, perched on the edge of her throne, lost in conversation with someone he didn't recognize: a tall, thin man sitting boldly on the king's throne. He stopped talking to look up at Tyrell and smiled smugly.

Isabelle giggled once more before turning to Tyrell. "Please do come, Tyrell. I would like you to meet a friend of mine. Aereon, please meet my Captain Guard Tyrell." Isabelle gestured in Tyrell's direction.

In one smooth motion, Aereon stood, bowed politely, and reached out to shake Tyrell's hand. He was a head taller than the captain, with broad shoulders that seemed disproportionate to his otherwise thin figure. Aereon was pale with cheeks and hands that looked reddened and chapped from a cold wind. His steel blue eyes were set deeply above a very long nose, and his thick disheveled hair was a black so dark it could've gotten lost in shadows.

Tyrell shook hands with Aereon, taken aback by how cold the man's grip was. "My pleasure, Mr. Aereon. From where do you hail?"

"From here and there," Aeron stated, but upon observing Tyrell's dark gaze, he continued. "But I've known the queen all of her existence."

"Really? She's never mentioned you," Tyrell said, instantly wary as he examined the man. Aereon moved with such incredible grace it was as though he had known how to walk a thousand years before anyone else figured it out. Tyrell instinctively knew he was very dangerous.

"Tyrell?" Victoria's voice came from the doorway. "Did you call for me?"

Before Tyrell could stop her, the princess entered the throne room. She walked to them, regarding Aereon with open curiosity. Aereon almost glided across the floor to greet Victoria, taking her hand and bowing deeply before kissing it. The longer Aereon held Victoria's hand, the more concerned she appeared to become.

"I am Aereon, and I am at your service. You must be Queen Isabelle's lovely daughter, Princess Victoria, and you are lovely indeed." His voice was filled with seedy intent, and Victoria yanked her hand from his. Aereon leered into her eyes, and the princess met his gaze straight on with an ice cold glare. "You are very...interesting," he acknowledged as he continued to leer at her.

"So, to what do we owe the...pleasure?" Tyrell interrupted.

Victoria shivered as Aereon slowly dragged his eyes from her to face Tyrell. "I am here to offer my unique and complete services as principal advisor to Her Majesty Queen Isabelle." As he spoke his hands were in constant motion, artfully swooping to communicate as much as his words. It was almost enough to distract everyone, but Tyrell wasn't fooled and saw the calculation behind Aereon's eyes.

"While I'm certain the queen appreciates all...information...provided by her subjects, you will need to do so through proper channels. I'm certain the guards can lead you exactly where you need to go," Tyrell suggested bluntly, hopeful that concluding this conversation would possibly conclude the man's visit. He waved the nearest guards over to Aereon.

The queen immediately raised her hand to halt the guards' advance. "That's enough, Tyrell," the queen said. "Aereon has given me the information we've been seeking."

"Oh?" replied the Captain Guard in disbelief, his eyebrows raised high into his forehead.

The queen stood slowly, regally, sure of herself now as if everything were back to normal. Her change in demeanor surprised Tyrell. Just an hour ago, she'd been overly anxious, seeming uncomfortable in her own skin. Yet here she was without the fidgeting, royally confident of her place, and apparently at peace.

"I was right all along. It's a conspiracy. Those magic-wielding fools have been creating an army of monsters." Isabelle descended the throne dais and approached Tyrell and Victoria. "All that time wasted, but now we can put a stop to it. Every single magic wielder outside of the castle must either be imprisoned or hunted."

Victoria paled, her hand resting on the bodice of her dress as if trying to keep her heart from leaping out. "But, Mother," she said, the words hesitant. "What proof could this stranger have possibly brought you that would warrant this harsh judgment?"

Victoria gasped as Isabelle's eyes met hers, her expression horrified. She brought her hand to her mouth to stifle a cry of alarm. Tyrell leaned in close to Isabelle. In the distraction of Aereon's appearance, he had completely missed it. The false eye no longer mimicked the queen's real one. A tempest now swirled within it—gray clouds in mists of white. The colors and textures inside the glass looked like a slowly brewing storm, spinning around a pitch black center.

"Thanks to Aereon, I now see everything."

29

Ivan hadn't returned by morning, and they resigned themselves to a search. After hours of looking, Hector discovered what may have been a trail, but the signs were faint due to the rain the night before.

"*Mr. Crazy* is probably halfway back to Unsel, to advise Isabelle they should ready the guillotines," Angst huffed to Hector, trying to catch his breath as they trudged beside a winding creek. Wet mud and clay stuck to their boots, weighing down their feet and tiring Angst. "This is really a waste of time."

"What you did yesterday was awful. The man obviously needs help," Hector reproached. "Do you really hate him that much, or are you only willing to be a hero for attractive young princesses?"

"It's not just him, it's what he represents," Angst responded, ignoring the slight. "The man is made of pure hate and bigotry, just like the establishment he represents."

Hector stopped to scrape some of the mud from his boots onto a nearby tree stump. "Are we talking about the same establishment you've wanted to be a part of all your life? Isn't this whole trip about you becoming a knight?"

Clearly Hector wanted to preach rather than discuss, but Angst tried to explain anyway. "It was. Well, it is. I do want to be a knight, but the difference is what I would do as a knight and who I would represent."

Hector set down one foot and rinsed off the remaining mud in the creek. "How much are you willing to sacrifice for this obsession, Angst? These are your friends. They aren't soldiers or adventurers. Dallow is right. Someone's going to get killed. Who are you willing to sacrifice first? Tarness? Rose? Me?"

"Probably you," Angst said with a wink before his voice became serious. "I'm not going to let anyone die. If anyone gets killed for my stupidity, it will be—"

"You both need to see this," Tarness yelled from the campsite.

Hector probably wasn't finished admonishing, which made the timing perfect, in Angst's opinion. After staring each other down for several seconds, they returned to the campsite. Several yards past the camp, they found Dallow, Rose, and Tarness watching Scar circle the black obelisk, his tail wagging rapidly.

"Did you see this last night?" Rose asked Angst accusingly.

"Sure, right after you stomped off." Angst sat on the nearby stone to catch his breath.

"Weren't you going to tell us?" asked Dallow, his tone similar to Rose's.

"I was going to say something after we had given up looking for Ivan. I didn't consider it an emergency."

"It would have been nice to know," Dallow continued to dig.

"Did you want to know how many times I got up to pee last night too?" Angst retorted.

"That's enough," Hector interrupted. "So we've found another obelisk. What do we do about it?"

"We follow it," said Angst logically as he stood. He moved behind the obelisk to better gauge the direction it pointed, the chiseled words 'Gressmore Towers' always facing him.

"Follow what?" asked Dallow, exasperated. The last of his patience seemed to have fled with Ivan.

"The path," Angst replied.

"You aren't going Ivan on us, are you?" Tarness asked. "Unless I'm missing something, I see no path."

"I think there's always been a path, and I might know how to find it," Angst said, allowing himself the tiniest bit of enthusiasm. "Everyone gather your gear. Come on." Without giving anyone the chance to question or argue further, Angst walked back to camp to grab his own satchel. His friends reluctantly followed with heavy sighs and wary looks.

They stood around for several minutes after shuffling about with purpose, quietly adjusting themselves and their packs, but mostly, they were waiting.

"Are we done looking for Ivan?" Tarness asked.

"I'm not a tracker, and everything has been washed out." Hector rubbed his scar. "It looked like he was headed west toward Unsel."

"In other words, we're done looking for Ivan," Angst answered firmly. He looked at everyone, giving them the merest of breaths to disagree, but nobody did.

"All right, Angst, what about us? I hope we're going to Unsel too," Dallow said in a tired voice, flicking blond bangs from his face.

"Scar, come here, boy," Angst called. The small lab happily obliged, wagging his tail and sniffing Angst's hand. Angst whispered to him, "If you really are the guide, now's the time. Show us where we need to go, Scar." The dog sat, happily oblivious to anything Angst had said. Scar's tongue lolled out the side of his open mouth, a bit of drool dripping to the ground.

Angst sensed the eyes of his friends boring into his back with impatience, and his cheeks flushed with embarrassment and frustration. His stomach quivered with anxious discomfort, and he squeezed his eyes shut. He was so tired of arguing and constantly having to prove himself. But here they were, in the middle of nowhere, with only a crappy signpost that was less than vague. They deserved more, he deserved more, but nothing 'deserved' came without earning it, so he tried something. Angst willed Scar to lead them. Just like he would reach for minerals to manipulate them, he mentally reached for Gressmore Towers and concentrated on that thought with all his might. For the briefest of moments, Chryslaenor's song stopped.

"Angst, your sword!" Tarness said, pointing at the now-familiar glow.

Angst opened his eyes to see Scar take off into the woods, in the same direction the obelisk pointed. Without a word, he followed. His friends stood motionless for several moments, looking at each other. Shrugging, Hector fell in line too, with everyone else trailing behind him.

They soon crossed the road that lead to Ravenhill and continued into the woods, though there was no clear path. For hours, they clambered over fallen logs and through muddy creeks. The terrain was exhausting, but they were all too tired to complain. Eventually, they reached a new road, freshly cut, and uniformly straight.

"This is unnaturally convenient," Dallow observed.

"Are you the one seeing conspiracies now?" Angst snapped at him. "You can't have it both ways, Dallow. Either the puzzle fits together or there is no puzzle."

Dallow had nothing further to say, out loud anyway, and his friends remained quiet as they reluctantly moved from rough forest to comfortable path.

They hiked for two days before approaching the crest of a tall hill. At the top of the hill, they had a magnificent view of tundra, stretching empty and desolate forever into the horizon. There was no sign of anything else. No animals, no Gressmore Towers, not even the Vex'kvette. The weight of this revelation forced Angst to his knees, squeezing him dry of energy and hope.

"I could have sworn, for a minute, that the sword...and the dog..." He let the words trail off as his knees sank into the moist hilltop.

Hector patted his shoulder once but said nothing as the others looked for dry spots to sit.

After several moments, Tarness finally spoke. "I guess this is it? Angst?"

"I guess," Angst replied bleakly. Scar barked and ran down the hill into the large expanse. "Now what?" Angst muttered. He shouted for the dog to return. "Come on, Scar." The young pup continued barking and running away from them.

"I'll get him then we can start heading back," Angst said in a low, defeated voice.

He made his way down the hill slowly, trying not to slip in the mud. Angst could barely discern Scar in the distance, and hadn't really been concerned until shadows rolled in like a storm. It didn't make sense. There were already clouds everywhere, and they didn't seem threatening. How could this area be darker than the rest? He looked up.

"By the Dark Vivek," he muttered before running back to his friends as quickly as he could.

When he finally arrived, they all looked at him like he had wasted enough of their time.

"Come on, you've…got…to see," Angst gasped, having left his breath far behind.

"What's going on, Angst?" Hector asked, concern on his craggy face. "Where's the mutt?"

"Now," he said, still huffing. "Come with me."

It would be easier to show than explain, and Angst was far too winded to do both. He impatiently turned to work his way down the hill, back to the darker shadows. When the others caught up, there was nearly an audible thud as their jaws collectively dropped. Somehow invisible at a distance, hundreds of black stone towers now loomed over them. The square base of every tower seemed to have grown from the very ground, reaching high into the sky, like fingers trying to grab clouds. Each one was large enough to contain a house.

They stopped at the periphery of the towers, silently attempting to absorb the awesome size and grandeur of the objects. The square pillars stood like rows of soldiers, towering over dry tundra in a military-precise line. Angst ran his fingers along the cold, smooth face of one pillar, and then into a vertical groove the size of his hand. These grooves appeared every few feet and seemed to be carved all the way up the stone face, similar to the obelisks yet much larger.

"So…are we here? Is this Gressmore Towers?" Angst asked,

breaking the stunned silence.

Hector shook his head in disbelief and scratched the scar along his chin thoughtfully. "I've been all over the world, and I've never seen, nor heard, of anything like this."

"How does something like this just...appear?" asked Rose in stunned disbelief.

Everyone looked at Dallow, who was lost in trance, his eyes glowing as he reviewed his internal catalog. It took much longer than normal. When Dallow's eyes eventually cleared, his face was starkly pale and he swayed with exhaustion, as if he had just finished running to Unsel and back. "I can remember only a few obscure references to black towers in poems, but those are from our oldest books. Some of which I can barely decipher."

"Any mention of danger, or monsters that eat nice people?" Tarness asked, only half-joking.

"None, fortunately. I can't remember reading anything that describes these columns or why they are here. It's like a forgotten myth come to life. The next thing you know we'll be seeing flying unicorns and fire-breathing dragons." Dallow laughed until realizing he was the only one. "Don't any of you read fantasy?"

"Who has time to read?" Rose answered, shaking her head. She looked haggard, her tone less than enthusiastic. "Do any of these towers have an entrance? I'm cold."

They spread out, circling some of the nearby towers in search of a door or maybe some stairs.

After some time, Dallow called out. "I found Scar, and he may have located an entrance."

They joined Dallow near the center of all the towers. He faced a pillar much larger than the others. It had no doors or other signs indicating an entrance, only a handprint surrounded by symbols carved deep into the stone.

"I don't recognize those markings. Do you know what they mean?" Angst asked Dallow.

"It's written in Acratic, a dead language," replied Dallow distractedly as he tried to translate them. "They say, 'Push to enter,' but I don't see any sign of a door."

Chryslaenor's song grew louder in the back of Angst's mind, as if in anticipation. Angst felt that the sword wanted him to do something, but was unable to translate the constant stream of music to something more recognizable, like words. Scar sat next to him, wagging his tail patiently. Angst approached the writing. He pushed on the wall, and to nobody's surprise, it didn't budge.

"Open?" he asked, and was again rewarded with nothing.

Rose laughed and rolled her eyes. "Why don't you put your hand there?" she suggested flatly, indicating the hand carved into the stone.

Angst reached out and touched the etchings. "Huh. Well, the hand is about the same size as mine." He placed his hand inside the one carved into the pillar. When nothing happened, he pushed gently. Finally, he leaned against it with all his weight. For a split second, it glowed, and Angst fell forward through the stone. Surprised by the sudden lack of wall, Angst tripped and dropped to his chest, landing on the floor of a dimly-lit room.

Angst crawled around to face the entrance, and reached out to find a wall. There seemed to be no obvious place to push his way through again. Just as he stood, Angst was pleasantly surprised to find Rose tripping through the entrance and landing right in his arms.

"Excuse me, ma'am. I am a married man," Angst drawled.

She rolled her eyes and shoved herself away, only to get bumped from behind by Dallow. The three quickly made room as Tarness came stumbling in. Hector followed, passing through the wall gracefully, a tail-wagging bundle of puppy in his arms. They all scoffed and rolled their eyes at his smooth entrance.

"What?" Hector asked defensively. "You didn't have to push, just touch and wait."

"All that's in here is a hallway," Angst reported.

"Figure that out all on your own, genius?" Rose asked tartly.

"You can go back to Unsel if you're going to be like that," Angst snapped.

"Why, do you need to send a love note back to your princess

girlfriend?" she said sharply.

Angst glared at her and was going to say something incredibly clever when Hector interrupted. "Kids, that's enough. Let's go."

They walked along a corridor illuminated by gently glowing orbs that hovered several feet from the ground, each small enough to rest in the palm of his hand.

"These things are incredible," said Dallow, poking at one with his finger. It rocked back and forth like a pendulum before returning to its original position.

"Is it magic?" asked Rose.

"Yes, but different than our magic. It had to be made with a spell, a sort of combination of magic and words," Dallow replied, respect in his voice.

At the end of the hallway was a wall with another carved handprint and similar symbols.

"Dallow, what does this writing say?" Angst asked.

Dallow made his way over to peer at the wall. "It says, 'Push to rise.'"

Angst put his hand in the etching, waited, and walked through.

"Can't we discuss these things before diving in?" asked Hector with annoyance.

Dallow shrugged. "You want to go next, Rose?"

"What, to be groped again when I fall through?" she said.

"He groped you?" Dallow asked, his eyebrows raised.

Rose rolled her eyes and pressed her hand to the wall carving. She too disappeared.

This time there was no tripping, and Angst stood further back. "That's where I appeared as well, so I'd suggest moving this way."

Rose walked over to him. He purposely bumped her with his shoulder in a teasing manner. "It's all a bit odd, isn't it?"

She smirked at him, and they were done apologizing. "I'm trying not to think about it. I just hope we're safe. I don't exactly have a giant sword for protection."

"Sure you do," Angst said.

Everyone followed, one at a time. This hallway mirrored the other, but unlike the first, it had a recognizable door at the end.

"What do we do now?" Dallow asked as they stood in front of the wooden door.

"It's a door. Open it," Angst suggested.

Tarness turned the handle. Momentarily blinded by bright warm sunlight, they all squinted and reared back before going outside. After days of dark, cloudy weather, their eyes adjusted to the brightness slowly. Beyond the door was a grassy courtyard filled with people. It took several seconds for the people to realize they had visitors, but they didn't seem surprised and watched in apparent interest as Angst and his friends walked onto the grass.

It was as if they had entered a dream, leaving the dreary grays of forest and suddenly walking into a world of color. A beautiful city surrounded them, blinding light reflecting off tall, white marble buildings. Each bore banners of deep blue with gold trim. A variety of richly colorful flowers bloomed from large planters smartly placed along every path. People in the courtyard were garbed in comfortable, bright-colored togas and sandals. They were all Angst's height or shorter.

"Look, we've found your people," Rose whispered to Angst with a mischievous smirk.

"Where did all of this come from?" Hector asked, his wolf-like eyes wary. He looked to Dallow, who simply shook his head while attempting to lift his dropped jaw.

A stunning young woman approached Angst. Her mane of light-brown hair hung gently over her tanned shoulders. She had a small nose and full lips, her smile dimpling her cheeks at seeing them. Her robes were deep blue, held together by a soft golden rope. As thin as Rose, she was several inches shorter than Angst. She stopped a mere breath away and looked up at him.

"Hi," Angst breathed with a broad smile. "I'm Angst."

She frowned and leaned her head to one side so she could better view Chryslaenor. Her expression reflected her surprise, and she walked behind Angst to get a better look. Angst eyed his friends, raised one eyebrow, and shrugged, politely waiting for the young woman to finish her inspection. She ran her finger along the flat of the sword, and several glowing symbols briefly appeared on the blade. Her entire face suddenly filled with happiness. She walked back around and gave Angst a lingering hug he happily returned, grinning at his friends the entire time.

"Here we go again," Hector muttered, shaking his head.

"What do you expect from people wearing bathrobes," Rose said tersely, assessing the young woman from head to toe.

The attractive young woman grabbed Angst's hand and rushed him through the courtyard. She was saying something in animated tones, but he couldn't understand a word.

"I think she's speaking in Acractic, but she's talking so fast I can't follow," offered Dallow as he scrambled to keep up.

She ushered them through the heart of Gressmore Towers, a full and busy city they'd unexpectedly found in the middle of empty tundra. Angst glimpsed roads and shops, all teeming with hundreds of curious people. As the group progressed, they slowly amassed a following of robed fans, each of them chatting excitedly. Five minutes later, they entered a large, official-looking building with twenty-foot-tall marble columns. Their entourage remained outside. The young woman guided them through various stone hallways, gripping Angst's hand the entire time, as though afraid to lose him.

She pushed through a large pair of ornate wooden doors, and they followed her into a library impressive enough to make Dallow squeak. Books floated around the room, approaching and departing an elaborately carved marble table at the center. At the head of this table sat a man who looked as solid as the stone pillars holding up the city. He wore armor similar to Angst's, though his was gray instead of black. His brown hair, streaked with white, was woven into a long braid. His tanned face was round, and his dark eyes appeared very tired. Next to him, a giant sword hovered on its tip, identical to the one on Angst's back.

When the man first looked up from the books he had been studying, he seemed distracted, as though lost in thought and annoyed at the interruption. The young woman spoke to him in rushed sentences, still holding Angst's hand. The man shook his head as though noticing everyone for the first time. He stood, and advanced toward them quickly. The man ignored Angst's proffered hand, walking around him to view Chryslaenor. After several moments, he forcefully turned Angst around and gave him an intense brotherly hug.

"Uh, I sort of liked it better when she hugged me," Angst said uncomfortably.

The man and the attractive young woman laughed. He patted Angst soundly on the shoulder and pointed at the sword. With no idea what the man was saying, he just smiled and nodded.

The man reached forward and removed the sword from Angst's back, holding it out in front of him to inspect it, as though it were his own.

30

To the best of common knowledge, Chryslaenor had not been picked up, used, or even swung about casually in recorded history. It had been considered a stunning feat for Angst to wield the sword. For this mystery man from a mystery city to nonchalantly take the blade from his back and lift it with such ease was dumbfounding. The older man smiled as he inspected the length and breadth of the beastly weapon. He nodded appreciatively and lowered the sword, setting it in its resting position over the floor.

Angst felt the cold chill of shock grip his heart that this stranger could wield his sword, and his face must have shown it. The man began talking, and while Angst couldn't understand him, he recognized the apologetic tone. He didn't know how to reply, and assumed it wouldn't be understood anyway. With a curious smile, the man pointed to his own identical sword and waved Angst over to it.

Angst looked at the other sword, hovering imposingly on its tip. He didn't understand what was expected of him until the young woman took his other hand. With a friendly smile, she led him to the sword, and rested his hands on the hilt.

*"**Dulgirgraut the Defender**."* The words echoed through Angst's head as he hefted the sword and held it aloft. It was different, this sword, much different. In spite of being identical in size, it seemed heavier and the weight felt balanced closer to the blade's tip. When Angst held Chryslaenor, it sometimes glowed

with shades of blue while Dulgirgraut's glow was dark green. Dulgirgraut's song wasn't the same. Chryslaenor often felt, and sounded, enthusiastic. There were always distant notes in Angst's head that seemed to elicit a sense of urgency. Dulgirgraut played a careful, more somber tune. Angst could sense why this sword was called the defender.

The man had set Chryslaenor on its tip to hover over the white marble floor. Angst lowered Dulgirgraut with the intent of placing it beside his sword. The thought of hefting two giant swords simultaneously made him chuckle, so on a whim, he reached for Chryslaenor. The man and woman yelled what must've been a warning, but it was too late.

Angst's muscles locked into place. It was like holding lightning in one hand and thrusting the other into freezing water. If the swords were brothers, they hated each other. An electric bolt from Chryslaenor tore through his right half and crackled around the outside of Angst's body. The attack stopped at his chest, where Dulgirgraut defended with painful wave upon wave of glowing green light. Angst was immobilized, unable to do anything but watch, immersed in sensation, as his chest prepared to explode. His teeth chattered violently as lightning wove through them. Thunderous reverberations crashed through his head, and blood trickled from his ears.

The young woman stood before Angst with her tiny wrists pressed together and palms facing him. Symbols haloed in yellow and purple light flew from her hands only to bounce off Angst's chest. The man muttered words and swept his arms in complicated movements. He stopped and reached for Dulgirgraut, attempting to wrench it away. He was instantly thrown into the air in a blast of green light. The man flew over the table and deftly rolled into a standing position. Nothing they did could free Angst from the feuding storms he held.

Finally, Tarness walked around to face him. "Sorry, Angst," his deep voice boomed over the chaos, and then he punched Angst hard in the face.

Angst

* * * *

Angst woke an hour later to find himself lying on the library table with the pretty young woman standing behind his head. The palms of her hands felt cold on his temples, and she was muttering something in their language.

"Hello," Angst said. His jaw was sore, and he practiced moving it around. He sniffed and smelled the coppery scent of blood.

The woman opened her eyes and looked down at him. Her shoulders dropped, and her face relaxed. She smiled tiredly at Angst and said something he couldn't understand then peered toward his feet where the older man stood. The man said something that sounded angry, but also made no sense. He shook his head. They were both frustrated, and the man spoke to her.

She walked around the table and took Angst's hand. "Um, how do I tell her I'm married?" he asked aloud.

She giggled and placed her other hand on his forehead.

"Wait, did you understand me?" he asked.

She said something that sounded like a different language than she had been speaking previously.

"Does that mean no? What if I said you're strikingly attractive and my wife would beat me if she knew I was holding hands with such a lovely young woman?"

She blushed a bit, and spoke again in what sounded like yet another language. The first language came from the back of the throat, the next rolled off the tongue silkily, and the third used odd clicking sounds.

"What if I said that attractive young women like you made me feel old and fat?"

The woman giggled once more. "I would say you shouldn't be so hard on yourself?" she said in an airy voice.

"Hey, I understand you." He pulled on the hand he'd spent so much time holding and kissed it. "Hi, I'm Angst."

She gently removed her hand from his and blushed again, very becomingly. She executed a little curtsy. "I'm Aerella."

Angst sat up slowly, with every muscle and joint screaming

in pain. He awkwardly swung his legs around to a sitting position where they dangled over the edge of the table. Scar made his way over and sat in front of his feet, waiting patiently. Angst reached down to pet him.

"I can fix language for your friends now," Aerella said. "I could understand yours fine, but it was complicated finding a translation. I'll go get them."

"Wait. You understood me all along?" Angst asked in surprise.

She winked and smiled before turning to leave the room.

"Everyone did," replied the man in a guttural voice. He sounded tired and wary. "No wonder your wife beats you. Is your name really Angst?"

"Heh, yes, yes it is." Angst leaned and reached to shake hands with the man. His friends entered the room and walked over to the table. Everyone seemed relieved that he was all right, but Angst could sense that they were all troubled by what had happened. He introduced them. "This is Rose, Tarness, Dallow, and Hector," he said, indicating each one in turn.

"It's a pleasure to meet you all. Welcome to Gressmore Towers. Please call me Anderfeld, and you've, uh, met my daughter, Aerella."

Daughter? Angst raised his eyebrows, and Rose snorted. Aerella had just finished touching everyone's forehead. "I'm sorry for any discomfort I caused by holding your hand for so long," apologized Aerella. "I needed some time with your language and physical contact makes the translation process quicker."

"Shame, and here I was hoping it's the local custom," Angst lamented facetiously.

"It's not," Anderfeld warned.

"What do you mean, the translation process?" asked Dallow, his curiosity hungry.

"The people here are from many different places. Magic imbued in the towers allows us all to communicate, but this requires a complex spell of translation." She handed Dallow a book. "I believe you were trying to read this while waiting for Angst to recover. You should be able to now."

He touched it, and his eyes flashed white momentarily before he handed the book back. "Fascinating. I was concerned something was wrong with me. Thank you."

"You're a reader?" Anderfeld asked.

Dallow nodded and smiled. "I would very much like to spend some time here," he said, looking at the books hungrily.

"I think that's an excellent idea," Anderfeld agreed, studying Dallow before turning to Angst. "But first I have much to discuss with Angst. Aerella, would you mind showing everyone our city? We can all meet again shortly at dinner."

She nodded and walked toward the entrance. "Please come with me," Aerella said cheerfully, waiting for the group to follow her.

Everyone paused uncertainly and looked at Angst.

"Think you can keep from dying for awhile?" Hector asked.

"I promise, no touching anything I don't understand. For now," Angst said with a huge grin. He held off wincing and groaning until after they'd left. "That really hurt."

"That's because, by all rights, you shouldn't be alive. Al'eyrn tend to pop out of existence when holding two foci at the same time." Anderfeld's thick gray eyebrows furrowed with confusion. "I don't completely understand why you're still here."

Angst had cocked his head to one side and attempted to clear out his ear with a finger. "I think the translation isn't coming across very well. Did you say Al-y-airn? What's a foe-key?"

"Al'eyrn and foci. Yes that's almost correct." Anderfeld observed him analytically. He walked around Angst, examining his armor, tapping it in several places with the back of a knuckle. He shook his head with frustration and sat hard in a sturdy, high-backed chair. Anderfeld put his large hands together and rested them on his chin thoughtfully. "Angst, what year is it?"

Of all the questions he had expected to be asked, this was not one of them. "Uh, well, it's 3039."

Anderfeld's expression had been one of deep reflection, but

this was immediately washed away by a deeper sadness. "Who passed the sword to you, Angst?"

"Passed? It was a decoration I grabbed in a moment of need." Questions were beginning to build in Angst's mind, but he decided to wait.

"A decoration?" Anderfeld asked with a mocking laugh. "After two thousand years, are all traditions gone? What about the other foci?"

"Two thousand years? Others? Anderfeld, I don't mean to be rude, but I don't know what you're talking about."

"The others. The foci, the armors, the tomes, the Vivek?" The blank look on Angst's face seemed to answer Anderfeld's questions, and he pointed at Chryslaenor. "This is all that's left?"

Angst looked over to where Chryslaenor hovered and merely nodded.

"Then the burden you carry is very great, Angst," Anderfeld said profoundly.

"It always has been," Angst said with a sigh. "I have questions, but I don't feel like we have much time. I can't say I begin to understand what's going on here," he looked around the room, "or even what you're talking about, but Ehrde is facing a crisis, and I think my friends and I are the only ones who can make things right."

"What's happening in the world? Please tell me," Anderfeld said patiently. He seemed to be a man used to listening, and giving counsel.

Angst explained what little he knew about the Vex'kvette and the creatures that had been created by it.

"It sounds to me like magic is breaking free again, but why would it need to?" Anderfeld's brow furrowed once more.

"Magic breaking free? Magic isn't even legal," Angst replied defensively. "Even the magical creatures have been hunted to extinction. Anderfeld, I don't know how things work here, but magic had almost been completely wiped off Ehrde until the Vex'kvette appeared. Now, magic creatures are back and eating people."

"That's what the fools get for trying to dam it up. It's like stopping a river. The water still has to go somewhere." Anderfeld slammed his fist on the desk. "Balance has to be maintained, and now it's being restored forcefully. What about your sword? How did you come by that? Tell me everything."

Angst told the story in its entirety, from lifting the sword to locating Gressmore Towers.

"So one of the most powerful weapons in the world had become your kingdom's biggest joke?" He chuckled mirthlessly. "Fate often has a cruel sense of humor."

"Where do the swords come from?" Angst asked.

Anderfeld sighed deeply. "They are the foci, relics of power and purpose. At one time, there were dozens, but these may be the only two left. I honestly don't know where they came from. I only know that they've always existed."

"You've used that term, Al'eyrn, several times. What does that mean?"

"It's the word we use for someone who bonds with a foci. You became Al'eyrn when you merged with Chryslaenor, giving yourself to your foci and becoming its conduit. It all comes together when the music starts making sense, doesn't it?" Anderfeld said with a knowing smile, as though Angst could relate to the experience.

They sat silently for a moment while Angst absorbed this information. He wanted all discussion of Al'eyrn and foci to end here. "Anderfeld, can you help us? I don't know how to stop what's happening, but my friends and I need assistance. We have no mounts and little time, but we have to find the source of this thing before more people are hurt."

Anderfeld nodded thoughtfully. "I believe we can help each other, but I require some time to research and think about what we've discussed." He stood and walked to the door. "First, let's eat. You're probably hungry after your...ordeal. I'd like to ask your friends some questions, and answer some of yours about Gressmore Towers."

* * * *

CHAPTER THIRTY

There was a polish to the evening. Everyone had enjoyed a warm bath and a fresh change of clothes as their own gear was cleaned and repaired. They filled the seats at one end of a long dining table with Anderfeld at the head. Angst made sure to sit directly across from Aerella, but unfortunately also within punching distance from Rose. Scar slept fitfully by a warm fire, which blazed behind Anderfeld.

The feast they enjoyed was both elaborate and exotic. Spicy roast bird with sweet meat, sugar-glazed vegetables, various types of breads, and enough wine to even make Tarness happy. Everyone was excited about their tour of Gressmore Towers, sharing with Angst some of what they had learned and about how large the city was.

After dinner, Aerella questioned them about the outside world—not only the restrictions on magic, which seemed to upset her, but the various kingdoms, politics, people, and events. She seemed hungry for details, and everyone provided what information they could.

An hour passed quickly as they discussed world history. Aerella finally paused to sip wine, giving Angst the opportunity to ask a question of his own. "How is it none of us have heard of Gressmore Towers?" He quickly followed up with, "No offense, of course."

Aerella looked up from her glass toward her father.

"This is complicated," Anderfeld began, taking a deep breath. "Angst, do you, or any of your friends, know what that is, or should I say, what those are?" He pointed to the swords, which hovered on point tip between the two men.

"No, not really. Stating the obvious, they're swords with magical properties that allow us to do things we wouldn't otherwise even attempt." Angst made eye contact with Anderfeld and decided to open up a little. "There seems to be something more in them, like a...consciousness buried in there, for lack of a better word."

Anderfeld nodded and smiled. "I don't know what they are

either, and I've had mine for over two thousand years. My father had it for two hundred years, as did his before him. Neither of them knew what it was or where it came from. Each generation has passed it along with whatever knowledge they could share. The rest has been learned from experience and bonding to become Al'eyrn."

"Al'eyrn?" asked Dallow. "Wait, did you say two thousand years?"

Anderfeld ignored him and continued. "We know what the swords look like, and what they can help us do, but let me share what we found Dulgirgraut to be capable of. Two thousand years ago, there was a war that had raged on for a quarter century, devastating every corner of Ehrde. We were attacked by forces far too powerful even for our magical defenses. I'd done everything in my power to stop the attack, and was near death when I made the mistake. I willed Dulgirgraut to protect my people at all costs."

Anderfeld paused and let out a deep sigh. "I remember saying that specifically, 'at all costs.' We've been here, just like this, ever since. Not a single day has passed for any living soul in Gressmore Towers."

There was a long pause before Dallow said, "That doesn't make sense. Where does the food come from?"

"Mr. Dallow, consider what I've said. Time hasn't passed. There's no tomorrow for us, only today. After dinner we will sleep, and when we wake, it will be today once more." Anderfeld's face was filled with concern and crushing guilt. "We've been living the same day, over and over, for two thousand years."

31

Ivan stumbled through the forest, holding his stomach with one hand and his cheek in the other. His face hurt all the way to his soul, and he couldn't stop uttering his new favorite curse. "Angst."

Lost in the woods and surrounded by looming danger wasn't the ideal setting to plan revenge, but there was some vague comfort in the anticipation of making Angst dead with his own hands. The magics…no, not just the magics, that *sword* would be the main obstacle in killing the man. Ivan's hatred for the sword was rivaled only by his abhorrence for Angst. This was no mere grudge. This hate was a living entity with angry tendrils coiling into every corner of Ivan's mind and body.

The stinging numbness in Ivan's cheek had spread to his forehead and scalp before crawling down his back like the lingering caress of an unwanted lover. He reached up to scratch the top of his head and pulled out another clump of hair. Ivan took a deep sobbing breath as he looked at the dark hair with bloody roots resting in his hand. That breath was filled with the sickeningly familiar smell of sweet honey and maple syrup. He was near the Vex'kvette.

Panic and disorientation swept through his body. Ivan's head throbbed, and he tripped over his own feet, sending him tumbling down a steep hill. He rolled uncontrollably, cursing at every rock or tree root he reached for and missed in an attempt slow his descent. The bottom of the hill gave way to a sudden drop. Ivan fell into open air before landing ungraciously on his belly in the softly glowing Vex'kvette.

It took several dazed moments to figure out that he would have to rise to continue breathing. He was covered from head to toe in the iridescent slime, which filled every breath with the vomit-inducing smell. Ivan rolled and struggled and was finally able to prop himself up enough to stand. The mud was thick to his knees, and attempting to plow through it in heavy plate armor took every ounce of his considerable strength.

He was still gathering his bearings when he realized the Vex'kvette was flowing like a river and he was fighting against it. The numbness that had been working its way down his back collided with a host of new sensations crawling up his legs. The glowing muck seeped through every opening of Ivan's armor as he struggled forward. Under his armor, his skin felt like curdling milk as the ooze traveled to his torso.

In a panic, Ivan struggled faster to reach the ledge. From the middle of the Vex'kvette, it had seemed scalable, but up close, the wall of dark wet mud was at least fifteen feet tall and went straight up. He wrestled with slick clay and roots and rocks for ten minutes until the sensation of drying mud on his chest became painful, as though the muck were trying to make its way into his very pores.

Ivan ripped off his gloves and frantically grappled with his chest piece. His hands were slick, making it impossible to unbuckle the armor. He tried reaching beneath the metal to wipe the orange goo from his skin, but felt like he was only rubbing it in.

Ivan cursed Angst once more. He needed room to breathe and space to take off the armor. It felt like a film of ooze now covered his entire body, and he was desperate to be rid of it. The other side of the river seemed level with the ground, just close enough to reach. With a deep breath, Ivan pushed away from the cliff wall and coaxed his muscles into wading back across the Vex'kvette. Halfway, the ooze was waist deep and the undercurrent pulled at his feet. Everything was so heavy. He was so tired it took all his energy and focus just to inch along the slippery ground. The smell choked away his remaining breath and, once again, tears streamed from his right eye, above the cheek Angst had attacked. Ivan felt himself give up as the Vex'kvette swept his feet from underneath him, engulfing him in glowing orange.

As he drifted along with the current, helplessly consumed by the ooze, his thoughts were on the humiliation wrought by Angst. It had been continuous, and embarrassing, and it hurt. He dwelled on these thoughts for what seemed like an eternity. They burned and roiled in his brain for days until, finally, the anger renewed his strength. He drew on this fearsome power to fight and claw to the surface. Ivan pulled his face free of the muck and drew a deep gasping breath. He crawled, slowly, so very slowly, to the nearby bank. When Ivan finally reached ground, he dragged himself out of the Vex'kvette with hands he didn't recognize and passed out.

* * * *

The castle was quiet. The usual hustle and bustle of soldiers and staff had been replaced by a somber wariness. Friendly nods and smiles were gone as people shuffled their feet and stared at the floor. An overwhelming sense of guilt had taken over, as though everyone had been pressured into helping a friend do something terribly wrong and now bore the weight of that secret. The sense of urgency had been replaced by a feeling of morose wrongness.

Rook entered the large throne room and cautiously inspected the perimeter. Guards stood between the tall marble columns that outlined the room. The queen sat on her throne, lost in conversation with the new advisor, a tall man dressed in bright clothes, who reached into the air dramatically with his hands as he spoke. The man sat to her right, resting on the edge of the king's throne. To the queen's left stood the princess, openly glaring at the advisor as though she'd caught him stealing.

Rook knelt before the queen and bowed his head. "I'm here to report, Your Majesty."

"Where is Tyrell?" Queen Isabelle asked tersely.

"He has taken ill. It seems—"

"Report, then," the queen ordered curtly.

"Every magic-wielding person we could find in the capital has been placed in the dungeon." Rook swallowed hard, and his shoulders struggled to hold up his armor.

"Excellent. How many of our soldiers were lost?" Isabelle asked, smoothing out her gold and crimson dress.

"None, Your Majesty," Rook answered.

"None? Were the magic wielders that incompetent?" the odd-looking man questioned, sounding a bit disappointed.

"I don't know." Rook paused, as he would've typically said 'Your Majesty' or 'sir,' but Aereon didn't appear to have a title. "It's, well, you see, they all came willingly."

"They what?" Aereon and Isabelle asked at the same time.

"We had expected a battle, even planned on casualties, but there was nothing. We didn't even have to bind them. They lined up to be taken." Rook shook his head in confusion.

"So...fine...then we are safe now. Right, Aereon?" the queen asked, seemingly hungry for her advisor's approval.

Rook coughed to clear his throat. "That's not all, Your Majesty."

The queen sighed, obviously wanting to return to her conversation with Aereon. "What else, Rook?"

"Something is wrong. They came willingly, but they refuse to speak and they won't eat," he said, trying not to shuffle his feet. "It's as though they aren't really there."

"You aren't making any sense. You said they were all in the dungeon!" Isabelle fumed.

"Yes, my queen. It's taken over a week to round them up. To go that long without eating...at least one should need medical care by now."

"Are they using magic to escape at night while staying in the dungeon during the day?" Aereon asked as he stood, rising from the edge of the king's throne.

"I don't know, but that's what I would assume," Rook said reluctantly, unwilling to share any information with this man.

"Then kill them," Aereon advised.

"Sir, they aren't even fighting us," Rook shot back.

"As the queen's advisor, shouldn't you investigate the situation yourself?" Princess Victoria interrupted.

Aereon looked at the princess, his gaze lingering as he painted her with his eyes and licked his lips before accepting her challenge. "Take me to the dungeon, soldier."

* * * *

Aereon followed Rook out of the room. As he departed, the queen became quiet and reserved, focusing on something far away.

Victoria shivered in disgust as she watched Aereon leave. "Mother?"

Isabelle didn't respond. Victoria leaned forward to inspect the glass eye and found a maelstrom of dark angry clouds.

"Mother, you have to stop this. There's no reason to imprison the magic wielders. It's madness. He wants to kill them!" Victoria proclaimed urgently, hoping to snap the queen from whatever held her attention.

"It's for the safety of Unsel. You'll understand when you're older, child," Isabelle replied distractedly.

Victoria stood in front of her mother and grabbed her shoulders, forcing the queen to face her. "How could you trust this stranger? How could you let him sit in Dad's seat? You've threatened war for less."

Isabelle's brow furrowed for a moment then she blinked rapidly as if coming out of a trance. She made brief eye contact with Victoria before gasping loudly. The queen cowered and winced, and light flashed in the glass eye. The flashes stopped, and Isabelle became distracted once more.

"I'm finding Tyrell, and we're going to fix this," Victoria announced in disgust and stormed out of the throne room.

Angst

* * * *

When they arrived at the dungeon entrance, Rook was shocked it didn't stink. The stench of torch oil and sweaty prisoners had always stolen Rook's breath. But now it was as though someone had freshened it with spring air from a mountaintop. He led Aereon down several flights of stairs to the underbelly of the castle. The advisor had said nothing since leaving the queen, but appeared more and more wary as they descended.

"Why do castle builders always have to bury dungeons so deep underground?" Aereon asked rhetorically.

"Sir?" Rook glanced at the advisor. "I suppose to keep people from escaping."

Aereon grabbed the back of Rook's armor and pulled the soldier to a stop. "I didn't require a response from you. Now show me to the prisoners. I want to be in and out of this vermin-infested hole as quickly as possible."

Rook took a deep breath, barely restraining his desire to beat the man unconscious. "I couldn't agree more."

They arrived at the bottom of the stairs to find a burly guard in dark leather armor sitting at a table. "You'll need to sign in for him, too, Rook."

Rook signed a thick book to get access for himself and Aereon. The guard checked the signature, nodded, and stood to unlock a sturdy iron door. Aereon knocked on the door as they passed through, as though to verify its durability.

In spite of torches every ten feet, the dungeon was dark, cold, and clammy. Unlike the castle, which had been built from various colored stones, the dungeon was more like a cave that had been carved out of the solid ground. They walked down a long stone tunnel with more iron doors on both sides. At the end of the hall was a door much larger than the rest.

Rook stopped in front of it and faced Aereon. "This is where we've been keeping them. It's the largest cell and typically reserved for groups of rioters." He opened the door to show an enormous cavern-like room that held several hundred people.

Everyone looked up at their arrival, but they remained oddly quiet.

For the first time since leaving the queen, Aereon acknowledged Rook as though he were a person. "Thank you," he said with a greasy grin. "Please allow me a few minutes to question some of the prisoners."

"Go ahead," Rook offered, gesturing to the magic wielders with his hand.

"I mean to say, I would like a few minutes alone with them." Aereon's grin wasn't as friendly now, and he moved his arms about oddly as he spoke, as though painting a picture in the air with his hands.

Rook smelled something strangely familiar, something distracting, like a perfume. Then he remembered it was the flowery scent his wife had often worn before she died. A sadness entered his soul, but then he shook his head to clear the memory. It took a minute before he could focus on Aereon. "I'll need approval from the queen before I can leave you here alone. Unless I'm locking you up, of course."

Aereon smirked. "You're an intelligent man with a strong will. I respect that. Let's go back to the queen and ask for approval. She seems to be a patient woman with spare time for bureaucracy."

Rook considered this before finally relenting. "Five minutes. That's it. If I hear anything I don't like, I'm coming in," he warned.

* * * *

Aereon smiled triumphantly, and Rook left, closing the door behind him. Most of the prisoners ignored Aereon, sleeping or pacing or scratching at the dirt. Two men sitting in the middle of the room looked up. One was old, his tan linen clothes well-worn and a gray beard covering most of his wrinkled face. The younger man's light brown hair was matted with sweat. He stood and wiped his hands on his coarse homespun shirt.

"What do you want?" the young man asked defiantly.

Aereon looked away from the young man to observe the others. "There aren't any prisoners in here, except for you two."

"Wait—"

Aereon pointed three fingers at him, and the young man flew to the wall, slamming against it silently. He attempted to yell, but no sound escaped his mouth, and he struggled against a constant barrage of wind that held him in place. The other prisoners instantly blinked out of existence. The older man stood and waved his arms in circular motions. A pitch black hole opened beneath Aereon's feet.

"I see," Aereon said as he hovered over the hole. "So he created the image of fake prisoners while you provided the real ones with the means to escape. I wonder where this portal would've sent me." He casually moved aside to solid ground. With his other hand, Aereon pointed three fingers at the older man, lifting him into the air. The two magic-wielders clawed at their throats, gasping for breath. Aereon brought his fingers together, and the men silently slammed into each other face-first. Their bodies continued to smash together until their hands dropped from their throats and hung limply at their sides.

Aereon lowered his hands, and the men fell to the ground in a heap of blood and dust.

"Guard, come quick," Aereon called out leisurely.

Rook pushed through the door and looked around the room. He ran to the two men at the far side of the prison cell. "Where are the others? What happened?" Rook efficiently rolled the men onto their backs. Their faces were broken and gushing blood.

"It was very odd. I asked a few questions, they began attacking each other, and everyone else disappeared," Aereon said with feigned innocence. "Are they all right?"

"Alive, but I don't know for how long," Rook said, eyeing Aereon warily from across the room.

"I believe they were using magic to trick the guards this entire time. We must inform the queen," Aereon declared.

Rook nodded reluctantly. "I agree, but we should hurry. I should send the physicians down here as well."

CHAPTER THIRTY ONE

* * * *

Rook and Aereon left the room, closing the door behind them. After several minutes, the ground shuddered beneath the two injured captives. The dungeon floor loosened like sand, and the men sank into the ground. When they were completely submerged, the shaking stopped, leaving no sign anyone had ever been there.

32

"Do you mean to tell me you're reliving the same day over and over again?" asked Tarness in disbelief.

Anderfeld nodded.

"If this is so, how would anyone even realize it?" Dallow asked, his brow furrowed beneath his blond bangs.

"Most living here don't, but for me, there's the book." Anderfeld looked miserable, like he was revealing every skeleton in his closet. "The book you saw me reading when you first arrived. It, too, seems to be magical. Whatever I write can be read the next day. Every morning, I start by reading the first page, which explains the curse, and then the last. The more I read, the more I remember...well, more like vague, dusty recollections of memories. Then I begin researching a way to escape this...prison that saved our lives."

Angst's eyes were wide. "You mean to tell me you think those...things did this to you?" He pointed at Dulgirgraut and Chryslaenor hovering beside each other in the corner.

"I believe Dulgirgraut tried to protect us, Angst, but something went wrong. Maybe it was too much for even foci to resolve." Anderfeld pulled on his face with his hand, as though attempting to wipe away his weariness.

"So how can we help? What can we do to break this curse?" Angst asked.

"Please excuse me," Aerella stood abruptly and left, apparently upset.

Anderfeld waited for her leave before replying. "I don't know that there's much you can do, Angst. I have some theories I'd like to discuss with you all tomorrow." He drank some wine. "I may be able to help *you*, though. There's much I can teach you of your sword. Tomorrow I would appreciate the opportunity to fence a bit and show you some of what I've learned from Dulgirgraut. Maybe I can give you some pointers, so you can avoid some of my mistakes."

The offer was surprising, but how could he refuse? "Um, thank you. Your help would be most welcome."

Anderfeld stood. "I need to make notations in the book before going to bed. I'll try to be thorough, but you may have to spend some time reminding me what transpired today."

"Of course," replied Angst, at a bit of a loss.

Anderfeld left. A young man entered and offered to lead them to their rooms for the night.

"I'll catch up with everyone shortly." Angst went in search of Aerella. Something didn't feel right.

* * * *

Aerella stood on a white marble balcony overlooking the city. She'd obviously been sobbing, and was now trying to catch her breath.

"I'm sorry if I'm interrupting," offered Angst as he approached her.

Aerella seemed surprised to see him, and wiped her eyes quickly. "I apologize. It was rude of me to leave so abruptly."

"Not at all. It sounds like you don't often get guests," Angst said in a quiet voice.

"Only once every several thousand years or so. I guess I'm out of practice," she said, trying to make a joke. She brushed the long mane of hair off her shoulders.

"You have to be the most attractive two-thousand-year old woman I've ever met," Angst said with a broad smile.

Aerella giggled politely. It was a pretty sound that seemed to contradict her expression. "Mr. Angst. Does your wife know what a flirt you are?"

"She admonishes me for it frequently, yes."

She stepped close to Angst, close enough to remind him of Victoria. Aerella shivered and looked frightened. Since she'd first held his hand, Angst had felt an uncomfortable connection with Aerella. He'd wondered if it was the sword, and that her own father held a similar blade. Now he felt like the wrong person—that maybe Dallow should've been here to share some wisdom, or Hector to cheer her with a bit of roguish charm.

"What is it? What bothered you so much that made you leave?" Angst asked.

She looked up at him and parted her lips. He did not lean forward to kiss her, but instead stepped back slowly. Her lips closed, and she shivered again. "You understand so little of our nightmare. You see, you could have kissed me." She moved forward once more and spoke in a quiet voice. "You could still kiss me, or hold me, or slap me, or rape me, and tomorrow I would never know." Aerella began to cry again.

Angst pulled Aerella into a comforting hug. She sobbed into his shoulder, but after a short time, she calmed. "Thank you, Angst. I wouldn't have expected you to do any of those things, but you have to understand what we're facing. I will never know all the wonderful or terrible things I've done over the last two thousand years, and I can't live with it anymore."

"I want to help, but I don't know what to do," Angst said, gently pulling away. "Is there anything that will remove this curse?"

"My father seems to think so," Aerella hesitated, on the verge of breaking down again but deep, calming breaths seemed to help. "Just remember, the sword chose you for a reason. Most of the foci select people who want to be heroes, Angst. Becoming a hero requires sacrifice."

"So I'm learning," Angst said under his breath. "Do you know what he wants of me?"

"I really can't say."

The tears streaming down her cheeks stopped him from asking any further questions about her father or Gressmore.

"Is there anything I can do for you?" he asked, hoping for even the tiniest chance to hero something this evening.

"Um, would you mind holding me a little bit longer? If I happen to remember today, I'd like the memories to be happy."

"Well, I'm not one to argue with my elders," he said with a wink, and she giggled.

Angst gave her another long hug that didn't feel as awkward as the first one. Maybe he'd passed a test...but would she remember that tomorrow? She sighed a lot, her sobs calmed to breaths, and she finally pulled away.

"Mr. Angst, be sure to tell your friends to wear their armor to bed," Aerella warned sincerely.

"Our armor? What happens if we don't wear it?" Angst asked, confused once again.

"Maybe nothing, but I'm not completely certain. I do know you weren't wearing these robes when you arrived, and you may not be wearing them tomorrow morning when you awaken."

* * * *

"*It's freezing!*" yelled Rose, waking everyone within earshot.

Angst's eyes popped open, and a grin crept across his face. A quick look at their surroundings confirmed Aerella's warning. They lay on the cold ground, scattered about the entrance of Gressmore Towers.

Angst meandered over to Rose, who was shivering so hard she was barely able to hide her nudity. On one knee in front of her backpack, she was desperately trying to cover her sizeable breasts with her left arm while yanking out clothing with her right. It didn't help that Scar was sniffing her ear with his wet nose. "What happened? Why are we on the ground?" Rose asked, sounding furious.

Dallow walked over to stand by Angst, eyed a mostly naked

Rose, and quickly spun away. "It, uh...well, it seems," he stuttered, "we've been expunged. Whatever curse causes them to relive each day kicked us out with nothing but our belongings."

"Can I lend a hand?" Angst offered generously in an overly polite tone.

Rose was fumbling to pull on her leather britches with trembling hands. She'd given up covering her breasts in favor of expediency. "Ass! No, just...turn around, would you? How did you guys get dressed so fast anyway?"

"Um, we're very efficient," Angst replied, sounding quite innocent, and turned away as slowly as possibly.

Hector showed up and immediately started laughing. "Didn't you tell her to change last night?" he asked before Angst could stop him.

Rose stood there for a moment, glaring at him before shivering her way into her top. "Har har. Fast dressers," she said through chattering teeth. She glared at Angst and Dallow while slipping on her boots. "Don't talk to me today."

Angst grinned triumphantly, but Dallow looked shocked. "What did I do?"

"Old Man there planned this, but you looked," Rose snapped. She turned her back on the three and walked away.

They all shared quick, boyish grins. "That was clever," acknowledged Hector. "How did you know she sleeps naked?"

"Doesn't everyone sleep naked?" Angst asked.

"Eew, no," Hector answered. "On a different subject, do we go back up there?"

"Yes, we go back in," Angst confirmed.

"Angst, what are the chances we get stuck up there forever? What happens if the curse takes us in as well?" Hector asked.

"Anderfeld thinks he has information we can use, and I'd like to try and help them as well," Angst stated.

Dallow coughed. "While I hate to admit it when Angst's right, the coincidence of Gressmore Towers appearing, and someone living there with another sword like Angst's is too much to ignore. I agree that we need to go in."

Angst smiled at Dallow in appreciation. "I can't imagine what could be accomplished if everyone supported me like that all the time." He slapped Dallow on the shoulder and gathered his things.

Tarness and Dallow followed his lead and left to grab their packs.

"I wasn't actually done discussing this yet," said Hector, the only person not putting stuff together.

Angst looked over his shoulder at Hector. "You can discuss it up there with us, or wait until we come back, it's up to you."

* * * *

They all met at the entrance, where Rose kept her back to everyone. She slapped her hand against the carving and was the first to pass through.

Dallow glanced at Angst. "I think you really pissed her off this time."

"I'm sure she'll get over it soon enough." Angst pushed into the dark room only to trip over something and fall flat on his face. He turned in time to see Rose pull back her foot.

"Oops," she said, and did a fake little curtsy while covering her mouth.

Before Angst could reply, Dallow had stepped through and tripped over Angst, landing on his stomach. Hector soon joined the pile of men at Rose's feet. Rose lost herself to laughing when Tarness stumbled over the three just as they were starting to stand. Scar barked, his tail wagging excitedly at this game and happily licked a few faces. After several minutes of gathering gear, rubbing bruises, and waiting for Rose to catch her breath, they made their way to the other entrance.

"Is this going to go on all day between you two?" Hector snapped at Angst and Rose loudly.

"Yes," Rose answered in her sweetest voice.

Everyone replied with grunts.

"Do you think we'll have to go through the introductions and translations again?" Tarness asked.

"I hope so. The translation was my favorite part of the visit," Angst replied eagerly.

"It depends how detailed Anderfeld's notes are. I'd guess they'll have to translate, but will most likely be expecting us," Dallow answered.

* * * *

"Is it always sunny?" Angst asked as they entered the bright courtyard. Aerella was already waiting for him. He held out his hand with a smile and a nod.

"That's right, you didn't get the tour yesterday. Angst, this place is amazing," Dallow said excitedly. "I couldn't begin to explain how any of it works, but the stone towers hold the entire city over the clouds."

"Wow, that's... I don't even understand that." He turned away from Dallow to face Aerella and smile. "You don't remember anything from yesterday do you? You're still strikingly attractive."

Rose patted Angst's shoulder. "Don't you remember anything from yesterday either? She can understand everything you're saying."

Angst had forgotten, and Aerella giggled at Rose's comment. Rose took the woman's hand from Angst. "I'll help her with translation today, while you go get maimed," Rose said wryly as she pointed at Anderfeld. "I hope it hurts."

The courtyard had cleared of people, and Anderfeld stood across from them, looking formidable. He'd shown up in full armor and already held Dulgirgraut in front of him with both hands. Anderfeld was baring his teeth like an angry dog, apparently hungry for this 'fencing' match, which made Angst wary.

"Are you sure I can't stay back and watch you two hold hands instead?" Angst said to Rose out the corner of his mouth.

"Ha. No. Now don't die, just get injured, and I may forgive you." She shoved him forward.

Angst kneeled to pet Scar, who sat next to him. "You stay

here."

Tarness gently grabbed Scar by the scruff of his neck. "I'll hold onto him, Angst. Good luck."

"Get him, Angst," Hector and Dallow said in support.

Angst looked at Rose and Aerella one more time before removing Chryslaenor with a sigh. Fighting against monsters, or people without giant magical swords, had been a challenge. Angst always felt at odds with Chryslaenor, trying to balance what he wanted to do with what the sword wanted him to do. In spite of this, Angst didn't remember ever being nervous about a pending fight. Until now.

Anderfeld advanced then stopped about twenty feet away from Angst, lowering Dulgirgraut. He bowed politely and said something Angst couldn't understand. Angst mimicked the bow but said nothing in response. Anderfeld lifted the sword again, this time holding the enormous blade horizontally in front of his face, as though preparing to defend against the first attack. He nodded. Angst nodded as well, locked his jaw in place, and ran at Anderfeld like a blur.

A streak of green light from Dulgirgraut cut through the air as Anderfeld met the first blow. Chryslaenor struck the other blade with a loud clang, appearing to shatter the green light in an explosion of colorful sparks. The giant swords blurred together in a maniacal dance of blue and green. Angst swung and parried, attacking and defending a constant barrage of crashing blows.

This was the first fight that truly felt like a challenge, and yet Angst held back until he realized Anderfeld was merely testing him. The older man didn't even seem to be trying. At this frenetic pace, it didn't take long for Angst to tire. Anderfeld deftly blocked a swing aimed at his head and held the sword in place, giving Angst a moment to catch his breath. A fair-sized length of Anderfeld's long, braided hair dropped to the ground, inadvertently sliced off by Chryslaenor. The older man smiled smugly, and Angst's frustration rose. He let Chryslaenor take over a little, but drove the fight with his will and growing frustration.

Chryslaenor led him forward, forcing Anderfeld to take a step back, and then another. The shower of sparks grew increasingly bright, obscuring his view, and burning the grass around them in a ring. There was a resounding crash, and both men flew back. Anderfeld landed on his feet with Dulgirgraut in the same horizontal position as before. Angst slowed himself by kneeling and extending his right foot. He dug a path of grass and dirt as he skidded to a stop.

At the very moment Angst was going to rush forward, Anderfeld lowered his sword and threw out his hand to signal a stop. Angst remained on one knee, attempting to control his rapid breathing and hold onto consciousness. Aerella ran over and placed her hand on his forehead. She stared at him with an odd expression, as though both impressed and concerned.

"Are you okay?" she asked, and he understood her words.

"I think I'm just old or something," he said between gasps before standing shakily.

Anderfeld was already in front of him, a broad hand extended to help him up. "That was a fine duel, Angst. It's been a very long time since I've gotten to enjoy such a match."

"Sorry about your hair." Angst pointed to the braid.

"It will be back tomorrow," Anderfeld replied with a smirk.

"Why aren't you out of breath?" asked Angst, disgusted with his own performance. "I hope I wasn't that bad."

"Not at all," Anderfeld said, patting him on the shoulder. "It's one of the many things we need to discuss, though. I never would've imagined one could use a foci, much less fight like that, without bonding." He shook his head in disbelief. "It took this fight for me to realize, Angst, but it seems you are not yet Al'eyrn."

33

"Gressmore was a city like any other, well, in the sense that it rested on the ground," Anderfeld began. "We were one of four cities scattered throughout Ehrde. Each was a place for the magi, or magic wielders as you call them, to study and live in peace," the large man explained as he paced around his library table.

Dallow was touching every book on the nearby shelves, desperate to absorb their contents as quickly as he could. Anderfeld hefted an old leather-bound volume that had been sitting by itself on a nearby podium. He closed it and placed it under one of Dallow's hands. Dallow blinked rapidly, surprised by the book's sudden appearance. His breath caught and his eyes widened momentarily. "Oh," he breathed, and the white glow from his eyes faded to their normal shade of brown. "Thank you."

"You're welcome." Anderfeld grinned then clasped his arms behind his back and resumed his pacing. "Gressmore was the oldest of the mage cities, and had the largest population. Most here can do magic, but not all. It isn't a trait like hair color or the shape of someone's nose. Your son, Angst, may look like you, but that doesn't guarantee he can wield magic."

"I don't have a son," Angst replied, more defensively than he had intended.

"Of course. What I meant to say was if you did have a son, he may or may not be able to wield magic," Anderfeld clarified quickly, looking slightly concerned that he may have touched a sore spot. "Everyone is welcome...or should I say was welcome?" He sighed. "There had always been peace until the foci started to appear." He dropped his hands to his sides in a gesture of helplessness.

Anderfeld stopped in front of Dulgirgraut and spun it like a top. He watched the sword turn as he continued his story. "There's no record of their arrival; they merely started to appear. Weapons, armor, and jewelry, all greatly enhancing the wielder's abilities, imbuing them with power no one had ever imagined. There were maybe thirty foci. Both the foci and the Al'eyrn who could wield them were coveted. It was the pride of a mage city to host multiple Al'eyrn, and it was that pride that started the war.

"Most foci seem to choose people of quality with good intent, but once bonded, the power corrupted some. They were all treated like royalty—or worshipped, if you were crazy enough to live among the Fulk'han." Anderfeld shook his head at this notion and then stopped the sword from spinning.

"People who couldn't wield magic were scared, and rightfully so. The war of Al'eyrn devastated Ehrde for decades, and only a handful of Al'eyrn bothered themselves with defending people that couldn't wield magic. At one time, Vex'steppe was the richest country in all of Ehrde. The devastation wrought by the war killed tens of thousands that lived there, leaving nothing but desert behind."

"Is that what happened? You were attacked by another mage city?" Hector asked as he mindlessly ran his finger along the scar on his jaw line.

"No, we were actually attacked by wyrms, beasts from yet another war. Wyrms belch a sort of liquid fire. Every mage city was suddenly defending themselves against forces beyond magic. To protect Gressmore, the Al'eyrn who lived here lifted the city on giant pillars, too high for crawling wyrms to attack. You may have noticed the blackened base of our obelisks? They were originally white until fire darkened them."

"Do you mean dragons? I thought they were only myths,"

Dallow said skeptically. "They also had wings in every story I've read."

"Yes, we started calling them dragons once they grew wings. Only weeks after Gressmore found its new home amongst the clouds, the attacks began again. By then, the dragons could fly." Anderfeld shuddered at the memory.

"All appeared lost, until father asked Dulgirgraut to protect us," Aerella said sadly.

"That's awful," said Rose.

"Have you ever tried leaving?" asked Dallow.

"Of course," Anderfeld replied with heaviness in his voice. "But walking outside the towers is the same as going to sleep at night. You still wake up the next morning in your bed to relive your day."

"So how can we help? Maybe if Dallow can make his way through all these books, he can learn something you can use," Angst offered.

"I'm going to see to lunch." Aerella excused herself, once again avoiding this conversation.

"If Dallow could help, or if you have any suggestions, we would be grateful." Then Anderfeld abruptly changed the subject. "I'd like to discuss what you're dealing with, and Angst becoming Al'eyrn."

"Can I go help with lunch instead?" Angst joked.

"I've never heard of someone not willing to bond with a foci. I'm surprised it hasn't killed you yet," Anderfeld said with concern.

"Actually, he's died several times," Tarness interjected. When Anderfeld's eyes widened with disbelief, Tarness continued. "It's happened twice that I know of, and always after long battles."

"Chryslaenor must be keeping you alive. That would explain your uncanny ability to continue living when you do something you shouldn't." Anderfeld seemed amazed at this revelation.

"Why do I have to bond with it? I already have one wife. I don't really care for another," Angst said, attempting to cover his exasperation with humor.

"You could've fooled me," Rose heckled under her breath.

"Bonding with Chryslaenor will imbue you with its power and its knowledge." Anderfeld sat up, expanding his chest with pride. "You will become one, a unified team with almost unlimited resources."

"But why do I feel if I let that happen, I have to give up part of myself?"

"Because you will. You have to sacrifice some of yourself." Noticing Angst's concern, Anderfeld continued, "But only to become more of who you truly are."

"And what if he chooses not to become Al'eyrn?" Hector asked.

"I could tell during the duel that Angst had become upset, and that's when he truly challenged me." Anderfeld faced Angst. "Under the right circumstance, it would even be possible for you to beat me, but I'm not the toughest opponent you will face. You can't rely on the timing of emotional outbursts to save you. There's too great of a chance that you and your friends will face true danger. I also fear that the foci will burn you out, that you'll die too many times for Chryslaenor to bring you back."

"What do you mean you aren't the toughest opponent we'll face?" Angst asked, feeling his body tense. "Do you know something about what's out there?"

Anderfeld shook his head and sighed. "Please remember what I've said about bonding. You won't succeed without becoming Al'eyrn. That's all I'll say on the matter."

"Good," Angst said with a winning smile. "About the Vex'kvette…"

"Without more information, I don't have any solid answers for you, but I may know how you can find the source of it."

* * * *

Aerella had returned with lunch. After sharing the light midday meal of bread and cheese, Anderfeld walked across the room to a wide wooden door and beckoned everyone to follow. It creaked loudly as he struggled to push it open. "This is an old project of mine started before the wars. I never finished, so it has some limitations, but I believe with practice it will help you find some direction."

He ducked to keep Dulgirgraut from bumping the top of the door jamb then raised his hand. A small orb floating at his feet glowed, followed by another, and then a third until a winding path of stairs was illuminated before him. "Be careful, there's no rail on the left side."

"If you're afraid of heights, don't look down," Aerella recommended as she followed her father. She lifted her blue robes to step carefully.

Hector was the first through the door, followed by Dallow and Tarness. They all gasped and Dallow called back, "Angst, you'll want to stay close to the wall for this one."

Angst walked through the doorway to find a long flight of stairs spiraling down around an enormous cylindrical room with a dark center. Stone stairs jutted from the walls, and a loud echoing click announced his first step down. After taking several more steps, Angst made the mistake of kneeling to inspect them. They appeared to be carved of shale, and should've been far too thin to hold much weight. Between each stair was empty space and below them, a very long drop into the dark.

Angst stood and tried to go back up the stairs only to find Rose standing behind him with a broad grin on her face. "Problem, Angst?" She moved closer to the open edge of the stairway and looked over at him. "Oh, wow, you really need to see this." She leaned over further and wobbled slightly.

"Rose!" Angst yelled as he grabbed her waist and pulled her to the wall.

She laughed so hard she was forced to sit on a step and catch her breath. Angst was holding onto his chest, his heart racing. Tarness had made his way back up the flight of stairs, quickly followed by Dallow and Hector.

"Oh, what now?" Hector asked as he eyed Rose.

"Angst isn't afraid of heights, he's afraid of other people falling," she informed them after her chuckles became manageable. Rose fluttered her eyelashes at Angst. "My hero!" she proclaimed then collapsed into laughter again.

"That wasn't funny!" Angst grunted and shoved his way past everyone to descend the stairs.

Hector was shaking his head. "You two never stop. Come on, we need to catch up before—"

The room was suddenly flooded with light, as though the roof had been removed and sunlight now poured in. Except it wasn't pouring in, it was pouring up. A massive glass dome covered the entire floor, with a giant fiery orb at its center, as though the sun had been captured and placed inside.

Anderfeld was waving everyone down the stairs. "Come, you'll want to see this," he said, pride clear in his voice.

The stairs ended at a ten-foot square platform where Anderfeld and Aerella stood. Dulgirgraut rested on a short, glowing cylindrical pedestal in the center.

"This helps channel some of Dulgirgraut so I can operate the memndus," Anderfeld said excitedly.

"I'm not completely sure I follow," Dallow said, tilting his head in curiosity.

"What my father is trying to say is that this memndus," Aerella pointed down at the dome, "can make a map, of sorts, but you need a foci to control it."

"You'll see, you'll see." Anderfeld waved Angst over to the platform. "Come. You'll need to watch closely so you can learn how to use it."

Angst carefully stepped onto the platform. Aerella took his arm and smiled. "It's fine. You'll like this."

"I'd recommend everyone else back up against the wall," Anderfeld said then waited for them to follow his instructions. Spread along the exterior, they all took a stair and pressed their backs to the cold stone wall. "Fine, and here we go."

Anderfeld turned away from Dulgirgraut to face two white obelisks that stood on the edge of the platform. They were similar to those that had guided Angst during the journey, except that these bore carved hand imprints like the one at the entrance of Gressmore Towers. Anderfeld placed one hand on each obelisk and then, hunching his broad shoulders forward, leaned into them.

The platform gently lifted away from the wall, and Angst was grateful for Aerella's arm. She continued to hold on as they floated around the dome. The small glowing orbs that had lit the stairs dimmed to nothing and an almost reverential hush filled the room.

Still pushing against the obelisks, Anderfeld gazed at the dome and focused with intent. The sun within the globe pulled away, shrinking to the size of a child's ball. Darkness surrounded the ball and seemed to push it to the far end of the dome, until the sun was completely out of view. Now the entire room was dark and the dome filled with stars.

"Pretty, don't you think?" Aerella asked.

"Very," Angst whispered. Then he paused and added, "The dome is nice too," making Aerella giggle.

A blue and green orb came into view, moving slowly until it reached the center. The orb quickly grew until half the hemisphere filled the dome.

"Is this Ehrde?" Dallow asked from the stairs, loud enough so everyone could hear.

"It is, but my Ehrde from two thousand years ago." Anderfeld leaned his head forward and shut his eyes in concentration. Four lights appeared on the map like distant stars. "This is the last known location of the four mage cities. You can see Gressmore here," he said as the northern-most light became brighter.

"Can we see the other cities? Can we look closer?" Dallow asked excitedly.

"As I said, I never finished the project. My hope is that if Angst can figure out how it works, you may be able to identify the source of what you call the Vex'kvette from this distance."

He removed his hands from the obelisks, and the hovering platform returned to its original place near the stairs. Anderfeld took Dulgirgraut from the glowing pedestal, and the dome instantly darkened. The small orbs illuminated the stairs with their cool light once again. Everyone along the stairs let out a collective sigh as though they'd been holding their breath while watching a dangerous performance.

"That was simply incredible," Angst said with admiration and wonder. "You made that?"

"I did." Anderfeld seemed pleased with Angst's appreciation. "Are you ready to guide the memndus?"

Angst looked at Aerella, who nodded at him encouragingly. "Sure. I'll be amazed if I can figure it out, but it doesn't hurt to try. Uh, does it?"

Anderfeld shook his head.

Angst set the tip of Chryslaenor in the center of the pedestal. After several anxious moments, a white glow appeared from the pedestal, the small orbs around the room dimmed, and the sun returned to its place inside the dome. His shoulders relaxed a bit.

"That's a good sign," Angst said under his breath.

Movement within the memndus was jerky as Angst attempted to navigate the view of Ehrde. After some time, an image of their planet once again appeared. It was spinning rapidly and seemed out of focus.

"This should be the Ehrde you know from your time, but you will need to concentrate," Anderfeld urged Angst patiently.

The globe slowed until it stopped spinning completely, and a trickle of sweat dripped down Angst's neck. Ehrde filled the dome as it had for Anderfeld.

"Excellent, Angst, you're learning fast," Anderfeld acknowledged. "I believe that is your Vex'kvette right there." He pointed at an ugly orange scar that crisscrossed the landscape like a spider web.

A headache was forming, and the light from the dome hurt his eyes as he opened them.

"It would appear that the greatest concentration of the Vex'kvette can be found near the capital of Fulk'han," Dallow said.

"If Fulk'han is in the same place I remember it, I would have to agree," Anderfeld stated.

"Can we see closer?" Angst grunted, concentrating on keeping the image of the globe still.

"You could if I'd finished it," Anderfeld said apologetically. "It has that potential, but..."

Angst's body shook as he forced the dome to zero in on the image.

"Angst, it really isn't supposed to do that. Please stop," Anderfeld said, placing a firm hand on Angst's shoulder.

Ehrde seemed closer though the image jerked about violently. A mountain appeared, and then a tree, and finally the base of Gressmore Towers.

Anderfeld was trying to pull Angst away from the obelisks. "What are you doing? You could break it!"

"It'll be back tomorrow when you relive your day. Let me be!" Angst yelled.

Anderfeld let go of Angst's shoulders, grunting in frustration at the abuse to his memndus. Rose, Dallow, and Hector knelt and held onto a stair as the entire room began to shake. The dome continued to flash random images of treetops as though looking through the eyes of a bird that occasionally blinked while in flight.

"Everyone hang on!" Anderfeld shouted.

"To what?" Tarness asked, gripping tighter to his stair and reaching for Rose to hold her in place.

The shaking suddenly stopped as the dome broke free of its base on the floor. It pulled away from the room, revealing an outline of the bright clouds and blue sky Gressmore towered over. Angst was gasping for breath, not only holding the giant dome in place, but guiding its internal map to a destination. After several very long minutes, an image of the castle in Unsel appeared. It flashed and then changed to show the inside of the castle and, finally, Princess Victoria pacing in her chambers.

"You have got to be kidding me! All this to catch a glimpse of the princess?" Rose said, her voice exhausted.

With a growl, Angst focused until the image adjusted to show the princess pacing in front of Heather.

"She's safe. They're both safe," Angst said with relief, gasping deeply. He let go of the image and the dome. They watched as it pulled away and tumbled into the clouds below, leaving nothing but the view of open sky and supporting obelisks instead of a floor. "But why is Heather at the castle?"

* * * *

"I was certain Anderfeld was going to kill you," Hector said the next morning, his words muffled by a mouthful of breakfast.

"I sort of thought he was more surprised that his memndus could do all of that," Dallow said in amazement. "Though, I think we would've been better served if you'd showed us more precise images of the Vex'kvette source."

"I needed to know that Heather was okay," Angst said matter-of-factly.

"That's who you were checking on?" Rose asked.

"We'll go back today and ask to use the dome one more time," Angst said ignoring her. "Since they relive every day, I'm hoping its back in one piece and we can get a better view of the Vex'kvette."

* * * *

At the courtyard entrance, they were greeted by Aerella, Anderfeld, and a team of red-robed men. Anderfeld was once again dressed in full armor, but this time his expression was angry and a thick green aura surrounded Dulgirgraut.

"Good morning," offered Angst. He held out his hand to Anderfeld, who replied curtly in the language they couldn't understand, refusing to take Angst's hand. He turned away, and Angst was surprised to see that the large man's long braid was still missing. Had he cut it off again?

Angst shrugged and looked back at his friends. "Odd. I guess we start from scratch one more time. This is my favorite part anyway." He offered his hand to Aerella.

She stepped away from Angst's hand, seeming upset to the point of tears. The red-garbed men joined hands and muttered something under their breaths. Their eyes glowed ominously.

"This isn't the same as yesterday at all. Wait, I can't move!" Hector exclaimed, struggling, though nothing seemed to restrain him.

"I don't understand! What's happening?" Angst looked around at his friends, who fought against their invisible shackles. He was the only one who could still move. "Aerella?" He looked at the young woman, but she turned her back on Angst, tears streaming down her cheeks. "Anderfeld, what's going on?"

Anderfeld looked upset as he pulled his great sword from his back and swung at Angst. Instinctively, Angst ducked and drew Chryslaenor. "I'm sorry I broke your dome, but is this really necessary?"

Anderfeld instantly became a blur of movement, and their swords met with a crash, showering those nearby in blue and green sparks. Anderfeld hammered away at Angst, and it took every bit of Angst's concentration to defend each blow. When he swung back, Angst felt like he was beating a steel wall with a hammer, and it hurt to the bone.

Angst lunged at Anderfeld's midsection and was easily parried. Anderfeld was a master with the sword, an Al'eyrn with years of experience. Every one of Angst's attacks were readily met or blocked.

After several minutes, Angst tired. The fight drained him, and wracked his body with exhaustion. His sword reached through his arm, singing to his mind, begging to help. It was foreign, and intrusive, making the battle within as challenging as the battle with Anderfeld.

Anderfeld still looked upset, and attacked with a ferocity Angst had never experienced. Angst's arms were quickly losing their strength, and he knew it wouldn't be long before Anderfeld overtook him. At the point when all seemed lost, his eyes met Anderfeld's, and he saw sadness. Anderfeld blurred past Angst and buried his sword deep in Rose's chest. The look of shock on her face was soon replaced by the distant stare of death.

"No," he said in a very quiet voice. His body began to shake.

Anderfeld slowly pulled the sword out. It was covered in her blood, and her lifeless body fell helplessly to the ground. He raised Dulgirgraut over Dallow's head, ready to strike.

"*No!*" Angst yelled in fury. Chryslaenor's song burst into his brain, filling his body with so much energy it burned. In the time it took Angst to blink, he found Chryslaenor buried to the hilt in Anderfeld's back.

Anderfeld exhaled one last time. "I'm sorry, Angst. Thank you."

Anderfeld fell to the ground, and Gressmore Towers was gone.

34

Victoria paced the length of her room, complaining loudly about her mother's recent nonsensical decisions. The princess flung her thin, pale arms about with stiff, angry gestures, pausing occasionally to pull up the sleeves of her dark green silk dress. Her room was painted in warm ivory and gentle pink, pretty and understated. The path Victoria walked was a clearing between small piles of scattered clothes from that morning's attempt to find the right thing to wear.

Heather sat on the edge of Victoria's bed, listening patiently. These "conversations" had become a daily ritual since Heather came to live at the castle. The princess would invite her into her room several times a day, and proceed to stomp about in frustration. It was everything Angst had told her, and any small concern Heather had hidden about the relationship between Victoria and Angst was now completely and utterly quashed.

Victoria stopped to face Heather, pausing briefly to catch her breath. "Now he won't even let me in his room!"

"It sounds to me like Tyrell is very ill—" Heather began patiently, collecting loose strands of curly brown hair then clasping it all together into something more manageable.

Victoria quickly cut her off. "He's not that ill. Tyrell's locked himself up for the last week because he's upset and thinks Aereon's replaced him."

"*Has* Aereon replaced him?" Heather asked, raising an eye-

273

brow.

"No. Well, maybe for a moment, but not really. He can't." Victoria placed a hand on one hip and gestured with her free hand. "This is hard to explain because it isn't common knowledge. There's an accord, of sorts, between Tyrell and my mother. He's more than just Captain Guard."

"You mean...they... Are you trying to say they're romantically involved?" Heather asked as diplomatically as she could.

"Oh! No. Well, I don't think so." Victoria pondered this for a moment before continuing. "Tyrell is the queen's champion. He's made the oath to protect her till death. It's a tradition for the queen and king to choose champions."

"So one day you'll also choose a champion?" Heather asked, secretly concerned that Victoria may have already made the choice.

Victoria's dark thin brows furrowed in thought. "I hadn't really thought of that. I guess I will."

Heather wanted to change the subject. "Tyrell's always seemed to be a man who lives by the book. I think honor actually flows through his veins. If he felt your mother was in danger, he would do something."

"That's the very reason he won't rise against her, she doesn't *appear* to be in any danger. Still, I need him to see what's going on, to see how much Mother has changed." She sighed and plopped onto the bed next to Heather. "How do I make him see?"

"Victoria, you are the royal princess, are you not?" Heather prodded as though this should be enough.

"For all the good it does me." Victoria pouted, pulling at a loose string on her dress.

Heather had learned quickly that reasoning with Victoria when she was in a snit did not work. She also found that the princess was easily offended, forcing Heather to choose her words carefully. She took a deep breath of bravery before stating in a voice devoid of emotion, "Fetch me some water."

Victoria whipped her head around to stare at Heather in disbelief. "What did you say?"

"You heard me. Fetch me some water." Heather looked at the princess coolly.

"No," her voice incensed and eyebrows raised.

"Why not?"

"Not only was your manner rude," she said, without hiding her indignation, "but that's not my job. I don't 'fetch.'"

"Then what is your job, Victoria?" Heather asked, hoping the point would be understood quickly before there was room for misunderstanding.

"I'm the royal princess, heir of Unsel. My job is to learn how to rule so I may one day become queen," the princess stated, arching her back automatically.

Heather smiled as friendly a smile as she could, hoping to relax the tension. "Then what would the queen do?"

"She would order the guards away and command Tyrell to..." Victoria's shoulders dropped as the obvious pervaded her thoughts, and she smiled sheepishly at Heather. "I swear, I'm usually much smarter than this."

"Of course, dear, you've just never been put in this position before," Heather said with relief. "Now go kick Tyrell out of bed and command him to make things right."

Victoria nodded as she stood. "Thank you," she whispered, giving Heather a quick hug. "Would you mind staying to help me change?" Without waiting for an answer, she walked to her large closet to choose appropriate attire for yelling at Tyrell.

"It's time for Angst to come home and have his job back," Heather muttered under her breath.

* * * *

Unwelcomed sunlight poured through the windows to slap Tyrell awake. He groaned loudly and looked over to see Victoria sitting in his favorite reading chair. She was resting in the high-backed seat with her elbows on the worn armrests and her fingers pressed together against her chin.

"Victoria. What are you doing in here?" Tyrell demanded weakly as he attempted to block the light.

"Get up," Victoria commanded.

"I told the guards not to let anyone in," Tyrell mumbled, trying to ignore her.

"I dismissed your guards, now get up!" This time she was much louder and sat straight in the chair.

Tyrell winced and wiped several beads of sweat from his long face. He'd never felt so sick, and couldn't seem to catch his breath. But ever so slowly, Tyrell sat up in bed. Covers fell from his shoulders, revealing several old scars slashed deep across his muscular chest. He turned to set his feet on the floor, and remembered he was in undergarments. She blushed furiously but continued to glare at him.

"It isn't appropriate for you to be in here, Victoria. I'm going to see you to the door so I can get some rest." Tyrell rested on his knees to hold himself up.

"You may address me as Your Majesty. Get dressed."

Tyrell leaned his head to one side until there was a noisy pop, then rubbed his neck. In spite of the sweat and fever, he was mostly certain this was real and not a hallucination. His eyes were more or less focused, so he looked at the young woman. She was in formal attire, wearing a full-length burgundy brocade dress. The outfit had enough embellishments that he wondered if Victoria hadn't raided her mother's closet when choosing her outfit. She was even wearing her tiara.

"Listen to me, young lady—" Tyrell began with a bit more energy.

She immediately cut him off. "You are failing my mother."

That startled him from his stupor. "Wh-what?" He gaped at her.

"You failed her weeks ago when she was attacked, and you're failing her now," Victoria snapped.

"You don't understand," he pleaded.

"No, you don't understand, but you will. Either you get up, get dressed, and meet me in the hall in five minutes or you will be relieved of your commission as Queen's Champion and dismissed from the castle." The princess stood and glared at him once more before calmly walking out of the room.

* * * *

Four minutes later, a furious Captain Guard stepped through the doors of his room. He straightened his dark navy tunic and swiped at the sweat dripping from his light brown bangs. He looked awful, and inwardly, Victoria dreaded doing this to him.

"Where to, Your Majesty?" he asked curtly.

Victoria fought to keep the sympathy out of her eyes. She now had a sense of the true burden her mother bore as queen. "Follow me," she commanded and led Tyrell down the hall.

They made their way through the castle halls without a word. Victoria could feel Tyrell glaring daggers at the back of her head. The Captain Guard was angry and ill, his breathing strained with every step. She could only hope his anger would fuel the strength he needed to face what was coming.

They stopped at the hallway that led to the dungeon entrance, and found a long line of bedraggled people waiting to enter. Most guards reluctantly urged the prisoners along, but several appeared happy and taunted their captives.

Tyrell stepped in front of the princess and walked to a guard. "What's going on?"

"Sir?" the puffy-faced guard asked in a flat tone, his confusion indicating that Tyrell should know the answer already.

Graloon stopped before Tyrell and the guard. His hands were shackled and a trickle of blood from an ugly cut on his large bald forehead was drying on his cheek. He spat on the floor in front of Tyrell. "You really think this is going to protect the queen, locking all of us up? We aren't the ones who attacked her!"

The guard jabbed Graloon in the stomach with the bottom of his halberd, making the man grunt loudly and bend over in pain. Several of the prisoners' hands glowed ominously. Graloon raised his hand and shouted, "No, not like this."

Tyrell grabbed the guard's arm before the man could strike Graloon again. "Stop. That isn't necessary. Who ordered this?"

"Aereon presented us the queen's order several days ago. This is the last of the magic wielders." The guard did not strike Graloon again, but didn't lower his weapon either.

"Where would I find Mr. Aereon?" Tyrell asked curtly.

"He's usually with the queen, in the throne room. Sir."

"I'm going to say this once," Tyrell yelled to everyone present. "If a single guard harms one of these prisoners in any way, every guard in that man's regimen will be shackled and thrown in the dungeons." He glared at the guard in front of him. "Do I make myself clear?"

The guard remained quiet but lowered his weapon. Tyrell faced Victoria, still angry but not at her. "I'll apologize later, Your Majesty, when I can do so properly. Thank you. Now, I would recommend you stay in your quarters until I've seen this through."

35

Angst woke shaking. The ground beneath him was terribly cold, but that wasn't the only thing making him tremble. He felt feverish, and his head throbbed as though he were sick. He pushed himself to his hands and knees and looked around. Angst was still at Gressmore Ruins, the ancient remains of a city that had long ago passed into history. He began to sigh with relief until he realized something was wrong. Where was Gressmore Towers? Flashbacks of his recent visit to Gressmore flooded his thoughts.

Conflicting images and memories assaulted his mind. Memories of a long journey to Gressmore Ruins seemed to occupy the same space in his thoughts as a journey to Gressmore Towers. The pounding in his head became excruciating as more conflicting images filled his thoughts. He sought help from his foci, desperate to break free from this war in his mind. Several feet away, a glowing Chryslaenor stuck out of the ground. He crawled to the beacon and used it to pull himself up. Angst stood and yanked his sword from the mud.

He ignored the ruins and attempted to concentrate on blurred memories of Gressmore Towers. The steady throbbing in his head coalesced into a single, sharp point of pain. When he tried to sort through memories from both journeys, the one that happened and the one that didn't, the pain became intense. Something warm and wet trickled down his cheeks and pooled over his lip. When he reached up to brush it away, he found blood dripping from his ears and nose. Angst shivered uncontrollably before doubling over to empty the contents of his stomach, and then collapsed.

* * * *

Hours later Angst woke with a cool hand on his forehead and a mass of warm fur breathing slowly at his side. His right arm was numb where Chryslaenor rested on it, and Scar was curled up against him. Angst tried, desperately, not to dwell on the fact that he now had two distinct memories fighting to occupy the same time in his mind. Even thinking about it made his vision blur, his stomach roil with nausea, and the throbbing in his head intensify. Focusing on one journey, the trip to Gressmore Towers, helped calm the storm of memories, and his stomach, but it was a struggle.

"I tried to push it off your arm, but it wouldn't budge," a pretty young woman said, appearing worried. "It was glowing for a while, but stopped when your ears and nose stopped bleeding."

Angst sat up at the behest of the woman tending him. He lifted Chryslaenor from his arm as he stood. Scar's tail wagged sleepily as the pup also woke from his nap. The painful battle of memories dispersed as he held the blade aloft. He remembered the towering obsidian pillars. He remembered holding this woman's hand. He remembered fighting. There was another sword like his. Panic set in, and he looked about the ruins frantically.

"Rose!" he yelled. He stumbled forward, hoping to find his friends, hoping to find Rose. It took all his concentration to focus, but he remembered that other giant sword had been shoved into her chest. He remembered her blood. Was it possible for her to heal from that? Panic clutched his throat at the thought of her death. In his distraction Angst tripped over Tarness's leg and barely caught himself. He placed Chryslaenor on his back and knelt by his large friend. Tarness was breathing, but didn't wake when Angst rolled him over to his back.

"Tarness, are you all right?" Angst asked quietly as he gently patted his friend's face.

Tarness muttered something that sounded like "Maarja" then rolled to one side and curled into a ball. Several drops of blood fell from his nose onto the grass.

"Leave him be, Angst," the woman advised as she approached him.

Looking at the attractive young woman hurt, as though she didn't belong here. She offered Angst her hand, which he took out of habit. "Aerella?"

She smiled weakly, looking almost as lost as Angst. "I'm glad to see you're all right."

"I'm not all right. Nothing is all right," Angst barked, looking down at Tarness. "Is it?"

"Tarness will be okay. He just needs to rest."

Angst nodded and looked about, collecting his thoughts. It was midday. A cold mist had settled about them and the dark clouds overhead looked on the verge of cutting loose. He needed to gather his friends and make camp before sunset. Angst stomped away and began searching frantically through the ruins. It was a mess of giant, weatherworn black stone, broken pottery, and pieces of statues half-buried in the tundra. Scar ran ahead, sniffing at the ground, and Angst instinctively followed the lab pup.

"What are you doing?" Aerella asked, trailing close behind.

"I'm looking for my friends," Angst said loudly as Scar led him around a corner to find Dallow. The dog wagged his tail with pride, and Angst rewarded him with a pat on the head. Dallow was balled up on his side, shivering from the cold or possibly struggling with the same conflicting memories of their last few days. Angst knelt beside his friend and lifted him with a grunt.

"What's going on? What happened to us?" Angst asked Aerella as he stumbled forward with Dallow in his arms.

"I don't know how much you remember, so this will be hard to explain," she began. "After the memndus fell, you and your friends left Gressmore Towers. My father willed Dulgirgraut to keep us both awake through the night so we would remember your visit. It took all his strength."

"Your father," Angst fought to sift through his warring thoughts to find a name, "is Anderfeld?" Angst winced with the effort as he laid Dallow near Tarness.

"Yes," she replied with a catch in her voice. "He told everyone at Gressmore that you and your friends were enemies. When you arrived, the guards had been ordered to detain your friends and wait while he dealt with you."

Angst shook his head in confusion. "That makes no sense. Why would I be an enemy? I remember admiring Anderfeld...I think."

Angst had the feeling she was going to say something he didn't want to hear, and he clumsily stumbled away again in search of the others. Scar once again took lead, and Angst followed. Aerella scrambled after him, pulling at her blue robes as they caught on bits of ruins. She was quiet for a while, trying to catch her breath.

"He liked you as well, which made the whole thing so hard for him. For both of us," she said, her words ending in a sob. "He'd tried everything to break the curse. He willed Dulgirgraut to stop it. He even killed himself several times only to wake the next morning as though nothing had happened."

Angst found Hector sprawled on his stomach, his legs jerking spasmodically, blood pooling in his ear. With another loud grunt, he slowly dragged his friend back to Tarness. After setting Hector beside Dallow, he leaned forward on his knees to catch his breath.

"Aerella, I barely remember any of it... I remember you, a little, and a fight. Rose died, and I killed..." Angst stood straight and peered at Aerella, though she wouldn't look at him. "Your father. He killed Rose! I lost my temper, and I killed Anderfeld." His voice trailed off.

Aerella was openly crying now. Gasping for breath. She wouldn't turn to face him, and was holding herself as tightly as she could. Angst stood by her, quite helpless. He hesitantly rested his hands on her shoulders and waited.

After several very long minutes, she wiped her face and turned to him. Her eyes were filled with two thousand years of sadness. "It wasn't your fault. I can't forgive you right now, but it wasn't your fault, Angst. You saved my people."

"But I killed..." Before he could finish, she touched his mouth to stop him. He gently pulled her hand away. "How did that save your people?"

"It broke the curse," Aerella said between sobs. "But something went wrong. He thought Gressmore Towers would be here, now. I believe killing him sent Gressmore back to the beginning and changed time."

"That doesn't make any sense," Angst barked, dropping her hand. He leaned over to pet Scar. Squeezing his eyes shut, Angst willed the dog to find the one person he really needed to find. "Scar, bring me to Rose."

Scar's brown eyes momentarily flashed blue and he barked before running back into the maze of ruins. Angst pushed past Aerella to follow. She appeared ready to cry again but composed herself before running after them.

"I could tell how much you care for her, and I knew she was the one. I knew her death would force you to action," she tried to explain.

"Shut up!" Angst growled as he moved faster to get away from her.

"You hadn't allowed yourself to bond with the sword. Without that anger, you would never have been able to kill him," she said between deep, gasping breaths.

"Shut up!" he yelled, waving her away.

"Don't you see, Angst, the only way to break the curse was to kill my father with a foci. You never would've willingly killed him. It's not in your nature," Aerella pleaded with him.

"So you had him kill Rose? That was the only way? That's insanity!"

Scar barked and wagged his tail as he sat next to Rose's body.

She lay on her stomach, sprawled unnaturally. She was so still. Angst dropped to his knees, and his eyes welled with tears. As gently as he could, Angst rolled her onto her back and lifted her.

Rose lay in his arms limply, and Angst carried her body back to the others. Who would keep him grounded now? Heather was his love, Tori fed his ego, and Chryslaenor gave him power. But it was always Rose who slapped him on the arm and reminded him how very human he was. Guilt slowly carved a pit into his stomach as he looked at her. "Rose, I'm sorry."

Rose's eyes opened wide, causing Angst's heart to skip a beat. "What?" she asked. Her shock softened and her voice became dreamy. "Angst?" Rose raised a hand, nearly touching his face, then allowed it to fall to her chest and went back to sleep.

"I had the Red Guard create the illusion of Rose's death," Aerella said so quietly Angst had to watch her mouth so he wouldn't miss anything. "It was the only way to trick you into killing him."

His memories were becoming clearer, but his emotions were more conflicted than ever. Angst had been used. His friends had been put in danger. Rose had died, and then he found her alive. Angst had killed an innocent man. This storm of thoughts and memories were an all-consuming tempest that could easily wash him away. He shook his head like a dog shakes off water, took a deep breath, and sighed it all out.

"Are you okay?" Angst asked Aerella.

Startled, she looked at him with disbelief. "I'm not certain I'll ever be okay. I don't understand why I'm here, or what I'll do. I'm forcing myself not to think about all of that."

"Everything happens for a reason," Angst said simply.

"Aren't you upset with me?" Aerella asked, obviously dumbfounded by his sudden change in attitude.

"I'm absolutely furious at being used, and distraught at having killed...an innocent man, but my friends are safe," he said, relief and exhaustion tempering his voice. He looked down at Rose in his arms. He'd never picked her up before, and was shocked at how light she was.

Aerella was still distraught. "I'm alone. What will I do?"

"You'll come with us. I need you," Angst said, nodding at his slumbering friends. "And I have a feeling they'll need you too."

"I doubt your friends remember anything," she said apologetically. "They may remember over time, but it will take weeks, or months. Or they may never fully remember."

"Then it sounds like we'll have to rely on each other," Angst said as he carefully lowered Rose next to Dallow.

Aerella nodded bravely.

"Let's see if we can find our things. They need blankets and a fire to be comfortable while they rest this off."

36

Tarness grunted and moaned, rocking from side to side with his eyes squeezed shut. Rose wrestled with her blankets, and they seemed to be losing. Hector coughed and pressed hard on his temples with the heels of his hands. It had been a very long night. Angst and Aerella tended to everyone until dawn when fevers broke and their faces stopped leaking blood.

"What's happening? I feel sick," Dallow said in a hoarse voice as he sat up. "Why aren't you sick?"

"I was," Angst said quietly, "but that was almost a full day ago."

Angst was reluctant to approach Rose, who was on her feet before the others and assisting in spite of being a bit grumpy. He wanted to give her the biggest hug ever, but knew she would just be confused, so he kept himself busy. Aerella and Angst brought water to everyone, helping them through the worst parts of their recovery. At first, his friends blindly accepted Aerella's presence, but soon began to question her as the effects of Gressmore slowly wore off.

"Not that I don't appreciate your assistance, but who are you?" Hector asked Aerella.

She looked at Hector thoughtfully. "For now, the best explanation I can offer is that I'm with Angst."

They all looked over at Angst. Rose rolled her eyes, and Dallow shook his head.

"Now you're finding them in the middle of nowhere?" asked Tarness.

"What does he mean by that?" asked Aerella, raising an eyebrow. She stood quickly and straightened her blue robes.

"This should be interesting," Rose scoffed as she sat on a nearby stone, crossing her arms and waiting for Angst to explain.

"All kidding aside, I would really like to know why she's here and why we're sick." Hector stood shakily.

"Angst, you really can't tell them what happened. I don't think it would be safe. They don't have foci to protect them," Aerella said, gently placing a hand on his shoulder.

Everyone asked questions at the same time, each one louder than the last, fighting to be heard.

"I don't understand!"

"What is she talking about?"

"What happened?"

Angst wanted to answer with a definitive, "Shut up!" Instead, he struggled with patience while they struggled for answers. As he waited for quiet, Angst looked at each of them talking over each other and fighting off the effects of Gressmore. He was responsible for this—for their pain, and for the danger he was dragging them through. Angst shivered as a cold fear crept along his skin. He was so grateful they were safe, that Rose was alive, but for the first time since leaving, he was truly scared for them.

Angst stared at Rose instead of avoiding her. It wasn't his usual typical childish playful gawking or serious contemplative look. This was worry on the cliff's edge of panic, specifically for her. He shivered again, and everyone became quiet.

"Angst, what's wrong?" Rose asked.

Angst tore his eyes away from her. "Nothing. Nothing's wrong. Actually, when everyone's feeling better, it's time to head home."

"Wait, what?" Tarness asked, looking around at the others.

"Dallow was right. Mission accomplished." Angst feigned a smile. "I need to go find Scar. When I get back, I'll help all of you pack up." Without another word, he turned away and walked into the ruins.

* * * *

Aerella started to follow, but Rose grabbed her sleeve. Rose squinted, concentrating on her face, struggling to recognize her. "You're Aerella, right?"

Aerella nodded. "Yes, Rose. I'm surprised you already remember."

"It's starting to come back, but thinking about it hurts." Rose shook her head as if to clear it. "Leave Angst be, for a bit. Dallow or I will go chase him down after he's done pouting."

"All right, but maybe just Dallow should go," Aerella said politely, pulling her long mane of brown hair back from her shoulders. "If your memory is healing this fast, I have a feeling you'll understand soon."

Rose looked at Aerella, perplexed, but reluctantly agreed.

Tarness seemed baffled and rubbed his large hands together in frustration.

"What's wrong?" Dallow asked as he wiped a bit of sweat from his brow.

"Did I hear Angst right or am I still sick?" Tarness asked. "Did he say 'I'll help all of *you* pack up?'"

"That's what I heard too. Pretty odd if you think about it. Like we'd let him go by himself," Dallow answered. Everyone looked at him in surprise. "I may have been opposed to continuing, but I'd never actually leave him to do this alone. If he's determined to see this through, I'll be there with him."

The stubble on Hector's scraggly chin had become a beard, but the scar along his jaw still showed through the hair on his face, making him look even more dangerous than before. "Since our leader is off living up to his name, I'll go ahead and ask. Does anyone have a suggestion about transportation? We're obviously going somewhere, and we're probably late getting there."

They looked at each other, sharing shrugs or curious glances.

"Do we have enough gold to buy mounts?" asked Tarness.

"Maybe," replied Hector, leaning against a piece of old fallen obelisk, "but from who?"

"I wish we could just appear where we need to go," suggested Dallow, "but nobody's been able to port for centuries."

Aerella stepped directly in front of Dallow. She squinted and balled her hands into fists that shook. Then she simply wasn't there anymore. The briefest moment passed, and Aerella popped into view several feet away. Everyone jumped or yelped in surprise.

"It's fine for short distances, and I can teach you how to do it, but it's an exhausting and slow way to travel," Aerella said, a bit out of breath.

"Who are you?" Rose demanded. "I mean, I know your name, but what are you doing here?"

Aerella looked at Rose. Without a word she reached forward and plucked one of Rose's long red hairs.

"Ouch. What was that for?" Rose said, grabbing her head. She stood quickly and leaned forward as though preparing to tackle the other woman.

Aerella cupped the hair into her hand and whispered to it. Her hands began glowing yellow as she spoke in Acratic. Dallow watched and listened very closely, obviously taking careful mental notes. After several moments, Aerella opened her hands and let the hair blow away.

Rose was still rubbing her head. "Well, that was useful. Next time try pulling hairs from your—" Rose's jaw dropped.

A bright red buck was galloping toward them. It veered slightly as it approached and then stopped beside Rose, as if waiting. This deer was like no animal she'd seen. Its body and legs were formed from thin strands of sapling branches, and the red hue came from flowers that bloomed all about the buck's body. Leaves rested on its back like a saddle, and its eyes seemed to be made of rippling water. The creature was stunning.

Aerella walked beside the buck and patted its neck. "This is your swifen. Consider it a mount made of elements that represent you and required a part of you to create. It will be yours for-ever, Rose, appearing whenever you call. After I teach you, of course."

Rose touched the flowers gently, and the buck shivered. "It's beautiful."

Aerella smiled. "Who's next?"

Tarness, Dallow, and Hector all raised their hands and stepped forward simultaneously.

Tarness's steed was magnificent—an enormous stallion as solid as its rider and seemingly formed from the obsidian and marble ruins. Hector's swifen was an angry-looking panther shaped from dark, wet sand with frightening silvery eyes that flashed ominously in the light.

Dallow stopped Aerella from calling his swifen, and plucked a hair from his own head. He cupped his hands around it as he'd seen Aerella do and looked to her for confirmation. She nodded encouragingly and motioned him to continue. Nothing happened the first two attempts, but after some counseling from Aerella, a tawny gazelle with tall horns strode toward him and nuzzled his shoulder. Dallow's swifen appeared to be carved from dark hardwood, and the saddle was made from lighter-colored wood-en shavings.

"Thank you so very much," Dallow said excitedly as he hopped onto the back of his gazelle. "That was my first spell."

Aerella nodded at him. "You learn very quickly, but I think it's time you find your friend."

* * * *

Angst swung his sword at nearby undergrowth then swung again, and then, with a grunt, swung a third time. He poured his frustration into every motion. Small trees and bushes splintered and with each strike, leaves flew up into the air. He inadvertently hit a nearby rock, splitting it in half. Upon inspection, he found Chryslaenor undamaged. He then attacked everything he could reach.

The sword wasn't giving him any magical boost. Angst wasn't moving with unbelievable speed, or dancing with uncanny accuracy, he was simply hitting things. After several minutes, tiredness overtook him, and his mind wandered. He thought about how he'd driven Ivan away. He thought about Tori. How desperately he missed Heather. Of Anderfeld, an innocent man, dying at his hands. About Rose being…being killed. He could still see her sliding off Anderfeld's sword, blood dripping from the blade. He'd failed to save her, and now he felt helpless to protect any of them. Angst struck out with the sword again.

"Is this helping?" asked Dallow.

Angst startled and turned, instinctively pointing Chryslaenor at Dallow's face. He quickly lowered it. "No, but eventually I'll work it out of my system."

"It usually doesn't take this long for your tantrums to pass. What happened over the last three days?" Dallow sat on a nearby stone and prepared to listen.

Angst had lifted the sword to begin relieving more frustration. "If I tell you before you remember naturally, it could make you even sicker than you feel now. Or that's the impression I get from Aerella. So on top of everything else, I can't even share what's going on with one of my oldest friends."

"I'm starting to feel much better," Dallow said encouragingly. "Why don't you put the sword to rest and tell me."

"Well, let's see," Angst said challengingly, pointing Chryslaenor at the ground and leaning on the giant sword. "In the last three days, I watched Rose die, I was tricked into killing an innocent man, and I broke time."

Dallow reeled at this for a moment then rubbed his temples. "Rose died? Changed time? I don't understand." He looked about, as if confused by his surroundings.

"See? And I haven't even told you any of the details," Angst said in frustration.

Dallow did his best to take it all in while fighting the effects of Gressmore. "What makes you think you can do this alone?"

"What do you mean?" asked Angst defensively.

"Everyone back at camp feels like you plan to dismiss us," Dallow replied. "Everything that's happened to this point has been a struggle. Everything that's happened has required us all to work together. If it's going to get worse, what makes you think you can do it by yourself?"

"I don't—" Angst lost his words at the sight of Dallow's wooden gazelle in the distance. "What in Ehrde is that?"

Dallow whistled, and the gazelle trotted over. He crawled on-to its back. "This is my swifen. Not bad, huh? Let's go make you one."

* * * *

It took Aerella three attempts —each time yanking out one of Angst's coarse hairs— before she could get his swifen to appear. When it arrived, everyone looked at it, perplexed. The swifen was an awkward-looking ram that was fat in the belly yet had very long legs. The 'elements' part didn't work out very well as the creature was covered in bits of shoddy, rusted metal squares that appeared hammered together like a patchwork quilt with sharp edges.

"Just what every hero needs," Angst muttered as he stepped away from the monstrosity. His swifen kept bumping him with its horns.

"Aw, Angst, it looks like you made it yourself," Rose said with a laugh.

"Every time it moves, it sounds like its dragging a bag full of weapons," Hector observed dryly.

"Maybe it could use some oil," Tarness offered helpfully. "Where to next?"

Angst sighed. "Well, now that you're all feeling better, it's best for you to go back to Unsel and warn everyone of what's going on out here." He reached out to pat the side of his swifen.

"What about you?" asked Rose, her voice raised an octave or three.

Angst avoided looking at her. "I have something to do. I'm sure I'll be right behind you."

"You aren't a good liar, Angst. Not to me." Rose stood right in front of Angst, making it hard for him to look away. "What are you going to do?"

"You don't understand," Angst said loudly, still avoiding her eyes. "You have to go!"

"You're right, I don't understand." She stepped inside the circle of personal space most people allowed. "Why don't you explain it to me? To us?"

"I can't," he replied, finally looking at her.

"You can't what?" Rose asked unrelentingly.

"I…" Angst took a deep breath, fighting back the emotion that suddenly choked his throat. "I can't keep you safe. Any of you. You don't have one of these stupid things to protect you," he thumbed roughly at Chryslaenor over his shoulder, "and I'm not good enough with it." In spite of his efforts at control, he was now yelling at his friends. "You may not remember the last few days, but I do. I can't…" There was a catch in his breath, and he stared into Rose's large brown eyes. "I saw you die, Rose. That can't happen again. I couldn't live with myself…"

She inched forward and cautiously held him for a moment. Dallow, Tarness, and Hector all moved closer as well. Angst sniffed and stared at the ground while stepping back from Rose. "Quite the hero, huh?"

"You're doing fine." Dallow patted him on the shoulder. "We're all with you, Angst, whether you like it or not. So where to next?"

Angst wiped his eyes and nose, embarrassed at his outburst. The silence around them was overwhelming, and he finally nodded. "It looked to me like we need to go to the capital of Fulk'han," he said, seeking acknowledgement from Aerella.

She nodded in agreement while summoning her swifen, a majestic-looking white tiger made of flower petals.

"Unless these *swifen* are incredibly fast, we've got a long trip ahead of us," Hector said with a smile. "Shouldn't we get going?"

37

The forest floor shook violently as he stepped forward. The ground gave way under his foot, though he couldn't truly recognize it as his own. He didn't like looking at his feet, or his hands, and the only reason he'd even consider glancing at his reflection was morbid curiosity about how much he'd changed. In spite of everything, he'd never felt this good in his entire life.

He heard a scream, and stopped to look down. A lone woman on the highway had dropped to her knees at the sight of him. He was always surprised at how much smaller they seemed since the change. Ivan leaned forward to hold her still and noticed his hand was almost large enough to wrap around her waist. He wondered, for a moment, if he was still growing. This thought soon passed as he studied her. Ivan savored the way she groveled and shook with fear, almost appearing to be worshiping him. It felt right, yet there was something missing. She was frumpy, her clothes were disheveled, and her short red hair unkempt from work and travel. The woman was older than he liked and puffy with weight. Ivan didn't want her to look this way, so he would change her just like he'd changed.

Ivan concentrated. Her hair became a brighter red and poured from her head to lengthen past her waist. This made her look up in surprise, and she squeaked out small whimpering sounds. The hair attached itself to her back along the spine, like a horse's mane. She shuddered in pain, but only started screaming when a long tail grew from the base of her spine. He chuckled to himself as her cry of anguish reached him. The woman fell to her side, rolling and roiling on the ground as her skin color changed from pale blush to light yellow then orange and pink before finally settling on a deep shade of purple.

Now on her stomach, the woman tried crawling away. He gripped the end of her new tail between two fingers and yanked. Flipping onto her back the woman kicked away while trying to pull her new tail free. She opened her mouth to scream and a long snakish tongue shot out. With both hands she pushed the tongue back in and kept her mouth covered. Her eyes widened in horror, and continued widening until they were unnaturally large for her face. Then she screamed once more as her body began to reform. Bones crunched and muscles tore loudly as Ivan adjusted her shape to his liking.

He was almost finished, she was just about perfect, when a flock of small birds darted past his face, distracting him. Ivan swung his monstrous arm to wave them off, and a black cloud filled with sparkling lights, like stars in the night sky, trailed behind his hand to engulf the departing birds. When Ivan finally returned his attention to the woman, it was too late. He'd stopped her metamorphosis before finishing, and now she lay still on the ground with blood pouring from her mouth.

Ivan admired his latest creation, but there was still more that could be done. Larger breasts, thinner waist, and maybe the next one he changed could be a bit taller. They should also live; they would all be so much more fun alive. He kicked her aside like discarded trash and continued down the long road to find another one. He was only a day away from the Fulk'han capital, and wanted to have everything just right by the time he got there.

* * * *

Tyrell's lungs rattled painfully as he huffed for breath. He gripped his chest and quickened his pace as he approached the main hallway to the throne room. Just as he began to turn the corner, a hand around his mouth pulled him back. The hand was as gentle as it could be under the circumstances, and smelled clean. It was only that, and decades of training, that kept Tyrell from defending himself and gutting Rook. Which was fortunate because in the time it took Rook to say "shhh," Tyrell could've killed him. Twice.

Tyrell glared at Rook and pulled the other man's beefy hand away. He was about to warn Rook never to do that, ever again, but the man was pointing to the adjoining hallway. Tyrell followed Rook's finger and peered around the corner to see a tall, lanky man facing away from them. Aereon. Tyrell reached for the sword at his belt, ready to dismiss this "advisor" from the kingdom permanently. Rook grabbed Tyrell's hand to stop him, shaking his head. He pointed once again at Aereon and the hallway.

Tyrell reluctantly turned to watch. Aereon's arms flailed about more wildly than usual while his torso stayed perfectly still. Tyrell wanted to slap the man for looking so foolish. The flailing continued for several minutes, accompanied by clicks and whistles. Then the odd movements suddenly stopped, and Aereon knelt into a deep bow.

Behind Aereon's bowed head, a short, husky shadow turned to look around with quick jerky movements. Something about it was disturbingly familiar. Aereon didn't budge as the shadowy form took flight and zoomed down the hall, past the corner where Rook and Tyrell hid. In the light from their adjoining hallway, Tyrell caught a glimpse of purple feathers and a silvery steel beak.

Rook nodded in acknowledgement when Tyrell turned to look at him in surprise. Rook jerked his head in the direction of a nearby room, the Captain Guard nodded and followed.

"Good timing, sir," Rook said after closing the door behind him. "It's good to see you up and about."

"You can thank Princess Victoria for that," Tyrell said between short breaths. "I think we have a queen in that one," he said in response to Rook's questioning look.

Rook smiled at this, and then frowned. "No disrespect meant, sir, but you look terrible."

"That would be exactly how I feel," Tyrell sank down on a nearby plush chair and gripped his chest. They were in a lavish sitting room, where important guests often waited to visit the queen in her throne room. Elaborate tapestries adorned the walls and kept the room very quiet.

"Was that it? Was that the creature that attacked the queen?" Rook asked Tyrell, gesturing with his thumb over his shoulder.

Tyrell nodded, feeling a bit better after sitting. "I hope so."

"I don't understand," Rook said, cocking his head to one side. "What do you mean you hope so?"

"I truly hope there's only one of those things," Tyrell said, sitting up straight. "What were you doing, Rook? How did you happen to be here?"

Rook smirked mischievously. "I don't trust him, Captain." When Tyrell nodded in agreement, he continued. "I don't like how he entertains the queen, I don't like how he leers at the princess, and I don't like how he speaks to us." He pointed a finger up and made a circle, 'us' meant everyone who worked at the castle. "So I've been following him, or it, or whatever he is."

"What do you mean, it?" Tyrell pressed.

"Well, sir, no disrespect to Angst and his friends, but Aereon seems to be like the magic wielders, yet even more bizarre," Rook's voice trailed off as he looked at the closed door. He remained quiet as footsteps passed by outside the room and continued down the hallway. "I think there may be magics here."

"Magic...or something," Tyrell agreed. "So what makes you think this?"

"People do crazy things when he's around. I think he tried to make me do something." Rook pulled back his helm and scratched at his light, curly hair before replacing it. "I smelled...well, I smelled something that made me want to leave the room we were in, that made me want to leave everything, but I was able to shake it off." Rook appeared to struggle with the memory.

Tyrell gave him a moment then asked, "So you think it's magic?"

"I don't know," Rook replied sincerely. "I've seen Angst move rocks and Hector flip around crazily while fighting five men at once, and I know those things are magic. Something about this just feels different, sir. I'm sorry, but that's my gut," Rook said carefully, as though it were inappropriate to mention these concerns to Tyrell without providing some sort of proof.

Tyrell nodded and smiled. Everything was beginning to make sense, but he needed someone else to come to the same conclusions. "I believe your gut could be correct, but don't stop there. What else has happened? Who could fight this?"

Rook's brow furrowed contemplatively, and he spoke slowly, as though putting the pieces together. "Angst was the only one that could fight the gamlin, I was told because he could do magic. Almost everyone he's traveling with can do magic, and they were sent to find what's been causing all of this."

"Go on," Tyrell encouraged.

"So magic wielders would be the only ones able to defend us." Rooks eyes grew wide. "And the magic wielders are all in the dungeon!"

"If we live through this, Rook, I'll see you promoted," Tyrell commended.

"Thank you, sir," Rook said proudly, straightening and clicking his heels together. "What do we do next?"

Tyrell stood, trying his best to control his breathing. "I believe it's time to remove Mr. Aereon from the castle."

"Then let's take him out!" Rook said enthusiastically.

"I'll take care of him. I actually have something else for you to do," Tyrell said with some concern. "But I can't command you to do this. There are risks."

Rook didn't falter. "Anything for Unsel," he answered.

* * * *

One of the large throne room doors opened slowly, and Tyrell entered. His hands were behind his back as he casually made his way to the queen. Aereon sat at the edge of the king's throne, and looked up at his approach. He frowned and stopped waving his arms long enough to scratch his head in confusion.

Tyrell scanned the room and saw four guards on each side, standing at attention near the marble pillars. The queen looked away from Aereon to flash Tyrell a brief smile but immediately returned her attention to Aereon. Despite her distraction, Tyrell bowed upon approach.

"Why, Tyrell, I'm surprised to see you up and about. I thought you were on your deathbed," Aereon said as Tyrell straightened. "How are you feeling?"

"Like this." In one fluid movement, he pulled out his sword and buried it deep in Aereon's chest.

Aereon grabbed at the sword, his eyes large with surprise, but Tyrell held it in place.

The queen screamed and covered her glass eye with one hand. "Tyrell, what are you doing? Guards, stop him!"

"No! Guards, stand down!" Princess Victoria commanded from the doorway.

The guards stopped moving, confused by the conflicting orders. Victoria walked toward them with confidence, surrounded by an aura of determination.

"Tyrell," she said in a firm voice. "Finish him!"

38

The swifen were fast. Unbelievably so. What should have taken two weeks had taken two days, and they were now a half day from the Fulk'han capital. The nerve-wracking speed at which the creatures traveled made everyone clench their eyes shut and hang on for dear life. The swifen didn't appear to mind the rough terrain as they dodged trees and animals and casually leaped over the trenches and chasms carved by the Vex'kvette. Hector reveled in this new form of chaos, but only Aerella seemed capable of simultaneously riding, talking, and not panicking.

The trip left Angst weary and shivering. He sat on a large stone jutting out from a wet grassy hillside near the highway. Angst pulled the edges of the traveling cloak Tori had given him in an attempt to fend off the damp fall morning. He hadn't used the cloak much, as it was made for much colder weather, and everyone had rolled their eyes at him when he tried to put it on, and it smelled like strawberries. At the moment, though, he didn't care. Wrapping himself inside felt like a comforting hug, and the scent of Tori's perfume reminded him of home.

Rose stood next to him on the stone and scoffed the sight of the cloak. "Comfy?" she asked as she squinted and braced herself against a cold fall wind.

"Quite. I'm certainly not shivery like you are." Angst lifted the cloak to make room for her. "Come on in. There's room for three."

"Three?" Rose asked, and Scar popped his head out from underneath Angst's other arm, startling a laugh out of her. She hesitated, looking warily at the offered closeness until her teeth started chattering. "Fine," she said and huddled next to Angst, wrapping half the cloak around her.

He turned away to hide a brief smile at her apparent sacrifice. "You know, I would be the last one to complain about your travel clothes," Angst said, nodding at her tight leather breaches and bodice, "but those aren't exactly ideal for this weather."

"You know I don't have anything else to wear," she replied with narrowed eyes.

"You're welcome to use this." Angst tugged on the cloak around their shoulders. "But I may ask you to share when we stop since that seems to be when I get cold."

"Wouldn't your princess girlfriend get upset?" she asked tartly. Scar had moved around Angst to nestle between them so they would both have to pet him at the same time.

"Oh, probably," Angst said with a smirk.

"Then I would love to borrow it," Rose replied with a broad grin.

Angst let out a bark of laughter. He looked into her dark eyes for a brief moment before turning his attention to Scar.

"Things have been really odd since Gressmore. Usually you're gawking at me, and now you can't make eye contact," Rose observed. "Why is that?"

"Aerella said it wasn't a good idea to share the details. She said that everyone's memories should come back on their own." He paused. "But, it really bothered me to watch you die."

She nodded slowly, waiting for Angst to look at her again. "I guess now you know how I feel when you die."

Angst bobbed his head back and forth, both absorbing and accepting the statement, but saying nothing.

"Your newest girlfriend seems obsessed with the whole bonding-Al'eyrn thing. That and she kept asking me about what I could do with magic. I didn't tell her."

"She means well," Angst said with a shrug. "We could probably learn a lot from her if we had time. What's she arguing about with Dallow?"

Rose gave a snort of annoyance. "Whether or not magic is an element. She's trying to convince him that it is, and he's being stubborn since he's never read anything about that," Rose explained.

"Wow, that's really interesting." Angst frowned. "Actually, it's not. Who cares?"

"Obviously Dallow does," she responded then placed her hand on Scar's nose. "Scar isn't doing so well. He's starting to remind me of Ivan."

"He's hitting on you and being offensive?" Angst teased.

"Don't be stupid," Rose snapped. "He seems to get weaker as we get closer to the Vex'kvette source."

"Scar appears healthier when he's close to Chryslaenor, but I don't know what else I can do. It isn't like I can leave him behind." Angst looked over at the others. "I'm going to see if they're ready to go yet." He stood, leaving Rose and Scar wrapped in the cloak.

"...drink water, you walk on earth, you breathe air, you use magic," Aerella was saying in a slightly strained voice as Angst approached.

"Next you'll be telling us magic is alive. I bet it doesn't like being used," Hector prodded.

Aerella became incredibly serious. "All elements are alive, and they don't like being controlled. There absolutely has to be balance or they start fighting until balance is restored."

Hector laughed, until he looked around and realized nobody else was laughing.

"Magic is the most dangerous of them all. Even more dangerous than fire. It's constantly changing to keep from being trapped. Now magic interacts even more differently than I remember. While we can still call forth swifen, the way people *are* magic now makes no sense. Tarness, and Hector, are completely alien to me."

"I get that a lot, honey," Hector heckled, making all of the men laugh.

"You don't understand. It's as though magic...found a way out after being ignored for so long. Angst uses magic the old way, as a means to an end. Tarness, and you, seem to be imbued with magic."

"I get that a lot too," Hector replied snappily, waggling his dark eyebrows and taking a bite of dried meat.

Aerella rolled her eyes. "This doesn't worry you?"

"Can I change it?" Hector asked.

"Not in any way I'm aware of." Aerella avoided eye contact and brushed her long hair from her shoulders.

"Then what good does worry do me? Not to mention, I like who I am, and what I can do." Hector grinned at her mischievously while raising both eyebrows. He looked at Angst. "You okay, old man?"

The song in his head was becoming louder, with blaring notes, most off-key. Angst dropped to one knee and covered his ears to focus. The song was jarring, but he needed more. Angst looked at Chryslaenor and said aloud, "What do you want?"

"What is it, Angst?" Dallow asked.

"Something's wrong...Hector," Angst said, making a circling motion with his finger to indicate the area around them.

Hector sprinted toward a nearby tree and scurried up before Aerella could even stand, and she shook her head in amazement. Angst remained still, concentrating to quiet Chryslaenor.

"If you'd allow the bonding, you would understand what it's trying to tell you." Aerella gently rested her hand on his shoulder. "It's only trying to communicate, and you can't speak the same language without becoming Al'eyrn."

"Thanks, but Chryslaenor and I are only dating...just friends with benefits, nothing serious," Angst replied, attempting to ward off any further discussion.

Hector dropped down from the tree to land nearby. "Trouble," he said, pointing at a large flock of birds flying toward them.

"What's the matter, Hector, afraid of a little bird crap?" Tarness asked dryly.

The black cloudy mass was only minutes away. Little black dots seemed to ebb and flow like the tide. En masse, the shadow lifted up and then down, a beautiful display of organized chaos, like any group of small migratory birds.

"Everyone get close, now!" Aerella yelled. It seemed to take forever as they waited for Rose to carry Scar off the rock. "Angst, watch what I do very carefully, because when I can't sustain it, you're going to have to."

He didn't understand, but nodded. Aerella leaned forward and grabbed at the air, as though catching a feather, and held it tight. She waved her other hand in complex patterns above her fist. When she stopped moving and opened her hand, a small clear ball hovered over it. The ball quickly grew to surround them in a semi-transparent dome.

The flock was on them just as Aerella finished her spell. At first it sounded like the gentle patter of spring rain. One hit the dome with a *pat* then another with a *tick*, followed quickly by a couple of *thud*s. Within moments, the storm arrived. The flock darkened the skies as the birds dove straight at them, moving too fast to see what kind they were. Even the ones that apparently died on impact were quickly pushed aside by the constant barrage.

Sweat beaded Aerella's forehead. "Angst, you'd better start now because I can't hold out much longer."

"Start? Start what," Angst yelled over the storm of birds and Scar's barking. "You waved your arms around and then those things were bouncing off air."

"Weren't you watching?" Her eyes opened wide. She looked angry and tired.

"Watching you do something that apparently hasn't been attempted in two thousand years. Sure, let me get right on that!" Angst snapped in a panic.

"Angst," she was gasping for air, "we don't have time for this. I can't..." The dome shimmered, and a deep crack crawled from the top to spider web around the sides. "Hurry!"

"*Aaaargh*," Angst yelled in frustration then pulled Chryslaenor from his back and jammed the point deep into the ground. The ground shook violently, someone screamed, and Scar yelped and barked. Just as Aerella collapsed from exhaustion, they were engulfed in darkness. The storm instantly quieted, and they could hear only a muffled patter that sounded far away. The air around them quickly became stuffy and thick.

"Oh, right. Air," Angst stated matter-of-factly.

Several small holes appeared near the ground opposite the onslaught of birds. The light was barely enough to illuminate the interior of their solid dome shield. Angst pulled the sword from the ground and looked at his handiwork. "Heh, I made a dome too."

"Angst, what is this made from?" asked Tarness, tapping the interior with his knuckle.

"There's ore in this hill, so I pulled it up through the ground. I didn't understand how to make the dome out of air, but I can do about anything with rock and mineral, so here we are." He smiled, nonchalantly resting one hand against the thick barrier.

"How did you know the ore was there?" asked Aerella, barely visible in the darkness. She was breathing very heavily and sounded as though she were still resting on the ground.

"I knew as we approached. I always know. That's my...uh, that's part of my thing."

"Magic has changed," Aerella said, letting out a deep sigh. "This really is amazing. What kind of metal is it?" she asked, indicating their covering shelter.

"More importantly, how can we get out? I hate small places," Rose said from the middle of the group.

"It's not like you take up much space," Tarness quipped.

Aerella conjured a ball of light, which hovered near her on the ground. They could all see that the dome had been mostly formed from gold.

"Wow... So, why are you working?" asked Dallow.

"I wish it were always this simple to find gold," Angst said, patting the dome. "I can't choose what kind of ore is in the ground."

"Is it done yet? Are they gone?" Rose asked. "I don't hear anything outside."

The constant patter of attack had finally stopped. Chryslaenor's song had been a sort of warning, so Angst concentrated, a little, to see if the song was still angry. He was rewarded with a barrage of musical excitement as the sword reacted to his attentions. It was several moments before it calmed again. None of the music made sense, but it was different enough that he felt confident the attack was over. Angst focused again, creating a door-sized opening in the dome.

The sun was bright, and the cool air was refreshing despite the wind. Rose tried to push past everyone, but Hector blocked her passage. She seemed angry, and Hector shot her a warning look. "Rose, I'm not playing. Just wait while we make sure you aren't going to get eaten or something."

She waited impatiently, hugging Angst's cloak tightly about her.

Angst nodded at Hector and Tarness, and the three of them stepped out with their weapons at the ready. They moved carefully around the dome to find their attackers lumped in an unmoving pile.

Angst gently poked at one with his sword so they could get a better look. A black disc rolled away from the pile, circled on its edge like a dropped coin, before coming to a wobbly stop.

"I thought they were birds!" Hector exclaimed.

Angst flipped it over then over again with his sword. "It has no mouth that I can see, no eyes. I think we were just attacked by giant game pieces."

"Ha! What exactly were we afraid of?" Hector walked to the black disc and nudged it with his foot as one might do to see if something were truly dead. The front of his boot sank into the disc, and color immediately washed from his face. When he pulled back, every bit of his foot that had entered the disc was gone, including the front of his boot and part of his big toe. Hector didn't scream, though his foot was now gushing blood, but he immediately sat on the ground.

"Hector, wait!" Tarness yelled, rushing to catch his friend.

This time Hector let out a wail as he inadvertently sat on another disc. Tarness and Angst rushed to his side to lift him off the ground. Hector was now bleeding heavily from both his foot and his rear. Angst quickly scanned the area and found a clear spot where they laid Hector gently on his chest.

"Rose, I need you!" Angst yelled.

Rose came out, followed by Aerella and Dallow. "What now?" she asked testily and then paused to stare at Hector. "What *did* that? That's disgusting!"

"Stay away from the hole...things, those black discs, and get over here," Angst yelled.

She tiptoed past the pile, still staring at Hector. It was as though someone had carved a perfect circle out of his rear, leaving behind a pool of blood. His wounds were bleeding freely, and he grimaced in obvious pain.

Angst grabbed her shoulders to get her attention. "Rose, he's losing a lot of blood! He's going to die."

"Angst? Angst, I don't know if I can..." Rose was obviously petrified and began stepping back.

"No, it's too much!" Dallow interjected.

"You have to! Please!" Angst pleaded, grabbing her arm to stay her retreat.

"This is going to hurt a lot," Rose said, dropping to her knees. She closed her eyes and gripped Hector's bare arm with both hands. Rose screamed in pain, and her leather breeches and boot were instantly drenched in her own blood.

They all watched in amazement as Hector's toe grew back and the hole in his rear closed. His bleeding stopped, muscles knit together, and skin formed over the injuries.

Dallow pried Rose's hands from Hector's arm as the scar on his chin began to fade and appear on her face. "Rose, that's enough. You saved him." He held her close as she sobbed through the pain. It was several minutes before anyone spoke.

Rose whimpered, but it was apparent that much of her own healing was already taking place.

Hector rolled over to look up at her. "Rose, I didn't know you could... I'm sorry. Are you okay?"

She gave a little nod and buried herself in Dallow's arm once more.

Angst paced, feeling absolutely helpless. He looked at Aerella, who was shaking her head in wonder. "I've never seen healing like that—"

"Would you stop it?" Angst snapped loudly, making everyone jump. "Quit being amazed with us like we should be studied. Quit analyzing us. We don't need any more of you acting surprised. We need help. I don't care if magic is an element, or if it's some crazed beast that needs to be beaten down. We need to understand how to keep this from happening again."

He stepped over to one of the holes and plunged Chryslaenor deep into its black center. It melted into orange and black smoke, leaving no other trace of its existence behind. Angst sighed deeply, wearily, as he realized that the hundreds of discs lying about would probably have to be removed the same way. The work just never seemed to end, no matter where he was.

He peered over his shoulder at everyone. "This is going to take hours. Hector and Tarness, check the road and surrounding area for anything else odd. Aerella, please help Dallow tend to Rose." He turned around and got to work, because that was what he did.

39

"I think this counts as odd," Hector said, looking down at the disfigured woman sprawled unceremoniously across a deep rut in the road. She was lying on her stomach, a long cat-like tail poking through her mane of red hair. Hector reached forward with his foot to nudge the purple body when Tarness stopped him.

"Maybe best not to put Rose through that again," he said in warning. Tarness unsheathed his sword and used it to press against an arm.

"Good idea," Hector replied thankfully. Noticing that the sword hadn't disappeared, or been eaten, Hector crouched down next to the woman and lifted the tail. It was stiff with death. "I'd say she's been dead for a day. Looks like another victim of the Vex'kvette."

"I don't think so," Tarness argued as he removed his helmet and rubbed his dark bristly hair in thought.

"What do you mean?" Hector asked, letting the tail drop. "She's obviously not human. Not anymore, anyway."

"I've seen the animals that survive the Vex'kvette," Tarness said. His thick brow furrowed as he studied the body. "They either come out a mess, or they don't come out."

"She certainly doesn't look normal." Hector said.

"The monsters we've seen come out of the Vex'kvette usually change into something scary, like two animals mashed together.

They also don't have genders." Tarness knelt to get a closer look at the body without touching anything. "This woman was changed into something perverted, but not scary. And she is definitely, well, a she. It's like the Vex'kvette tried changing her into something and she died while it happened."

"Would you get the others?" Hector asked, feeling both frustrated and confused. "I'd like to see if I can find anyone else this may have happened to."

"I'll be right back." Tarness replaced his helm and called forth his obsidian stallion.

* * * *

When everyone arrived thirty minutes later, Aerella immediately dismounted her white tiger to examine the purple woman. She rolled the woman onto her back and muttered spells in Acratic while waving her hands over the length of the body. When Dallow approached, she spoke more slowly so he could follow, but didn't stop. Silver glimmering dust hung in the air where her hand had been.

Rose limped over to join the group, carefully stepping down into the deep rut where everyone stood. She looked shaky and paler than usual.

"Uh, thanks Rose," Hector whispered. He reached up to the scar on his chin and then teased, "I'm still not sure why you would want to try and remove my handsome scar though."

"Do you want another one?" she asked with a weak smirk.

Aerella continued casting her spell. She withdrew a small dagger from her side and used it to puncture the woman's chest. The glimmering dust spiraled and collected, becoming a sparkling whirlpool that poured into the hole Aerella had made. The purple woman sat up abruptly, and everyone jerked out their weapons. She stared straight ahead with large golden eyes. Aerella held out a hand to signal that weapons weren't necessary.

"Our new Takarn has shown his face," said the purple woman. Her voice was hollow and distant. "He made me his, but I was not strong enough."

"What happened to you?" Aerella asked with concern.

"I was walking home when I found Takarn. We've been lost for so long, and now he has come. I began to worship him when he gave me this." She opened her arms and looked down at her body.

"This is bad," Tarness said under his breath.

The woman began to lie down once more.

"Who is he? Who did this to you?" Angst asked the woman. When she didn't respond, he looked up at Aerella. "Can't you make her tell us more?"

"Angst, I'm sorry. There's nothing else I can do," Aerella apologized, watching the woman return to her prone position.

Angst held the brightly-glowing Chryslaenor over the body. Bones cracked as he shoved the blade into the purple woman's chest in the spot Aerella had with her dagger only moments before. "Who did this to you?"

Her eyes opened wide, and she screamed, "Takarn comes for you, Angst!" Her body shuddered one last time before dissolving into dark orange and black smoke.

"That, uh, well, that's not really what I expected," Angst said as he wiped Chryslaenor clean on nearby grass.

"You aren't supposed to desecrate bodies like that, Angst. It isn't right," Aerella whispered, obviously horrified.

Angst wanted to snap at her but took a moment to calm himself with a very deep breath. "Thank you for the help, Aerella, but we needed to know more. At least she wasn't left like that."

"You were right," Hector said to Tarness. "It wasn't the Vex'kvette."

"Oh, I would've been okay to be wrong about that," Tarness replied.

Dallow, looking suddenly panic-stricken, backed away from the body as he moved his hands in a large circle. He pointed at the ground around them, outlining the rut in which they stood.

"Dallow, what is it?" Angst asked.

"I thought we'd been standing in wheel ruts this entire time,"

Dallow said, stepping out of the four-inch deep groove. "These aren't ruts. They're footprints."

* * * *

Their swifen trotted along the highway, following the five-foot-wide prints that lead to the capital of Fulk'han. The deep grooves in the road were shaped like a cloverleaf without the stalk, as though three giant horse hooves had been bound together and stamped into the ground every ten feet.

Hector and Tarness rode in front to keep watch, discussing what creature could leave such prints and how large it must be. Rose once again rode with Dallow. She rested against his back, flushed with exhaustion.

"It's too bad you can't take some of our health instead of taking our injuries. I know everyone would share," Dallow said, sounding apologetic.

"That's sweet, Dallow, but it doesn't work that way. I can't even control it," Rose replied with a sigh.

Angst rode in the back with Aerella, his swifen banging and creaking loudly. He watched his friends while petting Scar, who rested awkwardly on his lap. The dog's breaths were quick and shallow, and every so often, he let out a whimper. Angst had tried to will Scar back to full health, but without success. The Vex'kvette was too close and too overwhelming for the small pup.

Every few minutes, Aerella attempted to say something, but he cut her off.

"It's not going to happen, so forget it," Angst snapped before she could complete a thought.

"I don't think you realize what we're facing," Aerella pleaded, her airy voice filled with concern.

"I don't think any of us realize, including you. How can we? I'm so frightened for my friends, I could vomit," Angst said quietly as he gripped his shuddering stomach through the cool chainmail. "The last thing I want is even more magic in my life.

I'm not bonding."

"I think we're facing Magic. I think it's the element come to life, and I don't think you—"

"We've got more friends," Tarness yelled from ahead, interrupting Aerella.

Angst sped up, both to avoid Aerella's constant chastising and to see what Tarness had discovered. This woman-creature was a darker shade of purple, her mane of hair a brighter red. She still had a cat-like tail, but this woman also had three clawed protrusions for feet. Her eyes were even larger, and her naked purple breasts obscenely huge.

Next to her lay the body of what was once a man. His skin was dark gray, and his body muscular beyond comprehension. His torso and arms were twice the girth of his legs, and his feet shaped like horse hooves. The gray man's hands had been unnaturally stretched, resembling a monkey's paw with three fingers and sharp claws.

Aerella walked over to them, ready to cast her spell once more, but Angst gently grabbed her hand in mid-air.

"There's nothing more we can learn from these fanatics," he said with regret in his voice. She looked away as he plunged his sword into each of the victims, leaving behind the dark orange smoke.

"What do you mean by fanatics?" asked Rose, new worry on her face.

Dallow looked at her with surprise. "You don't know? It's the reason everyone is so wary of the Fulk'han. They've always been a fanatical people, choosing a new god to worship every decade or so. We've been fortunate that the last hundred years they've been worshipping agricultural gods created from their own imaginations, like a god of wheat or a god of milk, and not a god of war."

"Haven't you ever heard the joke, 'we're all safe until they worship a god of cannibalism'?" Tarness asked.

"I have, but ignored it. I thought it sounded stupid," Rose replied.

"That joke is older than I am," Aerella informed everyone. "I mean that they've been this way for thousands of years. Many wars have been lost to the Fulk'han. You don't want to war with fanatics."

"So, we keep following these footprints, and finding more bodies that look like they didn't survive a swim in the Vex'kvette. What if the creature who owns these footprints is changing people? What does it mean if the Fulk'han start worshiping a walking Vex'kvette?" Rose asked, and nobody answered.

"Let's keep moving. I want to get this over with so we can go home," Angst said as he remounted.

* * * *

They all remained quiet as dread and inevitability joined them on the trail to the capital. Discarded purple and gray remains of failed attempts to change people lay scattered along the path like breadcrumbs. Every half mile they found another man or woman, each a slight variation from the last. Each time, Angst dismounted and destroyed the bodies. While waiting, Dallow described the differences he noticed between each body they found, and Tarness nervously announced that the clover-shaped prints in the highway seemed to be getting larger.

It was late afternoon when the capital came into view. Usually, Fulk'han was a beautiful city set on a tall hill for all to see at a distance, known for its lanky spiraling towers painted dull yellow to match the surrounding limestone houses and shops. Everything in the city was tall and thin. The buildings surrounding the castle were at least three or four stories high, as though the city kept growing up rather than out.

Today, however, it was a fearsome sight. The city lay in the middle of a maelstrom. A dark orange and black storm brewed overhead, a slowly twisting hungry thing that seemed ready to consume everything it covered. Occasional bolts of lightning shot down from the storm, blasting pieces of ground or building into the air. They heard the echo of thunder and an occasional scream. Cobwebs of glowing orange Vex'kvette streamed from every edge of the city, pouring down the hill and spreading across the surrounding landscape.

They stopped a mile away to observe the chaos, in awe of the obvious power emanating from the place.

"That's a new look for the city," Hector said, taking a deep breath.

"I don't feel welcome," Dallow added.

Angst turned around to face everyone, his noisy mount clanking with every move. He petted a barely breathing Scar, who lay nearly lifeless in his lap. "Look, I really don't think you all—"

"Can we just get this done?" Tarness asked, still warily eyeing the city.

Everyone nodded in agreement, though Aerella's eyes pleaded with Angst, begging for him to become Al'eyrn.

Angst shook his head to deny her yet again and handed Scar over to Rose, who took the sick pup with a nod. He lifted Chryslaenor from his back and held it high. Turning his swifen about, Angst galloped forward in a rattling charge.

They rode the remainder of the highway with adrenaline pumping, looking to each other for encouragement and steeling themselves in preparation of the unknown.

"Angst, hold!" Hector yelled in warning and everyone slowed.

The purple woman standing alone at the edge of the city was alive, unlike the others they had found. Her bright red hair flowed along her back to her knees, and a furry cat-like tail twisted about her long legs. She watched them with her unnaturally large golden eyes, and smiled vapidly at their approach. Darker violet spots, like large freckles, covered the tops of her arms and front of her legs.

"So, what, is their Takarn a fifteen-year-old going through puberty?" Rose asked, looking the woman up and down with a sneer.

Angst dismounted and walked toward their greeter. She

seemed unconcerned at his approach and merely swung out her curvy hip as she shifted her weight from one clawed foot to the other.

"Whoa, Angst. That might not be such a good idea," Hector warned.

"Really, I've got this," Angst said, turning to quickly wink at his friends. Rose closed her eyes and Dallow covered his face with his long fingers.

She was easily a head taller than Angst. Her breasts were enormous and unnaturally buoyant, dramatically disproportionate to her tiny waist. Angst's cheeks and ears flushed as her cat tail wound in and out of his legs. Everything about her was uncomfortably erotic.

"Are you okay? Who did this to you?" Angst stuttered.

The woman's thickly-lashed eyes blinked several times in apparent confusion. She looked at the group then turned her attention back to Angst.

"Hi," Angst said with a grin, attempting a different approach. "I'm Angst."

Her eyes opened wide, and she snapped her head back and yelled. Her high-pitched, trilling scream was quickly followed by thundering sounds and trembling earth. Angst was forcefully knocked to the ground before he saw them coming. He looked up and made eye contact with an angry creature towering over him.

The monster was as tall as Tarness and twice as wide. Its entire body was dark gray and covered with leathery protrusions like a turtle's shell. Sharp, silvery eyes were hidden within the darkness of a diamond-shaped bone helm. Its enormous muscular arms were long enough to reach its knees, and it lifted Angst effortlessly. The monster either wore armor, or bones had grown outside its body to protect its chest and ribs.

Angst braved a quick look at his friends to find they'd all been caught unawares. Tarness had thrown one of the monsters aside and was grappling with three more. Hector ducked and rolled between two as they grabbed for him. Rose, Aerella, and

Dallow were each being held but were otherwise unharmed.

"Everyone stand down," Angst yelled.

"What?" Tarness and Hector snapped at the same time.

"They were expecting us, and I don't care to fight hordes of these things to make our way through the city," he explained.

The gray man set him down and nodded, as if it understood.

"Can you talk?" Angst asked.

The creature gave no response other than a shove to move Angst into a line with his friends. Rose picked up Scar on her way to join them while everyone else dismissed their swifen.

"I don't think getting captured is your best idea," Hector whispered behind Angst.

"I have a feeling we're going to need to save our energy," Angst replied, glancing one last time at the purple woman as they followed their "guides" into Fulk'han.

The city was ominously quiet, as though the dark storm overhead demanded obedience and silence. The only sounds came from their feet on the gravelly walk, or the occasional clap of thunder. They hiked through the city for fifteen minutes as they approached the center of the maelstrom.

"Any plans?" asked Tarness.

"I'm working on it," Angst replied.

"As long as there aren't any more purple women involved, maybe he won't be so distracted," Rose snapped.

"Right. With three weeks of adventuring experience under my belt, how could I possibly make any mistakes," Angst retorted rolling his eyes at her.

There *were* more women, and men, thousands of them throughout the city. The men all looked identical—enormous, gray, covered in bone armor and turtle shell, and ready for action. Unlike the uniformly gray bone men, the women had skin tones in a variety of pink, purple and blue hues.

The grey men and colorful women stepped aside, making a path that led to a roughly-cut stadium, a crater carved deep into the center of Fulk'han. Hundreds of the bone men circled the makeshift stadium, shoulder to shoulder with their heads lowered. Along each step going down into the center, women rested on their knees and bowed deep in worship.

"I was here only months ago," Hector remarked as they were led down long stairs into the center of the stadium. "As shoddy as everything is, I don't understand how they could remove the capitol building and replace it with this so quickly."

"I think that did it," Aerella replied, fear quivering in her voice as she pointed at a twenty-foot-tall statue in the middle of the city.

"A statue did this?" Dallow questioned in disbelief as he took in the sight.

It was an ugly thing. From a distance, it seemed roughly human, carved from black stone and tightly wrapped in giant purple worms. Up close, the black stone glimmered, like there were stars trapped in that darkness. The purple worms were large tubular things that slithered around the body.

"Angst, the feet!" Tarness yelled, pointing at the statue's feet. Three of the tubes had merged together in a cloverleaf shape at the base of its legs, exactly matching the footprints they'd tracked only hours before.

Just then the statue turned its head and rose from a coarsely-hewn obsidian throne. The grotesque purple tendrils were in constant motion around its body, as though fighting to contain the starry sky hidden within. It still had the general shape of a man—legs, feet, arms, hands with fingers, and a head. The creature's face hovered in front of the head, like some horrific masquerade mask floating in the air. The head and face angled down to look at them, its eyes widening as the face sneered.

"Uh, hello? I'm Angst," Angst called, with his hand cupped to the side of his mouth.

The creature leaned forward, placing its tendril-covered hands on its knees for support. The mask stopped within feet of Angst and spoke. "Hello, Angst," it said, its deep booming voice reverberating through the stadium.

Up close, Angst could finally make out the face. "Ivan?" Angst asked in shock. "Ivan, what happened? Are you all right?"

The thing that used to be Ivan straightened and laughed. The sound rolled like thunder, and several bolts of lightning struck the ground around the stadium. "All right? I've never felt better, and I have *you* to thank." His words dripped with a mocking tone.

"Me?" Angst asked bewildered. "How?"

"That night you sent me away, you drove me into the Vex'kvette." Ivan looked down at his arms and hands. "Now I have power like you, Angst. You see, not everything that comes from the Vex'kvette is a monster."

It was the wrong thing to say. All the anticipation, and fear, and concern that had built up in Angst burst out as laughter. This laughter was not the gentle guffaw that could be hidden with coughing, or a quickly-contained chuckle. This was an uncontrollable belly laugh that came from the depths of exhaustion.

"I don't think that's a good idea," Dallow warned Angst.

"Not a monster?" Angst asked, wiping his eyes.

Before Angst even had time to pull his hand from his face, Ivan's arm swung down in a purple blur, backhanding Angst into the air and over nearby buildings.

"Here we go," Hector yelled.

40

Tyrell didn't enjoy killing, but he couldn't help feeling relieved and justified as Aereon writhed at the end of his sword. The tall man struggled, gripping the blade with both hands, his eyes squeezed shut. Tyrell's relief was soon replaced by concern when the writhing and noises continued for far too long. Aereon suddenly stopped moving, his eyes popped open, and a seedy grin crept across his face.

"You really have no idea what you're dealing with." Aereon's chest transformed into smoke as he stepped to one side. Tyrell's blade passed through, leaving no sign of impact or injury.

There was no time for shock. Aereon moved so fast Tyrell didn't even see him unsheathe the rapier. Only years of experience let Tyrell block the thin sword mere inches from his face.

"Fancy," Aereon taunted. "That would've killed most."

Tyrell didn't banter without purpose and took the opportunity to study his opponent. Aereon was no blademaster, but he was unnaturally fast, and accurate. The man's overall nonchalant attitude had led Tyrell to dismiss him as a true threat, but that was a mistake, perhaps a deadly one. Aereon didn't bother defending himself when Tyrell swung, and Tyrell's sword passed through him easily as he switched forms at will.

"That isn't magic I recognize," Tyrell commented between short breaths.

"Who said it was magic?" Aereon answered with an evil,

knowing grin.

Tyrell spun around to block another swing as he heard Aereon pop into form behind him. Aereon was too fast, appearing and disappearing randomly around Tyrell. Instinct, raw skill, and desperation kept Tyrell alive. Neither man could successfully land a blow, but only Tyrell seemed to be tiring. He continued fighting while inching toward the door, hoping to draw Aereon away from the queen.

Aereon suddenly appeared between Tyrell and the door, looking quite pleased with himself. "No escape for you. This is too much fun." But as Aereon plunged with his rapier, the steel end of a large halberd struck him upside the head.

Victoria swung at Aereon again and again, each blow making painful contact with his head or torso. Tyrell took advantage of Aereon's prolonged solidity and drove his sword into the man's stomach. Aereon seemed momentarily disoriented as Victoria and Tyrell continued to attack together.

Aereon muttered something, and instantly a second rapier appeared in his hand. He spun wildly. Victoria dove to the ground and rolled away as gracefully as she could in her formal attire. Aereon's blade found flesh, striking Tyrell in the arm again and again, blood pouring from each new wound.

After seeing Aereon attack the princess, the guards posted around the room rushed forward.

"That's enough!" Aereon yelled, obviously no longer amused.

He raised his right hand, dramatically pointing outward and turning it in small circles. The princess and the guards flew against the throne room walls. The few guards still conscious hovered helplessly several feet over the floor.

Tyrell's sword arm was useless. Blood trickled down the sleeve of his dark navy doublet. He transferred the sword to his other hand.

"I grow tired of this, Captain Guard." Aereon stood in front of Tyrell and thrust the rapiers back and forth so quickly that his arms were only a blur of motion. He stopped to admire his work.

"That should do it."

Tyrell patted at his wet doublet. In a daze, he looked down to see dozens of holes in his chest, like large pinpricks, each dripping blood. He dropped to his knees, still holding onto his sword, feeling both surprised and confused.

Aereon leaned forward and whispered in his ear. "You are a fool. So worried about your queen inside that you didn't even notice what was happening to your kingdom outside the castle walls."

Aereon took the sword from Tyrell's hand, lifted it high, and slashed down at the man's neck.

* * * *

It was an ordinary Monday morning for the capital of Unsel. In spite of the recent upheaval that had driven the magic wielders away or into prison, people still needed to eat, and commerce commenced. Kertac had always been a produce vendor in this market and drew comfort from the normalcy of his life. He didn't understand nor care to acknowledge anything that didn't fit into his daily routine. Kertac's greatest concern was the weather.

After thirty years in the produce industry, he could gauge where to set that day's prices based on temperature, humidity, and cloud cover. If weather was turning bad, he may not receive a shipment and could raise his prices. Perfect weather was the worst for business, most customers finding things to do other than shopping. He waited all year for days like today, cool enough to keep his produce healthy, but not cold enough to drive away customers. They were already starting to gather at the edge of the market, waiting for the vendors to open.

Kertac looked over at the prospective buyers and was grateful that people were so easily swayed by fear. Recent arrests and rumors of attacks by monsters had driven shoppers to buy more food than they normally would have. Fearing war and inevitable scarcity, people naturally began stockpiling resources, and that was good for business. He wrung his large hands hungrily. Maybe, in spite of the nice fall day, he could find another excuse to keep prices up. Kertac sought his excuse in the skies, hoping for a sign of rain or, even better, an early snow.

One particularly dark cloud loomed near the city, and his hopes swelled. "Looks like a rough storm," he muttered to himself with a greedy smile. Kertac continued watching the cloud, startled by the speed of its approach.

He shook his head, rubbed his eyes, and inspected the produce displayed around his table. That odd cloud made him uneasy, and the increasing buzz of people around him reflected his worries. Though he really didn't want to, Kertac looked into the sky again, in spite of himself. The cloud was growing, and now seemed mere minutes away. Others followed his gaze and looked up to watch in trepidation as the cloud slowed. Kertac looked away and started packing his goods, for once unconcerned about bruising the fruit. He stopped abruptly when he heard the first loud thud. Someone screamed, and there was a crash as one of his tables collapsed.

"Guards!" Kertac yelled. He began recovering what he could from the mess. He crouched to retrieve pieces of smashed pumpkin, searching for anything salvageable. Instead, he found what had destroyed his table. The ravaged body of an old woman lay on the cobblestones, unmoving amidst various bits of produce. Her face and throat bore wide raw gashes and her eyes were gone.

"Kertac!" Old Mulson called out from the next booth, his lifelong competitor and nemesis. "Help!"

Kertac tore his eyes away from the woman to see Mulson's body crumple to the ground. "Guards," he croaked once more in fright.

He was torn. Should he help his neighbor, save his food, or run for his life? He sought guards only to find they, too, were under attack. A mass panic presided over the market. Everyone was running or screaming as hundreds of winged creatures dived from the sky. The monsters lifted people off the ground and flew away, or killed them where they stood.

"I don't understand! What's going on?"

A loud clicking noise behind him made Kertac whirl around. A large majestic bird with a dark crimson breast and velvety purple wings approached. The bird was half his height, and broad. Its legs were thick and blood dripped from its long metal beak. It screamed at him, and a feathery fan of blinking eyes popped up from its head as it dove at his face.

* * * *

Angst had to lie in the rubble and think about things for a moment. Like skipping a stone across a lake, Ivan had flung him into the city, and Angst remembered bouncing along the top of several buildings before rolling off the roof of a third and finally landing hard on the ground. It could only be magic, blind luck, or a combination of both that kept him alive. Sadly, neither had kept him from the pain. Every muscle in his body felt as though it had been ripped out and replaced several times with a bent fork.

The pain helped him focus, however, and he remembered that his friends were in danger. With a loud groan, he stood and picked up Chryslaenor, returning the giant blade to his back. Angst was too disoriented to run, so he called forth his swifen. The unfortunate-looking ram-thing made its way through the debris loudly and Angst threw his leg over to mount with a painful cringe. His friends were easy to find; Angst merely followed the noise. It was louder than any jousting tournament he'd ever attended.

His mind raced as he approached. Angst thought of Heather, and of Tori, and even of Wizard's Revenge. At this moment, he truly longed to be back where there was at least some small bit of normal left in Ehrde, a place where his friends could be safe. Home, or anywhere but here, where their lives were threatened by absolute chaos in its purest form.

A dark center had formed in the storm directly over the stadium, the clouds surrounding it like an apocalyptic halo. Before Ivan had smacked him over nearby buildings, the newly-changed Fulk'han had filled every level of the deep limestone risers circling the arena. Now the risers were empty as Fulk'han creatures swarmed to attack his companions in the center. Angst rode down into the maw, unnoticed amidst the chaos, in spite of his clattery swifen.

From behind Ivan, Angst saw Tarness muscling back scores of gray men, like a seawall defending against lashing ocean waves. Aerella stood several feet to his left, one arm maintaining an invisible barrier against throngs of the purple women while painfully bright rays of light shot from her other hand, directly at Ivan.

Rose and Dallow fought the creatures who made it past Tarness or Aerella, clearing a path for Hector, who was cutting loose.

After returning to the middle of the group, Hector briefly checked to make sure everyone was safe before jumping back into the fray. He leaped onto Tarness's shoulders and launched himself into the air. He threw knives that were pulled from who-knew-where, each of them striking a different target with deadly precision. Hector landed on the fresh heap of corpses and rolled to his next victim, whom he dissected with a short sword Angst had never seen him carry. Hector was a whirling frenzy of movement, and no enemy within reach lived for more than a breath's time after his approach. Even from this distance, Angst could see the larkish smile on his old friend's face.

Angst had been advancing slowly, analyzing what used to be Ivan. He was waiting for an opportunity to strike when Ivan suddenly beat on Aerella's invisible barricade. His monstrous arms rose high into the air and landed with enough force to shake the surrounding ground. Aerella winced at the impact, withdrawing her attack on Ivan to reinforce the magical barrier with both hands. Ivan's fists pummeled at the shield, and Aerella screamed. A crack began to form along the edge, like the one created by the phantom holes.

Realizing there was no ideal time to bring the fight, Angst barreled forward on his ram. He raised Chryslaenor high in the air and yelled, "*Ivan!*"

His mount moved quickly, allowing Angst to ride up behind the monster. He sliced into the thick purple cables where Ivan's calf had once been and continued riding to carve into the other one. Ivan immediately stopped beating on Aerella's shield and grabbed at him. Angst leaped off the ram, tumbling out of reach, and swung wildly at the giant arm as it passed, carving into the back of Ivan's hand.

Ivan's legs had already started to heal, oozing together as the worm-like exterior reformed to contain the darkness held within. Ivan continued swinging his great arms, grabbing desperately for Angst. But Angst kept just out of reach, dashing in to stab Ivan's foot.

This was nothing like attacking a disoriented monster fresh from the Vex'kvette. Ivan was fast, too fast to see clearly, and he moved with intent. What remained of Ivan after the metamorphosis—his training as a knight and his instincts as a fighter—only added another layer of threat to the raw power he wielded. The training made him dangerous and the power made him unpredictable.

"Enough!" the Ivan-creature yelled, his voice echoing off the arena stairs. In a blur of motion, he stepped back and caught Angst up in his hand, lifting him high into the air.

Angst couldn't breathe in the crushing grip. He struggled to pull Chryslaenor from its trappings in the cold violet hand. With every ounce of power he could muster, he yanked his blade free and buried it deep into the hand that held him. Ivan pulled Angst away with his left hand, leaving the giant sword buried in his right.

"No!" Aerella yelled. She allowed the shield to dissolve and pointed both palms at Ivan. A barrage of harsh light and symbols shot from her hands, striking Ivan in the chest.

"I'm done with you," Ivan said to Aerella with a sneer. "You don't even belong here!" He lifted his right hand and a gaping vortex opened in the middle of his palm. A geyser of the nighttime sky contained within Ivan's body poured out, engulfing Aerella in cloudy stars. She screamed and struggled as the stars twisted and swirled. The mass rolled, consuming itself until there was nothing, taking Aerella with it into the void.

Ivan held Angst in front of his face. "I'm so glad you came back for more!" Ivan said maniacally. He lifted Angst over his head and threw him to the ground, hard.

There was a loud snap as he landed, followed by several sickening pops and rips. Blood gushed from his thigh where his femur had broken and torn through his skin. He screamed in anguish, unable to stand or move. Scar was lying next to him, whimpering pitifully. The pup seemed to be growing as bubbles spewed from the scar on his side. Angst crawled to his lab but stopped when he heard a booming grunt. Ivan pulled and tugged at Chryslaenor, rocking it until he was able to remove the blade from his hand. The sword seemed incredibly heavy, but Ivan held it up high like it was his own. Ivan looked at Angst, smiled smugly, and swung down.

* * * *

The blow sounded like a melon being sliced in half, and was loud enough to make everyone stop fighting. Rose was the first to scream as Chryslaenor lodged in Angst's face. It had cut through the helm, and Ivan had left it there. Angst fell back to the ground. His right leg bent awkwardly and his arms twitched and jerked.

Hector roared in rage as he tried to pull away from the battle, but the horde of Fulk'han surged through their defenses. Aerella's shield was gone, and Tarness had stopped fighting, gawking in shock at Angst's body.

"Don't kill them yet. I want them to suffer like I did," Ivan ordered. He placed one giant cloven foot on Angst and yanked Chryslaenor from his face. Angst continued to shake and seize. "Bring them all to the dungeon, including him," he commanded, nudging Angst with his foot. "Make sure they can all watch the hero die."

41

"Rook, if you don't tell me what's going on, I'm going back to my room!" Heather warned, holding her burgundy dress out of the way as she jogged after the soldier.

Rook stopped at the intersection of two hallways and looked around to ensure they were alone. "Tyrell asked me to release the mages and said you could help. I don't understand why I'm supposed to let them go or what you can do, Heather."

"Won't we get in trouble for setting them free?" Heather whispered.

"Yes, probably. Tyrell didn't explain, but I trust him," Rook assured her.

Heather considered this. Angst had spoken highly of Tyrell and of Rook, and she finally agreed that Tyrell wouldn't put her at risk without good reason. "Let's go."

Rook nodded his appreciation and led the rest of the way to the dungeon entrance. They followed the long flight of stairs down into the bowels of the castle. Before the large iron door, four guards stood at attention as they entered the room.

"Where do you think you're going, Rook?" a meaty looking guard said with a growl.

"Step aside," Rook commanded. "I outrank you, soldier. I don't need your permission to enter."

"Aereon delivered the queen's order this morning. Nobody's allowed in without his consent."

"Let me see that order," Rook demanded, his voice getting louder.

"Actually, sir, we're supposed to deliver anyone that comes down here without approval directly to Aereon," the guard said threateningly. Two of the others started moving behind Heather. "You'll both need to come with us."

Rook reached for his short sword, but Heather placed her hand on his before it cleared the sheath. She looked at the man who was threatening them and smiled. He blinked several times and then smiled back. Heather continued to smile, and the guards stopped moving. Everyone stood very still as she walked around the room. The men, including Rook, seemed entranced, watching her every move.

"I think everyone should go stand against the wall over there and wait for a while," she said, pointing at the nearby wall. Rook and the guards happily made their way over. Heather held Rook's hand. "Not you, dear. You get the key and unlock the door."

Rook appeared to think that was a great idea and proceeded to open the iron door leading to the dungeon cells.

"You should all wait there until we get back," Heather gently advised the guards standing against the wall. Everyone nodded their heads in complete acceptance of the notion.

After making their way through the iron door, Rook shook his head as if waking up from a surprise nap. "What...what just happened?"

"Angst says I have an infectious personality," Heather answered, smiling fondly as she thought of Angst. She sighed. "Anyone nearby gets caught up in my state of mind at the moment. If I need help, they help. If I'm upset, they become upset."

"You could have anything you want!" Rook said in shock as they made their way down the long dungeon hallway.

"How do you think I got Angst to marry me?" Heather replied coyly.

Rook stopped in his tracks. "Are you serious?"

Heather laughed out loud. "No."

Rook started laughing too and then covered his mouth.

"Sorry, I can't control it when I'm laughing," she apologized. "And what I do doesn't last long after I move away. It's a proximity thing."

"Wait. Exactly how long?" Rook asked, looking back at the iron door. Two of the soldiers had already entered their hallway. He grabbed Heather's arm. "Run!"

They ran to the large cell holding the magic wielders, hastily unfastened the lock, and heaved the heavy door open before the guards arrived. When the two soldiers pushed into the room, they found a dozen angry men and women standing in front of Rook and Heather, their hands or eyes glowing ominously. The soldiers backed out of the cell slowly, as if it were a room filled with vipers, all expression and color dropped from their faces.

"We'll be back with more!" one yelled after closing the door.

"What's going on, Heather? And why are you with this guy?" Graloon said, looking at Rook with disgust.

"He's on our side, Graloon," Heather said, placing a hand on Rook's arm. "We're here to set you free."

"You're doing a great job so far," Graloon replied, rolling his eyes. The old barkeep had an ugly purple bruise along the side of his face.

"He has a good point," Heather agreed, turning to Rook. "Now that I've gotten you in, what's your plan on getting us out?"

Rook scratched at stubble on his chin. "I'm, well, uh, I'm working on that part."

"Wait, you don't have a plan to escape?" Heather asked in exasperation.

"I thought the thing you do would help with that," Rook said, waving his hand around to indicate magic in general. "Tyrell wasn't very clear about it."

"It won't work if they bring a lot more. There are limitations," Heather said with a sigh.

"There has to be someone in here that can help us leave without fighting our way out." Rook looked around at the surly people gathered in the large cave-like room.

The ground shuddered as the floor in the center of the room loosened like sand. Everyone stepped back as two men appeared—an older bearded man with well-worn linen clothes and a young man with light brown hair wearing a homespun shirt—the two wielders Aereon had found 'fighting' in this same cell.

"You two! Where have you been?" Rook asked in surprise.

They both peered at Rook with distrust. The older man spoke. "There's no time to explain right now. Graloon, will your bar have any problems accommodating us if we all appear at once?"

"No problem at all. Welcome back, Andec," Graloon said to the older man with a gratified smile. "You too, Jace."

Andec nodded then yelled, "Everyone brace yourself."

"For what?" Rook asked Heather, panic around his eyes.

Before she could answer, a dark circle appeared in the floor beneath them, and they fell. It was like missing a stair, the drop was just enough to make Rook's heart skip a beat. Within a blink, they were in Graloon's bar, unharmed.

"Do you want to explain why you were sent to release us?" Graloon asked Rook.

Rook looked around in amazement, still shocked by the sudden relocation. "Tyrell sent me, but didn't have time to explain why."

"It's because Unsel is under attack!" Jace announced.

"What?" Rook exclaimed in disbelief. He ran to the door and opened it then cautiously stuck his head outside. Looking up and down the cobblestone road, he found it completely empty. As he turned around to tell everyone, something slammed into his back, knocking him to the ground.

Rook rolled over to find one of the large steel-beaked birds preparing to attack. He scrambled to stand and pointed his sword at it. The bird flew at his face. Rook ducked and stabbed at the beast's chest. Striking the bird was like hitting a metal shield hanging on a stone wall. His sword bounced off.

"Only magic can kill these things!" he yelled, remembering what Tyrell had told him.

Before the bird could attack again, a bolt of fire shot by Rook's right ear. The creature squawked loudly as it burst into flame and cooked to cinder. Rook peered over his shoulder to find an attractive middle-aged woman standing behind him, her arm extended and her hand glowing scant inches from his cheek.

"Thanks!" he said with genuine appreciation, yet still eyeing the glowing hand warily.

"You're welcome," she said, smiling at him. She pulled her hand away from the side of his cheek and placed it behind her back as though to hide an obscene disfiguration.

"Can anyone else do that?" Rook asked excitedly. "If Unsel is being attacked by those things—"

"You mean to tell me we're supposed to defend the very kingdom that put us all in prison?" someone yelled from the crowd. Many others nodded, echoing the sentiment.

"In the queen's defense, she has been compromised," Rook pleaded.

"I'll vouch for that," Heather said supportively. "I don't believe it was her decision to throw everyone in prison."

"And the same person influencing the queen's decisions is the one who's brought about this attack," Rook explained to the magic wielders.

"I'll fight," declared the woman who'd killed the bird, still smiling at Rook.

A handful of others stepped forward, though some with obvious reluctance.

"There's no time to wait," Rook said, taking the lead.

"Where do you think you're going?" asked Heather, grabbing his shoulder to hold him back. "You can't fight those things."

"I need to get back to the castle. Tyrell and the princess have to know what's going on out here."

"I can send you back." Andec stepped forward.

Before Rook could object, a dark circle appeared at his feet. Heather stepped into the circle to join Rook, and they vanished together.

42

Dungeons are the same everywhere. Cave-like hovels where the cold and the stench seep into their captives' pores while sucking the life and hope out of them. The dungeon cells in Fulk'han were similar to the ones in Unsel, except they had chains with shackles. Those shackles now held Rose, Tarness, Dallow, and Hector against the walls of a cell, their wrists bound high just enough overhead to make sitting awkward and standing uncomfortable. They'd passed the point of tears and anger, leaving them frustrated and filled with regret. Hanging along the back wall of the cell was Angst.

Like the others, chains held his arms aloft. The Fulk'han guard who'd shackled the body had attempted to position Angst's head so it leaned back against the cold stone wall where everyone could view the horrific wound. Fortunately, jerking muscle spasms kept forcing the head to loll forward. So the guard had left him, hanging by his wrists. Even hours after the battle, his body continued to shudder on occasion while blood and fluids dripped from his face.

Ivan had given the guards instructions to set Rose closest to Angst, so she would have the best view. She was the only one struggling against the iron cuffs, her wrists in a state of constant healing and her arms caked with dry blood. Angst was just out of reach. Frustration itself could wiggle between the space of her finger and a spot of exposed skin on his right leg. She yelled in anger, cursing loudly and making the guards outside laugh.

"Rose, let him go, he's dead," Dallow said quietly, his voice filled with regret.

"Then why is he still moving?" Rose snapped at him.

"You think it's the sword, don't you?" Dallow asked her, shaking his head. "You think Chryslaenor is somehow keeping him alive. Rose, didn't you see? His skull was split open. Angst is dead."

She ignored Dallow and kept reaching, fresh blood trickling down from her left wrist once more as she stretched and pulled against her restraints.

"What will happen if you do make contact? Even if he is alive, there's no way you could survive all that healing," Dallow pleaded.

"What would you have me do? Just hang here like you three?" She flashed everyone a bitter look. "So what if I die healing him? Ivan is going to kill us anyway, or worse."

"What choice do we have, Rose?" Tarness's voice was heavy with defeat. "Even if I did break us free, we can't fight off Ivan's entire army of creatures."

The door opened, and two large gray men entered the room. The first looked around at them with an evil grin then licked his lips hungrily when he saw Rose. He walked over to her and removed her boots. The second guard unlocked her shackles.

"What are you doing, you freaks? Leave her be!" Hector yelled as he stood and fought against his restraints.

The second gray man lumbered over to Hector and slapped him across the face with his clawed monkey hand. "I do what Takarn commands!" he said in a scratchy, toneless voice. The man returned to Rose and finished removing her bindings. The other guard pulled at her breeches. "Our Takarn says even though your magics might resist, he's figured out how to change you. Soon you will have gifts like the other women."

Rose's heart raced like a rabbit, and she flailed, striking the one man's chin with her freed hand while kicking the other.

The first gray man backhanded her, and she collapsed.

"Leave her clothes on. We can strip her in front of Takarn," he snapped.

The Fulk'han who'd been attempting to remove her clothes gripped her bare ankle. Its very touch made her feel sick as he began dragging her out of the cell. Rose clawed at the ground to reach Angst, but the gray man pulled her in the opposite direction.

"Maybe Takarn will let me keep you as a pet, after he's done," the first guard said with a raspy chuckle.

A chain link snapped as Tarness swung at a gray man's face. The punch was hard enough to crack the bone helm. The gray man tripped over Rose and fell into Hector, who was ready. Hector wrapped his thick legs around the guard's throat and twisted until there was a loud snap. The guard dropped to the floor, lifeless.

Tarness struck the second guard in the stomach. The gray man reeled back but still maintained a hold on Rose's ankle. It was just enough. Rose saw her chance. She dove forward and made contact with Angst.

"No!" Dallow pleaded as he watched helplessly.

Rose squeezed her eyes shut, waiting for pain and death. There was a grotesque crunching sound. The gray man holding her ankle screamed and collapsed. She looked back to see that his head had split into two pieces and bones from his right leg had torn through his skin. Rose stared in shock at the guard's broken body before slowly turning to look back at Angst.

* * * *

Angst stood. He reached up to his healed face and shuddered. He looked at Rose with all the gratitude that could fit in his eyes then held his right hand high in the air. The shackles around his wrists wrenched open as he willed the iron to break apart. Still raised over his head, his hand glowed with an aura of a bright blue light. The ground and walls shook and a distant scream reached them. Though the sound was indistinct, he knew it came from Ivan. A crack opened above Angst in the ceiling of their dungeon cell. Chryslaenor, dripping with purple ooze after being forcefully torn from Ivan's grip, slowly lowered through the new opening into Angst's waiting hand.

"Yes," Angst whispered. He let go, completely, and allowed the sword to bond and make him Al'eyrn. Lightning poured from the tip of the blade, showering him in arcs of blue and white light. Everyone in the room squeezed their eyes shut, turning away from the brightness.

Angst experienced a sudden moment of clarity, an epiphany that seemed as if it would never end. He gave part of himself to the sword, sacrificed a piece of that which made him Angst, and replaced it with Chryslaenor. Moments passed as the bonding seeped into his being. A single tear dripped down his cheek at the loss, followed by an intake of breath as he realized all he'd gained in return. Chryslaenor's song filled him with knowledge and experience. He knew how to use the foci, and he knew how to defeat Ivan.

"Angst, are you..." Dallow began, but let the words trail off.

Angst opened his eyes, now glowing bright blue from the infusion of power. He looked at each of his friends, and his heart filled with rage at the state of things. "Everyone stand back," he said in a voice that echoed around the room, a voice not quite wholly his.

The remaining shackles and the iron door transformed to sand and cascaded to the dungeon floor. His friends shuffled away to stand against the far wall, still weak and disoriented from their confinement. Angst made a swatting gesture at the dungeon roof. Every particle of ground and building over them shattered and flew into the sky. He drew a circle around himself in the dungeon floor with Chryslaenor then stepped into the middle. The circle wrenched away from the ground, a gliding stone platform that rose and carried him through the ceiling.

* * * *

Determination and anger flowed through Angst's veins. He'd had enough of his friends being abused, he was sick of unknown wild magics, and was done being dead. Angst's jaw set around his gritted teeth. He shook with fury as the platform made its way to Ivan. He crouched to steady himself, gripping Chryslaenor's hilt.

The great sword sang proudly, apparently eager to communicate with an Al'eyrn for the first time in millennia. It flooded the Chryslaenor part of his mind with songs of history and spells and other foci. Angst took it all in with deep breaths and fierce vigilance. It had been only a brief time since Ivan had utterly destroyed him. In spite of what Angst was gaining from becoming Al'eyrn, Ivan was incredibly powerful and now bolstered with the confidence of victory. His bonding had just happened, it was too new, and Angst realized this battle would require every ounce of his resolve.

Angst's stone platform flew over the city, and he soon spied Ivan. The monster stood in the middle of his makeshift stadium, smugly looking over the crowd of worshiping Fulk'han, satisfaction consuming his large face. Scar had once again transformed into the giant monster dog. He sat next to Ivan, stoic and unmoving, though Angst thought he saw the briefest of tail wags at his approach. Ivan studied the platform as it came into view. The confused look on his masquerade face changed to concern, and finally disbelief when he realized it was Angst.

"Why aren't you dead?" Ivan asked incredulously. His booming voice was a dark echo in the ominous silence of his stadium, and the Fulk'han worshipped even more vehemently, bowing faster and deeper, in fear of their new god.

Angst lifted Chryslaenor and pointed it at Ivan's face. Ivan *tsk*ed and shook his head mockingly. Angst urged the platform to inch forward slowly, dramatically, while still holding his blade aloft. Ivan sneered at his arrival as though Angst were a gnat preparing to battle a mountain. Angst spun in one giant arc, slapping Ivan on the cheek with the flat of his enormous blade. There was no muscle behind the strike, no magic, and no way monster-Ivan could've felt actual pain. But the memory of Angst's previous assault struck deeper and harsher than any mere cut.

In an instant, Ivan's haughty look of omnipotence became one of shock and anger. Ivan reached up to swat Angst away, only to find his blow deflected by the invisible shield of air Angst had fashioned, thanks to Aerella's attempted lesson.

"How many times am I going to have to do this before you figure it out?" Angst spat. "We want you to leave!" Chryslaenor met Ivan's cheek with a loud, humiliating slap as Angst spun once more.

Ivan roared in fury, and swung to punch at Angst like some petty brawler. Angst let the shield drop and sliced deep into Ivan's hand. It split down the center to the wrist. Ivan yanked his hand away and stepped back to cradle his new wound and assess the situation. The purple tubes reformed around the damage, though much slower than Angst remembered earlier wounds healing.

"You were an appalling failure as a knight. That's why Isabelle dismissed you from Unsel!" Angst yelled, spinning once more to slap the giant.

Faster than thought, Ivan grabbed Angst with his uninjured hand and lifted him high into the air. Ivan paused to gather all his strength, winding up to throw Angst down harder than before, but stopped abruptly, howling in pain. Scar had leaped at him, sinking his large fangs deep into Ivan's leg. The beast dog jerked its mouth from side to side, pulling out wiggling purple cables, exposing the darkness within Ivan. Scar shook his prize bits of Ivan like a puppy with a toy. Ivan was reaching down with his injured hand to bat Scar away when several large boulders rained down and pummeled his back.

Distracted by this new attack, Ivan let go. Angst dove with Chryslaenor before him, sinking the great blade into the monster's breast. Angst held onto the sword, riding it to the ground while cleaving the Ivan's left flank like a butcher.

"You can't do this! I am Magic!" Ivan screamed in disbelief

as he reeled back.

Angst landed on his stone platform, and immediately rose high into the air. "You're going crazy in there again, aren't you, Ivan? Can't you even do this right?"

Ivan was becoming disoriented. Distracted by the barrage of insults, he kicked at Scar while trying to dodge the whirlwind of boulders and pieces of building Angst threw at Ivan's back. He definitely wasn't fighting like an omniscient god; Ivan fought like a man.

When Angst's platform reached Ivan's head, he dove blade-first into the other side of Ivan's chest, cutting deep into the monster's muculent hide. Angst gripped tight as Chryslaenor tore into Ivan's right side, rending a new gash that reached from the monster's chest to his leg. The platform was already rising to catch him before Angst hit the ground.

Ivan instinctively held pieces of his ravaged body together, gripping both of his sides. Scar spat out his wormy plaything and bit deep into Ivan's other leg while Angst rode his stone disk into the air once again. The onslaught of giant stones continued to attack Ivan. The monster Ivan looked around for someone to come to his aid, but the Fulk'han had already begun to flee.

"Look around you, Ivan!" crowed Angst. "These people you violated don't worship you! They worship what you're failing to hold inside. I'm going to show them all who you truly are!"

"I'll show you what I really am!" Ivan roared in a thunderous voice filled with desperation. "I'll show you how much power I can wield!"

Ivan let go of his wounded sides and threw his head back. He reached for the clouds. A whirl of darkness spun downward from the eye of the storm, and the clouds lowered into his grasping hands.

Angst heard screams from below and looked down from his platform to watch the Fulk'han escape. Even Scar had leaped up the stairs to move away. The ground quaked violently. Cracks appeared all around the stadium, growing larger until the very floor beneath Ivan gave way. Ivan hovered over an opening large enough to swallow him whole. Vex'kvette bubbled through the opening, billowing black and orange, rising until it met Ivan's feet. Purple wormy appendages shot out from Ivan's back and shoulders, reaching toward the sky in a desperate attempt to absorb more power. His feet and legs widened grotesquely as they absorbed the magic infused in the Vex'kvette.

Angst watched calmly as he urged his stone platform forward. Ivan's masquerade face filled with panic as he realized what he'd started. He now brimmed with power he couldn't control. Angst lifted Chryslaenor high over his head.

"You don't want to do this, Angst!" Ivan pleaded.

"Yes. Yes, I do!" Angst leaped off the stone disk and swung down with every ounce of power he could summon. Angst willed himself to the ground, pulling Chryslaenor through the center of Ivan's body, cleaving the monster's chest open. The purple worms that held Ivan together flailed wildly, unable to reform around the dark power contained within.

"If you destroy me, Magic will just find a new host! Someone you won't fight!" Ivan cried.

"What? Wait!" Angst said as he reached his platform on the ground.

Angst urged the stone slab to quickly move out of the stadium. From a hundred yards away, Ivan looked like a giant shadowy tree with roots of orange and black, and leaves formed of dark clouds. The center of the monstrous tree undulated and writhed, shaking with power. The thing released an inhuman scream as he exploded, bursting out like a tree struck by lightning.

Angst winced and ducked as giant chunks of purple monster deflected off his air shield. When he was able to look again, the front of the tree was gone, husked out by the great element of Magic, leaving behind a vibrating pillar of black and orange. Angst moved forward to get a better view of this new oddity. Resonating with power, the entity formed a solid beam of dark light which reached higher into the night sky than Angst could see. He could sense its presence. Angst veered to his right as it began to move.

"That's not at all what I was expecting," Angst mused aloud in dumbfounded wonder.

The ten-foot-wide pillar of dark light crept out of the remains of Ivan. Haltingly at first, the pillar picked up speed as it advanced out of the stadium and into the city. Everything in its path crumbled as it ripped through Fulk'han and away from Angst. The pillar quickly reached the edge of the city and shot out of sight.

Angst rolled his eyes and sighed deeply, bracing himself. His stone platform would be too slow to follow the black light. He willed it to the ground and cast the spell to call forth his swifen.

The ram had changed, as Angst had. His swifen was now muscular, solid, and looked fast even when standing still. Light from Chryslaenor reflected off the ram's polished steel hide, and it pawed at the ground, snorting with determination, as if asking why they hadn't left yet.

"About time," Angst said as he jumped onto the ram's back. "Go!" he yelled, pointing Chryslaenor toward the path of destruction newly carved before them. In a blur of silver, the ram launched itself forward in pursuit.

43

The sword stopped mere inches from Tyrell's neck, vibrating painfully in Aereon's hand. The Captain Guard had already braced himself for death. A death in battle, protecting the crown of Unsel, protecting Isabelle, was more than he could've asked. That would be an honorable death, and he'd been ready. As he slumped to the floor, weakly holding his chest together as blood seeped out, Tyrell wondered if death hadn't just arrived in person.

Never in his life had he seen such a beautiful statue. She'd grown from nothing to ten feet tall in an instant, seemingly formed of the same off-white marble that made up the pillars. No detail was left unfinished. Her short locks of curly hair, her fine stone eyelashes, even the veins of marble that accentuated her muscular arms and sturdy jaw had all been chiseled to life. A marble toga hung from the statue's right shoulder and tied at her waist, where it flowed below her knees. Tyrell could see creases where the toes bent, and delicate toenails carved neatly into them. The most talented sculptor ever to walk Ehrde would've given up their trade at the sight of her perfection. Then run for dear life when she began to move.

The statue jerked Aereon's sword free and squeezed tight, snapping it in half. She surveyed the room. Victoria and the guards were pinned against pillars and walls, all staring in shock at her appearance. The queen gazed into nothingness, distracted by the whisperings of the stormy eye. Tyrell lay on the ground behind the moving statue, his life blood pouring out onto the throne room floor. The statue's eyes narrowed with anger and distrust as she hunched down and leaned forward to peer at Aereon. She snapped the sword into fourths and dropped them at his feet.

"No! I claim this place!" Aereon said defiantly, once again wielding long rapiers. Oddly, he wasn't taken aback by the statue's presence or ability to move. As if pride and arrogance had made him invulnerable, Aereon didn't back down.

The stone woman stood to her full height and reeled back, laughing at his challenge. Her laughter was the cold sound of rocks skipping on a shallow creek. "Give up now, young host. An Al'eyrn comes, and he brings your death," she warned him, her voice like a mountain, powerful and beautiful.

Aereon's eyes widened in response. He raised his dual rapiers and lashed out in frustration, spinning wildly. The blades slapped the statue across her waist a hundred times in the blink of an eye. Each blow sounded like a blacksmith attacking an anvil. Sparks and smoke rose from the statue's waist, but the attack ended quickly when Aereon realized she was ignoring him. With a smirk, she turned her back to Aereon and knelt by Tyrell. She lifted him gently and walked to the nearby wall, setting him down, away from Aereon and his attempted battle.

She returned to the center of the throne room. Aereon had dropped his rapiers and raised both palms to face her. Moving his arms in rapid circular motions, he took one step forward, leaning into the attack while bracing himself against the floor for balance. His arms picked up speed. Wind pummeled the statue as the force of a thousand gales flew from his hands. The throne room doors burst open with the sudden change in pressure, but the statue smiled as though merely enjoying a cool spring breeze. She tilted her head to look behind Aereon. With a nod, the marble floor beneath him turned to sand.

Aereon's footing instantly gave way. He slid, a startled expression on his fierce face, and then flew back into a nearby pillar. Screaming in pain, Aereon lost his focus. Victoria and the guards dropped to the floor, no longer pinned against the walls and pillars by his will. The guards nearest Tyrell quickly made their way to him to assess the damage done.

"In a hundred years, your wind may erode no more than a thin layer of stone. Thus has always been the results of battle between the elements of Air and Earth!" the statue informed Aereon. "There is nothing you can do here. Your meddling is finished."

"You are no host!" Aereon accused, pointing a finger at the statue. Panic filled his face at this realization, and he drew in a ragged breath.

The queen screamed and grabbed at her eye. She looked around the room wildly, confused and desperately lost. Victoria tore her gaze away from Aereon and the statue woman, and ran behind pillars, attempting to avoid notice as she made her way to the throne. Cautiously, she knelt by the queen. Moving her mother's hand aside, Victoria carefully lifted the eyelid covering Aereon's stormy eye.

"Victoria, what's going on?" the queen sputtered, slowly coming out of her stupor.

"The storm is gone!" Victoria said in astonishment.

"I am not a host," the statue replied to Aereon.

"There are rules! I was told there are rules!" Aereon's rapiers were forgotten. He stomped around like a spoiled child. "You can't be here! I was promised these people were mine." His hand swept around the room, but his gesture seemed to include all of Unsel.

"The rules have just changed, little host," the statue said as she grabbed the collar of Aereon's jacket, lifting him from the ground. "And I would guess your services will soon no longer be needed."

* * * *

Twelve magic wielders stood outside the Wizard's Revenge, empowered but unprepared. Andec was scared for the others. He was far too old for battles with monsters, but hoped his presence would temper the unrestrained excitement he saw in the younger eyes around him. The prospect of letting loose abilities that had been mostly hidden their entire lives was intoxicating. He feared that would lead to reckless mistakes.

"This is too easy!" he cautioned loudly, creating a portal in front of a lone bird. The portal closed before the attacker had completely passed through, leaving the front half to crash into a nearby building while the rear fell sloppily to the ground. "I thought there were hundreds of these things."

Several moments later, a flash of shiny metal talons and purple plumes flew toward them. Janda casually torched it with another bolt of fire, almost removing the ear of the man in front of her. Her eyes apologized in response to his wide-eyed stare.

"Everyone face away from the center when attacking," Andec barked in a tired and hoarse voice. The lack of monsters was disconcerting, making him tense. He waved the group to follow him across the abandoned cobblestone walkway. "There's an alley ahead that will take us to the main road."

The magic wielders bunched together like a small mob rather than a troop of trained soldiers. They huddled behind their old leader en masse until forced to walk shoulder to shoulder through the thin alley. The temperature dropped to a violent shiver, intensified by their situation. The alley had little debris, amplifying the sound of each step against the close walls. Several times Andec stopped to turn and shush a young man in the back who couldn't stop muttering to himself in his nervousness.

When they reached the end, Andec didn't yell "halt" like a military procession, nor did he hold up his hand in warning. He simply made an odd hissing sound, as though the words strangled in his throat, unable to edge out past his tongue and teeth.

The dim light of sunset reflected off thousands of purple velvet wings and thin metallic beaks. The large birds blanketed the entire road leading to the castle. Each of them shuffled about, pecking at the ground like geese in a field. Several of the birds made loud shrilling sounds and stabbed at each other with their long beaks.

"What are they doing?" asked Tanden, a middle-aged bookkeeper. He leaned forward, squinting to better discern what was going on.

Andec paled and turned away from the birds. He attempted to urgently wave everyone back down the alley in hopes they could safely return to the Wizard's Revenge, but it was like pushing back the tide. The small mob leaned toward him, craning to get a better look.

"Th-they're...they're eating," Janda said brokenly, covering her mouth.

The monster birds feasted on carcasses of horses and people strewn over the main road. Andec continued trying to usher everyone back, but couldn't dislodge the foothold of morbid curiosity. The nervous young man in the back finally got a good look, and forcefully emptied the contents of his stomach. The retching sounds were loud enough to garner the attention Andec had hoped to avoid.

Most of the birds flapped their wings nervously, the sound like a roar as they lifted into the sky. They hovered over their dinner, giving an unobstructed view of the grotesque remains. The monster birds closest to the alley peered with evil intent then raced on their metallic clawed talons toward the magic wielders.

With every ounce of courage he could muster, Andec stepped around the corner of the building, making room for others to attack the approaching foes. The magic wielders formed a line along the wall of an old brick building.

"*Now!*" Andec commanded.

The earth shook, startling the mass of birds charging them. Janda cast beams of fire, shearing several birds into pieces. Her sister, Nikkola, fought with similar beams of black light. Tanden shook as he reached out with two cupped hands. He focused on a target and squeezed his hands together. Space seemed to shrink around the bird as it was crushed from all sides.

"Don't fight just one at a time! We need to kill faster!" Andec yelled as the magic wielders fended off the birds, each in their unique way. But he was already tiring—the portals he created were becoming smaller and now only absorbed a target or two.

Others faced the same dilemma. Good intent does not make up for inexperience. The fifty monster corpses lying before them were not enough to stop, or even slow down, the rapid march. Andec leaned forward, placing his hands on his knees as he panted to catch his breath. When the attacking flock was only ten feet away, he looked at the ground then closed his eyes tight. He heard the monsters' excited screeches and braced for the inevitable.

But he was still panting, still breathing, and there were no screams of pain from his companions. Andec looked up to see that the first wave of monstrous purple birds had apparently disappeared. He turned to Nikkola with a confused expression and pulled on her sleeve.

"Just watch. You won't believe this," she said, shaking her head.

Another wave of birds approached. The cobblestones beneath the birds shifted, rippling like water as gamlin burst from the road to grapple with the purple birds, forcefully pulling them into the ground and out of sight. One of the gamlin crawled up through a cobblestone to stand before Andec. The creature looked at him with its red eyes, and its small human-like face smiled. It clicked its long bear claws together several times before nodding at him. As if this were enough, it turned and dove back into the hard ground. Andec cautiously swept his foot over the cobblestone into which the gamlin had disappeared. It was solid once again.

"I guess we have reinforcements," Andec declared with renewed energy. "Keep fighting!"

"What do we do about those?" Nikkola asked, pointing up. The mass of birds now darkened the sky overhead.

"Aim!" Andec responded, directing his next portal into the sky.

* * * *

"Stairs would've been nice," Tarness joked as he pulled himself through the hole Angst had created. He reached down and grabbed Hector's hand to hoist him up.

"Does someone want to explain to me what just happened?" Hector asked loudly, grunting as Tarness effortlessly yanked him through the opening.

Dallow folded his hands together so Rose would have a foothold. She remained quiet as she carefully stepped up, holding onto his head for balance. Rose hesitated at taking Tarness's proffered hand.

"We don't have time for this, Rose. I'm not hurt, now come on!" he commanded angrily. He grabbed her hand before she could pull it away and lifted her.

"I didn't know what would happen, after that..." She looked at the gray man whose head had been split asunder when she healed Angst.

"Now we know," he replied in his deep voice. "You did good."

"You did better than good. That was amazing, Rose! You saved all of us!" Dallow enthused. "And it looked like Angst bonded with Chryslaenor. I wonder how he's doing."

His question was answered by a distant roar from Ivan.

"Sounds like he's doing what he always does," Hector said, shaking his head. "Let's go see how bad it is this time."

Within moments, they'd mounted their swifen and were following Hector through Fulk'han. They rode at a careful pace as he attempted to find a safe passage away from Ivan's followers.

"Are you all right?" Dallow asked Rose.

She nodded slowly, still assessing the effects of her healing. "Actually, I feel great." Not only had she transferred Angst's wounds to the creature, but she wondered if she hadn't rid herself of some as well.

There was an explosion followed by screaming. The clouds above them spun and dissipated as though drawn to the middle of the city. The ground nearby shook, and without a word, Hector rushed to the main road toward Ivan's stadium. They stopped at the side of the road as hundreds of Fulk'han approached, all running away from Ivan.

"Now what?" Hector asked, reaching around his armor to find a weapon. He pulled out a small skinning knife and stared at it. "I have nothing. Anyone else?"

Before anyone could speak, the Fulk'han arrived. The group moved closer together, but the mass of odd-looking creatures just ran by them and continued down the road. Within ten minutes, the stampede had passed, leaving them mostly alone again.

"That's not good," observed Tarness wryly.

There was another explosion and a wrenching scream that sounded like Ivan.

"At least it isn't Angst," Dallow offered. "Why are we waiting here? He may need our help!"

A giant Scar, with glowing red eyes and covered in bony protrusions, followed close behind the throng of fleeing Fulk'han. He'd reverted to the monster they'd found in the woods.

"Oh no," said Rose sadly.

Scar stopped in the road and turned to look at her. His three tails began wagging as he lumbered toward them. Rose instinctively covered her head, but the beast stopped several feet from her. Instead of attacking, he dropped a large chunk of dark purple Ivan at her feet. Obviously proud of his catch, Scar sat with a thud, his tails clearing debris from the road.

Rose looked up and smiled warily. "Good dog," she said, reaching out to him.

Before their eyes, Scar quickly shrank down to his puppy size and walked to Rose for some love. She looked at Tarness, Hector, and Dallow for affirmation that it was safe, but they gawked in silence, stunned by the sudden transformation.

"Ugh, you need a bath," she said as she dismounted and cautiously petted Scar, rubbing the back of his now furry ear.

The ground shook again as a ten-foot wide beam of darkness slowly approached them. They pressed their swifen tight against a nearby building. It was so close, Rose felt hairs rise along her arms and the back of her neck. The raw power was palpable, destroying everything in the dark pillar's path. It picked up speed as it passed them.

Hector dismounted and was the first to step into the road for a better look. He glimpsed the dark beam as it sped away from Fulk'han like a shot arrow. Then Angst's solid steel ram tore past him, a mere foot away. The wake from Angst's charge pushed Hector forward several steps.

"That was Angst!" he said with a fist in the air.

"Do we follow him?" Dallow asked.

"Can we follow him?" asked Tarness.

Rose walked away from the group to approach one of the remaining Fulk'han. The pink-hued woman writhed on the ground, moaning in pain. Tears streamed down the Fulk'han's face. Rose leaned forward to see if she could help.

The woman was muttering in a strained voice, "He killed Takarn. He killed Takarn."

Rose stood quickly and hurried back to the others. "They think Angst killed their god. We need to leave, now!" she yelled, scooping Scar into her arms.

Rose and Hector quickly remounted their swifen.

"Hang on tight, everyone. Let's try to catch up," Hector said with a battle-wild look in his eyes.

44

Fast was an understatement. Lightning crawled in comparison to the swifen's flight, which was as instant as your life flashing before your eyes after making a bad mistake. Angst had chased Magic through the night and into the break of dawn. Chryslaenor and the ram were glowing in tandem as miles flew by in seconds. At some point, he'd decided to start referring to the powerful beam of darkness as Magic, because what else could it be? Hadn't Aerella tried to warn them, warn him, that Ivan had become a host for the awesome power Angst now chased?

Foolishly, he'd taken a swing at the dark pillar as they sped out of Fulk'han. Angst had been close enough to make contact, and hours later, his right arm was still somewhat numb and prickly, as if it had fallen asleep. In spite of his attempt to attack, Magic seemed to be ignoring Angst, perhaps not considering him a threat. He'd resolved to continue the chase and try to stop it before it claimed a new host, but he didn't have a clue how he could stop this element come to life.

He was tired, lost, and had no idea where he was going. And he was alone. Angst wished and willed for his friends to join him. He begged Chryslaenor to help them catch up, but he couldn't spare even the briefest look over his shoulder.

At times he rode so fast that the landscape around him was only a blur. Indistinct images of trees and rivers all flew by as Magic carved a swath across Ehrde to a destination only it knew.

There were also moments that would burn in Angst's mind forever. Brief periods of surreal horror when the dark beam of power slowed, as though ensuring those unlucky souls in its path would experience fear in the face of death.

Angst would try to ride beside Magic, desperate to warn people away, but it was useless and only gave him a better view. He watched them disappear into the beam, gone forever. Families, pets, houses, all instantly destroyed within Magic's insatiable hunger. It was almost worse to watch the survivors, and not be able to stop and explain. An old man whose dog was killed, children who lost their parents, and a woman with long, dark blue hair, who stared at Angst with such hate that he felt cold to the bone, as if he'd been standing outside in freezing rain.

They never slowed long enough for Angst to concoct a solution. He focused on staying close to the beam while simultaneously wrestling with the constant barrage of information from Chryslaenor. The foci seemed desperate for Angst to know everything right now. Angst only wanted to know how to stop Magic, but the music provided him with no direct answer.

He laughed out loud as he pondered this situation. Even with all the power at his command, everything Angst had imagined would make him a hero, here he was, still fighting for what he wanted. It was the worst case of 'be careful what you wish for' he'd ever heard of, and the laughter left a bitter taste in his mouth.

Even before Chryslaenor, his day-to-day life had been a constant struggle, and he'd longed to reach the life he knew should be his. Now he realized that life came at a terrible cost. Aerella was dead, Gressmore whatever-it-was-called was gone, Angst had died more than once and was certainly headed for another brush with death. That one more death might leave Heather alone, and the thought sickened him. Why did everything have to be a battle? Why did every battle require so much sacrifice? So much of *his* sacrifice?

Angst inhaled sharply as he and Magic crested a hill, where

the morning sun rose over a distant Unsel. His exhaustion momentarily dissolved into gut-wrenching panic. Ivan had said that Magic would find a new host who Angst wouldn't fight. There were only two people currently in Unsel he couldn't lift a finger against, and his mind immediately filled with images of their faces. Heather and Tori. He willed the swifen ram to speed up as a surge of nervous energy coursed through his body.

Magic couldn't be killed, only contained. Angst remembered the story told by the Nordruaut Jarle, and Chryslaenor's song confirmed it. In a sense, it had been trapped in Ivan, but Angst couldn't wait for Magic to find yet another host he'd have to destroy. There had to be another way.

Even from this distance, Unsel did not look healthy. Plumes of dark smoke rose from buildings all around the great city, and a wispy cloud hovered above it. Angst couldn't help but wonder what else he would face there, and Chryslaenor answered. In his mind, Angst saw a vision of the city at war. Magic wielders fought alongside gamlin against hordes of large dangerous-looking birds. He shook his head in disbelief. How was he supposed to stop this attack while he also captured Magic?

The beam of power had already reached the edge of the city, ripping apart homes and buildings. Everything in its path was instantly vaporized. People, animals, trees—all gone the moment Magic passed, unyielding in its apparent focus on the castle.

At this speed, the destruction was almost too much to absorb. As he crossed the threshold into the city, Angst was surrounded by death and chaos. He glimpsed magic wielders, people he knew, defending themselves against the bird creatures. He roared with anger and pulled Chryslaenor from his back, drawing strength from its great power. Instinctively, he reached up to the sky with his mind, desperately searching for something, anything that could help.

Angst found what he was looking for. He could feel the thousands of birds flying overhead or scurrying along the ground. Every one of them had claws and beaks made of dense metal. He reached out for all of them, every single bird he could find, and pulled down.

The strain of using magic on so many creatures over such a large area hurt almost as much as having his face cleaved. Angst clenched his teeth in pain as he forced them into the ground. The bird creatures screeched in panic and flailed helplessly as their beaks crashed into cobblestone roads. Those nearest Angst died on impact, their metal beaks yanked from the birds' heads and pulled deep into the earth. Those farther away were driven into the ground, their heads buried but their bodies still above the surface, left to flop about, waiting for death.

The attack had taken only moments, but the effort used up the last of his energy. The merest bump, and Angst would've slid from his swifen. He couldn't even return Chryslaenor to his back because his arm was too weary.

Why did it always have to hurt? Why did everything require sacrifice? Rose had almost given up her life to save him, to save all of them. He'd had to sacrifice part of himself to bond with Chryslaenor. What would he have to sacrifice to keep Magic from making Heather or Victoria its new host? Sacrifice. The realization almost struck him like a physical blow. He proposed an idea to Chryslaenor, and the sword's sad song indicated that his idea could work.

The pillar slowed when it struck the castle, the deafening crash resounding through the city. Walls collapsed inward as the foundation disintegrated in Magic's path. They were destined for the throne room. He drew in a deep breath and struggled to lift himself to crouch on the swifen, urging it closer to the powerful beam of dark light. He was almost close enough to touch it, close enough to feel the intense power emanating from it, like an electrical current coursing along his skin.

The two giant throne room doors flashed out of existence as the dark beam passed. Angst heard screaming as everyone in the room scrambled back. There was no more time. As he commanded the swifen to stop, he leaped forward with all his might, diving into the beam with Chryslaenor held before him. He wrenched, and pulled, and fought against his mind until his bond with Chryslaenor tore free.

It had never been done before, a bond like this had never been willfully broken, and dislodging it was like pulling the cork from a drain at the bottom of the ocean. The foci was starved for Al'eyrn, for any connection, and Chryslaenor immediately latched on to the element of Magic. Angst flew into the heart of the dark tower of light and planted his sword deep into the center of the throne room floor. He flipped over Chryslaenor, crashing through a tall man and a statue woman to land on his back. His momentum carried him across the floor to the stairs before the throne, smoke rising from his tattered armor.

Angst wondered if he was going to pass out or die again, but when he opened his eyes, he saw a familiar face. "Hi, Tori," he said with a tired but grateful smile.

She looked at him in stunned amazement. "Hi, Angst," she replied, clearly relieved.

He rolled over to watch as the dark pillar of Magic shrank to a pinprick then disappeared. Dark lightning crackled along the edges of the great blade. Angst slowly stood with a loud grunt and limped over to the sword. Magic was once again trapped, held inside the foci until it found a way out. He wanted to lift the sword, but the faintest of sounds, no longer a full chorus of music in the back of his head, told him no.

"What's happening to Aereon?" Victoria asked in surprise, pointing to a man at the other end of the room.

"Who?" Angst asked.

The tall man who had broken his fall screamed and rose from the ground. Aereon dropped the two rapiers he'd been holding as a whirlwind engulfed him, lifting him several feet into the air.

"I did not fail you!" Aereon tried to reason with some unknown force. "I can still do this!" Another scream tore from his throat, and he fell to the ground in a crumpled heap.

A tall statue of a beautiful woman walked over to Aereon and nudged him with a foot. "It is done," she declared in her great voice. She turned to face Angst, looking him up and down. She smiled, nodded once, and then dissolved into the stone floor like a waterfall flowing into a lake.

The queen screamed in pain. One of her eyes popped out, fell to the ground, and smashed into a thousand pieces.

"Would somebody please tell me what's going on?" Angst asked wearily as he took in the madness surrounding him.

Rook rushed into the throne room with Heather close behind. She ran to Angst and threw her arms around his neck, nearly knocking him over in the process. She was crying and almost incoherent as she whispered, "I love you," over and over in his ear. Angst forced himself not to cry as waves of her, and his, emotions collided. He held Heather close and soon realized he had to lean over to embrace her. He pulled away to look down and saw the small bulge of life growing in her belly.

"Yeah?" he asked as his eyes became wet with tears.

Heather could only nod and hold him even tighter.

Rook dashed over to kneel by Tyrell. "He's still alive, but barely."

The queen had one fist balled up against her eye as she stumbled over to Tyrell. She dropped to both knees and took his hand in hers. "I couldn't do anything. I'm so sorry."

Tyrell's eyes fluttered open. His mouth opened like a fish gasping for its last breath, but no words came out.

Hector, Tarness, Dallow, and Rose rode into the room. Their swifen glowed from Chryslaenor's infusion of power, and they slid to a halt just before reaching the great sword. His friends looked beyond exhausted from the long trip, harrowed by the incredible speeds at which they'd traveled. They dismounted clumsily as their sore muscles protested the change in positions for the first time in half a day.

Angst gently separated himself from Heather and made his way to Rose. "I need you," he said.

Before she could protest, Angst grabbed her wrist and brought her to Tyrell and Queen Isabelle. Rose looked at the queen's eye socket and winced. She knelt by Tyrell and inspected his wounds without touching him.

"Angst, I can't heal him. I would try, but it's too much. It would kill me," she said, still looking over Tyrell's body. His eyelids drooped with the heaviness of death, though he fought to keep them open.

"Please," Isabelle pleaded of Rose. "If there's anything you can do."

"Can you transfer the wounds to someone else, like you did for me?" Angst asked.

Rose thought about this and then nodded. "I think so."

Victoria stood over everyone, listening intently.

"She can remove wounds by taking the wound on herself," Angst explained to the princess, "or transferring the wound to someone else. Whoever she transfers these wounds to will die."

"Take me," Rook offered, holding out his hand.

"Thank you, Rook, but I have someone else in mind," Victoria said, her eyes narrowing. She looked across the room to Aereon, who was still reeling from whatever had happened to him. "Guards, bring that man over here!"

45

EPILOGUE ONE

They were already here. Angst couldn't remember the last time his friends had beaten him to Wizard's Revenge, but there they were. Not in worn armor or tattered travel clothes, not exhausted from the stress of survival. They were in fresh clothes that suited them, perfect for drinking and carousing, and well rested. He smiled, and his heart filled with warmth. Angst gripped Heather's hand, and together they made their way through the crowd.

Bar patrons began clapping even before they reached their seats. Several at first, and eventually more, until everyone at the bar was applauding. Angst smiled, and held out his free hand for everyone to stop. Then he relented and encouraged it for a moment, which made everyone laugh. Finally, the room became quiet. Heather stepped aside and made her way to the table. Angst looked around the bar to see the magi who'd survived, and those who'd defended Unsel in her time of need. He couldn't put into words how proud he was.

Graloon approached, handing him a goblet of port. Angst raised the cup and called out, "To Unsel!"

"To Unsel!" was the hearty reply. The brief toast was enough, and the crowd returned to their conversations.

Angst clasped forearms with Tarness and Hector from across

the table. Dallow stood to embrace him in a manly hug. Rose remained seated, looking up briefly to smile at him. Angst hugged her anyway, making her pull back defensively. Since healing the queen several weeks ago, she continued to wear a patch over her right eye. He looked at it with concern, but she quickly turned away.

Before Angst could ask Rose how she was doing, Graloon patted his back with a heavy hand. "So is it true, Angst? Tell me it is," he boomed.

Angst turned to face the old barkeep. "Changes are indeed coming, my friend. The queen wants guards who can wield magic. More restrictions are being lifted. Real, actual progress."

Graloon waved the bosomtastic server over, and grabbed the bar towel from her shoulder. Heather and Rose looked at each other, rolling their eyes and shaking their heads as she walked away. The barkeep patted at his eyes with the towel. "It almost feels like we're being set free." Graloon wandered back to his place behind the bar with happy tears in his eyes.

"The kingdom is safe, Ehrde is safe, and we're safe!" Hector proclaimed, raising his flask, and they all raised their cups to toast once again.

"What about you, Angst?" Tarness asked, already deep in the keg. "Are you going to finally be knighted?"

"No," Angst replied in a surly tone. "Chryslaenor remains in the throne room, trapping magic, or whatever that thing was. No sword, no knighting."

Hector, Tarness, and Dallow were instantly in an uproar, complaining on his behalf. After a rash of insults to the queen and several long draws of port, Angst finally responded.

"It's not over yet, but really, I don't care anymore," he said, looking at Heather, patting her stomach. "Maybe my adventure is going to be at home for a while."

Everyone toasted once more. Dallow suddenly stood.

"Do you have to go already?" Angst asked.

His tall friend heaved a carafe off the sticky bar table with a jerk. "Just grabbing a refill. I didn't want Rose beating up the waitress because we're empty."

Rose flashed him a look without much heat. She obviously wasn't feeling well. As Hector began regaling Heather with a tale about Angst ending up covered in monster when they saved Rose, Angst took the opportunity to question his friend.

"What's going on? You don't look like yourself," he asked worriedly.

"I'm fine. Healing the queen wasn't like anything else I've done," Rose said in a reserved tone. "It was different than healing that wound on your face."

"May I see?" Angst asked, reaching for the patch.

"No!" Rose snapped, slapping his hand. Obviously realizing her response was too sharp, she softened. "No, Angst, I'll be fine."

He nodded at her but still worried.

"You're a bit broken," she said, expertly changing the subject.

"Pardon?" he asked in confusion.

"When I healed you in the Fulk'han dungeon, even though the wounds transferred from you to the guard, I got a pretty good dose of Angst." Rose's thin eyebrows furrowed as she looked at him. "Everyone's missing something in their life, everyone has a hole that needs filling. But yours is like a deep pit."

"Eh, I'll be fine, too," Angst said, shrugging off her insights.

"Even now, without Chryslaenor?" Rose asked, but knew from the look on Angst's face he was done with this conversation. "If you want me to try and heal you again, I will."

"Thanks, Rose," he said gratefully. Angst looked at her eye patch once more. "But I think you have a bit of healing to do for yourself first."

"I thought you weren't supposed to flirt with girls when your wife is around!" Tarness slurred loudly from across the table.

Heather laughed, and everyone joined her, though involuntarily. She stopped abruptly, covering her mouth with her hand. She spoke between her fingers. "That's never stopped him before."

"Angst, I'm still not clear on how you beat Magic. How do

you fight an element?" Dallow asked, ever curious.

Angst took a deep breath as he reluctantly thought of the battle with Ivan. "Magic made a mistake. It chose a host that was already broken. Ivan had been defeated before he became a host. In Fulk'han, I fought Ivan, not magic. I beat him down with his own insecurities, and he finally gave up. I'm not proud of that, but didn't have much choice."

Angst looked down at his drink and took a long draw before continuing. "That thing that came out of Ivan was the element Magic, and it went looking for a new host. Someone I wouldn't fight. It's an element, which means it's impossible to kill. The only thing I could think of was trapping it by sacrificing Chryslaenor."

"Sacrificing?" Dallow asked in surprise. "You're still Al'eyrn, aren't you?"

It was the conversation that he wanted to avoid more than any other. All of his life, Angst had wanted to be a hero, and the sword had given him that missing component. Giving it up had been the single hardest thing he had ever done. It wasn't only the pain of removing the bond, or the emptiness that removal left behind. There was a storm of questions that gathered strength every time they snuck into his head. Why now and not when he was younger? Was sacrificing Chryslaenor the only way to save everyone? Would the emptiness ever leave? How could he possibly be a hero now? And to make it worse, he could still hear the faint whisper of Chryslaenor's song.

In the end, Angst merely shook his head. Everyone became quiet at this revelation. Heather placed her hand on his shoulder in support.

He looked up and smiled. "Like Hector said, we're all safe. Isn't that all that matters?" Angst said with feigned cheer. "The entire adventure was almost everything I always wanted. I would have it no other way. Thank you." Angst raised his glass to his friends, and they responded in kind.

Rose stood. "I need to get some rest before starting my new job tomorrow."

"That's right, you're working for the princess now." Dallow stood to give her a brief hug. "That should be, uh, interesting."

"Heh. Handmaiden. I like how that sounds," Angst joked.

Rose and Heather struck him on both shoulders.

* * * *

"I'll see everyone next weekend," Rose said, tossing a final glare at Angst. She walked through the crowded bar and left the Wizard's Revenge. The air outside was brisk, and Rose looked about to find the cobblestone street momentarily empty. She took a deep breath and leaned against the building. With one shaky hand, she reached up to her right eye and pressed firmly on the patch that covered it. After several moments of concentrating, the itch behind her eye went away, but she knew it would return. It always did.

46

EPILOGUE TWO

There was an awkward moment after the first hug. Their embrace was brief, and Angst stepped back and took her in. Her light pink dress was a touch more formal than he was used to seeing her wear, and this was the first time she'd worn a tiara to one of their meetings. Something about the way she carried herself made her seem older.

"Hi, Tori," he said. Her reaction told him she hadn't been called that since he left.

"Hi, Angst." She looked him over several times. "You've lost weight."

Angst patted his tummy and glanced down, making a comical expression that made her giggle. They were both quiet, and he could feel that things were off. He'd missed her, at times longed for her friendship, and her need of him. But it had been a very long month apart, and the moment was surreal. Things felt out of sync, so he stepped forward and hugged her again for only a little longer than he felt was proper, to urge everything back to familiar ground.

"What was that for?" she asked, her eyebrows gently furrowed.

"Does there need to be a reason?" Angst answered.

Her frown deepened and she stepped toward him. Angst

forced his shoulders to relax. "Tell me about your adventure," she asked.

Angst surveyed the maiden's courtyard. "It's going to take a while. Won't we get in trouble?"

She smiled and shook her head. "There are no more secret meetings. My mother knows we're both here, though I'm pretty sure she always did. I think you've earned her trust."

He nodded slowly, not completely believing her, then they both sat on a stone bench near the fountain. She moved close so their knees were touching, and Angst let it all out. For the first time since returning, he shared every minute detail he could remember. Until now he'd only told highlights. Heather was more excited about being pregnant than listening to the boring details. The queen and her cabinet wanted only specifics on dangers and the changes to Fulk'han. Nobody else had asked, so he was grateful that he could finally share everything. Victoria paid close attention to every word, never once questioning or interrupting. By the end, he was exhausted, and relieved, as though a great burden had been lifted.

When he was finished, it was Victoria's turn. The awkwardness of their time apart passed as she told him most of what had happened in his absence. Tori excitedly skipped back and forth between what she felt, what had taken place, and what she'd remembered later. The one solid bit of information he absorbed was that she'd taken charge and was proud of what she'd accomplished. He was proud of her too and told her so. By the end of the conversation, things were almost back to normal.

Angst was curious about Aereon and his abilities. About the bird creatures that had attacked Unsel. Victoria interrupted his thoughts before he could launch into his questions.

"What about Chryslaenor?" she asked with concern in her voice. "How are you, now that it's gone?"

Angst instinctively looked over his shoulder for the giant sword that was no longer there and sighed deeply. "It's hard to explain. When I gave up Chryslaenor to trap Magic, I had to rip it out." Angst shivered and squeezed his eyes shut. The wound still felt so fresh. Tori rested her hand on his supportively. "I gave up part of myself to bond with Chryslaenor. The part that I let go was replaced with the sword. When I removed the bond, when I wrenched it out, there was nothing to fill the hole.

"Now, I feel like I did when I left," he said in a very sad voice and was immediately embarrassed. This was far beyond their normal scope of conversation. He was supposed to be listening to her and the trials she'd gone through, not pouring out his pathetic insecurities.

Angst looked away and saw the patched crack in the fountain, the one he'd created when he first met Victoria. "Your gifts were kind. Though Tyrell had some concerns about the origins of the cloak."

"How is Rose?" she asked, trying to change the subject.

"She's healing more slowly than usual, but otherwise she seems fine, I think," Angst answered, surprised by the question. There was a brief pause in the conversation, and Angst took this moment to consider. Something had been nagging him throughout the trip, and he wondered if this was the right time to broach the subject. It was against his better judgement to make things weird between them, especially here, back where they started. But, he never admitted to having better judgement. "Speaking of Rose, you were right that I needed her."

Tori's eyes grew round with surprise, but she quickly smiled to cover the reaction. "I figured you'd need someone to flirt with."

"Well, that too, but thank you for sending her," Angst said, watching her response closely. "I wouldn't have made it had she not healed me in the dungeon."

"I'm so glad she was there then," Victoria said with a smile. She moved her knee away from Angst and began to inch away from him on the bench.

"You know, you were right about me going on this mission as well," Angst stated matter-of-factly. "Everything turned out fine, for me, for the kingdom. It was the greatest adventure of my life."

Victoria stood and took a step back. His suspicions were correct. He stood and stepped closer to the young princess. "I also thought it was interesting that you knew Heather was pregnant, even before she or the physician did. Thank you for keeping her safe at the castle."

The princess seemed troubled. Her eyes darted around the room for some escape, and she continued backing away from Angst. He didn't stop, didn't give her any space. "It was also very convenient that Heather was here to help release the magi locked in the dungeon."

Victoria was shaking her head and placed her hand on Angst's chest to keep him away.

He reached into his pocket and pulled out the marble rose. Angst handed it to the young princess. "You knew I'd bring this back."

"No," she whispered.

"How much can you see, Tori? How much of our future can you see?" he challenged, raising his voice.

The princess stopped moving and dropped her hand in defeat. "I can see everything," she finally said in a very quiet voice.

Angst let that hang in the air and seep into his mind. "You knew all of it was going to happen. When I first found you here in this courtyard? You knew I could wield Chryslaenor? That I would bond with it after losing the battle with Ivan? You knew about the attack on Unsel?" Angst bit off every question, the thought of being used like that was crushing. "You knew that I would have to give up being a hero?"

Tears streamed down the princess's cheeks as she sobbed, clutching onto his tunic. She closed her eyes and lowered her head as she nodded in silent agreement with every harsh accusation.

"That's why you've been friends with me all these years," he railed. "Because you already knew how I could fit—"

"No!" she said firmly, and her head snapped up. Victoria stabbed a finger at him. "Don't you dare accuse me of using you. I can't control what happens or doesn't happen. I only see things that could happen! You are my friend, and when I saw that you could have what you wanted, that you could be a hero, and it would save Unsel... I swear I didn't mean to use you."

The words trailed off, and the princess started to cry in earnest. Angst felt awful. This wasn't what he'd intended. He pulled Victoria close and held her. "I'm sorry," he said consolingly. "I just...I thought you trusted me, that we shared everything. I shouldn't have assumed."

After several long moments, Victoria began to calm down. They made their way back to the bench and sat. "My mother and Tyrell are the only ones who know...what I can do," Victoria said quietly. "I'm sorry I didn't tell you. I didn't want Mother to hurt you or Heather if you found out."

He reeled at the thought of Isabelle holding this over her young daughter. It must have been a horrible burden, and it made him despise Isabelle even more.

"I may not have the sword, but I also haven't forgotten everything I learned. I don't think she can hurt me now, Tori."

She looked up at him, her long lashes blinking away tears. "I'm glad you know," she said. "I've always wanted to tell you."

"It certainly explains a lot," Angst stated. "Not only the dramatic changes in laws over the last ten years, but some of the decisions you've made, and some of the things you do." He looked down at their knees, which were touching once again.

Victoria blushed. "The future comes to me in dreams, but it's like looking at a large map on a table. I only see the entirety of what might happen. When I'm awake and near someone, physically, I see pieces of that future and their part in it." She sighed deeply and her shoulders slumped with relief. "The closer I am to you, the more clearly I can see your futures. I can see what could happen, what will probably happen, and sometimes, unfortunately what the person wants to happen."

Angst's eyes grew with surprise and alarm, which made the princess laugh. "You must think I'm a dirty old man!"

"Only sometimes." This made her laugh even harder, and it was Angst's turn to blush. She caught her breath, looked at his reddened cheeks, and began to laugh again. Good tears were now streaming down her cheeks.

"No. No, really. I think you're sweet. Most of the time," Tori said coyly. "I've been close to people who are truly depraved, and your worst imaginings don't even compare."

"Seers are rare, Tori. It must be a burden to know everything that could happen," Angst said with concern, while also, perhaps, trying to change the subject.

Victoria practically bounced with excitement and had to take calming breaths before speaking. "I don't know what people will choose to do and how that affects their future. Some things are just going to happen, like the attack on Unsel. But you wouldn't have wielded Chryslaenor without Ivan at the party, so I made sure he was there. That was for you, Angst, so you could be a hero!"

Angst stared at her in amazement as he began to understand just how powerful the young princess was. They sat next to each other for long minutes, staring off in deep thought. He was very aware of the fact that their knees were still touching, and thought about pulling his away. When he decided not to, when Angst decided it was safe to trust Victoria, she smiled.

"So what happens next?" Angst asked.

"I don't know," Victoria replied with worry in her eyes.

"I don't understand. I thought you just told me you can see the future?" Angst asked.

"I couldn't see Aereon's future, only a little of what he was actively thinking," she said with a delicate shudder. "I can see pieces of your future, and of mine, but I honestly don't know what's going to happen to Unsel. Something is changing in Ehrde."

"So you don't think this is done yet?" Angst asked, unable to hold back a smirk.

"What are we going to do, Angst?" Victoria asked with sudden concern. "You may have trapped Magic within Chryslaenor, for now, but what about the other elements? We've already been attacked by Air, what about that statue and the gamlin? Was that

Earth? What happens if the others come? You aren't Al'eyrn anymore. What are we going to do?"

"I've been thinking a lot about that," Angst began. He raised his right eyebrow mischievously. "And I have an idea."

About the Author

David J. Pedersen is a native of Racine, WI who resides in his home town Kansas City, MO. He received a Bachelor of Arts degree in Philosophy from the University of Wisconsin - Madison. He has worked in sales, management, retail, video and film production, and IT. David has run 2 marathons, climbed several 14,000 foot mountains and marched in Thee University of Wisconsin Marching Band. He is a geek and a fanboy that enjoys carousing, picking on his wife and kids, playing video games, and slowly muddling through his next novel.

To learn more about David and his writing please visit his blog:

www.gotangst.com

Angst and his friends return in the sequel:

Buried in Angst

Available now!